BLISSED

A CHARMING ROMANTIC COMEDY

PIPPA GRANT

Srishti
PUBLISHERS & DISTRIBUTORS

Srishti Publishers & Distributors
A unit of AJR Publishing LLP
212A, Peacock Lane
Shahpur Jat, New Delhi – 110 049
editorial@srishtipublishers.com

First published in India by
Srishti Publishers & Distributors in 2024

First Published as The Husband Games by Pippa Grant writing as Jamie Farrell in 2014

10 9 8 7 6 5 4 3 2 1

By arrangement with Pippa Grant, through BookEnds Literary Agency.

This edition is for sale in Indian Subcontinent only.

Printed and bound in India.

Chapter 1

Natalie Castellano had spent the better portion of the last five years in the shadow of happily ever after. Usually it came from the family bridal boutique or the Knot Festival committee, sometimes from the five-story wedding cake monument standing guard over downtown Bliss. But today?

Today, it came from the man who had broken her fairy tale.

He was back, and if the Queen General got her way—which she always did—he was back to stay.

Bliss was giving Natalie the blues. In more ways than one.

She wove through the crowded foyer of St. Valentine's Catholic Church, focused on two goals: be invisible, and avoid CJ Blue. All two hundred million of his relatives—or possibly only fifty or sixty or them—filled the foyer and blocked her path to a stained-glass door leading outside. It wasn't just a door. It was escape. Escape from the well-dressed crowd, escape from the overpowering perfume of wedding flowers, escape from her own memories and regrets and guilt.

She clutched her sewing kit in her slick hand and stopped when yet another pastel-clad woman sporting a corsage stepped into her path. Natalie ducked her head and dodged right. "Excuse me," she murmured.

The last few years, she'd gotten good at being invisible at weddings.

More like she'd gotten good at not making appearances at weddings at all. Were it not for today's high-profile guest list—both the bride and groom had spent the last several years touring with the bands of some mega country music stars—Natalie wouldn't have left the bridal boutique to do an emergency fix on a veil she hadn't sold.

For CJ Blue's sister.

Nevertheless, Nat couldn't pass up the chance to represent Bliss Bridal among a crowd like this. The boutique couldn't buy this kind of publicity.

The boutique couldn't buy any publicity lately. Not in Bliss.

If the Queen General caught Natalie here, though, publicity would be the least of Bliss

Bridal's problems. So Nat had kept her name to herself in the bride's quarters and dropped a few generic Bliss Bridal business cards in the room. And now she was alternately keeping her head down and scanning the crowd while she zigzagged for the door. Dress, dress, dress, tuxedo.

Check the hair—no red—keep going. Dress, dress, dress, tuxedo.

Fifteen more feet, and she'd be outside. Then a dash across the parking lot, and with any luck, the Queen General would never know Natalie had been here.

Four chattering women stepped into Nat's path. She dodged left and bumped into the chalky ivory wall. Another two women approached from her side. She slid along the wall until she was boxed in by a closed wooden door, a table holding church bulletins, and a group of women more fragrant than a bride's bouquet. Fourteen more feet, and the crowd was swelling around her like jellyfish. "Excuse me," she murmured again.

The back of her neck prickled. Then the backs of her knees. A tinny taste tickled the back of her tongue.

Oh, shit.

What was she doing here? She should've been setting up a wedding cake somewhere.

But there she was, the Queen General herself, marching through a crowd that parted for her like trees splitting in a tornado. A tornado headed away from Natalie. For the moment.

Marilyn Elias, Queen General of Bliss, had more power than the mayor. Probably more power than the governor of Illinois. As chairperson of the entire Knot Festival, she oversaw the annual week devoted to Bliss's celebration of its very purpose—weddings and marriage and bliss. She managed the subcommittees responsible for every Knot Fest event from the parade to the bridal expo to the Husband Games, Bliss's final festival event where men competed in a series of challenges—like lawn mowing, dishwashing, and wife-kissing—to be named Husband of the Year. And she did it all with the single-minded, take-no-prisoners drive usually reserved for dictators, bridezillas and cartoon villains.

Natalie hugged the wall, one eye straining to follow the QG, the other on the outer door she could barely glimpse now. She had to escape.

Now or never. "Excuse me," she said.

Her voice drowned in the normal pre-wedding chatter. She tried to shift around the table, but the crowd pushed her back against the door.

The QG stopped near the chapel entrance. Natalie could tell because the shuffle of bodies stopped. But she had another clue too. A big one, towering over the female-dominated crowd, his back to her.

A man. In black. With red hair.

A word entirely inappropriate for a church squeaked through her lips. Forget escape.

Nat had to hide.

* * *

A man didn't grow up with eleven sisters without learning how to effectively duck the squawking, and CJ Blue thought he had outdone himself today. He was equal parts impressed and horrified at the depths to which he'd sunk in his quest for an estrogen-free zone. But between his sisters and mom in one room screeching about a ripped veil and the multitudes of aunts and girl cousins lurking around every pew—all giving him the how-you-doing-you-poor-thing look—a guy had to take what he could get.

What he got was a gift from God Himself. An empty confessional.

His brother, Basil—Father Basil to the members of his newly assigned parish of St. Valentine's here in Bliss—said confessions were mostly done face-to-face now, so the room was never used.

Bonus: Basil was tied up preparing for the wedding mass. No one would look for CJ here.

But just in case, he made himself at home behind the screen in the red vinyl lounge chair on the priest's side of the dimly lit room. Everything smelled vaguely of christening oil. The muffled murmur of a crowd told him the rest of his relatives were arriving. He'd escaped just in time, so now he could pop back out at the opportune moment to witness Saffron's nuptials while avoiding the relatives asking his feelings on his sister's decision to have a destination wedding here. Of all places.

They always added of all places.

But until the ceremony, he had a comfy chair, blessed semi-quiet, and a God-given reprieve from guilt and condolences and memories. After the ceremony, he had about twenty-four more hours of family obligations, and then he could hit the road and leave this all behind.

Again.

He set his watch alarm, closed his eyes and pictured the sunrise he'd experienced at the summit of Mount Kilimanjaro a week ago. As he was about to doze off, the door on the other side of the screen wrenched open. A louder hum of female voices wafted in on the draft. Just as quickly, the door clicked shut and CJ's peace was restored.

Momentarily.

"Oh shit shit shit," a woman said. Her voice rippled with the kind of panic CJ expected from the bride today, but her husky undertones were too low for her to be any of his female relatives.

Perhaps the confessional hadn't been a gift from God after all. "If that's what you need to do, but not right now, please," CJ said.

Her shriek splintered his last hopes for peace. "Ohmigod!" his intruder gasped. "Not generally, but hey, if that's what you want to call me, I'm game." "I—you—what?"

He'd learned his lesson about that tone when his sister Pepper got him with the tailpipe off Basil's first heap of junk. Which meant goading his unexpected visitor was a bad idea. He covered the family jewels and settled deeper into the chair. “Never mind. Like I said. Wrong guy.”

She inhaled a ragged breath. “Sorry. Sorry sorry. I thought this was an office.” A shadow moved behind the screen, as if she were heading out.

Guilt nipped at his chest.

Probably a good thing she was leaving, whoever she was.

But the shadow stopped. If he were looking close—which curiosity might’ve encouraged him to do, but through only one eye, because he still wouldn’t have minded that nap—he might’ve seen the shadow’s head drop.

Heard a wobbly breath. For courage?

Sympathy added a few prickles to the guilt. “Nah, not an office. It’s more personal than that,” he said.

“More… personal?” “As personal as it gets.”

She started muttering then, words he wouldn’t have been able to understand even if he had been able to see her face, but the acoustics in this room were impressive and he did have a lifetime of experience with translating irritated-female. Not that he cared to translate. He’d let her mumble herself out, she’d leave, and he’d get back to dreaming about where he’d been and where he was headed next.

“I’m sorry?” he said. Because he was an idiot.

“Right, right. Get out so you can do your business.” Her shadow hovered at the doorway. His business. Sleeping. Avoiding relatives. Not asking her questions.

Not thinking about Serena and weddings and how the confessional suddenly smelled like oranges.

Just like Serena had.

His other eye slid open, along with one of those psychological wounds his sisters had spent the last fifty-eight hours talking at him about. “My business?” he prompted the woman.

Because it was better than thinking about oranges.

“You know what?” she said. “What if I just cover my ears? I can’t see anything, and everybody does it, so what’s the big deal?”

Whatever the lady thought everybody did in here, CJ was fairly certain this wasn't it.

Besides, he knew for a fact he never did what the room was designed for, and he suspected most of his sisters avoided it whenever possible too. Plus that whole majority of the world that wasn't Catholic. "No need to cover your ears," CJ said. "I, ah, do it quietly."

"You know what else?" she said. "Most buildings would at least have the courtesy to put a big sign on the door. So you can't miss it."

A sign for what?

CJ straightened. The orange scent was fading, and his mind was engaging in a puzzle. This was good.

Better than where his mind had been headed. "In my experience, the people who want to use a confessional don't need the sign."

"A con—oh, God." A hollow knock sounded, like a head hitting a door. "Shit! I'm sorry. Didn't mean to say God. Really."

His chuckle caught him off-guard. Of all the things he thought he'd be doing today, laughing inside a confessional wasn't one of them. "Ah, you're forgiven."

He didn't so much hear her suspicion dawning. He smelled it.

Familiar odor, that. Sort of like a bad pork chop on top of department store perfume, set off by female intuition and probably hormones too.

So much for funny. Still better than oranges. "Are you the new priest?" she said.

"No, ma'am. Just a single guy too early for a wedding."

More voices echoed on the other side of the wall, louder and closer. He couldn't make out the exact words of the conversations outside, which gave him hope the confessional was as private as it was supposed to be, but he should've been whispering.

Basil would be pissed if he found CJ in here like this, and CJ still had enough respect for the collar that he wouldn't suggest they take it out back to settle the grievance.

"You're hiding too," the woman said, the husky back in her voice. Distrust? Or was she intrigued?

"So few places to do it effectively," he said.

If she got the hint, she ignored it. "Are you in the wedding?"

"Nope." Dylan, the groom, had more best friends than CJ had sisters. Cleared him of all responsibility. Didn't even get asked to be an usher.

Or maybe Saffron didn't want to pick any more of his scabs. "Why so early?" his intruder asked.

"I was in housekeeping's way." He could've stayed at the rectory, but Basil's housekeeper was stopping by with her very single daughter. "You?"

"Oh, I'm not here for the wedding. Not to attend the wedding. The bride had a problem with her veil. All fixed now. So I should get going."

She didn't move. Not her shadow, not her scent—which was getting more orangey again since the suspicion had left her voice—not even her breath seemed to move.

CJ waited. Held his own breath.

"You having some trouble with somebody out there?" he asked. He didn't know jack about any of these musician types Saffron and Dylan had invited today, and he wouldn't tolerate it if a single one of them made any of his sisters or cousins or nieces uncomfortable.

"Oh, no. Not today. Exactly. It's just—" She blew out a shaky laugh. "Hey, this is a confessional, right?"

Basil would have his head if he didn't cut this off right now. "Technically there has to be a licensed operator for it to actually be a confessional." "Licensed operator?"

"Licensed from God. I'm not. Just a normal guy here. You sure nobody's giving you grief?"

"I'm fine," she said. "I'm just hiding from the Queen General and her latest poster boy." "The Queen General?" Which one of his sisters fit that description?

More like which one didn't.

"Queen General Marilyn," his visitor said. "Supreme ruler of Bliss and chairperson of Knot Festival."

The words Knot Festival twisted CJ's stomach, and the room seemed to climb ten degrees hotter. He tugged at his bow tie. The woman kept talking.

"According to the Queen General, divorced women don't belong in Bliss's bridal business, and divorced women don't belong at Knot Fest, and divorced women especially don't belong at high-profile Bliss weddings."

He couldn't tell if it was bitterness or regret coloring her words, but he would happily worry about someone else's problems if it helped him ignore the itching beneath his undershirt. "You live your life according to your rules or hers?" he said.

"The last time a divorced person tried to buy a shop on The Aisle, the Queen General was so displeased she made the town flood."

He stared at her shadow. Her words were English, but when she put them together like that, she might as well have been speaking alien.

Normal for a woman. But he'd take crazy woman-talk over Knot Fest talk and memories. He stretched out again. He could get her started, then doze off while she rambled. He was good at grunting go on noises in his sleep.

God bless his sisters. "Do tell," he said.

"She probably didn't actually cause the flood," the woman said. "But she did keep the divorced guy from buying the shop. She jacked up the price of joining the BRA—"

CJ coughed. "The what?"

"The Bridal Retailers Association. All the businesses on The Aisle belong." The Aisle. Right. This crazy town called their main street The Aisle.

"The QG runs The Aisle," the woman said. "So when this divorced guy tried to buy the party supply store, she went apeshit. She ordered the mayor to host a special Wedded Bliss Celebration that spring, married people only."

"So not you?" he said.

Because he was oddly fascinated that Bliss wasn't perfect.

His new whatever-she-was did that delicate snorting thing again. "She had the governor sign a proclamation naming Bliss the most family-friendly city in Illinois because of the Wedded Bliss thing. Most Married-est Town on Earth, and she won't let anyone forget it. You don't want to know what she did to discourage people from getting within four shops of the place this guy wanted to buy. And when he didn't leave fast enough for the QG, the town flooded. He opened a shop somewhere north of Chicago instead."

"And you want to live here… why?"

He knew better than to question a woman about her logic. But since this woman had invaded his confessional, he kept making rookie mistakes. He braced himself, waiting for the inevitable You couldn't possibly understand. That one drove him nuts.

Instead, she dove right into the last psychological wound his sisters hadn't hit yet.

First there was the soft sigh. Then her shadow drooped, and her voice did too. "It's home."

The sentiment echoed in the small room, her longing overshadowing any of her frustrations or regrets.

Home.

A hot shiver prickled the back of his neck. His parents' farm down near Peoria would always be home, but not like the home the yearning in her voice spoke of.

Her home sounded like family and kids and happiness. Like meatloaf and mashed potatoes.

Birthday parties with kazoos and paper hats. Pets and chaos and laughter.

Or maybe he was imagining what he'd always wanted.

The confessional was hot as hell. Even his balls were sweating.

"I've only lasted this long because my parents have done so much good for the community," she said. "They've buffered me."

Self-loathing. Now that was a feeling he could relate to.

He felt her shuddery breath rattle his own rib cage. He needed to stop her, maybe crash through the screen and dive out of the room into safer territory. But he'd seen his sisters in action enough to know her ears were becoming intake valves to keep her mouth running, and her brain had already launched into dump-all-my-problems-on-the-innocent-bystander mode. She'd follow him until she said her piece or until she sucked every last molecule of oxygen from the entire church.

And he still had a few dozen female relatives waiting to wallop him with pity outside that door.

"But my mom's gone now, and I know I can't live here forever. I've made some mistakes. But I'd like to do a few more things my parents would be proud of before the Queen General destroys me." The yearning was back in her voice, and it did more to scrape CJ's wounds raw than his sisters had managed in all of the last four years.

"So if you don't mind," the woman continued, "I'll just hang out here a few more minutes, and then she and her new Knot Fest poster boy can go ride off on their righteousness while I keep my mom's shop going."

The defeat and anxiety and sadness in the confessional were making it hard to breathe. He had an overwhelming desire to offer her a hug, and an equally strong desire to hasten her departure from what was supposed to be his haven.

He gripped the armrests on the chair, his palms sticking to the wood. "Takes a hell of a lot of balls to live like that."

"You mean a hell of a lot of idiocy? I should've left months ago. Those games she played with the divorced guy? It's my turn. She rewrote the Golden Husband Games rules so her Exalted Widower is eligible to be named Husband of the Half Century. And you know what? He's the reason my husband left me." CJ squeezed his eyes shut.

He hated the word widower almost as much as he hated mention of the Husband Games. Five years ago, after eloping here, he had played. And despite not knowing much about being a good husband himself, he'd won.

He shoved the memory away and latched on to the injustice done to his partner in hiding. Some guy destroyed her marriage? And now would get honored for it?

What kind of place was this? “Want me to kick his ass?”

“No!” Her shadow swayed. “Please. I wasn’t here. You didn’t see me, we didn’t talk. I don’t exist.” She chuckled, but there was nothing funny about it. “And to think, most of my life, I wanted to be her.”

A shaft of light broke through the room, and a cool draft whooshed a swell of conversation over the screen.

“Ma’am?” Basil intoned in his holier-than-thou, constipated way. “Can I help you? Are you lost?”

“No,” she said quickly. “Yes. I mean, we were just—Yes, actually. Yes, I’m lost.” There was silence. Then—“We?” Basil said.

Hell. CJ squinted at her shadow. Don’t look this way. Don’t look this way. Don’t—

Too late. “CJ?” Basil said. “If you’re in there—” “Yeah, yeah,” CJ grumbled.

“CJ?” the woman said. And if he wasn’t mistaken, there was some horror lingering beneath her words. “CJ Blue?”

Odd. Both being recognized in a Bliss confessional, and that it would be horrifying. “At your service,” he said.

Basil’s long-suffering sigh made an unfortunately familiar appearance. “Marring the sanctity of the confessional, CJ? Low, even for you.”

This, at least, was normal. “If God’s everywhere, how can one room be more sacred than anywhere else?” He liked yanking Basil’s chain, and besides, Basil’s predictable “very disappointed in you” theological lecture would be a welcome reprieve.

Instead, another female voice broke in. “Natalie. I wasn’t aware you were Catholic. Or invited.”

“Veil emergency.” CJ’s confessional intruder—Natalie, apparently—mustered more cheer than a hoard of drunken elves, making CJ think he’d imagined the horror. “Can’t have a disappointed bride in Bliss, can we?” Natalie said. “Guess I found the wrong room.”

Yes. Yes, she had.

"They're in the cry room," Basil said. "It's that way." "Thank you! Enjoy the wedding."

A shuffling told CJ his hiding companion had just left him to the wolf in priest's clothing and whomever the new mystery woman was.

Thank God.

"We'll talk later," the woman said. Even though Natalie had hit all his sore spots, CJ felt a twinge of sympathy.

Sounded like somebody was up for an ass-chewing. "Something you'd like to confess, Princess?" Basil said. "Jackass," CJ muttered.

"Careful, little brother. You're still in God's house."

True, but it was one more bit of normal he desperately needed. Besides, if he didn't react to the nickname, his siblings were more likely to call him by his real name. Their parents, free-spirited nature lovers that they were, had named all thirteen of their children after spices. Basil had gotten the only decent male spice name. God bless Rosemary for insisting on calling CJ by his initials, and God bless, well, God for not gifting his parents with any more sons.

CJ scooted around the screen and out of the confessional, ignoring the holy look of severe disappointment that generally kept people from mistaking CJ for his eldest sibling. The woman with Basil was somewhat familiar. And not just because she looked vaguely like Hilary Clinton. She was dressed in a white power suit and had neatly styled short hair with so many different shades of color in it—most occurring in nature—that he wasn't sure if she was blonde or brunette, though the sag beneath her chin suggested a natural gray.

Given her erect posture and the silent demands for acquiescence to whatever she was obviously about to say, he was surprised any of her skin had the audacity to droop out of formation.

A tingly sense of foreboding had more than just his balls sweating now. Basil clicked the confessional shut.

"Mr. Blue," the woman said, "I have an exciting honor to discuss with you."

CJ scrubbed a hand over his face. Honors in Bliss weren't his thing anymore. Whatever it was, he didn't want it. Wasn't so easy to say so, though. Something about the woman made his tongue want to say yes despite the fact that his brain, and one or two of his other favorite body parts, was screaming no! Took a swallow or two to find the appropriate deflection. "Appreciate the sentiment, ma'am, but I'm afraid I don't have the necessary respect for the collar."

While the woman tittered—which was a demonic kind of sound—Basil's pious disapproval hit epic proportions. He puffed his chest, showing off his own collar. "Don't flatter yourself."

"Mr. Blue." The woman offered CJ a hand so smooth it glowed, her pale blue eyes both inviting and scary as hell at the same time. "I'm Marilyn Elias. By the power vested in me as chairwoman of Bliss's Knot Festival, I hereby invite you to participate in the Golden Husband Games."

Marilyn Elias. Chairwoman. Knot Festival.

Queen General.

No. No, not just no. Hell, no.

CJ opened his mouth. No. One word, two letters. He could say it. He had to say it.

The Queen General blinked rapidly several times. Her eyes went unnaturally shiny. "The entire committee, of course, wishes your wife could be beside you. Such a tragedy." Suddenly she had a handkerchief in hand, dabbing at tears he suspected were made of cyanide. "But we believe you, a widower of a decorated military heroine and one of our most popular former Husbands of the Year, deserve the opportunity to compete to be crowned Bliss's Husband of the Half Century." Marilyn turned to a couple CJ hadn't noticed lurking behind her. "Surely you know what a wonderful husband this man was."

CJ's world twisted another crank. They weren't random wedding guests.

They were Serena's parents, Bob and Fiona. CJ's in-laws.

He hadn't seen them since her funeral. He'd planned to stop by their place tomorrow. Say hi. See how they were doing since the flood, since Bob's battle with cancer last year.

But there they were—here, now—at his sister's wedding with the Queen General of Bliss, waiting for him to accept or decline a reenactment of his wedding week.

This time without his bride.

Fiona smiled a watery, wobbly, this-would-mean-the-world-to-me kind of smile, her mouth wrinkling in the corners, the sag under her eyes suggesting she'd aged more than four years since the funeral.

Bob watched him with hopeful expectation, and CJ saw Serena's ghost pleading with him through her father's tired eyes. *You promised. You promised we'd come back here and have a big party with our families for our fifth anniversary.*

The Queen General—apt name, that—turned back to CJ with a beseeching look that was ruined by the freaky don't-fuck-with-me quality behind her tear shine. "Please, Mr. Blue. Please do us the honor of agreeing to participate in the Golden Husband Games in your wife's honor."

The niggling thought he'd been suppressing burst forth. He cast a glance around the vestibule, but the suddenly nauseatingly irritating Natalie was nowhere to be seen.

A sea of his sisters in their green bridesmaid dresses were, though. All his cousins. All his aunts. A handful of Dylan and Saffron's musician buddies.

All watching him. Waiting. Judging him. He couldn't breathe.

"Let us help you honor Serena's memory," Marilyn Elias said.

This woman could take all his sisters together in the contest for crazy-scary. Hell if he'd be anybody's poster boy—Poster boy.

Natalie had been bitching about CJ.

The Exalted Widower. The Queen General's poster boy. None of them had a clue what they were asking.

Who they were asking.

"I'm certain he'll be honored," Basil said.

CJ stepped back, but the plaintive hope brightening Fiona's weathered face made him choke on his denial.

"But of course he'll have to give it due consideration and consult his calendar," Basil continued.

The Queen General beamed. "Of course, my dear CJ. Of course. And the Knot Fest committee will be pleased to offer you any assistance necessary in making your decision. Do enjoy your sister's wedding today. And call me if I may be of any help." She slipped a card into his vest and retreated out of the church, his relatives giving the woman a wide berth.

He didn't want to call her.

He didn't want to stay in Bliss.

He didn't want to play in the Golden Husband Games.

Living with eleven sisters, though, CJ had acquired more than his share of knowledge about women. And he knew what he wanted didn't matter. This Queen General woman had a plan. A plan for him. He could fight it all he wanted, but the truth was simple. His future was no longer entirely within his own control.

* * *

Natalie was in her car, a cathedral-train-length away from escaping St. Valentine's parking lot when the Queen General stepped out of the front of the church and into the path of Natalie's car. Nat wanted to keep going. She still hadn't caught her breath or calmed her heart after the horrific realization that she'd just bared her soul to CJ Blue. All of her soul.

That she didn't belong in Bliss.

That she once wanted to be the Queen General. That he wrecked her marriage.

The QG was going to kill her.

Hang her from the center gazebo on the Bliss courthouse lawn with a giant D tattooed on her forehead and a Divorcees Be Warned, Thou Art Not Welcome in Bliss sign pinned to her dress. Because obviously Natalie would be in a dress. An ugly-ass, second-hand black bridesmaid dress, most likely.

There was some appeal to the thought of letting her car run over Marilyn.

But the car stopped of its own volition under the power of the QG's frosty glare. Possibly because the car knew in a match between it and the QG, the QG would win. Or maybe the car stopped because

Natalie didn't much like the idea that her son could grow up visiting Mommy in prison.

Still, that would be better than his growing up without her at all. Was it possible to die of mortification? She hadn't yet, but the day was still young.

She threw the car into park and rolled her window down.

"Miss Castellano." Disdain dripped from the QG's turned-down, painted lips.

Natalie swallowed hard. Her mother had led the Husband Games subcommittee for the Knot Festival, reporting to Queen General Marilyn for almost as many years as Natalie had been alive. By tradition, Natalie should've inherited her mother's place on the committee. It was how things were done in Bliss.

But the QG had denied Natalie the privilege of formally continuing her mother's legacy.

Were it not for Dad, Natalie would've had no role in Knot Fest at all. Instead, he'd convinced the QG to let Natalie represent the Castellano family for one last Knot Fest in Mom's honor.

The QG had ultimately relented and put Natalie on the janitorial subcommittee. Being the QG, she had the capability to do worse.

Much worse.

Especially after catching Natalie in a confessional with CJ Blue.

She swallowed once more, harder. "Mrs. Elias, nice to see you again."

"It is my pleasure," the QG said, not sounding pleased in the least, "to present to you the news that Mr. CJ Blue has been invited to play in the Golden Husband Games."

She stopped and peered at Natalie expectantly, as though Nat was supposed to burst into a round of applause and make a few catcalls for a kiss.

"Fantastic," Natalie said. The chorus of shits and dammits in her head were quickly adding up to a few more dollars she owed Noah's college fund. Today had been very profitable for the little guy.

"I'm not interested in your opinion, Miss Castellano," the QG said. "I'm informing you so that you understand that he will accept his invitation, and that you will have nothing further to do with him for the duration of his stay in Bliss. If I ever catch you in a compromising position with him again, I will not only remove you completely from the Knot Fest committee, but I will also do everything in my power to remove you from The Aisle. Are we clear?"

As clear as the ice forming in Natalie's veins. "Yes."

While the QG had formally taken the Husband Games job from Natalie, the truth of what Natalie was doing was a bit stickier. And if she were completely—and no doubt publicly—removed from the Knot Fest committee entirely, the golden anniversary of Mom's lifelong pet project would be nearly impossible to secretly keep afloat.

Nat never wished she'd stayed married to Derek, and she never wished she hadn't had Noah, but being divorced was a pain in the ass.

And that was a dime she'd happily give Noah's college fund.

"We all have to live with our choices, Miss Castellano. I suggest you give your future wiser consideration than you have your past. Starting now."

If Natalie had a couple do-overs, she'd fix a lot of things. But she didn't have do-overs.

She had do-your-bests.

She also had an ugly suspicion that her time of doing her best in Bliss had just been shrunk like cotton in a dryer.

Once again, she was letting her mother down.

The QG stepped back from the car, gave a regal nod, and tucked her forearms behind her back. "Enjoy your afternoon, Miss Castellano."

Natalie nodded meekly. She pulled away at a fraction of the speed her heart was racing.

Mortification and regret were still giving her soul indigestion, and while she'd developed a pretty thick hide over the last five years, her eyes and throat burned as badly as they had at her mother's funeral.

A nice afternoon? Not in Bliss.

Chapter 2

Natalie's favorite black pencil skirt and Mom's pearls weren't a total cure for the way her day was going, but she indulged herself with a quick trip home to change into them anyway.

Because she needed something to get through the rest of today.

Not only was her heart still doing the turn-yourself-around part of The Hokey Pokey from the confessional incident, but she had issues to deal with at the shop. Fewer brides were booking appointments, the coffee maker was acting up, and today, one of the bridal consultants had called in sick. She couldn't call Dad back from his grandpa-grandson playday with Noah so she could hide from her life and her responsibilities. Not when there was so much to do to keep the boutique running.

Not to mention the Husband Games.

After all her parents had done for her and Noah, she owed it to them to keep her life together. She owed them a hell of a lot more than she could ever repay.

So fifteen minutes after she left St. Valentine's, she pulled on her everything's-fine-here mask and marched into Bliss Bridal.

Since the flood three years ago, the entire boutique had been redone. Better lighting, faux marble floor, bigger dressing rooms, better layout, bigger selection of accessories, more efficient kitchenette and comfier chairs for the bridal parties that came along for the bride's big shopping day. The second floor, where the bridesmaid dresses and the in-house seamstress shop were—which was where Natalie had happily hidden after her divorce and before her mom's passing—was bigger, brighter and fresher too.

But the one thing that hadn't changed was the way the shop smelled of wedding cake. Because they shared a wall with Heaven's

Bakery, which was run by the QG. Natalie's steps faltered just inside the boutique, and her stomach flopped.

The boutique wasn't hers. It had been her mother's, now her father's, and one day—probably one day soon—he'd discover it wasn't doing as well as she pretended it was, and he'd sell it. And Natalie would have to find where she belonged in the world.

Because it wasn't here. Not in Bliss's wedding business. Not with the QG next door.

Amanda, Bliss Bridal's floor manager, paused with an armful of dresses on her way toward the front dressing room. "Big mess up in alterations over that doggie maid of honor dress, but I think they have it under control now. Two brides canceled their appointments tomorrow.

And you have visitors in the office." She took two more steps, then looked closer. "Nat? Everything okay?"

No. "Great. After you're done, hop online and start commenting on next week's brides' Pinterest boards. Be people to them—you know, connect personally. That's harder to cancel." She swung herself back into motion, her heels making staccato clicks to the time of a John Legend love song filtering softly through the room. No time to dwell on her latest mistakes.

She'd make another one soon enough, and she'd need her energy to deal with that.

The office and kitchenette were through a door behind the checkout counter. Since Natalie had taken over more and more of her mom's duties while Dad retreated further and further from boutique life, she'd relocated from her spot as head of alterations upstairs to her mom's old office. In the six months since Mom died, this was the first time she'd had unexpected visitors.

Much to her relief, they were welcome guests. "Jeremy! Gabby!" Her eyes welled unexpectedly, and she stepped into the room to hug them each in turn. "How are you two?"

Jeremy was Natalie's favorite bartender at Suckers, her favorite bar in town, though she'd been too busy for months to stop in for a drink. He could've been a stunt double for The Rock, and he'd saved

Natalie's hide when he'd agreed to be Bliss Bridal's bachelor for the annual bachelor auction last Christmas.

Gabby was his polar opposite—a petite blonde with more brains in her pinky than most people had in their whole heads—but she'd won him at the auction.

And today, she was sporting a new diamond.

A thick knot of something entirely too close to envy lodged in Natalie's throat. The welling in her eyes morphed into something with a sting. She latched onto Gabby's left hand, twisting it to make the rock sparkle. "Oh, beautiful." Didn't matter how hard Nat blinked, she couldn't entirely clear her vision.

They both smiled, more at each other than at her. They'd join the ranks of married Bliss, and they'd live their own happily ever after. And Natalie would be happy for them. "When's the big day?"

"The Saturday after the Games," Gabby said.

"Would've been her parents' anniversary," Jeremy added. Gabby shushed him. "It's a very practical date."

"Mm-hmm."

Natalie wasn't entirely following the nuances and hidden messages in their conversation, but she knew the look. The I've-found-the-only-one-for-me look. The we-make-each-other-right look. The I-love-you-above-all-else look.

This was what Bliss was supposed to do for couples. Nat cleared her throat. "So you need a dress."

"No, I—" Gabby started.

"Yes," Jeremy interrupted. "She needs a dress."

Natalie suppressed a smile. She'd grown up here in the boutique, and while it was unusual, this wasn't the first time she'd seen a man have to insist that his bride get the dress of her dreams. Knowing what she did about Gabby and Jeremy, Nat guessed cost was an issue. Gabby was finishing school and working part-time down the street at Indulge, Bliss's premiere chocolatier, and Jeremy worked as many shifts at Suckers as he could pick up.

"We give a good family and friends discount," Natalie said. She reached for a stack of catalogs on the shelf behind the pressed-wood desk. “Peek through these. See what jumps out at you. We’re cutting it close for a June wedding, but we’ll make sure you get your dress.”

Gabby’s smile drooped until any hint of bridal exuberance evaporated from the room. “I’m not good at this kind of thing.”

Jeremy took the catalogs from Natalie and put them on the desk. “Her grandmother was making her dress.”

Was.

Natalie knew all about was. Her eyes subconsciously drifted toward the front of the shop, where her mother had collapsed right beside the checkout counter. That was Natalie’s was.

“I’m so sorry,” she murmured to Gabby. “I hadn’t heard.” “Can you finish it?” Jeremy asked.

Gabby’s head jerked toward him. Her face scrunched up, her cheeks and nose went from pink to fuchsia, and her upper lip twisted. “I don’t need a dress to get married,” she said.

Nat’s chest constricted.

Jeremy pulled a beat-up point-and-shoot digital camera from the pocket of his Levi’s and handed it to Natalie.

“Jeremy,” Gabby whispered. “You deserve your dress.” “We can’t afford it.”

“We’ll make it work.” “It’s just a dress.”

Jeremy didn’t answer, just stared at her with an intensity that made Nat shiver. His mouth didn’t move, but he was saying something to Gabby. Something deeper than words.

Natalie diverted her gaze and occupied herself with looking at the pictures on the camera.

The dress was far from complete, but it was pinned well enough for Natalie to see it wasn’t complicated. She imagined it was supposed to be a simple, old-fashioned, 1940’s era dress—probably similar to what Gabby’s grandmother had worn on her own wedding day.

Before Natalie’s mom died, Nat had quietly taken the occasional major modification and from-scratch jobs for out-of-town brides. Their secret, Mom had called it. A way for Natalie to use that fashion design degree her parents had paid for. Mom’s way of trying to give Natalie her full dream.

The last few months, without her mom as a buffer between the indignity of Natalie's divorcée status and the Queen General's rules of Bliss propriety, Nat had mostly done her best to keep a low profile. And that had included closing the door on her secret favorite projects.

Not making waves so she could last on The Aisle long enough to finish Mom's work on the Games. Or trying, anyway.

But this—making Gabby's dress—this could be her last chance to connect her name to anything in her hometown.

"Your Nana would want you to have the dress," Jeremy said.

Gabby swiped the back of her hand over her eyes. "I have you. That's worth a million dresses."

"If I can't give you your Nana at our wedding, I'm going to give you the dress she wanted you to have." He pinned Natalie with a dark-eyed, silent order. "Can you do it?"

"Jeremy," Gabby said again. "We can't afford it." "Nat?"

"She's busy," Gabby said. "We can't ask her to take this on too."

Natalie had the boutique to keep afloat. The Games to plan. Noah to keep fed and clothed—and she liked to see him on occasion too. She did not have time to take on another project. Especially if there was any chance of the Queen General hearing. Gabby and Jeremy weren't Aisle people, but they were one of the success stories from the last bachelor auction, which would put them on the QG's radar. Natalie could be accused of sewing divorce cooties into Gabby's wedding dress. Wouldn't that be fun? She was hanging by a frayed thread here already.

Jeremy had one giant arm tucked around Gabby, who was watching Natalie as though she held the key to giving her back her grandmother.

Natalie was leaving Bliss. She might as well leave with a bang.

"Of course," she said to Jeremy. Because if she looked at Gabby again, she'd see herself in those first few days and weeks after Mom passed away, lost and sad and angry, but Gabby had something else.

She had a future with a man who loved her. She had hope. Natalie swallowed hard. "Bring me everything you have." "Really?" Gabby whispered.

"For my favorite couple? Absolutely."

Gabby tackled her with a hug. "We'll repay you for this," she said, her voice wavery and watery. "Thank you. Thank you so much."

"I got you covered, Nat," Jeremy said.

Natalie squeezed Gabby back. "Not necessary," she said.

Because nice as a little extra cash might be—especially given the state of Bliss Bridal's financials and a few things she'd done for the Games—having friends who trusted their wedding dress to her was worth so much more.

After Jeremy and Gabby left, Natalie checked that everything was running smoothly—if a bit slowly—out on the showroom floor and upstairs. Then she tucked herself into the office to answer the most vital Husband Games e-mails—one from the farmer in charge of the sunflower field, the other from the web design company that was setting up the voting page for one of the Husband Games events. The rest she saved for after Noah was in bed tonight, and she set to work on payroll.

Thirty minutes later, she needed a Tylenol. An hour after that, she wanted a whiskey sour, but since she was shaving her own salary down to the bare minimum to pay the rest of the employees, she couldn't afford a drink, much less the cash she owed Noah's college fund.

If sales didn't pick up, they wouldn't make it to Knot Fest. And she didn't know how she'd tell Dad.

Mom had been the primary force behind everything at the boutique. Dad had been on hand during busy times when Mom needed him. He was fabulous at convincing brides they looked beautiful in their gowns, and he'd supported whatever Mom needed supporting in her various Knot Fest and Bridal Retailers Association commitments. But mostly, he'd taken care of Natalie and Lindsey while Mom kept the boutique running.

Natalie pushed aside the keyboard and rested her forehead on the pressed-wood desk.

She'd grown up watching her mother work at her grandmother's classy antique walnut desk in this room, but the flood had taken it too.

In some ways, it was nice, how much the flood had taken. How much had changed. When Natalie left her hometown after Knot Fest for whatever the future held for her and Noah, it wouldn't be the same town she grew up in.

Maybe she would miss it less.

Or maybe all her happy memories would be swallowed by the last six months. If today were any indication, the next two months would only be harder.

Knot Fest crunch time.

She also had to find the time to make Gabby's wedding dress and somehow keep Bliss Bridal in the black.

Discover the key to invisibility so she wouldn't have any more run-ins with CJ Blue.

Even if by some miracle CJ resisted the QG's mind control and left town, Nat would still have the memories of today's mortification. That was enough to last another five years.

The worst part was, until she'd known who he was—when she'd thought she was talking to one of the normal wedding guests—she'd thought he was a semi-decent guy.

Not only was she a fool, she was a fool who kept repeating her own mistakes. "Are you a princess?"

The little voice out on the shop floor startled her. The shop girls and the bride-to-be giggled and oohed and aahed over Natalie's little minion. He was back from his playday with Grandpa, and he was working his magic. She straightened and pulled the keyboard back to its place. Her dad poked his head into the office.

In his prime, Arthur Castellano had been just shy of six feet tall, with thick, jet-black hair and a hooked nose. He'd lost a couple of inches in height as he'd aged, and his thinning hair was closer to salt than pepper these days. Since Mom died, there was a light missing in his eyes. "That's my princess, always working too hard," he said.

Natalie tried to smile, but she'd used up her faking-it quota already today.

"Someday I'm going to marry a girl as pretty as you," Noah said, still out on the floor, "and then"—Natalie didn't have to see him to know he'd be leaning forward, holding his arms out while his dark hair fell in his eyes—"I'm going to kiss her."

He was the perfection in Natalie's life. The absolute perfection.

Over another chorus of squeals and awws, Dad chuckled. "Gonna have to give that kid a commission."

Natalie's heart hiccupped. He'd said the same thing about her at that age, and look how she turned out. "Darn child labor laws," she said. "You two have a nice afternoon?"

"We went to that indoor fun center over in Willow Glen."

"Bet Noah loved that. Did Lindsey go?" Lindsey, her older sister, lived and worked in the trendy little city half an hour away. Close enough to visit, far enough to not violate the Queen General's No Divorce Attorneys Allowed edict.

Both the Castellano girls loved following the conventions of their hometown. Dad's lips slanted down before he shook his head. "She's working."

No big surprise there.

Dad jerked a thumb out toward Noah's voice. "Tell you what, that little guy takes after his grandpa. Should've seen him in the batting cages."

"He hit a ball?"

"Nah, not just yet. But he's got a good swing in him." He bent to sit in the corner chair and let out an old man grunt. "Looks like business is good today."

Natalie hid a wince. "Mm-hmm." She fiddled with the mouse, debating the wisdom of showing him the payroll. He hadn't double-checked her work since Christmas, said he trusted her, but sooner or later, she needed to tell him the truth.

That she was failing Mom—and him—one more time.

Another round of titters erupted out in the shop. "I like the sparkly one!" Noah said.

Nat's breath caught. She'd let him down too. She started to stand. "I should rescue the customers."

"Let the girls watch him a minute." Dad reached over to push the door mostly closed. His eyes took on a glossy sheen. "Been thinking a lot about the shop lately. 'Bout the future."

Natalie's chest squeezed and her legs gave a shudder. She gripped the seat of the folding chair that served as the desk chair and lowered herself back into it, slowly licking her lips. She'd known this was coming.

But did it have to come today? "Yeah?"

"Really become obvious lately I can't do this forever." His self-deprecating chuckle boomed louder in Natalie's ears than it should've. "Guess I haven't been doing it anyway the last few months. Probably longer, but I suppose you've figured that out."

"Dad—"

"No, no, it's the truth. But you've impressed me. Made this a whole lot easier, to be honest. Your mother was always proud of both you girls, but she'd be glowing to see what you've done since she's been gone." His voice cracked. He pulled his glasses off and wiped his eyes on the sleeve of his shirt.

It was hard enough to breathe past the lump in her throat, but Natalie's heart was stuck somewhere between swelling and twisting, adding an extra pressure in her chest.

She hadn't done anything near as well as she'd let him think she had. And he had a point.

If they were selling, they needed to do it now, while the shop was still worth something.

How would she keep the Games afloat then? "Dad, it's okay. I know."

"It's not just the shop." He was still talking to the floor. "I know it's not easy on the committee, but you've shown them all that you belong here despite your circumstances. I'm proud of you, honey. Real proud of you."

He was proud of her for being a fraud. She didn't fit in on The Aisle. She didn't fit in with the Knot Fest committee. She pretended she did for him. So he wouldn't worry over her. So he wouldn't worry over the Games. So he wouldn't worry over the boutique.

Dad drew a shuddery breath. "And that's why I want you to have the shop." Natalie bolted so straight her neck popped. "I—you—what?"

No. No. He wouldn't be this cruel. He wouldn't offer her the one thing she couldn't keep.

Not today.

She'd failed her parents enough already. She wouldn't run her mother's boutique into bankruptcy too. Not when they could sell it while it was still worth something.

He gave her a sideways glance. "After all you've done the last few months, I know it's what your mother would've wanted. Fourth generation in the family boutique business. You've earned it, honey. Figure it's about time I get out of your way."

The room was shrinking. It was shrinking, and it felt like someone had taken blowtorches to Natalie's ears. "Now?"

He gave the floor a halfhearted smile. "I know. Should've done it months ago. Truth is, I wasn't ready to face retirement. Thought I'd have your mother here with me when the time came. Everything we thought we'd do—" He shook his head. "Doesn't matter. What matters is, the boutique is yours."

"But—"

"Now, don't worry about Lindsey. I'm heading over to talk to her tomorrow. See who she'd recommend to draw up the paperwork."

Worry about Lindsey? Natalie was stuck on the part where Dad thought she could own the shop. His delusions were sweet, but they couldn't fix Bliss, and they couldn't magically keep the shop profitable.

Not as long as Marilyn Elias ran the town. "Dad, listen—"

"Lindsey's a logical kind of gal. Got her own thing, doesn't want the family business. We've always known that. But we'll work it out if she has any concerns."

It took effort to push air past her constricted throat. "I'm not worried about Lindsey."

For the first time since he'd shut the door, he looked at her, really looked at her. His eyes tightened, his head tilted. "Natalie? What's going on?"

Caught.

She needed more time to put her thoughts together. To explain this rationally.

To figure out what her future would hold once Knot Fest and the Golden Husband Games were over.

To come clean, but still make him think this was her choice. "Just getting hungry," she said. "Makes it hard to concentrate. I was thinking about dinner. How's Italian sound? Noah keeps asking for Cloudy with a Chance of Meatballs, and I make a mean can of SpaghettiOs."

"Natalie…"

She hated that warning note in his voice. She hated worse that her decisions in life meant she couldn't smooth it away. "I could stop at the store for some frozen garlic bread."

Dad's eyes narrowed to dark slits. "Is someone giving you trouble?"

Natalie would've rather taken a flogging before she had to explain to him that she'd failed him and Mom again. And she'd done that herself. Maybe the QG was behind some of it, but she could've tried harder. Sought better advertising. Experimented more. Offered better sales.

Stayed away from high-profile weddings where she'd known CJ Blue would be in attendance.

Except the truth was, she'd done most of those things. In a lot of ways, she'd done them better than La Belle and Mrs., the other two boutiques in town. But neither of the others were having problems. The Queen General was still winning her war to keep divorced people off The Aisle.

Dad's interference would do nothing more than earn him the same kind of heartburn Natalie had. He'd already served his time on The Aisle. This wasn't his fight anymore. It was Natalie's, and the truth was, it was over.

She stood and moved toward the door. "It's fine, Dad. Just been a busy week."

"That's not the problem here, though, is it?" His voice crunched through her ears like tires on gravel. It wasn't a question. It was an accusation.

She'd never wished so hard her mother were still here to smooth things out.

But Mom wasn't, and Natalie could never take her place. But Nat could be a grown-up.

Accept her place. Own her mistakes. And move on.

Natalie opened her mouth and forced her dry tongue to form the seven words that would probably make three generations of her mother's family split the seams of their coffin liners.

"I think you should sell the shop."

Dad's face turned a shade of gray Natalie hadn't seen since the summer he coached softball and Kimmie Elias smacked a line drive into his dad parts. He shook his head so hard his hair shifted. The gloss in his eyes turned to brittle glass. "Excuse me?"

Natalie almost buckled. Just kidding! she'd say. Except she wasn't. "You should sell the shop." Her voice wavered with her conviction. "It's the right thing to do."

The heater kicked on, and the first blast of semi-cool air from the vents overhead sent a shiver between Natalie's shoulders.

The angry vein throbbing in her dad's forehead made her knees quake. "The right thing for who?" he said.

Uh-oh. That was the calm voice that came between the warning zone and the danger zone. Natalie gulped. "For all of us."

"It sure as hell isn't the right thing for me!" He stood and pounded on the metal filing cabinet by the door, one of the few things that had survived the flood. "You think I spent my whole damn life working your mother's dream so you could prance around here and tell me this shop isn't good enough for you? That you don't give a damn about how we fed you, clothed you and sent you to college? That you want to wash your mother's legacy down the crapper?"

Righteous indignation and her own temper snapped Natalie straight. "You think this town will accept me as a business owner? I have to work twice as hard as every other person on this block as it is, and the shop's not even mine."

"That's bullshit and you know it."

"It is not and you know it." She held up her left hand and pointed to her bare ring finger. "I don't wear the right accessories to belong here, and I never will. And what about Noah?"

"What about him?"

"You and Mom had each other. I hardly see my son as it is right now. What happens if I'm running this place solo? When do I get to see him then?"

"So hire someone. We can afford it. Dammit, Natalie. There are solutions if you just think about it for a while."

"Oh, so now you want to give the shop to someone who can't think? Brilliant. Just brilliant."

"Don't you turn this on me—"

"You're turning it on me! I'm trying to do what's best for everyone, but you're too stubborn to consider that maybe it's time we sell and move on." She was vaguely aware that the love songs constantly pumped into the shop were getting louder, which meant the customers could hear and the girls out on the floor were trying to cover, but she didn't care. She wasn't the bad guy here. She wasn't the good guy either—that wasn't a crown she would ever wear in Bliss—but Dad was way overreacting.

"Do you have any idea what you're asking me to give up?" he said.

"You think I want to do this? That I want to walk away? I don't have what it takes to make this shop work. You think I wouldn't change that if I could?"

"I think you quit every time anything gets hard, that's what I think. Damn it, Natalie, when are you going to grow up?"

Natalie pointed out toward the floor. "About five years ago, if you didn't notice."

"I noticed." Dad stalked toward the door, then turned back around. "Should've happened to Lindsey. At least she could take care of a child on her own."

Natalie sucked an icy breath through her nose.

Despite everything, Dad still thought she was the same immature brat who'd ignored everyone's warnings and gotten married because of a ridiculous idea that she could transform Derek into the man she needed her husband to be. She was an Aisle princess; he was a second-generation mechanic from a broken home. He'd been dark and dangerous and bold—no other man had asked her out those first two years after she graduated college. But he'd also shown a soft side, writing her poems and picking wildflowers for her. And she'd decided to save him from his sorry, non-Aisle existence, and finally fulfill her destiny of getting married in the process.

Turned out, she was the sorry one.

Still was. Probably always would be. Her own father thought so.

She blinked back the cold sting of tears. "You know why I don't want the shop? It's because this town doesn't want us. If they don't want me, fine. But what about Noah? He hasn't had a single playdate since Mom died. I had to cancel his birthday party because Marilyn made sure no one would come. I'm doing this for him."

"You're doing it for yourself and using him as an excuse."

Natalie flung a hand out and wished she had a filing cabinet to hit. "That's right. I'm the horrible one. Well, Dad, you raised me. So what does that say about you?"

A tension hard as granite settled in the room. Natalie's lungs seized. Dad's forehead vein visibly throbbed. He lifted a finger to the door. "Get out."

Natalie deflated. There she went, screwing up thank you all over again. "Dad—" "I said, get out."

She needed to apologize, but he pointed harder at the door, his eyes shiny, his throat working overtime.

She snagged her coat and purse and scurried out of the room before she could make anything worse. Amanda gave her a funny look, and Natalie realized her cheeks were wet. Noah barreled around the high register counter. “Mommy!”

Her heart squeezed, and she dropped down to his level. Her reason for living shot into her arms, a streak of blue dinosaur shirt and brown hair and love. He must’ve had another growth spurt overnight, because his legs seemed to barely dangle a foot off the floor when she stood up with him. He hadn’t been that tall yesterday. But he was still solid and warm, and he still smelled like little boy sweat. She buried her nose in his dark wavy hair. “Hey, baby boy. Let’s go home. You want some spaghetti?”

“Can my meatballs be made out of dinosaurs? Because Grandpa says if I drink my milk I’m a cow. So if I eat dinosaurs, I’m a dinosaur, and I want to be a dinosaur. Can I be a dinosaur?”

“You can be anything you want to be.” And it was Natalie’s job to make sure he could. She’d screwed up everything else. She couldn’t afford to get this one wrong too.

Chapter 3

The liquor might've been free at the wedding, but at least it was squawk-free across town at an off-the-wall joint called Suckers. Tonight, CJ's headache demanded that his frugal side shut the hell up and let him indulge.

He had fulfilled his familial duties at the wedding reception—made Bob and Fiona comfortable, danced with the obligatory percentage of female relatives, suffered through the requisite number of not-so-subtle inquiries as to his emotional state, warned Dylan of the consequences of mistreating his new bride, spent his allotted hour making sure Gran didn't goose any of the waitstaff—and now CJ was happily seated on a red leather stool at the steel semi-circle bar breathing guilt- and in-law- and family-free air.

Several of the bride and groom's big-shot musician friends had staggered in looking for females who weren't related to the bride, all dropping names like Toby Keith and Tim McGraw and Billy Brenton to attract the attention of the single women in the bar.

They could have 'em. CJ was done with women today.

Feeling like he didn't fit into his family anymore might've been bothering him too. He'd been too slow to keep up with the friendly jabs and inside jokes flowing around him at the wedding, and his mind kept drifting back to the confessional. The more he thought about all of it, the more pissed he got.

If he hadn't escaped the reception, his mood would've ruined what was left of Saffron's big day. Too bad he wasn't able to escape himself.

One seat over on his right, a tallish older guy with salt-and-pepper hair and a mulish,

I-wanna-get-shitfaced expression was concentrating on a full shot glass. CJ had taken himself around the world the last few years, tending bar to pay for his next BASE jump or scuba dive or hang gliding trip, and he had a solid feeling this guy wasn't where he belonged.

Made for good odds the guy wouldn't want to make chitchat. Perfect.

But CJ had barely gotten his own drink from the big tattooed bartender when his privacy got shot to hell. To his left, Basil appeared and inhaled an audible, about-to-open-his-mouth-and-be-annoying kind of breath. "I suppose it's my duty as your arm man to enlighten those poor young ladies as to the unlikelihood of your bank account supporting your buying them a drink."

"Wing man," CJ corrected without thinking. He lifted his Jameson to his lips, purposely not looking at Basil or the ladies. If he ignored them all, they wouldn't be there.

"Might want to check them out," His Holy Piousness said. "Never know where you'll find a woman willing to support you in the manner in which you've become accustomed."

CJ supported himself just fine. Man didn't need possessions to have a life, and he'd had a hell of a good time the last few years. Lived more in those years than most people did in a lifetime.

Basil gave a holy sniff. "Can't recall if you like brunettes or blondes better, but you've got your pick over there."

It was like having one of his sisters here. Should've picked a different bar. One four or five states away.

"The brunette's naked," the Holy Annoying One said.

"Does God approve of setting your brother up with an exhibitionist?"

"God's willing to make some concessions if that's what it takes to nudge you along the path to adulthood."

CJ gave a brief thought to slugging Basil, but decided against it. Conduct unbecoming of a former Husband of the Year and all that. Least he could do for Serena and Bob and Fiona was to behave himself, especially so close to their hometown.

But paying the bartender to knock out some of Basil's pompousness had some merit.

Or it would have, if CJ could afford it. His bank account was in a valley after his trek up Mount Kilimanjaro and the subsequent plane ticket home for the wedding.

The Jameson, though, was worth every penny.

Especially since his plans to leave for Utah tomorrow were now delayed. His sisters had volunteered him to clean Bob and Fiona's gutters. Bob had looked just pallid enough by the time he and Fiona headed home to Willow Glen that guilt had convinced CJ to stick close for another day or two, see what else they needed done.

Work in mentioning that he wouldn't play in the Games. Couldn't do it without a wife anyway. That would be a reasonable excuse.

One he should've thought of hours ago.

"If you're determined to forever be homeless," Basil said, as if each word pained him, "that room you're staying in at the rectory is open for the foreseeable future."

CJ grunted over his drink. Most of the family would scatter back across Illinois tomorrow or Monday—only a couple of them had moved more than a few hours from the Peoria area in the middle of the state—but Basil's diocese had sent him here to Bliss a few weeks ago. He liked to gossip and henpeck as much as the girls. Another two nights would probably kill CJ, but a free room wasn't something he was in the position to mock.

"My congregation has a soft spot for lost souls, and I could use someone to do my laundry and dishes," Basil added.

"Sounds like you could use a wife," CJ said. "I hear they're overrated."

"Your housekeeper's daughter is single. I'm sure God would understand." "Didn't you used to be funny?"

"Were we at the same wedding today? Because hell if anything's funny after that many hours with that many women."

Basil's cheek twitched, the pious holiness equivalent of a belly laugh. CJ shook his head and lifted his glass. "To shitty days, man."

"You two don't know shitty."

The guy to CJ's right was sizing him up as if he were trying to decide whether CJ was worth the effort it took to look at him.

"Arthur Castellano?" Basil said.

The older guy dipped his chin in acknowledgement. "Our condolences on your wife's passing."

CJ had lost the bow tie a good while ago, but the prickly heat around his neck came back, along with some extra pressure where he'd once worn his wedding band.

Arthur looked down at his own finger, and a lost hopelessness blanked his expression. He snagged his shot glass with a wobbly hand and tossed the drink back in one inexperienced motion.

His face went a nice purple color complementary to the neon track lighting above the bar, and he coughed out a long, dry, tongue-out cough that spoke of a man having his first run-in with bottom-shelf whiskey.

"Ho-oly fish sticks," Arthur gasped.

Basil gave CJ a nudge. "How about you help the man out."

"Don't ever take one on the house unless you know what they're pouring," CJ said. Helpfully.

But Basil shot him one of those pompous don't-be-an-ass looks that magnified when Arthur slapped a fifty down on the bar. "Keep 'em coming," he called to the big guy.

The second bartender, a guy so old he probably farted ashes, scowled over at them as if they'd already stiffed him on his tip.

Arthur wheezed out a chuckle. "Go on, Huck," he said to the old guy. "Try and throw me out. My money works here."

Huck's rheumy blue eyes bulged, and his hunched chest puffed out. The crowd went noticeably quieter. Not silent—Saffron's wedding guests didn't seem to notice the chill descending—but several patrons in non-formal attire stopped to watch.

The old guy pointed a finger at Arthur. The other bartender stepped between them. He looked about CJ's age, but the dude could've pounded CJ into the ground with just a thumb.

Said something. CJ wasn't a small guy either.

The big dude slid Arthur's fifty off the bar and gave him an unreadable look. "Money's good here, attitude ain't," he said. "Don't want to throw you out, so simmer on down."

Arthur leaned around him to eye the old guy one more time, then slumped, arms crossed.

The big dude refilled Arthur's shot glass from a bottle of Jeremiah Weed. Conversation in the bar went back to normal levels, but Arthur was still getting curious glances.

"They don't like my kind in here," Arthur said to CJ. "Mine either," Basil said.

CJ choked on an unexpected laugh. Old pompous-pants was getting funny in middle age.

Wrong—CJ had served many a priest in many a bar—but funny. "Your kind?" CJ said to Arthur, though he had a suspicion getting the guy going wasn't a wise idea.

Couldn't seem to help himself today.

"I own a shop on The Aisle. Huck there"—Arthur nodded at the barkeep—"isn't a fan of the wedding industry."

"Why not?"

"Guy's been divorced three times and has a bar called Suckers in the most married-est town on earth. He caters to the underground wedding haters and single groomsmen. Makes his reputation on not liking the likes of me."

"Bliss Bridal?" Basil said to Arthur. The older man nodded.

Basil nudged CJ again. "I believe you met his daughter this afternoon."

Took a minute for CJ to register what Basil meant. But when it registered, it registered big.

CJ wasn't even drinking and he choked.

Arthur grunted. "Which one?"

The crazy one probably wasn't the right answer. Neither was the infuriating one. And God help them if that didn't narrow it down. "Natalie."

Arthur's jaw tightened. "She welcome you to Bliss?" "Suppose you could say that."

Basil coughed. CJ knew that cough. It was a cover for the fact that Basil had once again momentarily become reacquainted with his sense of humor.

Old Pompous Pants had no idea how not funny the whole situation was.

CJ might not have been the poster husband that the dear old Queen General wanted him to be, but he damn sure hadn't chased anyone's husband away or wrecked anyone's marriage.

Other than his own.

Arthur downed his next shot. His eyes bulged, his skin went red from his top shirt button to his receding hairline, and he wheezed out a series of raspy coughs. "Holy Toledo," he gasped.

The big bartender hid a smile, and CJ felt an affection for the bar take hold. Not warm enough for him to care that there was a Help Wanted sign over the mirror, but warmer than it had been five minutes ago.

"You got kids?" Arthur said to CJ after he'd wheezed himself out.

"Bunch of nieces." And another couple of punches to the gut every time someone asked him that.

"Do yourself a favor. Let that be enough. Kids got a way of messing with a man." So did women.

"Problem with kids," Arthur said, "is they develop opinions. They take all your hard work for granted, then throw it all back in your face when you're down. Never say thank you for putting clothes on their back, food on their table—"

"Or for walking uphill five miles in the snow both ways," Basil said with utter seriousness. "Carrying a hundred pounds of their crap on your back," Arthur agreed. "And then they blame you for needing therapy."

"I think he knows Ginger," Basil said to CJ.

Ginger, the third oldest Blue sibling and the most open about her visits with her shrink. If CJ had followed Basil and Rosemary, he'd need a shrink too.

Probably did anyway.

The big dude passed another shot up the bar, then lumbered away.

"Her mother would've known what to do." Arthur pressed his palms into his eyes and let out a shuddery breath CJ recognized all too well. "Always knew better than I did. With both of 'em." He tossed his third shot back almost as if he were getting the hang of it, but he still wheezed out a string of dry coughs.

This would get ugly fast. CJ flagged Huck. "How're your nachos?"

The old dude sized him up. Slid another suspicious look to Arthur, then to Basil, then back to CJ.

It occurred to CJ that Huck knew who he was. CJ glanced around the bar.

The locals weren't watching Arthur. They were watching CJ.

Openly. Curiously. Suspiciously.

All these people knew who he was, or who they thought he was. A military widower.

Husband Games winner five years back. The Queen General's new Knot Fest poster boy.

The man who wrecked Natalie's marriage?

Wasn't just hot under his collar now. Nope, he was itchy too. Itchy, confused, and borderline pissed. If CJ had wrecked Arthur's daughter's marriage, wasn't a chance in hell Arthur would be sitting here getting shitfaced with him. So somebody was mistaken. And it wasn't CJ.

He wasn't big on being accused of things he didn't do.

Especially when the accusations reminded him of things he had done.

Huck nodded to CJ and signaled the kitchen, making his gray Willie Nelson–like braid swing. "Nachos are good. Soak up the liquor too." He shuffled on down the bar, and Arthur grunted at the older guy's back.

On CJ's other side, Basil shifted in his seat, pulled out his phone, then sighed. "The twins lost Gran," he said. "Pepper's asking for reinforcements."

Hallelujah. Good excuse to get the hell out of here. Maybe get away from himself too.

But Basil clapped him on the shoulder. "Stay. Have fun. Make sure you're okay to drive yourself home."

Not a chance. And Basil probably knew it. "How about you point me to the nearest bingo hall, and I'll go find Gran," CJ said. Commiserating with a fellow widower—especially this one—wasn't on CJ's schedule.

Basil's eyes narrowed in devilish delight. He made an unmistakable take-care-of-the-drunk nod at Arthur. "I believe you're still in need of some penance, little brother."

Basil had no idea how long CJ had been paying his penance. And not for marring the sanctity of Old Holy Britches' confessional. "Somebody should tell God you're pinch-hitting for Satan," CJ said.

No denying the spark of humor lightening Basil's expression. "Curfew at the rectory is midnight."

Curfew on CJ's peace of mind passed about nine hours ago. "And make sure your new friend here gets home safe too."

CJ bit back a suggestion about what Basil needed to keep safe. But Basil knew the Bliss bingo halls better than CJ did, and his car was more reliable.

And the truth was, CJ couldn't leave a guy hanging in a bar with no safe way home. Not when he was only seventy percent sure the two bartenders would look out for Arthur. "Yes, Mom."

While Basil headed for the door, CJ sucked up his penance, pushed away his Jameson, dammit, and turned to Arthur. Sooner they got the widower's commiserating out of the way, the sooner they could get Arthur sobered up and both of them out of here.

Without any more talk about Arthur's crazy daughter. "How long's she been gone?" CJ asked.

Arthur scratched his ear. "Six months. Brain aneurysm. Never saw it coming." "You done this before?" CJ nodded at the shot glasses.

"Nope."

"Took me about four times before I realized it wasn't helping. Tell you what did, though. Skydiving."

"Skydiving?"

"When your wife dies fighting a war, you gotta find a way to prove she didn't have bigger balls than you. Skydiving did it for me." So he told himself.

"You stay married thirty-four years, you don't have to prove who's got the bigger balls. Just take it for granted she does." He swayed on his stool, then emitted a giggle.

With all those sisters, CJ knew a thing or two about giggles. Knew a thing or two about fast drunks too. "Those nachos?" he called to Huck.

The old man pointed to the kitchen. "Can't hurry good food. Keep your pants on."

Arthur's head dipped, and his goofy grin swung a one-eighty until CJ thought the dude might cry. "I shouldn't have yelled at her."

More guilt welled up in CJ's chest. "They forgive us, man." He hoped.

"Not Karen. Natalie." Arthur waved his shot glass at Huck. "It's hard on her, being on that committee. She's doing the best she can. Doing better than I could, even with her circumstances. I knew it, and I yelled anyway. She should've told me how bad things were."

CJ swallowed hard. "Women make us crazy." Seemed appropriate. And safe.

"Me and Karen, we were going to retire in another five or ten years and go see the world. Sell the shop. Didn't think Nat wanted it anymore. But now Karen's gone, and I thought Nat was fitting in. I can't—I wasn't—I can't sell it. That shop and our girls—they're all I have left of her. Can't win today. Just can't win."

They sat in silence until Arthur slanted an almost passably sober glance CJ's way. "You gonna play in the Games?"

"Not likely."

"Supposed to tell you it's good publicity for the town." Arthur wobbled on his stool, his voice wobbling with it. "Marilyn says we're showing our best colors when we honor a war widower. Tell you what, though, if I play, I'm gonna kick your ass."

No doubt most of the whole town could. "Thirty-four years, was it?" CJ said. "Thirty-four years. Damn good years."

"Eleven months for me, and she was deployed three of those. You tell me, who's a better representative of what marriage is all about?"

Arthur swayed. "Was she your everything?" For a while.

Until he screwed it up.

"Don't tell anybody I told you this, because it's bad for business," Arthur said, "but the only thing that matters is that she's your everything. The wedding, the legalities, the rings, the dresses and cakes and Games don't add up to a hill of beans. If you loved her with all your heart and you honor her memory with how you live your life, she was your everything. If not, get the hell out of my town."

CJ eyed his Jameson.

"Thirty-four years, she was my everything. But it doesn't mean shit, because I wasn't a big enough man to teach my daughters that lesson." He pointed a finger at CJ. "One day, son, you're gonna find yourself your everything. When you do, you tell her. And then you make sure you live it. Live it every day."

The big dude slid a heaping plate of nachos between them. Arthur dug in. "Good nachos. Should come here more often."

CJ wished he'd stayed with the squawkers. He hadn't been Serena's everything. And it was too late to fix it now.

Chapter 4

Natalie had thought multiple brushes with death-by-mortification were the worst part of her day, but living through Noah's meltdown over her not-as-good-as-Grandpa's reading of How I Became a Pirate took top honors.

As if she hadn't had enough reminders today that she was a failure. She needed one last kick from her four-year-old flesh and blood.

He had finally settled down, and she'd snuck back into his room to snuggle him until he drifted off in the middle of singing "Twinkle Twinkle Little Star" to himself. It would've been so easy to stay there with him, listen to his soft breathing, and let his snug body warm her chilled soul.

But she had a clandestine meeting about Golden Husband Games security to arrange with the Bliss Chief of Police, a handful of e-mails to answer from concerned Husband Games vendors who hadn't seen signed contracts yet, and probably an apology to issue to her dad. So she staggered downstairs in search of hot chocolate and perspective.

Instead, the first thing confronting her in the small office-slash–sewing room across the hall from Dad's bedroom downstairs was her dog-eared copy of Diana Gabaldon's Outlander.

Nat had started rereading it during a precious free moment last weekend, but today the thought of a copper-haired Highland warrior made her stomach attempt a full acrobatic routine. Cursing herself for not starting the new Mae Daniels book with its dark-haired, charming Southern hero instead, she shoved the book in the bottom drawer of the desk, then almost squashed Noah's favorite dinosaur when she flopped down in the chair.

She rescued the stuffed animal and set it on the edge of the desk. "Sorry, Cindy," she muttered to the orange stegosaurus.

Cindy stared back with disgusted accusations in her dark button eyes.

"Fine," Natalie said. "You make sure Mom's boutique doesn't fall apart. You keep her Games going. You play nice with the man who destroyed your marriage so the Queen General doesn't make you the victim of her next voodoo cake."

Cindy had the grace to look properly chastised.

It was entirely possible Natalie needed a shrink. How had Mom done this all?

One step at a time, Mom would've told her. Natalie hadn't known how big those steps would be, or how many obstacles she'd have to overcome.

This time, it wasn't an obstacle she could beat. It was an obstacle she had to walk away from.

Nat triple-checked a draft of an e-mail to the chief about Husband Games security. She wrote e-mails back to the trophy shop, the high school booster club, and the hardware store, assuring them their contracts hadn't been awarded elsewhere and suggesting they approach Bonnie and Earl Phillips at their flower shop this week with proposed agreements in hand. The QG, as head of all of Knot Fest, got to choose Mom's replacement for the Husband Games subcommittee. She'd appointed the Phillipses, and now everything was falling apart. But Nat knew the Knot Fest treasurers would handle payments so long as the vendors' contracts were signed, so Bonnie and Earl couldn't let that slip through the cracks too. Thank God Mom had gotten the sunflower field contract finalized before she died. Now if only the weather would hold up for the planting this week, and the rest of the spring so the plants could survive.

When her e-mails were done, Natalie considered curling up on the couch and waiting for Dad—they needed to have a rational, honest, heartbreaking discussion about the shop—but her usual second wind had kicked in, and she couldn't sit still.

So she pulled out her copies of Mom's notes about the Golden Husband Games and set to work making her own notes about what she needed to subtly put in motion next—permit applications, bus reservations, invitations, door prizes for the crowd, schedules, manipulating the weather, and a host of other things that weren't getting done—all without the Queen General getting wind of her involvement.

Natalie had made mistakes, but it felt good to be helping. Doing something right.

Honoring her mother—who had been Nat's strongest public and private supporter after her divorce from Derek—by finishing the work that had been the highlight of Mom's year.

After twenty-seven years of leading the Husband Games subcommittee, a position she'd inherited from her mother before her, it wasn't fair that Mom would miss the golden anniversary. But Nat was doing everything in her power to make sure the Games were as beautiful and brilliant as if Mom had done it all herself.

Dad still wasn't home when Nat finished her notes, and a book wouldn't cut it for relaxation tonight. She switched desks, grabbed her sketchbook, and powered up her sewing machine. Jeremy would drop off Gabby's dress tomorrow, but Nat had another project to work on. The same kind of projects she'd done anytime she got an urge to sew the last few months. Before long, though, her eyes itched like her lashes were made of the starched lace she was adding to a Cindy the Stegosaurus-shaped yellow bridesmaid dress. A veil-like haze ringed the edges of her vision. She set the dress aside.

Headlights flashed through the blinds.

Natalie's heart fluttered. "Please let us both be reasonable adults," she murmured to the ceiling.

She hadn't meant to belittle Dad's offer of the shop. She'd spent her entire childhood dreaming about the day it would be hers. Of the glittery accessories she'd order, of all the dresses she'd have in her own closet, of all the dresses she'd design to make her the richest, most famous, most envied shop owner on The Aisle. Possibly in the whole wedding industry.

Such a selfish dream, all wrapped up in ribbons and bows and blinders. She'd never considered that the price of owning the shop would be her mother's life.

Yet, she still wished she could keep it. That she could give Noah a stable childhood here.

That she could successfully compete on The Aisle.

But she wasn't meant to have a fairy-tale ending.

The car lights cut off outside. A car door slammed. Then another car door.

She whipped around to peer through the gauzy drapes. That was her dad's voice, but he wasn't alone. Two bulky figures moved past the window.

Wait—was Dad singing?

Yep, that was "Itsy Bitsy Spider" in a familiar baritone. Except when Natalie learned the song, the Itsy Bitsy Spider was supposed to go up the spout again, not sit and pout in his gin.

A second voice spoke low and deep. Dad laughed. Natalie heard the distinctive sound of keys being tested in the lock, and Dad laughed harder. His companion said something else.

Natalie darted to the front door and flung it open.

Dad grinned at her, one eyeball pointing more toward his nose than toward her. "Look, it's the top of my shit list."

He swayed, and his companion steadied him.

Natalie's stomach flipped inside out. A few expletives flew through her head, but this time, she didn't immediately calculate what she owed Noah's college fund.

Nope, this one was free.

Because her father, her own flesh and blood, had brought him home.

Look, Nat, Dad may as well have said, *this is what I always wanted in my children.*

Dad knew what had happened, and he'd brought CJ home anyway.

Everyone knew what happened, and they still glorified him. They picked him over one of their own.

Because he hadn't married the wrong person. That was all that mattered, wasn't it?

CJ stood there, unblinking, unhurried, and arrogant as if he'd been a Highland laird in that book Natalie had hidden from herself. He was copper-haired, tall and broad as the door, cocky as hell. While one side of his mouth hitched up, his grass-green eyes made a slow, intentional perusal of her body, from the headband holding her hair back, to her lips, to her black tank and cardigan, to her yoga pants, to her pink-tipped toes, and then all the way back again.

Sizing up the enemy.

She wished she had the luxury of sizing him up too. Instead, she swallowed her pride, and opened the door wider. "Come on, Dad. Let's get you to bed."

Dad took two Captain Jack Sparrow steps into the house, and his knees buckled. CJ snagged him before he hit the wood floor. "Whoopsh," Dad said on a chuckle.

Natalie's jaw locked down, but she forced it to unclench. This was her fault too.

She reached for Dad. "Thank you for bringing him home," she said to CJ's lapel. "I can take it from here."

Dad swatted in the general vicinity of her hand. "Itshy bitshy shpider don't need girl help," he slurred.

CJ cleared his throat. Natalie instinctively looked up. A dangerous amusement flickered from his eyes to his lips, and she felt an inexplicable pull low in her abdomen.

Inexplicable, unwelcome, and not as surprising as she wanted it to be. "He'll be okay soon," CJ said.

Maybe someone else's dad would be okay soon, but the liquor cabinet over the fridge held the exact same booze her parents had received as wedding gifts.

Except for those few open bottles she'd refilled as a teenager. "How much did he drink?" Natalie said.

CJ's grin turned a color of delicious that perfectly matched every last put-together inch of his solid, male body.

She disliked him more by the minute.

"Aw, Mom, can't a guy have a night of fun every once in a while? This man here"—he slapped Dad on the back, then shifted to prop him up again—"hasn't gotten shitfaced in years. When a man loses the love of his life, there's nothing like a night or two to drink until you forget. Then you move on. All he's been dealing with, he's had it coming."

Drool slipped out Dad's mouth. He swiped at it, clocked himself in the nose and knocked his glasses crooked, then laughed like Noah had told a bad knock-knock joke.

Natalie's roots radiated more heat than the heater. She stepped up to Dad's other side. "Bedtime. Let's go."

He swatted at her again and banged the entryway table instead, knocking flat his wedding picture that had been there since Mom passed—one of the few photos that had survived the flood. "Can't hold the fam'ly, can't hold me. Man gots friends, time like thish." Dad punched CJ in the ribs.

CJ didn't flinch. His gaze flicked to Natalie, and a fleeting memory of her own guilt at that long-ago Knot Fest tickled her conscience.

"Might want to get him a bucket," CJ said. "Sound good, Arthur? Bed and a bucket? Let's go, buddy."

With CJ's help, Dad made it farther into the house.

The Queen General would read Natalie the riot act when she got wind of this. And she'd get wind of every bit—how Natalie was a shithead to Dad at the shop, how Dad went who-knew-where to get drunk, how Natalie welcomed CJ Blue into her home in the dead of the night.

If she could start this day over, she'd poke herself in the eyeball with a sewing needle to avoid having to live through it.

But she didn't have that luxury. Instead, she had to attend to a drunken father and the QG's poster boy. A drunken father who'd earned his night out, and a poster boy she now owed for not allowing Dad to drive home drunk and possibly causing Natalie to bury both her parents within a year.

The thought made her breath hitch.

And maybe her general dislike of CJ thaw. But only a little.

She gestured toward a short hallway beneath the stairs. "His room's that way."

With the men headed to Dad's room, Nat ducked out to the garage, sucked in enough chilly air to numb her lungs, snagged a bucket, and wondered how the hell she could minimize tonight's damage.

She needed to stuff her pride back into the shadows and be a good little divorced daughter of Bliss, but when she got back inside, CJ was taking up Dad's entire doorway with his tallness and broadness and inherent Neanderthal-ness.

She might've gone a little tingly in some formerly dormant parts.

Residual cold from the garage. Her dormant parts were defrosting. Totally normal after going outside for less than a minute in early spring. Yep. That was all it was.

Nothing related to having an attractive, apparently capable, single man in her house.

Or related to thinking about what might've been her own role in the demise of her marriage. But she had enough problems without going there.

She put the bucket between her and CJ—a girl had to give some indication she didn't like having strange men in her home. Until he acknowledged recognizing her from the confessional incident or introduced himself, she would absolutely call him a stranger.

She hovered just beyond the door.

"Here, let me." CJ gave her an even more delectable grin. Hints at laugh lines creased the corners of his mouth.

"Arthur's not decent." CJ winked, and then the bucket was gone, her mouth was dry and she was staring at the closed bedroom door, wondering how the man who symbolized the worst wrong of her life was suddenly so manly.

She retreated to the living room and paced, rubbing her palms and listening to the occasional snort of laughter or verse of "Itsy Bitsy Spider."

CJ appeared a few minutes later. "All set." He plopped down on the couch and bent to untie his shoe.

Untie his shoe?

"You know what?" he said, seemingly oblivious to her sputters at his intention to make himself comfortable.

"I just realized," he continued, pulling a long, black-nylon-socked foot from his shoe and flexing his toes, "I didn't catch your name."

Wait.

He didn't catch her name?

He was playing, that much was certain, but an even more mortifying thought occurred. He didn't remember her from the Husband Games five years ago.

Just when she thought she didn't have any ego left to bruise. He had ruined her life, and he didn't remember.

Worse, he had ruined her life, and now he was making himself at home in her home, right beneath where her son slept. "What are you doing?" she blurted.

He dangled a set of keys. Car key, house key, shop key, all on the Bliss Bridal key ring Dad had used since the 1990s. "In case you hadn't noticed, your dad's not in any shape to drive me back to my car tonight." He plopped the keys on the end table, then went to work on his second shoe.

"You can't stay here."

He couldn't. The things the Queen General would do to Natalie if the Exalted Widower did the walk of shame from this house in the morning.

How could Dad not realize the implications of bringing CJ here? Oh, right. Because CJ had gotten him drunk.

CJ gave her a look that clearly said she was the fool who didn't realize he was the king of this castle, then patted the leather couch that was at least a foot too short for him. "Slept on a lot worse. You got a blanket?"

She gaped at him. There was a quaking in the pit of her stomach that she couldn't clench. "You can't stay here." She lunged for the keys. "I'll drive you back to your hotel."

Not the best option to leave Dad drunk and home alone with Noah, but she had to get CJ out of here before someone saw him. She'd be back in ten minutes. Noah and Dad would be fine.

CJ scoffed at her. "Lady, I have eleven sisters. No way in hell I'm letting you drive." Did he just—he did. The bastard.

She curved her lips into a tight smile. "I'm more grateful than you could know that you brought my father home safe, but I'd hate for an honored guest of Bliss to get pulled over smelling like you do."

"If my choices are the couch or you behind the wheel, I'll take the couch." He lifted a speculative eyebrow. "Unless there's a bed you wanted to show me?"

A pleasurable pang knocked on her dormant bits, which only made her want to show him a few other things. Like the door. Maybe with a side serving of humility.

She had to get him out of here.

A cab was out of the question. The Queen General would hear about that. Lindsey was half an hour away. Dad was drunk.

"Why are you doing this?" she half-whispered.

He stretched back on the couch, hands linked behind his head. His light-green eyes held hers for what felt like longer than her marriage had lasted. His words rumbled out low and rough, as if the question had made him as vulnerable as it made her. "I'm tired. Why are you doing this?"

For more reasons than she'd tell him face-to-face.

Thank God they weren't in a confessional tonight, or she might've spilled her guts again. "I know more about Bliss propriety than anyone should have to know," she said, giving herself a mental pat on the back for not adding because of you. "And I know you need to leave this house before I ruin your reputation."

He snorted. "What is this, the Dark Ages?"

"This is Bliss. And it's close enough to where your in-laws live that you might want to keep that in mind." It was a desperate play, admitting that she knew exactly who he was.

His body went rigid and his eyes flat.

Bullseye.

"My in-laws are fair-minded people," he said, the dangerous edge to his words making her shiver in both good and bad ways. "Is there anything else I should worry that they'd hear?"

Oh, no.

Not that.

Not tonight.

Nat's heart jumped into her throat and threatened to choke her. "No."

"You sure?" CJ said. "Because you sound just like this woman I met in a confessional today. She had a lot to say about a Queen General's poster boy, and turns out—unless there are two—I'm him."

Words wouldn't come. Because here, late, alone with him—and the undeniable knowledge that he was the type of guy who could kiss a woman and not remember it, and that she was the type of girl whose body was having a serious reaction to his tallness and broadness and general male Neanderthal-ness despite his being CJ Blue—she was too far out of her own skin to formulate coherent thoughts, much less put them into words.

"So that was you today." He stood, peeled off his tux jacket. "Looks like you and I have some unfinished business."

Her eyes tripped on the fit of his white dress shirt, and she had to force herself to look away and point to the door. No way, no how. The QG would kill her. And then bring her back to life, kill her again, follow her to hell, and do it a third time.

And then there was CJ himself.

Bad enough he didn't remember. The last time she'd seen him, the last time he'd touched her, her entire world, her entire life, had broken. It had taken him less than three seconds to strip her of everything she'd ever wanted.

She hardly had anything left, but what if he did it to her again? "You need to leave," she said.

He tossed his tux jacket over the back of the recliner, then assumed stubborn-male position: arms crossed, feet wide, expression growly. "Can't say to my face what you'll say behind my back?"

Natalie wanted to flinch, but she refused. "Feeling guilty?" she shot back instead. Wrong move.

He took a step toward her. A giant, manly, CJ-size step. She gulped. But she maintained eye contact.

"About what?" he said.

Hell with it. He wanted to talk? They'd damn well talk. "About destroying my marriage." But she had to admit that saying it out loud, to his face, didn't feel nearly as good as she'd hoped it would.

Damn it.

CJ took another step. His eyes went dark and ominous, his cheek ticking over his solid jaw.

"I don't feel guilty over something I didn't do."

Natalie matched one of his forward steps with one of her own. She didn't have his stature, but she refused to be intimidated in her own home. "Not having the decency to remember doesn't help."

"Or maybe you're a freaking nutjob looking to blame anybody but yourself for your problems."

Her face went white-hot, and before she realized she'd moved, he caught her hands mid-air, abruptly stopping her from shoving him.

"A feisty nutjob," he murmured, "but definitely a nutjob. Too bad. Waste of a pretty face."

The jackass was playing with her. And while there was a flash of amusement in the quirk of his lips, there was flat calculation in his narrowed eyes.

"Were you this much of an ass to your wife?" Natalie said.

His grip went lax, releasing her hands, and everything about him went still as death. His eyes, his breath, probably his very pulse. She felt it as surely as if it were her own. She'd hit a nerve. A major nerve.

She couldn't stop herself today, could she?

And what right did she have to attack his marriage? What good would it do?

She blinked at the floor, gathering her courage. I'm sorry wasn't a sentiment she'd ever been good with, but she'd crossed a line.

Several, in fact, by Bliss standards. Her mother would have been horrified. "Oh, don't do that," CJ murmured. "We're just getting to the good stuff."

His lethal tone sent a shiver from her hairline to her tailbone, but it wasn't fear. It was genuine intrigue. He wanted a fight.

She lifted her gaze again. His eyes, spindled with the red lines of exhaustion, were nonetheless sharp and glittering. His lips were tight, and he slowly rubbed his hands together.

"Because if you do that," he continued, his dangerous edge inspiring her second shiver of intrigue, "I might feel guilty for suggesting I did your husband a favor. And I'm not real big on feeling guilty."

The list of reasons continuing this fight was a bad idea was longer than the train of Princess Di's wedding dress.

But he didn't remember what he'd done. What kind of person forgot something like that?

She licked her lips.

His eyes went a shade darker.

"Must suck for you, then," she said, her voice low and husky and unrecognizable, "that you actually did me the favor."

A flash of teeth showed in his hard smile. "Interesting way of expressing your appreciation."

"Tell you what. When you remember what I'm supposed to be appreciative for, then I'll thank you properly."

His gaze took a slow meander up and down her body. "Define properly." Properly would be to wipe that blisteringly inappropriate speculation off his face.

But despite everything, his suggestive scrutiny was awakening her long-forgotten femininity.

She needed to cut this off right now. "Hard," she said. "Loud. Painful. Properly." "Too bad you're a nutjob, or you might be my kind of woman."

When his lazy, broody-eyed stare took another meander at her goods, she knew she was in trouble. Was it because she hadn't heard that smoky tone from a man in too long, or was it because she was extra-susceptible to CJ?

That had been the problem, hadn't it? "Too bad you destroy marriages, or I might've mistaken you for a decent human being," she said.

"Lady, I'm a guy. There's a lot of asshole under this skin. But I'm not a homewrecker. Never have been, never will be. So you and I, we're going to work this out. I've got too much respect for the institution to let you say otherwise."

Natalie's breath caught.

Hard not to be susceptible to a guy who said things like that.

A muffled, off-tune baritone cut through their staring match. "Twinkle, twinkle, little bar…"

She shot a glance down the hall. Her father's door was still closed. The singing faded, replaced by a slow, deep snore.

"You need to go," Natalie whispered. If they could wake Dad, they could wake Noah.

CJ shifted, putting himself squarely in her personal space. "You own this place? Because your dad told me to make myself at home."

"My father's inebriated. And whose fault is that?"

"Yeah, that's right. I forced all that liquor down his throat. You're a piece of work, you know that?"

"Would you keep it down?" Natalie hissed.

"Sure. As soon as you tell me what the hell your problem is."

"You know what? I'll call you a cab." She'd call Lindsey. Same thing. "Or," CJ said, "I'll ask your dad."

Natalie stopped with her hand on her phone. He wasn't talking about asking Dad for a ride.

Her chest ached. She should've stuck that sewing needle in her eye this morning. She'd done this day completely wrong.

The last six months hadn't been easy on any of them. Suddenly having to bury Mom, the injury of having the Golden Husband Games taken out of the family, explaining why Grandma was gone to Noah. And now she was on the verge of making tomorrow worse for not only herself, but for Dad too.

She dropped her phone back in her pocket and did the one thing she hated the most. She gave up.

"You kissed me," she said, but it was barely more than a whisper, because saying it was like living it all over again.

And while the fall-out had been horrific, there had been a moment in that kiss—maybe two—that haunted her for a different reason.

"Oh, that's bullshit," he said. "I didn't—"

He stopped himself. The sudden flare of his eyes suggested he might have remembered after all.

Nat scrubbed her hands over the goose bumps on her arms.

His brow crinkled. His gaze dipped to her lips, and then back up. Uncertainty and a hint of vulnerability had snuck past the hardness in his eyes. "I kissed you," he echoed.

Her head drooped as low as her self-worth. She stared at his socks on the tan carpet. "It was horrible," she said. "And you don't even remember."

The blind kissing challenge was the crowd's favorite event of the Husband Games. All the wives lined up on the outdoor stage set up at the Bliss High football stadium, and then one by one, their blindfolded husbands were led up to find and kiss the right wife.

Usually Dad had led the men onstage. Both Natalie's parents got credit for being chair couple of the Husband Games committee, but other than Dad's role as emcee of the event, Mom did all the work. Not that year, though. That year, Dad had come down with food poisoning and missed all the festivities.

Natalie had wished she'd done the same.

Instead, she'd been onstage when Mom led the men out. Natalie was first in the line of wives, itchy in her rayon sundress, her shoulders already stinging beneath the bright sun, her stomach jittery. She hadn't known yet that she was pregnant.

Derek had been third. She'd intentionally not rinsed out all her shampoo that morning so he'd be able to smell her. Sure enough, when he stood in front of her, his black blindfold a perfect match to his always-too-long raven hair, his nose had hitched in an irritated sniff. He'd given her a perfunctory peck on the lips—obligation over—then taken his place behind her while the rest of the husbands were led out to find and stand with their wives. Four husbands later, when Mom stepped onto the stage with CJ, he hadn't hesitated. As soon as he stopped in front of Natalie, he grinned big, his mouth wide and happy and tempting beneath his blindfold. Her stomach had dropped down—all the way down, until she felt pressure in places she had no business feeling pressure and tasted horror and fear and guilt in her mouth.

He'd said, "Hey, beautiful," then grasped her by the waist, pulled her into his big, solid body, and kissed her as if he were a caveman and she needed some clubbing.

She didn't remember if she tried to protest. If Derek did either.

She just remembered that CJ was half a tongue-swipe into her mouth when he stopped cold. The laughter of the crowd penetrated Natalie's ears. Lights danced behind her eyes.

Watching men screw this one up was a hell of a lot more fun than being the woman onstage he screwed up with. Also much less confusing. Especially given the escalating number of fights Natalie and Derek were having.

Fights over which movie to watch on a Friday night. Why the car was dirty. Who hadn't paid the bills. The grease and grime from his job that she couldn't get out of his clothes. Her obsession with expensive purses.

Her demanding that he play in the Husband Games. Him shouting that all of Knot Fest was stupid.

He'd written her poetry. He'd learned her favorite ice cream flavor. He'd taken her nowhere-near-subtle hints about getting the right engagement ring, which he couldn't afford, and married her because she'd convinced him they were soul mates. That she could give him a life he deserved. A better life. A happy life.

The life she wanted to dictate for him, since he was the only man in Bliss strong enough to brave dating her.

But he'd still thought the Games, the festival, her life were all stupid.

She'd felt pretty stupid then, standing onstage while a man who wasn't her husband kissed her.

CJ had pulled back, his lips screwing up in honest confusion. But then he flashed a grin in

Mom's general direction, blindfold still in place. "Nope, this one isn't her," he said.

Mom, the consummate Husband Games chairperson, had cleared her throat and given the crowd a knowing smile. "The point is to figure that out before you kiss her," she'd said into her microphone.

The crowd—a full stadium—had laughed harder, hooting and hollering and enjoying the hell out of Natalie's mortification. CJ had gone on to easily find his remarkable bride and kiss the stuffing out of her.

When Natalie finally worked up the nerve to turn around and look at Derek, he'd been white-faced and shaking. "What the hell, Natalie?" he'd snarled through thin lips.

"It's the Games" hadn't appeased him.

And there was a part of Natalie that didn't blame him.

He'd left the stage after the next husband was led up. Walked right out of the stadium. All the way out of her life.

Since then she hadn't had any contact with him that didn't involve a lawyer.

She also hadn't been kissed by another man since. And it hadn't bothered her for five years.

Until tonight.

"That was you?" CJ finally said.

She didn't move. Didn't nod, didn't blink, didn't breathe. She just willed him to leave. But of course CJ Blue, Widower Extraordinaire and Bliss's Poster Boy for All Things Maritally-Inclined, couldn't leave that alone. His feet came closer, and she could feel his breath. "There's something you need to know," he said.

Her own breath came out loud and uneven. He was entirely in her personal space, but she'd given him enough power as it was. She wouldn't back away, wouldn't let him see her agitation.

He tucked her hair behind her ear. Tension took hold of her body. She shuddered, looked up to tell him to stop, but he bent forward, his lips parted, a single freckle on his cheek drawing her attention while his lips got closer and closer and closer until—

"For future reference," he said, "I never kiss horribly."

And before she could blink or breathe or think, his lips closed over hers. His grip tightened in her hair, and when she should've protested or pulled away or kicked him in the shins, her body melted into his.

Kissing him was wrong.

But it was a different kind of wrong tonight. The I-hate-you kind of wrong. The I'm-a-mother kind of wrong. The I'm-only-kissing-you-because-I-miss-kissing kind of wrong.

He tasted exotic and spicy, like too much rum on a summer beach. His lips were soft and hard at the same time, punishing and forgiving, warm and cold.

And she wanted more.

She shouldn't have. Not five years ago, not tonight. But—God—kissing was so simple. So easy.

So wrong. She was so good at so wrong. And maybe, so was he.

Abruptly, he wrenched his hands away and leapt back. Chest heaving, he stared at her like this was her fault. Like he was the victim of a drive-by kissing.

Like she'd sucked out his soul. He wouldn't be the first one.

She put her fingers to her tingling lips.

Without another word, he turned away. Grabbed his tux jacket. Grabbed his shoes. And when he walked out the door, he shut it quietly behind him.

Once more walking out of her life as if he'd never been there at all. This time, though, she was certain of one thing.

This time, he'd remember.

Chapter 5

CJ got all the way to the corner before he stopped to put on his shoes and jacket. The night wasn't black enough, the air not cold enough, his world not solid enough.

Eleven sisters, and he had forgotten rule number one: Never engage in psychological warfare with a woman.

He was a moron.

Worse, he was a lost moron. He hadn't paid attention to which direction he went when he left Natalie's house. Couldn't remember which direction he was supposed to go either.

Damn woman had his brain all turned around.

He did a slow circle, looking for the massive wedding cake monument, but he didn't know which of the soft glows of light above the trees he should walk toward.

He looked back at the house he'd just left. Its windows were all dark now, but he still felt her eyeballs watching him.

That was all he needed to pick a direction and get moving. Lady was nuts.

Except she wasn't. Not completely.

You kissed me.

He hadn't seen that coming. Not coupled with the homewrecker accusations.

He remembered the part where he'd kissed somebody at those Husband Games. Right there in front of God and his new wife and his new in-laws. On an outdoor stage, the sun bright through his blindfold, with a couple thousand people watching and cheering and laughing.

She'd smelled like oranges, like Serena, but she hadn't kissed like Serena. He'd realized his mistake quickly.

And when he'd found and kissed his wife—the only other woman onstage who smelled of oranges, thank God—she'd pulled his blindfold off, peered up at him with sparkling eyes and a laugh that warmed him more than the sun, then whispered her proposed punishment for his mistake.

That had been a damn good night. One of their best.

He and Serena had met Bob and Fiona for breakfast the next morning. Other than a subtle squeeze in Bob's handshake, they'd both seemed amused as hell over CJ's mistake. Turned out Bob had kissed the wrong woman in the Husband Games the year he and Fiona got married too, and Bob and Fi had known each other a lot longer than Serena and CJ had.

Which was pretty much all it had taken to put CJ's mind at ease, especially after he won—which was something Bob hadn't done.

That kiss shouldn't have bothered him now. It had been an honest mistake. According to Serena, that kissing game was part of the Husband Games almost every year. And every year, men kissed women who weren't their wives. Sometimes on purpose just so they could apologize later.

But tonight, that kiss did bother him.

He wasn't guilty of that first kiss. Not to the extent she'd accused him.

But the simple phrase—you kissed me—had sparked suggestion. That he could win. That he could make her see how ridiculous she was being. He'd thought he could intimidate her.

Make her back down. Shut her up. Cleanse the additional guilt over his own marriage by making her admit she was wrong.

Instead, she'd taken him for all he was worth.

She'd kissed him back. She'd kissed him back, not just with her mouth, but with her hands and her scent and her whole body, and something inside him had flared back to life. Warmed him to the point he still couldn't feel the dark chill of midnight. Set his adrenaline pumping like it had the first time he'd jumped out of a plane.

Damn woman was pretty for a nutjob.

And why the hell was he thinking about a nutjob being pretty?

He muttered a few choice words to himself, then yanked out his phone. Of all his sisters, Pepper, Tarra and Cori were his first choices for a ride. Cori was still pissed that CJ had switched her iPhone language to Mandarin to shut her up about Serena at the rehearsal dinner yesterday, and he'd seen Tarra wander into Suckers with Billy Brenton's drummer half an hour ago. Which meant Pepper was CJ's best shot at a ride.

Bonus: she owned a GPS. And as far as he could tell, she wasn't pissed anymore that he had signed her up for that MisterGoodEnough.com dating Web site after her last breakup.

Ten minutes later, she picked him up on the corner.

"Too old to be partying like this, little brother." She was still in her bridesmaid dress, a light-green number that Saffron claimed to have chosen for the half of their sisters with red hair. Pepper's hair was dark brown, and were it not for her pale face and the dress peeking out from beneath her dark coat, she would've blended into the darkness.

CJ ignored the teasing. "Find Gran?"

"A resident wedding crasher offered to teach her how to polka. She called Cinna when she realized the invitation was a euphemism."

"Yes would've been sufficient."

Pepper's teeth flashed in the darkness. "But not nearly as fun. You want a ride to Basil's place, or your car?"

"Car." He wanted his own wheels accessible again. So he could get the hell out of here. "You sure it'll start?"

He cut her a silent shut up in the dark. His car was one of the few things he'd stored at their parents' house the last few years, and it ran just fine.

She grinned again.

Her clever little GPS guided them out of the neighborhood and toward the mutant wedding cake, away from Arthur, away from Natalie, away from that damn kiss.

Felt good getting some distance from the house.

Pepper turned onto the main downtown street—The Aisle—and cruised past wedding shop after wedding shop, the five-story cake monument in the rearview mirror, the courthouse lawn where CJ had said his own vows looming ahead, semi-lit in the darkness.

"This is a really cool little place," Pepper said.

CJ blew out a slow breath. They drove past ghostly awnings, empty parking lots, and shadows of concrete flower boxes along the sidewalk. As far as downtown America went, Bliss took top marks in quaintness. Pepper was a regional manager in the St. Louis area for some big bridal gown company. She was probably as enamored with the types of shops as she was the presentation.

They rolled past a bakery, then Bliss Bridal, with its well-lit display windows showcasing slender mannequins in flowing sleeveless wedding gowns.

CJ's nuts went into hiding.

"You gonna play in the Golden Husband Games?" Pepper said.

Damn women. "With what wife?"

"No worries," Pepper said. "I've already registered you for a dating Web site. FindYourSugarMama.com. If you're lucky, you can get hitched again before the Games. You have an applicant already. Her shrink says dating will do her some good, and her grandchildren want to see her happy."

So maybe she was still a little mad. "Ha ha."

"Actually, Ginger talked to Saffron's caterers, and they said widowers are being allowed to find a stand-in. Apparently these anniversary games are a big deal. Can't play unless you've won in the past. You know we'd all come cheer you on, right?"

"Are you arguing for or against my playing?"

"Jeez, Princess, who stole your tiara tonight?" She snapped her fingers. "Oh, hey, I know where you could get a real crown. At the Golden Husband Games."

"No."

"None of us saw you win the first time. Sage always said you were lying. Here's your chance to prove it once and for all."

Always could count on family to watch a man make a fool of himself. "Nice try. Won't work."

"There's something to be said for closure."

"All closed up just fine," CJ said, even though he believed himself as much as he expected his siblings to.

"So that's why you're hightailing it out of here as soon as you can."

He appreciated that his family wanted him to stay. He missed them in his own way when he was out and about in the world. But he didn't belong here anymore. He wasn't the same brother and son they'd known five years ago.

That man wouldn't have just gotten his ass handed to him through an ill-advised kiss with a nutjob.

"We miss you, CJ."

He was caught up enough in the pride he'd left at Arthur's house to almost miss the subtle tell in her voice. There was sincerity, but there was something else too—the I know something you don't know triumph.

A weary sigh rolled out of him, dragging his shoulders lower. "What is it?"

They were almost to the courthouse.

CJ averted his eyes, looked at Pepper instead, then wished he hadn't.

A passing streetlamp lit up the sympathy in her quick glance at him. "Fiona asked us not to mention that Bob's had a reoccurrence."

Hell. Bob and Fiona didn't deserve to have to fight this fight again. They'd suffered enough. Losing Serena, the flood, his first bout with cancer.

And they didn't have anyone else to help them.

When CJ had gotten word last year that Bob was sick the first time, he'd made the requisite inquiries about what he could do to help. Serena had been their only child. She hadn't had any aunts or uncles. Fi had told CJ they were fine. They had their church friends, they had their neighbors. It was all CJ had needed—wanted—to hear to keep his plans to hang glide Victoria Falls.

But CJ was here. Now.

"When's he start treatments?" CJ asked. "Last month."

Explained a few things. Put a few extra pounds of guilt and expectations in CJ's bags. Bob and Fiona wouldn't ask for help. But that didn't mean CJ didn't need to give it. "Basil told them you'd be staying here until Knot Fest," Pepper said.

Of course he had. Pompous know-it-all.

But it was hard to be mad at Basil when CJ knew he couldn't leave now. When his shit hit the fan, he had twelve siblings and his parents at his back.

Bob and Fiona had their friends and neighbors, but they deserved family too. And he was the closest thing they had.

Looked like CJ was sticking around longer after all.

* * *

Natalie wasn't sure if she was supposed to go to work Sunday morning or not, but since Dad merely grunted a hungover kind of groan when she knocked on his door, she packed Noah up and headed to The Aisle. She parked behind Bliss Bridal, her senses on full alert after last night's incident with CJ, and was almost inside when the back door one shop down opened with an ominous click.

The sweet scent of cake wafted into the alley and turned Natalie's stomach. Before the flood, she'd smelled it only a couple days a week, on cake-baking days. But now Heaven's Bakery sold cupcakes daily, and the smell was omnipresent.

Natalie couldn't escape the Queen General.

"Miss Castellano." The QG was channeling the full force of both the queenly and the General parts of her personality this morning. "A word."

Noah shrunk behind Natalie, which was all it took for her to find her spine and utilize it to stand tall. Nobody intimidated her little boy. "Good morning, Mrs. Elias. How are you today?"

"By the power vested in me as president of the Bridal Retailers Association, I'm afraid I'm the presenter of bad news," she said.

Cold, thick dread sliced through what little optimism Natalie had left for today. Marilyn had heard. She knew about last night. About CJ.

About the kiss.

It wasn't her fault CJ had shown up, dammit. It might've been her fault he kissed her though. This time. Maybe.

Noah's arm slinked around her hip. Nat had to pull herself together. He needed to know that his mommy could stare down adversity, so that one day he could too.

And she owed his college fund a few more dimes for the profanity acrobatics in her head. "Whatever it is," she said, "I'm sure we can fix it."

"I had a meeting with Mr. and Mrs. Gregory last night," Marilyn said, "and it appears Bliss Bridal's annual dues were misplaced."

Natalie sucked in a breath. The Gregorys were the treasurers and webmasters of Bliss's Bridal Retailers Association. "Misplaced?"

"They've been located," the QG said with a dismissive wave, "but the summer Guide to Bliss Brides has already gone to print."

"You're telling me Bliss Bridal isn't in the Guide." The mailing went out to thousands of brides all across Illinois, Indiana and Wisconsin. Exclusion meant even less visibility.

"That's correct," the QG said.

There went another full quarter to Noah's college fund. "But we're still listed on the Web site and in the e-mail newsletter."

Because they had to be. Three quarters of the boutique's Web site traffic came from BRA referral links. Bliss Bridal's Pinterest, Facebook and Twitter presences were solid, but most of their followers were past customers. Mom had never invested in other ads because they'd always had support from the BRA. Natalie didn't have the budget to play around with any advertising that wasn't a sure thing.

Marilyn's lips made a calculated turn toward mock regret. "Bliss Bridal was removed from the Web site when the dues didn't appear to have been paid in time."

"But we can be put back," Natalie said.

"Whenever Mr. and Mrs. Gregory have time to work on the Web site again. And the e-mail newsletter has already been sent this month. Very busy time, with Knot Fest just around the corner, of course."

"Of course," Natalie said. But only because fix it, you evil bat wouldn't help.

She would call the Gregorys' son, Max, to get Bliss Bridal re-listed. They'd grown up together and were moderately friendly. He did most of the web stuff in his parents' place.

A whole new generation was being groomed to take over The Aisle.

"Rest assured Bliss Bridal will be in the fall mailing," Marilyn said, but Natalie heard the unspoken if you're still here. The And you won't be Marilyn silently added was deafening.

Which meant it didn't much matter if Max got Bliss Bridal listed again.

"We look forward to it," Natalie said. Because it was what Noah needed to hear.

Marilyn conveyed a firm No, you don't with the barest waggle of her eyebrows, then disappeared back into Heaven's Bakery.

And Natalie breathed a sigh of relief.

Because if the Queen General had heard about CJ and Natalie last night, there would've been a bigger issue than Bliss Bridal's being excluded from the BRA's advertising.

Her skin prickled, and she cast a covert glance around the parking lot and across the street.

Paranoia, maybe, but the only thing worse than the QG hearing about something would be the QG witnessing something, and Natalie wouldn't rest easy until long after she'd heard CJ was gone.

She shivered.

"Mommy?" Noah whispered.

She herded him toward the door. "Hmm?" "I wish I was big as a dinosaur."

For all her personal problems in the last five years, she'd gotten the best reward in him.

She dropped and squeezed him in a hug. "Me too, sweetheart. Me too."

Inside the shop, Natalie shook off the feeling of being watched and put on coffee in the small kitchenette. She and Noah dashed across the street to the teahouse for fresh scones to serve as today's refreshments for their brides' entourages. Then she got Noah set up with crayons and a dinosaur coloring book at his little table in the corner of the office and powered up the computer. She had three brides to connect with on Pinterest so her bridal consultants could get a feel for their styles before their appointments this week, inventory to tackle and a certain kiss to not think about.

Two of those tasks proved easier than the third.

Amanda arrived just before eleven to get the rest of the shop in order. At noon, they opened for business.

Natalie jumped every time the door chimed.

She had no reason to think CJ would come here, but she had no reason to think he wouldn't either.

It had been a lot easier to dislike him before he brought Dad home. Before he made a point of demonstrating he was more than just the moment her marriage had fallen apart.

Before she'd caught on to the fact that he was a man. That kiss had been unexpected.

Unexpected and thrilling and horrifying, just as it had been five years ago. And, like five years ago, thoroughly guilt-inspiring.

At least this time, they were both single. As if that were any consolation, given the mess that was Nat's life.

But for all the problems he'd brought into her life, the man was right. He didn't kiss horribly.

"Mommy!" Noah said.

She jumped and dropped her fingers from where they'd been rubbing her lips, heat gathering in her cheeks. She'd meant to switch over to the inventory software, but instead, she was staring at the last bride's honeymoon Pinterest board. Noah was practicing his inquisitive half squint on her.

"Yes, sweetheart?" she said.

He pointed his purple crayon through the slats of the blinds on the back window. "Aunt Lindsey's here."

Lindsey—the taller, blonder, non–childbearing-hipped Castellano sister—finger-waved through the back window. Her nails were tiger-striped with neon green and pink, and they stood out over her fingerless ivory gloves. Natalie slipped to the back door and let her in. "No clients this week?" She gestured to Lindsey's nails.

"Hot date." Lindsey fanned herself. "Smoking, actually."

Her relationships resembled the life cycle of a fruit fly in hell—short and scorching. Most ended with her assistant breaking things off for her. Yet most of the guys she'd dated treated her like an old friend. She'd even been in a couple of their weddings.

"So he's getting dumped tomorrow?" Natalie said. "Pretty much."

Lindsey knew how to pick 'em. No complications there.

She wiggled her fancy fingernails. "I'm painting them back to normal tonight. Want to come over? I have sour mix."

"Can't. Knot Fest meeting."

"Aunt Lindsey, what's a hot date?" Noah leaned out of the office, wiggling a foot behind him.

Lindsey winked at him. "It's when you turn up the heater really high in your house and pretend you're at the beach."

His little dark brows furrowed over the crease between his eyes. "Did it catch on fire?" "Fire?" Natalie repeated.

"There was smoke," Noah said. "Right, Aunt Lindsey?"

The things Noah learned from his aunt. "How do you explain that one, Aunt Lindsey?" Lindsey's grin would've inspired jealousy if Natalie hadn't known the bags beneath Lindsey's eyes came from too many hours at work rather than one night of adult activities. "My electric s'more maker overheated," Lindsey said. "It was ugly, little man. Ugly." His lip trembled. "Can you get a new one?"

"Are you talking to the awesomest aunt in the whole world or what? Of course I can get a new one."

"And it'll make big huge giant marshmallows?" Noah's pure hope made Natalie believe marshmallows were the way to world peace.

Lindsey scrunched up her nose and twisted her lips to the side. "We'll see what we can do. You drawing pictures today? Think you can draw me a picture of a dinosaur in a wedding dress?"

Noah's cheeks split into a grin almost as bright as his eyes. "Yeah!"

He darted back into the office, taking a bit of Natalie's heart with him. For all the trouble she'd had in the rest of her life over her failed marriage, she wouldn't trade her past for the world. Because she'd gotten Noah. He was a damn good kid. And that was another dime she'd happily part with.

She wanted to scamper back to the office with him and color dinosaur pictures, but she had grown-up issues to face instead. She propped herself against the wall. Lindsey tucked her hands into the pockets of her ivory knit overcoat and leaned against the opposite wall. "You could've warned me Dad was hungover," she said.

"Is he still mad?"

"Mad is such a nebulous term." "Shit."

"You charge yourself double on Sundays?"

She needed to start charging herself half before she went broke. "I should've just said thank you when he offered me the shop." "Maybe. Maybe not."

"I appreciate that he believes in me." Nat didn't need to add the but. Because Lindsey knew. She wasn't very popular in Bliss either.

"He's packing for a little fishing trip right now," Lindsey said. "He'll cool down, you'll cool down, and maybe when he gets back, you two can be rational adults putting the pieces of your lives back together. Things change. Give him some time to get used to it."

Natalie gave Lindsey the seriously? look. Dad had spent four years denying Lindsey's law specialty until she marched into the house with police photos of a battered woman. Is the sanctity of marriage more important than her life? Lindsey had said. Society needs me to terminate unwanted marriages. Deal with it.

Since that day, he'd told everyone who asked that his younger daughter was in the family business and his older daughter was on a mission to save the world. Lindsey handled other cases too—adoptions, child support, prenuptial agreements—but when you grew up in the Most Married-est Town on Earth, the only thing that mattered was your respect for and participation in holy matrimony.

Lindsey shrugged. “What else can you do?”

Noah popped around the corner. “Aunt Lindsey? Do you want a pink or purple or green or red or blue dinosaur?”

“Pink with blue polka dots,” Lindsey said. Noah giggled and disappeared again.

Natalie scrubbed her hands over her cheeks. “Do you think he’ll forgive me for leaving?” Once the shop was packed up and sold, she would leave. Bliss was no place for a divorced woman to raise a son.

“Dad?”

“Noah. He’s finally adjusting without Mom here. What happens when Dad’s not there every day for him too?”

The last six months had taught her what she was capable of, but it also helped her realize something else.

One day Dad wouldn’t be around to be Noah’s role model anymore. What would she do then?

“You two will be fine,” Lindsey said. “You’re already doing a great job with him. Besides, you know I’ll fix whatever you screw up.”

Natalie squinted at her. She gave an unexpectedly bright smile, the kind of smile that usually meant she was wearing her favorite smiley face panties, and some of the tension left Natalie’s chest and windpipe.

“So,” Lindsey said. “The confessional, huh?”

“Oh, shut the hell up,” Natalie grumbled. No sense asking where she heard.

Everyone would’ve heard by now.

Lindsey’s grin got bigger, but there was a sympathetic bent to it. “So did you two have a nice chat? The story I heard was a little fuzzy on details.”

Thank God. Double bonus that Lindsey hadn’t heard about last night’s kiss either. “Let’s just say I said a few things I wouldn’t have if I’d known who I was talking to.”

“You didn’t know it was him?”

"He was behind a screen. I thought I was talking to one of the guys in Billy Brenton's band and that he was out in the foyer."

"Billy who?"

"The country rock—never mind." Lindsey hated country music. She wouldn't care who CJ's sister had toured with. "Point is," Nat said, "I'm never speaking to anyone again about CJ Blue."

Lindsey pursed her lips and repositioned herself against the wall. "How much cussing did you do?"

"Are we counting Oh, gods?" "You were in a church."

"And Noah's college fund is about full for the year." "You could just watch your language."

Natalie gave her the shut up eye again.

"Or," Lindsey said, "you could quit the Knot Fest committee." And there, Natalie suspected, was the real point of Lindsey's visit.

But she was wrong. Nat couldn't quit. Not with the shape the Golden Husband Games committee was in. Then there was her morbid desire to withstand Marilyn Elias's mental bruisings as long as she could. "I owe it to Mom to see the Games through."

"Mom would understand."

"Mom always understood." Natalie thumped her head back on the wall. The wall that had been in the family for three generations. The wall that had survived decades of bridezillas, a few tornado scares and the flooding three years ago. The wall that would never belong to her.

Natalie had grown up here, prancing about the floor in oversize bridal shoes, modeling tiaras, dreaming of the day she'd graduate from homecoming and prom dresses to her wedding dress. The beautiful wedding dress, special ordered just for her—with intricate bead- and lacework on the strapless, drop-waist bodice, the yards and yards of bunched white organza making her look as though she were floating in a cloud—then modified to add sequins and sparkles into the skirt.

The dress she'd burned three months later.

But it had been almost five years now. Five years, and a few lifetimes' worth of lessons from her parents and her son. Without

Mom, Natalie had come to realize that the shop wasn't something she should take for granted.

It was something she needed to own. Not the shop itself—she would never own the building, never own the dresses and accessories in it. But she needed to own her own history as she faced her future.

She needed to fit into herself again.

Hard to do when she didn't much like herself. "You know I never thought to tell her thank you while she was alive?" she said.

"She knew, Nat."

"Maybe. But there's no one else who knows these Games as intricately as I do." "So they'll learn."

Since her divorce, Natalie had known she wouldn't take over the family business when her parents retired. Divorced people didn't own shops on The Aisle. Period. Maybe if she'd gotten remarried, she could've kept the boutique, but Nat's short marriage had shown she wasn't cut out to be a wife. Natalie had still been her mother's biggest helper in planning the Games every year though. They'd all thought they would have more time before Mom needed to worry about a real replacement for both the Games and the shop. "They can learn next year. But there will never be another golden anniversary of the Games. This is the first year since the flood that the hotels are booked solid. Bliss is finally back in the destination wedding game. Everything has to be right this year. And it's not. Not even close."

Little boy giggles carried into the hallway.

Lindsey looked toward the office, then back at Natalie. Pointedly.

"Are you sure you're doing this for Mom?" she said softly.

Of course. Who else would she do it for? No matter how badly Nat wanted to still fit in Bliss, the QG had made it abundantly clear that Natalie was wasting her wishes. "How will Dad feel if the Games fall apart?" Nat said. "Mom's not the only one I've let down. I can save Mom's Games. I can do it for both of them."

"And then what?" Lindsey said.

"And then—" Natalie's throat clogged up and her breastbone ached as if her ribs were caving in.

And then she would be done. It would be time to move on. To truly say good-bye.

She inhaled and licked her lips. "I'll worry about that after the Games." "Nat—"

"I'll never have another chance to do this, Lindsey. Please don't be one more thing standing in my way."

Lindsey crossed her arms. "You're still only one person. Mom had a team behind her. You can't—"

"I can. I'm the only person who can do this right, and I'm doing it."

Noah darted out of the office. "Aunt Lindsey! I made you two dinosaurs!"

"Saved by the preschooler," Lindsey murmured. She went down on her knee to his level while he launched into the story of the epic tea party the dinosaurs were having.

Natalie ruffled his hair—he was adorably irresistible this morning—then caught Lindsey's eye. "Send him back in when you're ready to go. I have some work to do."

Lindsey nodded, but Nat had known her sister long enough to get the message behind the nod. Don't work too hard.

She'd take that into consideration. After Knot Fest.

Chapter 6

CJ staggered back into St. Valentine's rectory early Monday evening after spending the day cleaning Bob and Fiona's gutters over in Willow Glen. The rest of his family had scattered back to their respective homes and jobs, leaving just him and Basil in Bliss.

Him and Basil and the Queen General, who was perched as delicately as a Queen General could be at the edge of the stiff pleather sofa in the rectory living room. She held a basket of cake balls that were decorated like little brides and grooms. The fact that CJ even knew what cake balls were gave him serious concerns about his own balls.

"You have a visitor," Basil said.

His Holy Wimpiness snagged his newspaper and retreated across the creaking floorboards to the kitchen.

Never a good sign.

CJ took a step into the room. "Mrs. Elias." "CJ, my dear, do call me Marilyn."

With those predatory eyes killing the effect of her blinding white smile, he could think of a few other things to call her.

Like batshit crazy or scary as hell. Basil had God on his side, and even he was hiding. "Nice of you to stop by," CJ said.

She rose and offered the basket of cake balls, and CJ instinctively jumped forward and cradled the gift.

"By the power vested in me as Knot Festival chairwoman and as a direct descendant of the founders of Bliss," Marilyn said with every ounce of authority necessary to pull off the bizarre statement, "our community formally welcomes you into its loving folds."

CJ could see how God would be kinda helpless against this woman. "Ah, thank you," he said.

"As you'll be with us for a while, I wanted to offer my assistance in anything you might need." The Queen General gestured to the basket. "You'll find coupons and brochures for all of Bliss's best restaurants, nightlife, relaxation services, and adventure opportunities tucked in there. I've also prepared a job reference and character recommendation form, should you decide to seek employment or alternate living accommodations. Drop my name, and you'll have no issues with anything your heart might desire. We simply want you to be happy and comfortable as long as you'd like to stay with us here in Bliss."

He was in some kind of Stepford Wives: The Bridal Chronicles movie. "Thank you," he said again, glad he'd stifled his silent snort of disbelief when she'd said adventure.

If this was how she acted when he was on her good side, he didn't want to provoke her bad side. And that was more than a little jacked up.

"I do hope you'll stop by and see us at Heaven's Bakery," the Queen General continued. "My daughter is most eager to offer you her hospitality as well."

There went his ball sack shriveling up so high it bumped into his lungs. "Mm," he murmured.

The Queen General leaned in. A cold sweat flushed his body.

"The upstanding population of Bliss is at your beck and call," she said. "It will be my pleasure to introduce you around town, and I've already ordered the country club to begin plans for a welcome reception."

CJ swallowed. "That's not necessary."

"My dear CJ, we want to show you the very best Bliss has to offer. It's the least we can do to make up for any awkwardness you may have suffered upon your return to town."

So this was how deer felt when a semi came barreling down the road at them. Did she know about Saturday night?

He sure as hell hoped not.

She flashed another of those scary-as-hell smiles. "Do enjoy your evening, and call me if I can be of the least bit of assistance. I'll be in touch."

He saw her out the door, then took the cake balls to the kitchen, giving momentary consideration to burning them as a sacrifice to whatever gods had put that woman on the face of the earth.

Basil was tucked into the square Formica table, his red hair just visible over the top of his newspaper.

"Problem, Princess?" he said, back in full Holy Pompousness mode.

When CJ didn't answer right away, Basil peeked at him over the top of the paper.

"Something you need to confess?" "Nope."

No chance in hell.

"Make sure it stays that way," Basil murmured. "Wouldn't cross that woman without half our fairer siblings and God at my back."

"Pansy-ass." "God bless you."

CJ stifled an eye roll. Living with Basil made him twitchy, but he couldn't bring himself to take Fiona up on her offer of their spare bedroom either.

He already felt like he knew his in-laws better than he'd known their daughter. "I'm going for a run."

"Can't run from your life forever," Basil said behind his paper. "God bless you," CJ said back.

Best he could do these days.

He popped upstairs into the simple bedroom he'd been assigned, changed into the only pair of shorts and T-shirt he had, laced up his shoes, and set out to visit a few places Serena had introduced him to.

He was here. Might as well look into some of that closure his family kept harping on. He'd start small. Look. Maybe remember, maybe not.

But he got lost trying to find the football stadium where he'd played in the Husband Games and gave up on finding it. Might've been his subconscious's way of weaseling out of memories he didn't want to face. Might've been time had healed his wounds while he wasn't looking.

Or he might've been the pansy-ass he'd accused Basil of being.

CJ jogged through the streets of Bliss, not paying much attention to where he was going once he'd decided to actively avoid the courthouse and the stadium. He concentrated on nothing more than the ground beneath his feet, the burn of the just-this-side-of-chilly air in his lungs, and the strain of his muscles.

It hadn't been long since he'd gotten down from Kilimanjaro, and he'd trained hard for it, but that was no excuse to slack off. He had plans to hit Utah for some rock climbing soon as he was done in Bliss, and he wanted to stay in top shape.

Soon, he was approaching the monstrosity of a wedding cake.

That, he would never forget. On the rare nights over the past few years, when a beer and a persuasive companion had talked his story out of him, he'd always mentioned the wedding cake statue. A hundred feet high if it was an inch, with a fountain beneath the middle columned tiers of cake and staircases sloping down to fifty-foot columned cakes on either side.

He had the gear to climb it. He could pretend he was in the mountains. Had to be some kind of law or ordinance against scaling it, which would make it about the biggest adrenaline rush CJ could hope for while he was here.

He rounded a corner, and the full thing came into view. He hadn't paid attention the last couple of times he'd driven past it this last week, but today, he did. Looked just like he remembered except for the missing fountain. Must've been taken out by the flood.

A dark-haired little boy twirled on the flat surface beneath the middle statue, his navy jacket unzipped. CJ kept running, but he watched the kid, squinting to make out exactly what the boy was swinging around. Looked like some kind of stuffed animal with a horn and a dress.

Saw it all in this town.

He put his attention back on the road in front of him. St. Valentine's was another half a mile up the road, and he was stretching his limits. Hadn't eaten since Fiona stuffed him full of peanut butter and jelly sandwiches and apple slices at lunch.

A pop-pop-squizzz! shuddered at the cake, then a child's scream splintered the crisp evening air.

CJ whipped around. The little boy under the cake danced in place, shrieking and shielding his face while a spray of fountains erupted around him.

"Mommy!" the kid wailed.

CJ darted for him. He was almost there when a flash of denim and dark hair swooped across the fountain and grabbed the boy, hauling him up and hustling him to safety.

Holy shit. CJ paused.

Stumbled to a shocked halt, really.

Hadn't pegged her for having maternal instincts.

She put the kid down and dropped to her knees, petting his hair and pulling off her jean jacket to wrap around him. Her eyes lifted, momentarily locking with his, and something both vulnerable and indomitable flashed across her features.

Lungs heaving, muscles burning, CJ looked at the little boy again. Dark brown eyes.

Mussed dark hair. Lips curled in a howl of fear and pain.

He stumbled another step back.

"Cindy," the kid was sobbing. "Save Cindy."

Natalie looked back at the fountain. CJ did too. The stuffed animal lay in the middle, getting soaked. From one of the side cakes, an older woman in a floral print dress and Coke-bottle glasses waddled toward them in her orthotics. "Land sakes, ain't nobody told us the boy was playing there."

A squat, furry guy in need of a belt hustled around the other cake. The top two buttons of his blue uniform shirt gaped open. "Aw, hell," he said, then disappeared back around the cake.

CJ ignored them all and set out to play hero for Cindy.

His lack of fondness for Natalie didn't mean her kid had to suffer, and God only knew how long it would take to get the sprays shut off. He'd seen firsthand what water could do to stuffed animals.

He'd been responsible for it more than once in his childhood. And any other time, he would've smiled at the memories, but watching Natalie with her son, glimpsing her with the family he'd always wanted but would never have, it scratched something more raw than the rest of his scabs.

The spray shut off about the time he stepped off the splash pad with Cindy—an orange stegosaurus dressed in a lime green girly-ass dress that appeared to have taken most of the damage. The little boy had quit screaming, but he was visibly shivering under Natalie's coat.

CJ could sympathize. That water was like frickin' ice. But what had him totally off-kilter wasn't the water.

It was the way the boy's head was tucked into her neck, the way she smoothed her fingers down his damp hair, the way his lanky little body huddled into her as if she were his very world.

The purple smudges beneath Natalie's eyes had spread down her cheeks and her shoulders drooped so low her elbows nearly touched the ground. The rest of her was still completely put together—silky dark hair in place, blouse crisp, shoes unscuffed—but there was one major difference between Natalie Saturday night and Natalie today.

Today, there wasn't a thing nuts about her.

He also had the striking impression that he'd underestimated her. Probably shouldn't have attempted to fight her without half his siblings and God at his back. Given that ninety-two percent of his siblings were female, he doubted they'd take his side over a single mother's.

Especially after what he'd done Saturday night.

The older lady had circled the splash pad and now stood over Natalie. "Little fella gonna be okay?"

"Yeah." She smoothed his hair again without looking up at either the woman or CJ.

The woman shot a covert glance toward The Aisle, which extended straight out from the small park at the edge of the statue. "He need anything?" she half whispered.

Natalie shook her head. "Thanks. I've got it."

CJ approached and held the stuffed dinosaur out.

Natalie took it, gave it a small shake to get off the worst of the water, then tucked it between her and the boy.

"Thank you." She spoke softly without looking at him, which was somehow worse than if she'd found a way to blame him for her son getting caught in the water fountain too.

Coke-bottle glasses lady let out a small gasp. "Oh, dearie me. CJ Blue! How nice to meet you!"

She pumped his hand while Natalie stood and put her arm around her son's tiny shoulders.

"Let's go home, sweetie."

The kid patted the dinosaur's back, still shivering, still sniffling. "It'll be okay, Cindy. Mommy will fix you." His hands weren't visible for the length of the sleeves of Natalie's jacket, but he kept patting the dinosaur's back anyway.

While they walked away, an affection for the boy launched so thick and fast in CJ's chest, it practically gave him the Heimlich.

He could've had an adorable kid like this if Serena were still around. Maybe a couple. If he hadn't pushed her so hard to give up her career. If he'd tried to fit into the role of a military husband. If he'd taken the time to appreciate her commitment instead of putting his desires for his own career ahead of hers.

If he hadn't come home with a job offer in Atlanta and told her to pick.

The lady was still pumping CJ's hand as if he weren't standing in fifty-five-degree weather, soaking wet.

"We're right honored to have you with us here in Bliss, we are. I'm Vi. You come right on up here and we'll get you all dried off."

"Not far to get back to my brother's place. I'm good." He gestured up the road, but his gaze snagged on Natalie and how she bundled the little boy up into a charcoal Mazda 3 at the edge of the street.

"Those two," Vi said. "Doing the best they can, aren't they?"

CJ cocked his head at the older lady. She had a wedding ring on her stocky finger, some kind of ornate bird pin peeking out from beneath her gaping white cardigan, and she smelled like a pile of flowers two days past their prime.

"Ain't easy, what she's doing, but she's doing it," Vi said. There was definite respect there.

Interesting.

But not as interesting as getting back to the rectory. Out of the cold and back to the safety of somewhere he could suppress both old and new guilt. He squeezed Vi's hand. "Nice to meet you. Gotta get going."

"You sure I can't help you dry off, hon?"

Was it his imagination, or was she ogling his chest through his T-shirt?

"My Gilbert was built like you back in the day," she said. "Mm-mm, good memories. You stop on by again sometime, you can meet him. Wouldn't mind watching the two of you arm wrestle, though you'll have to go easy on him on account of his bursitis."

"Ah, I'll remember that." And he would. Unfortunately. He cast one last glance back at Natalie and her son.

He'd remember that too. Among too many other things.

* * *

Noah was up bright and early Tuesday with no sign of lasting trauma from his accidental soaking in the wedding cake splash pad yesterday afternoon. Natalie wished she could say the same about herself.

She was used to her brain pinging with to-do lists she'd never get done for the Husband Games, problems she couldn't solve at the shop, worries over whether Noah was getting enough vegetables or watching too much television. But since they'd left the wedding cake last night, she was fixated on replaying the image of a tall, broad, Highland warrior marching into battle against the evil waterfalls of doom to rescue a stuffed dinosaur.

He'd saved Cindy.

For Noah.

CJ Blue was making it very difficult for Natalie to continue to dislike him. And she suspected disliking him was the only thing saving her from liking him entirely too much. First he helped Dad, then Noah. She was willfully repressing the memory of talking to him in the confessional before she knew who he was. When he'd asked if she needed him to kick his own ass.

She'd never gotten many offers like that, and the sweetness of it had gotten buried beneath her mortification and horror.

Plus she'd be lying if she said he was a bad kisser. Not that she'd admit to anyone—herself included—how many times she'd found herself remembering that.

Noah was still bouncing around, happy as only a four-year-old could be when she dropped him at Mrs. Tanner's home day care. Nat was trying to focus on the positive—it was dark and rainy today, but Nat had gotten word that the sunflower field was planted yesterday, and Bliss Bridal had a full schedule of brides today. When Mrs. Tanner called before Nat made it to work with news that Noah had already spilled his juice and his spare clothes didn't fit anymore, she told herself this was also an excellent distraction from thinking about CJ.

So was running late.

Nat whipped around the corner to the alley behind Bliss Bridal three minutes before opening, then came to a screeching halt at the chain roping it off.

She muttered a cuss worth a dollar, but gave herself a fifty percent discount on what she owed Noah's college fund since she didn't have a whole dollar on her. Plus she would've stuck to a couple of quarter words anyway, were it not for the slick roads. She carefully backed out of the alley entryway, made a half circle around the block and drew up short—again—when she found the parking lot beside Bliss Bridal also chained off.

Damn it.

She was so friggin' tired of Marilyn Elias punishing her for things that weren't her fault.

Don't talk to CJ Blue, you divorced hussy. Natalie eyed the rain splatters on her windshield. Watched her wipers swish back and forth.

Peered up at the ominous clouds. Oh, God.

The Queen General had heard Natalie had been spotted with the Exalted Widower again.

She was going to bring back the flood.

A low grumble of thunder rolled in the distance.

No. The Queen General could not cause a flood. Again.

Natalie left her car angled between the chain and the street, blocking the sidewalk, and dashed through the rain on her heeled boots past Bliss Bridal and into Heaven's Bakery.

And promptly blinked against the pain of the blinding white everything inside. "Um, Nat?" Kimmie Elias said softly.

Natalie shielded her eyes against the harsh lights. Kimmie, a dishwater blonde with bright blue eyes, a smile for everyone, and a coping mechanism that Freud probably would've had a field day with, straightened behind one of the glass display cases of cupcakes. Her covert head-bob toward the kitchen fired Natalie's blood.

Kimmie hustled out from behind the counter and nudged Natalie toward the door. "I got a fortune cookie Monday night that said my workplace would be the epicenter of a new adventure," she whispered, "and nothing catastrophic has happened yet, so you should probably go before an earthquake or an asteroid hits."

Natalie shook her off. Had customers been present, she would've walked away. She was, after all, a representative of Bliss Bridal, and still a member of The Aisle. But the bakery was empty. "It's going to be the epicenter of tornado Natalie if your mother doesn't unchain my parking lot."

"I'm not kidding," Kimmie said. "It said epicenter. Fortune cookies don't say epicenter. I'll talk—"

"Miss Castellano," the QG interrupted, "may I help you?"

Her voice was soft enough, but the utter lack of disapproval and animosity in her was abnormal enough for Natalie to wonder if Kimmie was right about that asteroid.

There was a reason Natalie didn't visit Heaven's Bakery. The QG did a freakishly scary I'm-pretending-I'm-happy-to-see-you-but-I'm-actually-plotting-your-demise face.

Another grumble of thunder rattled the windows.

Natalie matched the QG's ramrod posture and pleasant tone. "Do you know anything about the alley and my parking lot being chained off?" They were both city property, maintained and kept by Bliss so there would be ample parking for all out-of-town brides without arguments among the business owners.

And they were both items that Marilyn Elias could manipulate with a simple call to City Hall.

"I believe the public works department is repaving them," Marilyn said. "There was an announcement in the paper."

Natalie's jaw popped from the effort of unclenching it. "It was repaved last summer." "The city deemed it a subpar job."

Nat bit her tongue until it hurt. She'd lost her temper with Dad, and look how that had turned out. She couldn't afford to give the Queen General any more motivation to speed up her campaign to destroy Bliss Bridal. "And how long will it take?" Natalie asked.

"I'm afraid the power of that knowledge has not been vested in me." Marilyn drummed a finger against her lips. "Although I may have heard speculation that it's usually only a week."

"Only?" Natalie squeaked.

"Once the weather clears," the Queen General said. "I have work to do. I'm sure the mayor or the public works department will be able to answer your questions."

Screw the mayor and the public works department. Natalie needed a place for her customers to park and a reason to lure them into the store.

The Queen General gave a regal nod toward the door. Natalie was dismissed. Like hell. She sucked in a lungful of courage, but two things stopped her.

The first was the QG's don't do it glare, tossed over her shoulder with the practiced ease of a woman with a lifetime of experience in ruling the town her ancestors had founded.

The second, though, was inspiration. The QG wanted to play dirty?

Nat could play dirty.

She spun on her heel and marched out the door—more confidently than petulantly, Nat liked to think—then got back in her car, drove to the parking lot across the street, and held her head high all the way back to Bliss Bridal, through the rain, across the shop floor, and back to the office.

The phone number was easy enough to find. And that drumming of her heart—that was satisfaction.

Satisfaction at not taking that woman's shit anymore.

The phone rang once. Twice. Halfway through the third ring, a pleasant voice answered. "Deppert County Health Department, where may I direct your call?"

"I have a complaint about a food establishment," Natalie said.

"One moment."

Nat crossed her legs, her foot jiggling, listening to Michael Bolton on the hold music. Her pulse surged until her arms tingled. She could hang up.

Forget revenge.

Keep to the shadows, let the QG walk all over her.

There were two months to Knot Fest, and then she'd never have to see the QG again.

But being divorced didn't make Natalie a thing. She was still a person. And Marilyn had pushed too far.

Michael Bolton went silent. "Deppert County Health Department. This is Susan. How may I help you?"

Natalie sat straighter. War, she reminded herself. This was war.

Still, she dropped her voice. And added a country twang to it. Because she never could shake the feeling that Marilyn had eyes and ears inside Bliss Bridal. "Hi, I was just in Heaven's Bakery in Bliss, and I heard one of the girls ask the scary older lady if they should toss the frosting that was out overnight, and she told them no, that they should use it as samples today. Is that sanitary?"

The silence on the other end of the line was so loud, Natalie could hear her own pulse. "Susan?" she said after a minute.

"Heaven's Bakery?" Susan repeated. "Yes, ma'am."

So Natalie hadn't technically heard that conversation. Today. Or exactly like that. But Kimmie had mentioned once over drinks at Suckers that Heaven's Bakery didn't always refrigerate their frosting—something about its safety because of the chemistry that was over Natalie's head—and Kimmie had also let it slip that not refrigerating the frosting was against health department code.

"Heaven's Bakery in Bliss?" Susan repeated again. "Yes, ma'am."

There was another long pause, and then Susan's sigh echoed through the phone. "Your name?"

"I'd prefer to remain anonymous," Natalie said. "Yeah, me too," Susan grumbled.

Natalie's conscience gave a kick. She kicked it right back. There were always casualties in war. Marilyn didn't hesitate. Natalie couldn't either.

"Tell me again exactly what you heard," Susan said.

Natalie repeated the story—it wasn't exactly a lie. She answered a few more questions—maybe adding that she'd sampled the frosting before hearing the conversation and that her stomach hurt now, to completely sell the story—then hung up.

Take that, Queen General.

So Nat's heart was still pounding, and her conscience still warbling out a feeble protest, but for the first time in weeks, she had something to smile about at work.

Smile?

Make that laugh.

Outright glee trickled out of her body. She tossed her short hair back and shoved up out of the desk chair, then turned to the door.

Her father stood there.

His lips were parted, his eyes pained, bewilderment making the wrinkles around his eyes stand out. "Dad," she stammered.

He cut a pointed glance to the phone on the desk.

The tidal wave of shit, shit, shits rolling through her head were too many for her to count.

A chill pebbled goose bumps down her arms.

His shoulders drooped. He blinked a couple times, shook his head. As though he couldn't believe how low Natalie had sunk.

"Guess you're right after all," he said sadly. "New owners are probably the best thing that could happen to the old shop."

He turned and walked out the door, leaving her alone. Alone, and miserable with her utter incompetence.

Chapter 7

CJ had worked a variety of bars—from a rooftop joint in Brazil to a polished study in an Irish castle hotel, to holes in the wall in a variety of holes—and Suckers sat in the middle of the spectrum. It smelled faintly like latex and stale beer, but the floors were clean and, despite the funky music and the pimpin' purple, red, and silver décor, the clientele—heavy on the ladies tonight—was the dependable Midwestern stock that didn't cause a lot of problems.

Felt good being back in his element. Slinging bottles, flipping tops, shooting the shit with the guys and charming the ladies. It had taken him less than ten minutes to convince Huck to hire him. He suspected not dropping Marilyn Elias's name had helped seal the deal. After about five minutes into his first shift tonight, he rediscovered his groove. One step closer to feeling normal again.

With positive cash flow back in his bank account, he was also one step closer to his next adventure. He'd be able to afford a ticket to Utah long before Bob was done with treatments, which meant he could also save up enough to tackle some of the more advanced climbs. Have a good bit ready for whatever he decided to do next. Maybe he'd finally get around to the Great Barrier Reef late this year.

Until then, he was gainfully employed and happy about it. Mostly.

Huck paused on his way past with a plate full of potato skins to nod toward the female-dominated crowd. "Ladies' night helping you out with that little problem yet, boy?"

"Don't know what you're talking about." CJ was already plotting revenge for whomever made his extended dry spell public knowledge. He would've preferred that it wasn't mentioned at all.

"Not so fast," His Holy Pompousness said from his seat at the end of the bar. "I put my money on next Monday."

CJ passed Basil an iced tea. "Does God approve of your betting on my unwed sexual activities?"

"God knows you'll fornicate anyway. The money goes to charity if I win. And I suppose I could look the other way if a few minutes of a woman's company made you more bearable." He took a sip of the tea, scowled, then pushed it back. "Put a hit of grenadine in that."

Huck pointed at Basil. "You go on and tell that sister of yours I want in for tomorrow. Anything after midnight tonight counts."

CJ took a moment to bask in the memory of a rogue chicken pooping on Cinna's head when she was seven. If he started a bet about her sex life—he shuddered—he'd be labeled a perv. She opened a pool on CJ's sex life and took a cut of the bets, and she was a brilliant businesswoman.

Jeremy shut the cash register in the corner. "Leave the man alone." He jerked a thumb at the kitchen. "Order's up."

CJ delivered a basket of jalapeño poppers to a clique that looked like a sorority reunion at the top of the bar, took three orders from the waitresses, then collected credit cards from another group who were heading out. On his way back to the computer, he checked on the blonde two seats up from Basil. When she'd arrived, she slung a soft ivory overcoat onto the stool to her right and set her purse on the stool to her left. Waiting on friends, CJ had guessed. But it had been thirty minutes, and she wasn't looking around for anyone.

Instead, she was pulling her locket along its thin gold chain, subtly shifting away every time someone approached her space bubble.

His sister Sage did that too. In Sage's case, it was claustrophobia. CJ nodded to her almost empty wineglass. "Refill?

"Not just yet." "Hungry?" "Still deciding."

"Holler if you want something."

Her eyes flickered, openly studying him, and his gut clenched like it did when his sisters got the same look.

She wanted something. Whatever it was, he wouldn't like it.

He retreated to the computer to run the cards, but watched while a clean-faced girl with a white glob stuck in her curly, dishwater hair popped in between the blonde and Basil. Blondie pulled her coat off the stool, and Curls slid onto it. There was something vaguely familiar about her. Blondie did another subtle shift, gave herself more personal space, but smiled comfortably at Curls. "Kimmie...?" Blondie fluffed her own straight, shoulder-length hair.

"Hey, Lindsey." It took Kimmie another hint or two before her hand flew to her head. "Oh, pumplegunker."

Eleven sisters, and he'd never heard that one before.

While he ran the third card, Kimmie worked at the goo. "We had to toss all our buttercream and start over after a surprise health department inspection yesterday," she said. "Guess I got some on me. I knew that fortune cookie was trouble."

CJ had too many sisters to touch that and too much wisdom to try to understand. Still, he stepped away from the computer to offer her some napkins. "What can I get you?"

An uneven pink stain spread up her cheeks, shaped like a sideways map of Africa. She flashed an awkward, toothy smile back at him. "I had a dream about you last night," she said. "You were a llama, but I still knew it was you. You had your name on your trunk."

There was another something none of his sisters had ever said to him. Pretty sure that was something no human had ever said before.

"A luggage trunk, or an elephant's trunk?" Lindsey asked.

"Elephant's trunk." Kimmie pulled a blob of frosting out of her hair and smeared it across the napkin.

Lindsey nodded as though this was normal. CJ scratched his jaw. "Huh."

Kimmie's eyelids flared. She dropped the napkin and grabbed the edge of the bar, smearing the buttercream on the shiny surface. "Oh, no," she whispered.

"Yes?" he said, painfully aware that whatever was wrong, it would be worse than if he had an elephant's trunk.

"My mother's gonna spit lemon juice when she finds out you're working here. Oh, no, no, no. This'll be worse than the chocolate ganache catastrophe of '09."

Kimmie's familiarity clicked. Despite the obvious personality differences between mother and daughter, CJ couldn't unsee it.

He retreated half a step. Basil's chin dangled so low it hid his collar in a rare appearance of the Holy Look of Disbelief.

Kimmie was a young Queen General. She didn't have the presence and the outfit, but there was no mistaking the solid jaw line, the high cheekbones, and the slant of her blue eyes.

The warmth in them had fooled him.

Lindsey was watching CJ again, and he had enough experience with women to know what her scrutiny meant this time.

He wasn't being judged on being an honored widower in Bliss. He was being judged on being a human being.

And she wouldn't give him more than one shot to do it right.

Tough crowd. Shouldn't have mattered, but there was something about Lindsey that put CJ on extra edge.

"Man's gotta work," he said to Kimmie.

Kimmie's head wouldn't stop shaking no. "I like coming here. I don't want it to close down. Did you apply at the country club? Or Melodies? You like karaoke, right? It's not always bad. Some of the brides and bridesmaids sing pretty decent. Sometimes. Mom would get you a job either place. Obviously she'd prefer the country club, and then we wouldn't have to worry about her expressing her displeasure by making the earth swallow Suckers whole. We're already on thin icing after that health department visit yesterday."

"Your mother can't control the jaws of hell," Lindsey said with exaggerated patience. "I'm pretty sure she can."

CJ looked to Basil, but His Holiness didn't correct Kimmie.

Jeremy elbowed in with a basket of nachos for the two women. "She can't." He pointed to Kimmie. "Ain't your mother's place to say where a man can and can't work." He switched his focus to Lindsey. "A woman either."

"No arguments there," Lindsey murmured. "She gives Natalie any shit, you let me know."

Lindsey gave a single nod, but she had one eye on CJ, and he was positive she caught his head whipping up toward his fellow bartender.

"Any more than usual, or any at all?" Lindsey said.

Kimmie paused in her headshaking. "She's always giving Nat trouble. You know how it is. Mom gets all I now pronounce you the divorced outcast on the committee, and Natalie gets all Bite me, and Mom gets all Does your mother know you talk like that? and Natalie gets all Bite me harder, and then we go home and do it again next week."

Lindsey pulled a nacho chip out of the basket. "Knot Fest is a beautiful celebration of marriage inside and out, isn't it?"

Her dry delivery should've been funny, but CJ was having a hard time shaking the paranoia that had come with knowing these women—and Jeremy—were on Team Natalie.

"Hush," Kimmie said. "She'll hear you said that, and then she'll make it worse for Nat." "Like hell she will," Jeremy said.

"She will," Lindsey said on a sigh. "And she'll blame Nat, and Nat will let her."

CJ inched down the bar. Still had five drinks to make, and this conversation was going places he didn't need to go too.

Kimmie hopped off the stool. "You know what? I have to go. If Mom finds out I know you're working here, this'll be worse than—well. It'll be worse. And I don't need worse."

"Stay." Lindsey gestured at CJ with a nacho chip. "Tell her you were here to convince him to play in the Golden Husband Games."

His Holy Obnoxiousness laughed. Actually laughed. "Good luck with that."

Kimmie leaned back into the bar, glancing between CJ and Basil. "Would you play?" she said to CJ.

He grabbed two glasses, shaking his head. "Pumplegunker," Kimmie said again.

The reflection in the mirror showed Lindsey patting the stool Kimmie had vacated. "Sit. Have a piece of coconut cream pie. Work on him some more."

Lindsey, CJ decided, was evil. Sort of like another woman—hell. He turned around. Looked closer. Patrician nose like a guy CJ had given a ride home to the other night. Brown eyes—lighter in color, but with the same undisguised judgment he'd seen on another woman recently.

And the same sharp pink lips that had turned his world inside out Saturday night. Jeremy's favorite customers were the Queen General's daughter and Natalie Castellano's sister.

This shift had just turned to shit.

But CJ had been in enough shit in his life to know it was better to shovel it than wade through it. "How's your nephew?" No sense pussyfooting around it.

Lindsey's lips curved into a smile. "Brilliant, adorable, and perfect. Runs in the family." Nope, CJ wasn't touching that one.

"Mom's bringing you cupcakes tomorrow," Kimmie said to CJ. "To thank you for being such a great representation of everything a Golden Husband should be. Somebody posted the fountain thing up on the blog. Now Mom's talking about making a special float for you in the Bridal Mar—you know what? I was leaving. Right now."

Jeremy gave a guy across the bar the just-a-minute sign. "Sit, Kimmie. Coconut cream pie's fresh. Extra coconut."

She groaned, but she slouched back onto the stool. "She's going to salt my caramels if I can't talk you into playing."

"And you—" Jeremy poked CJ. "Play." "Don't think so."

"I'd play," Jeremy said. "And I'd win." "With a stand-in wife?" CJ said.

"If that's what it took to show the world what she meant to me. Tell you what, I'd kick your ass too."

Probably would.

That didn't bother CJ.

But knowing CJ himself would've made a similar declaration five years ago put a crimp in his gut.

"You'd win if you were playing with another woman," CJ said. That part, he felt confident calling bullshit on.

“Ain’t about winning. It’s about honoring her.” A grin broke Jeremy’s dark stare. “Still kick your ass though.”

“Shame you can’t put your money where your mouth is.”

“Nah, but you can. Do it. Show the world what she meant to you.” He gave Kimmie a nod. “That help?”

These people were all nuts. “You ladies need drinks or not?” CJ said.

Neither Kimmie nor Lindsey answered. Kimmie had the grace to scrunch her nose like she was contemplating the question.

Lindsey, though, brushed her hair over her shoulder, all the while maintaining her overtly critical gaze. “You did love her, didn’t you?” she said.

Cheap shot.

Loaded shot.

Almost hit its mark. Didn’t quite, but it still left him this side of rattled. The Castellano women went for blood.

“Lindsey!” Kimmie hissed.

“Legitimate question. You all want him to play, but you haven’t asked if he deserves to.” “Of course he does,” Kimmie said. “Deserve it. Loved her. Love her. Pumplegunker.” Her face went splotchy again. “Don’t listen to her,” she said to CJ. “Sometimes she forgets to leave the divorce lawyer part at the door.”

“I’m asking,” Lindsey said, “for the good of Bliss. Your mother would be highly embarrassed to put all this effort into making CJ her publicity stunt only to discover in the middle of the Games that he didn’t love her.”

She was goading him. On purpose. Were she one of his sisters, he’d hit right back or walk away, depending on which sister and how much he deserved it.

But he couldn’t brush Lindsey off or fight back. Because she had a point.

He sucked in an unsteady breath and leaned into the bar. “Bad breakup?” he said to Lindsey. “Got a cure for that. Called Jeremiah Weed. On the house.”

Her good-natured laugh set his teeth more on edge. “Not necessary, but thanks.”

“Don’t let her get to you,” Kimmie said. “We believe in you. Right?” She looked at Basil, who had been remarkably unopinionated thus far.

There went the Holy Constipated Squint of Pain.

CJ pushed back from all of them. He had other customers to tend to. A paycheck to earn.

Places to go. “God can hear you thinking,” CJ said to his brother. “But it’s so painful to admit when you do something right.”

The one time His Holy Perfectness got something wrong, CJ couldn’t call him on it.

Basil heaved a holy sigh. “I suppose I can make an exception, though, if it will nudge you on the path toward doing something respectable with your time in Bliss.”

“Not playing,” CJ said.

Huck hmphed on his way past. “Damn shame.”

Jeremy shook his head. “Won’t get another chance, man.” “Final answer. No.”

“My mom’s gonna scramble somebody’s eggs when she hears about this.”

“I’ll tell her your good friend here talked me out of it,” CJ said. “Anything else, ladies?”

Kimmie’s face pinched tighter. “Can I get an orange juice with piña colada mix and that cherry stuff in a martini glass?” she said in a pained rush.

“You sure?” CJ said.

“It’ll be worth the weird dreams. Well, weirder dreams.”

He doubted the pie and the drink were the root causes of her issues, but if she hadn’t figured that out for herself yet, wasn’t his business to enlighten her.

He had enough problems of his own.

Like that lingering question over whether Serena would’ve wanted him to play. Wouldn’t find the answer here.

Wasn’t sure he’d find it anywhere.

* * *

Natalie had attended Knot Fest committee meetings in the ballroom of the Rose and Dove Country Club nearly every Sunday night this year. But tonight, the scent of roses and the sound of "The Wedding March" piping through the building gave her stomach an extra turn as soon as she opened the heart-etched door to the building.

She'd heard her counterattack on Heaven's Bakery was successful, but that was all she'd heard. She also felt more guilt at the work she'd caused Kimmie than victorious that she'd thrown something in the QG's life out of whack.

And since it hadn't rained since Tuesday, nor had any earthquakes struck or tornadoes plowed through Bliss Bridal, Natalie was very, very nervous about the retribution that probably awaited her inside these walls.

She was also sneaking in to the front half of the ballroom forty seconds late, being conspicuous when she needed to blend in, just in time to hear the Queen General's normal meeting opener.

"By the power vested in me as chairperson of the Bliss Knot Festival Committee, I now pronounce this meeting called to order. If anyone objects to this proceeding, speak now, or forever hold your peace."

Natalie eased the door shut with the precision of an overprotective mother, but heads still turned. The room was set for a sit-down dinner reception of about two hundred, but the Knot

Fest committee took up only the front quarter of the room. Near the back of the populated tables, Kimmie and a few other members of the janitorial committee subtly waved or nodded. By virtue of Nat's mother's position on the Knot Fest committee, the QG hadn't made a fuss over Kimmie's friendship with Natalie and Lindsey since they'd all come home from college. That would probably come to an end once this year's Knot Fest was over.

Yet one more disappointment. Natalie liked Kimmie. And not just because she was the only other single woman in the room besides the QG. Marilyn had been widowed by a car accident before Kimmie was out of diapers. As far as Natalie knew, that was the last time fate had successfully interfered in Marilyn's life.

Natalie tiptoed in her flats to the white linen-draped round table. She pulled her chair silently over the rich red diamond-patterned carpet and swung her seat to face the front. Kimmie handed her an agenda. "Are you okay?" Kimmie whispered. "I had this dream last night that you got swallowed by an armadillo and then had to mud-wrestle my mom in a vat of liver-flavored cake batter. So when you weren't here, I got worried."

"Sitter problems," Natalie whispered back.

Dad had disappeared after catching her calling the health department. Lindsey said he was back at his cabin. He'd bought the little structure on a pond aways beyond Willow Glen when Lindsey hit her teen years, claiming he needed an estrogen-free zone. Bonus for him that it didn't get cell reception, and he rarely remembered to check the messages on the landline.

Not that Nat had called to ask for help.

Kimmie snapped her fingers. "Sitter problems! Right. I should've warned you. I got this fortune cookie—"

"Sshhhh!"

Kimmie slunk back in her chair, her expression crushed like tulle beneath a runaway groom's getaway bike. Natalie glared at Elsie and Duke Sparks one table over. Duke whispered to Elsie during the meetings all the time. They could shove their sshhs up their telephoto lenses.

The Queen General cleared her throat and sent them all a warning glare that probably could've made a Marine crap his pants. Natalie joined Kimmie in slinking back into her chair. Respectfully. As if she'd meant to slouch.

She seriously needed to stay off the QG's radar. Marilyn motioned for the minutes.

Vi, long-standing Knot Fest secretary, stood. Her husband Gilbert grunted and thwomped his cane every time Vi read Motion Approved.

Max Gregory, sandwiched between his parents at the table in front of them, sent a sympathetic smile back Kimmie's way, then gave Nat a subtle nod. He'd put Bliss Bridal's information back up on the Bridal Retailers Association Web site for her this week.

And the QG could have that fixed again in seconds if she figured out the health department inspection was Natalie's fault.

Vi finished the minutes. The QG started roll call for the Knot Fest subcommittees. All the Knot Fest subcommittees. Knot Fest came one week a year, in June, but the committee—which, like the Bridal Retailers Association, was composed nearly exclusively of couples who owned businesses on The Aisle—ran other events throughout the year as well. The bachelor auction with proceeds going to the QG's favorite charity of the moment, generally women's shelters or a children's charity. The Snow Bride Expo to draw attention to winter weddings. The Battle of the Boyfriends every Valentine's Day. And that was just the winter months.

Bliss never stopped working toward those happily ever afters.

Of all the Knot Fest committees, the Golden Husband Games committee was most important. The Games brought the most publicity to Bliss, and their revenue was second only to the income from the Bridal Expo.

Bliss needed the Games to be a success. Especially this year. The golden anniversary of the Games, and the first year they had promise to be as big as they'd been before the flood.

The QG called on the janitorial committee. Claudia and Wade stood and reported.

Clean-up plans were ahead of schedule, garbage cans and Dumpsters had been reserved, the other committees had been reminded to keep potential waste with their giveaways and products to a minimum. And when the QG murmured a "very good," afterward, Natalie felt the sting of vindication.

She'd done everything Claudia had just reported.

She wasn't here for the recognition, but it wouldn't have been unappreciated. The QG called for the Golden Husband Games report. Natalie's heart cramped.

Bonnie and Earl Phillips stood. Bonnie was a pleasantly chubby lady in her late fifties dressed in floral print, Earl a squat, balding man trying out this year's beard fashion.

And until they'd been named successors for the Games, Nat had thought them nice enough.

Bonnie consulted her flower-decoupaged clipboard. "Madame Chairman," she said, "all's going well."

Earl nodded, and the two of them sat down.

Natalie's shoulders hunched with the effort of suppressing an outraged howl. Formal invitations should've been sent two weeks ago. The husbands couldn't just show up and play. Other years they could, but not this year. To compete for Husband of the Half Century, they needed to design team logos for T-shirts and commemorative merchandise. Sell tickets to the Games and the reception. Do interviews for publicity.

But first they needed to say they were playing.

And then there was everything else—trophies, supplies, advertising, and on and on and on—and it was all barely getting done.

Claudia and Wade shot Natalie an alarmed look. Other couples at other tables cast covert glances her way. Max Gregory coughed behind his hand, and a couple tables over, Luke Hart—Gabby's boss at Indulge Chocolates and another single son on The Aisle—stifled what looked to be a laugh.

This was a disaster.

Marilyn gave a regal nod and called for the Miss Flower Girl and Junior Miss Bridesmaid subcommittee reports.

"Mom's gonna flip their pancakes," Kimmie whispered.

Natalie buried her head in her hands. "She needs to make them do their damn job instead."

Dammit. She'd promised herself she wouldn't cuss tonight.

After another hour of old and new business and announcements, the Queen General tapped a spoon against her water glass. "If anyone knows of any reason why this meeting should not be adjourned, speak now or forever hold your peace." She paused a moment, then looked right at Natalie. "Miss Castellano. A word after the meeting."

She dinged her spoon against the glass once more. "I now pronounce this meeting adjourned."

The couples around Natalie stood, giving her a wide berth. Even Claudia and Wade took the long way around the table toward the door. "Janitorial committee meeting tomorrow at nine," Claudia said to the table at large.

They all nodded. The few willing to make eye contact with Nat gave her the maybe-we'll-see-you, maybe-we-won't eyeballs of doom. The rest of the couples—including Bonnie and Earl, who deserved Knot Fest Committee Detention far more than Natalie—gathered their things and headed toward the door, calling greetings and making plans with their other friends around the room.

Kimmie paused and squeezed Nat's hand. "Watch your pancakes, okay?"

"My pancakes need a drink." Natalie's head ached. Worse, though, her rebellious, I've-had-enough side was clawing its way out of that nice little bag she kept trying to suffocate it with. Again.

"Mom's looking this way. I've gotta run."

Yep, they were the target of the Queen General's attention. As if the tingly sensation of Nat's humanity being sucked out of her pores wasn't clue enough that they were being watched. "Meet me at Suckers if I survive," Natalie said to Kimmie, even though she desperately needed to spend time on Gabby's dress. "And if I don't, tell Noah I love him."

Nat had this coming. All things considered, she was lucky Bliss Bridal's walls were still standing.

And she couldn't think about that whole ordeal where CJ had kissed her a week ago. And then rescued Cindy the dinosaur.

Because the Queen General would read her mind, and then Natalie's pancakes would be toast.

Kimmie hesitated, but then nodded quickly. "Sure." She made a dash for the door. Natalie gathered her notes and stuffed them in her messenger bag, then sent a quick text inviting Lindsey to join them. She approached the Queen General's table as the last few couples escaped the room, their voices disappearing down the hallway.

"Good evening, Mrs. Elias," Natalie said.

"Natalie," the Queen General said in that commanding way that made Natalie wonder if she'd been Attila the Hun in a previous life, "is there any particular reason you've been interfering with the Golden Husband Games planning committee?"

Natalie opened her mouth. Closed it.

A slow fuse ignited the long trail of injustices she'd endured from this woman since her mother died. Her shoulders snapped back, and she swallowed the nasty bitterness that would've otherwise colored her words. "I'm sorry, I have no idea what you're talking about."

"So you deny coordinating security for the Games with the Bliss Police Department?"

Relief swept hard and fast through Nat's shoulders. Maybe too fast. This, she'd prepared for. "The Bliss Police Department was assisting me in making arrangements so that cleanup from Knot Fest will count as community service for anyone court-ordered to serve hours. While I was discussing the details for the janitorial committee, the chief inquired about when they might expect to hear from the Husband Games coordinator. I merely told him what my mother had shared with me before she passed."

Marilyn's hard-as-diamonds expression didn't waver. "I expect you'll refer any future inquiries to Bonnie and Earl."

"Of course. I mean, I did." Her brain telegraphed shut up now, but Natalie's mouth was already well on its way to opening for her foot. "I get the impression they're not doing their job though."

"It's not your concern," the QG said.

"It's all of Bliss's concern. Do you know what people are telling me? Questions about the voting software are getting no answers from them. The hospitality tents for the husbands and wives? Not reserved yet, and there's a big political rally in Willow Glen that day." Natalie's heart raced so fast, it could've beat a lion in a footrace. There was a line. A thin, fragile thread between improving the Games and destroying her own work to make sure the Games still happened. And

Natalie was riding up to that line with an out-of-control chainsaw. "The sunflower field? They don't even know where it is."

Marilyn's chest puffed. It was a slight movement, but it made her look eight times more intimidating than normal. "Once more, Miss Castellano, the Games are not your concern."

"The Games bring in more tourist revenue than almost any other single Knot Fest event," Natalie said. "They make Bliss unique. Bonnie and Earl are ruining them, and you don't care."

"I suggest, Miss Castellano, that you remove yourself from my business." The pointedness in the QG's cold blue glare took on a know-all, see-all, hear-all quality. "All of my business."

Nat swallowed her own tongue.

She knew.

The Queen General knew Natalie had been the one who called the health department. "I understand you were seen with CJ Blue at the wedding cake monument," the QG continued. "I believe I made my expectations of you clear."

Hearing his name, hearing the reminder that Nat wasn't worthy of his company sent a wave of conflicting emotions through her veins. She'd done a decent job of not running into him again since Monday, which had her both frustrated and relieved. And then worried about why she was frustrated that she hadn't seen him.

She had issues.

"Pardon me," Natalie ground out, "for not having the powers of premonition about where a grown man might be every minute of every hour of every day so that I can appease your ridiculous expectations."

Marilyn's expression went hard enough to crush diamonds. "For conduct unbecoming of a Knot Fest committee member, I'm placing you on probation from the committee. One more misstep, Miss Castellano, and I will remove you. Are we clear?"

I quit.

It was all she had to say. Give the Queen General exactly what she wanted so Natalie could live in peace. No Knot Fest committee meetings where she didn't quite fit in anymore. No more putting off finding whatever it was she'd do after Dad sold the shop. No more crossing this damn woman's path.

But Natalie couldn't walk away from the Games. Not when they were still her mother's legacy, and not when that legacy was on the brink of falling apart. She could still do something to make her father proud, and she could still do something good for the people of Bliss who weren't irrational, pain-in-the-ass Queen Generals.

She gulped down the Bite me rising in her throat, and gave a tight nod instead. "Yes."

The flick of the QG's finger dismissed Natalie. Nat knew better than to give her any more excuses to talk. She swallowed the lump of cotton in her throat. "Have a nice evening, Mrs. Elias," she said instead.

Because her mother taught her to have manners, even when she didn't mean it.

Chapter 8

Natalie was fuming so hard her windshield was fogged over by the time she arrived at Suckers. At the door, Lindsey gave Nat a once-over. "That bad, eh?"

Beside her, Kimmie nodded emphatically. "On the epic badness scale, it's like a forty out of ten to be called to stay after a Knot Fest meeting."

Natalie was too occupied picturing the Queen General dying a slow, painful death of suffocation by her own righteousness to do much more than just breathe.

Lindsey linked her arm through Natalie's. "Nat? You okay?"

"No." She couldn't stop shaking her head. "She put me on probation. Because I was publicly seen with C—with you know who. Bonnie and Earl are letting the Games fall apart, and I'm on probation for something that's not my fault."

Kimmie rubbed Nat's back. "Mom had a meeting scheduled with them the other day, but then we had a surprise visit from the health department, and she skipped it."

Oh, hell. "Seriously?" This was her fault.

"Uh-huh." Kimmie's nose scrunched. "It's weird, really. We have protocols in place. We practice for surprise inspections. We could've handled it without her. But she stayed. And she let them make her toss all the buttercream. You know my mother. She could've done some Jedi mind trick and sent the health department people away. I don't—oh. Oh." Kimmie's lips pursed. "Maybe that's it."

"What, menopause?"

"No, she hasn't hit that yet," Kimmie said.

Good lord. She could still get worse. Natalie shuddered. "Somebody has to do something about that woman. She used to be able to at least pretend she was human. But now she's just impossible."

"Well, since—never mind." Kimmie spun to the door. "Since what?" Lindsey said.

Kimmie sucked her lower lip into her mouth, then shrugged. "It's nothing. Just a death in the family recently." "Who?"

"Distant relative in Chicago," Kimmie pulled on the door. "Nobody you know. It's made Mom a little cranky. It'll pass." She winced. "Maybe."

Lindsey pushed the door shut. "That relative?" Kimmie blanched. "Wh-what relative?" she squeaked. "Ooh," Lindsey breathed.

"What?" Natalie looked between the two. "What?"

Lindsey hustled Nat and Kimmie into Suckers and toward a quiet booth in a corner away from the rest of the scattered patrons. The soft glow of the purple track lighting welcomed them back to a friendly place where Natalie hadn't been in far too long.

"Oh, look, the Bachelors are here," Kimmie said. Her voice was too high. She slid onto the bench facing the door, craning her neck to look back at Bliss's minor league baseball players who were crowded at the bar behind them, all laughing at something Natalie couldn't see.

Lindsey slid into the booth across from her. "Who got the bakery, Kimmie?" "Who—what?" Natalie sputtered. She climbed in beside Kimmie.

"Keep your voice down," Kimmie whispered. "How do you know about that?"

Natalie's heart hummed faster than her Singer on steroids. "Your mom sold the bakery?" So there would be a new owner. New blood on The Aisle.

New blood on the Knot Fest committee. Marilyn Elias's time was up.

Oh, God. Did this mean Nat could keep the boutique? "Half the bakery," Lindsey said.

Kimmie's eyes were so big they were in danger of falling out. "You do know."

"I have good sources," Lindsey said. "And, quite frankly, I'm tired of your mother bullying my baby sister. So give me a good reason to keep this to myself."

Her apologetic tone was probably meant to take the bite out of the threat, but Kimmie went paler.

Natalie leaned into both of them. She was breathing too fast and her hands were getting shaky, but she didn't care.

The QG's reign could be over.

Kimmie fidgeted with the zipper on her jacket, not making eye contact with Nat or Lindsey, her own breath uneven and her voice strained. "Didn't you ever wonder where she got the money to pay for so much of that first Knot Fest after the flood?"

Natalie's breath whooshed out on a single syllable. "Oh."

"She'll do worse than salt my caramels if she finds out you know." Kimmie sounded near tears. "She was going to buy it back, but Knot Fest didn't come back as strong those first two years, and it turned out the bakery's flood insurance wasn't enough to cover repairs, so Mom had to do something. She almost had enough saved up to pay off the debt, but then cousin Birdie bit the beaters, and—well, Birdie's will was… surprising."

"Heaven's Bakery has a new owner." Natalie could barely breathe, but she pushed the words out.

"Half owner. Uninvolved. In the bakery."

"How uninvolved?" Natalie leaned closer. "Is the new owner willing to get involved? Kimmie, how much do you know about running Knot Fest?"

Kimmie's cheeks were taking on her signature jagged flush. "You know what? I need a drink. Do you guys want a drink?"

She twisted in the booth, raised her hand, but then Lindsey spoke. "We won't tell anyone." Nat gawked at her sister.

Not tell anyone?

They would tell everyone. The QG didn't own the whole bakery. She was a fraud. And if she was a fraud, she didn't have any power.

"Stop, Nat," Lindsey said. "When word gets out that she sacrificed half her bakery for Bliss, she's the hero. So yes, we are keeping this to ourselves."

Natalie's jaw clenched so tight she felt it all the way down in her toes.

Why did Marilyn Elias always come up smelling like chocolate buttercream? "She can't treat people the way she does," Natalie hissed.

"And you need to focus on what you can fix and let go of what you can't." Lindsey pulled her coat off and set it in the booth beside her. "You want to show the old bat what you're made of? Be the bigger person. Keep getting your job done despite her. Do something she can't."

"And what, exactly, can't the Queen General of Bliss do?"

"She hasn't talked CJ Blue into playing in the Golden Husband Games yet, has she?"

Was she kidding? No.

No way in hell would Natalie convince CJ to play in Mom's Games.

Her face, her ears, even her hair went hot. So did some of her dormant parts. "What is wrong with you tonight?" she hissed at her sister. "Mom's last Games, Nat. What would she want?"

Dangerous question. "She'd want someone more capable than Bonnie and Earl running the Games."

"Natalie…"

Nat slunk back in the booth.

Mom would want CJ to play. Not only that, she'd ask him to do interviews with the Chicago Tribune. Get something picked up by the Huffington Post. Use his status as a war widower to leverage more publicity for the Games.

Though Mom, of course, would've had a softer touch than the QG was capable of.

"Are you sure you're doing this for Mom?" Lindsey said, gently as if she were talking to Noah.

Natalie squirmed. "I'm doing it for Mom and Dad."

Which meant she needed to respect the damn Queen General and be a good little in-the-shadows divorcée. No more calling in health department violations. No talking back. No making waves.

There had to be a better way.

"I'm supposed to flaunt my wares to convince him to play," Kimmie said, wincing. "If you could—you know—instead, that might be better. More effective."

Natalie sputtered out a laugh she didn't feel. "You want me to flaunt my wares for him?" As if she hadn't already. Then nearly broke when he rescued Cindy.

"If it'll work," Lindsey said lightly. "There's something to be said for psychological victories."

She was right.

If Natalie wanted to save the Games for Mom, she needed to make sure CJ played. "Yeah, and how about while I'm at it, I go ahead and offer myself as his stand-in wife."

"Mom would mix your nuts." Kimmie ducked her head again. "She has this crazy idea that he'll ask me to do it. Once we convince him to play."

Natalie shouldn't have cared one way or another who anybody played with in the Games, but the thought of Kimmie and CJ on the Husband Games field, together, competing in married couple events, rolled her stomach.

Lindsey's attention shifted to Natalie, perceptive and probing as only a big sister could be. "Miss Junior Bridesmaid all over again."

Natalie shuddered, and hoped Lindsey wouldn't figure out Natalie's real fear wasn't that she'd come in second to Kimmie, as she had years ago during Bliss's annual teenage talent show, but rather that she'd be jealous of Kimmie. In their school days, Natalie had been a big enough shit to hold it against Kimmie that Marilyn was her mother, which had caused problems more than once between Mom and the QG. Nat liked to think she'd grown up a little since then.

Kimmie was not only a good friend, she was as pure and innocent as her mother was queenly and General-ish. Kimmie deserved the kind of guy who would wade into a splash pad in fifty-degree weather to rescue a stuffed dinosaur.

Kimmie's mouth hinged open, and she suddenly slapped a hand to it. "Oh, Nat," she groaned through her fingers. "Me being friendly with him won't be awkward for us, will it? After—you know. Your history. It feels… disloyal."

Natalie blinked.

Kimmie knew about the kiss?

How the hell did anyone other than Natalie and CJ know about that kiss?

She threw her hands up in surrender. "Oh, no. You can have him," she said, perhaps with more force than the situation warranted.

Especially since Lindsey's eyes went narrower and her lips parted softly into a semblance of an amused, you're-going-to-regret-that smile.

And suddenly Natalie realized exactly what Kimmie thought was awkward.

The first kiss. The public one. The one Natalie had spent the last five years regretting. Kimmie gave a snorty laugh. "Like you'd want him, right? That would be awkward." "Exactly." Relief fueled Natalie's fake laugh. "Can you imagine? Oh, yes, CJ, I'd love to be your temporary wife. Especially since it's your fault my son doesn't have a father."

A glass of what looked suspiciously like whiskey sour plopped down on the table in front of Natalie, and Lindsey sucked in a breath.

Natalie half-choked on her own spit.

Large, manly fingers were wrapped around the glass. Large, manly fingers that weren't dark enough to be Jeremy's.

"Evening, ladies," a large, manly, not-Jeremy voice said. A familiar, large, manly voice that echoed through Natalie's body, from her roots to her toenails and every place—every place—in between.

She couldn't look up. Her face ignited so hot her skin should've melted off.

Kimmie made a sound between a horrified squeak and a guffaw. Lindsey had gone mute. Oh, God. Oh, shit. Natalie had to leave. If the QG heard—

No. Fuck the QG. Fuck probation. This was Natalie's bar. This was Natalie's home.

She was staying. She was having a drink, and she'd damn well finish planning the Golden Husband Games even if Marilyn Elias banned her from the face of the whole fucking earth.

Once she got over her mortification at getting caught mocking CJ right to his face. Again.

"Friday night, I dreamed you were a mushroom," Kimmie sputtered into the silence. "You make a much better llama. Is it weird that I keep dreaming about you?"

"You kidding?" he said. "It'd be weird if you didn't."

The friendly smile in his voice made Natalie like him a bit more, which made her hate herself a little more.

He nudged the glass in front of Natalie. "Whiskey sour."

A glass of white wine appeared, followed by a milky drink with a pink tint in a martini glass. "White zin. And a Kimmie colada."

"No rum, right?" Kimmie said. "It makes me break out. And recite dirty poetry. Badly." "No rum," CJ said. "Extra coconut and grenadine."

"Wow. You really know how to make a woman happy." She winced out loud, as only Kimmie could do. "I mean with their drinks. That's all I meant."

"I have a ninety-eight percent success rate with always knowing what will make a woman happy," he said.

Lindsey chuckled softly. "And how do you quantify that?" "Wouldn't you like to know," he said.

Nat wanted to know. She shouldn't have wanted to know, but she hadn't caught a whisper of him all week, and he was being flirty and relaxed and friendly despite what he had to have heard. She couldn't help herself. She wanted to know.

She risked a glance at Lindsey. Her older sister was giving Natalie a speculative look she generally reserved for nights of playing "Does This Couple Stand a Chance?"

Lindsey liked to claim she could see when a couple was a bad match. She had an uncanny success rate of predicting splits, but she rarely put effort into playing matchmaker. She claimed it didn't work that way.

That she was still looking back and forth between CJ and Natalie wasn't good. Not good at all.

It meant she hadn't spotted whatever she needed to spot in order to guarantee this couple didn't stand a chance.

This was bad. Very, very bad.

Natalie shoved her mortification back into that little box in her mind where she'd stored half of the last five years of her life, then put on her game face and looked up at CJ. His shoulders were extra broad in his green muscle shirt tonight; his biceps nicely showcased in his sleeves; his short hair still long and unkempt enough to give a girl dirty thoughts. "Thank you," she choked out.

His gaze locked on hers. Her throat went dry at the spark of a challenge lurking in the quirk of his lips.

As if he were challenging her to say it one more time—that he wrecked her marriage—to his face.

"For the drink." Natalie's face threatened to erupt in flames again, but she'd be damned before she'd let him see her sweat.

Again.

Not that she didn't deserve to sweat.

"Can we get some nachos please?" Lindsey said.

CJ held Natalie's gaze an eternity longer than he needed to. "Already on their way." "Not bad for a new guy," Lindsey said.

"Got orders to take good care of you." He still hadn't looked away from Natalie, and she felt more heat rising, except this time it was nowhere near her face.

It was much, much further south.

"You ladies enjoy your drinks. Food will be out in a few." He walked away, and Natalie buried her face in her hands.

"Don't tell my mom I said that thing about rum and the poetry, okay?" Kimmie said.

Lindsey sank back into her side of the booth. "Honey, we're not telling anyone anything that just happened here."

And thank the holy heavens that neither of them asked Natalie to explain it either.

* * *

CJ was unloading a tray of glasses from the under-the-bar dishwasher when Lindsey strolled back through the front door and headed straight for him. She wore the look of a woman who took his participation in her latest harebrained scheme as a foregone conclusion.

Hell.

Yeah, hell. That's exactly what this shift had turned into the moment she'd walked in his door.

And it had nothing to do with her, and nothing to do with Kimmie.

It had everything to do with her loudmouthed, sharp-lipped, wounded-eyed sister. Lindsey swung her hips onto the stool closest to him and gave him a smile he'd seen a thousand too many times from his sisters. That smile never ended well. "Could you do me a favor?" she said.

No right answer for that question, and he'd bet she knew it. "Depends on the favor."

She plopped a wallet on the bar and gave him a look of innocence that, fortunately, didn't come close to touching his sister Cinna's. Otherwise he might've fallen for it. "I found this in the parking lot and was hoping you'd know how to return it to its rightful owner."

It was a girly canvas number, pink with a strained black zipper, bulging as if its owner cleaned it out only after it burst while she was juggling groceries and a hungry, whiny four-year-old after a long day of work. Which he was able to picture less because he'd had that much experience with women, and more because he'd seen Natalie wrestle cash out of it fifteen minutes ago after refusing to hear that their bill was on the house.

Jeremy's orders, seconded by Huck, who had apparently used Lindsey's services once or twice. Maybe more, after he wised up and started getting prenups.

"How'd you get that?" CJ asked.

"Found it in the parking lot," she repeated.

"You know whose that is."

"I don't peek in wallets." She flashed him a smile that was remarkably friendly. "Hazard of being a lawyer. Nobody trusts us. But a bartender—everyone trusts you."

Her straight face was impressive. "Not everyone," he said.

"If that's how you feel, you should consider giving everyone a second chance to learn to trust you. They might surprise you."

"I think you're full of shit."

That earned him a full-on grin. "Appreciate the help." She swung herself down from her stool. "I'd return it myself, but I have to be at work early tomorrow. Long drive home still."

"What's your game?" he called after her.

"I hear you're a fairly smart guy when you're not trying to kill yourself jumping out of airplanes. You'll figure it out."

It wasn't until after she'd sashayed herself out the door that he picked up the wallet.

And noticed the gift certificate with Bob and Fiona's name on it. She'd paid for three months of maid service. His in-laws would appreciate this as much as they'd appreciated his work around their house the last week.

Son of a bitch. She could teach his sisters a thing or two. "What's she want?" Huck asked.

CJ pocketed the gift certificate, then held up Natalie's wallet. "Found this in the parking lot."

Huck tilted his head, making his left eye bulgier than his right. "That her sister's?" "Looks like." CJ pried it open carefully as he could and worked out a credit card that was clearly stamped with Natalie's name. He slipped it back inside and zipped the wallet. "Yep." "Heh." The grin on the old man's face wasn't endearing. He slapped CJ on the back.

"Thought she had that look about her." "What look?"

"Son, the lady just anti-eyed you."

Thirty years of living with sisters, and CJ had no clue what Huck was talking about. "English?"

"She don't disapprove of you with that wallet's owner. Ain't saying she approves, but her not disapproving means something round here." This whole town was nuts. "I'm honored."

"Should be. Usually she sticks to breaking 'em up. She goes to the effort of putting you together, she's feeling extra good about something. Wouldn't do that if she didn't like you."

"Or hate me." That made more sense. He thrust the wallet at Huck. "How about you take care of this."

But Huck shook his head and backed up. "Don't go listening to everything you hear. Nat made a mistake. Didn't burn down a bunch of houses, didn't drown a bunch of kittens, didn't sell drugs to any middle schoolers. Just made a mistake with who she married, 'cept unlike the rest of us commoners in Bliss, she gets to pay for it over on The Aisle every day. Got some respect for that."

CJ caught himself off guard when he realized he'd bit his tongue to keep from letting a Me too, slip out.

Despite her crazy-ass homewrecker accusation, he did have some respect for Natalie. She looked as though she hadn't slept since last Christmas, she was pretty high up there on at least two big shit lists—her father's and Marilyn Elias's—and yet, from what he'd heard, she kept pushing through.

Making things work. Keeping her family's business going. Helping other small businesses around town.

All while being a single parent.

"Might have a point," CJ said. "Doesn't mean her sister isn't wasting her time." Huck chuckled again. "You say you got eleven sisters of your own?"

"Yep."

"Then I reckon you already know your opinion on the subject don't add up to a hill of beans."

Wasn't that the unfortunate truth.

* * *

"Noah! Time to go."

Natalie tossed two bowls into the dishwasher. Milk splattered everywhere. She bit down on her lower lip to keep from thinking that nice four-letter word she desperately wanted to think, but she didn't have the money to put in Noah's college fund today.

She'd used up more than she had already, cussing all night over CJ and the QG when she should've been sleeping.

At least she'd made progress on Gabby's dress.

"Noah," she called up the stairs again. "Are your teeth brushed yet?" Her answer was a little voice shrieking the Stones' "Satisfaction." She went upstairs and peeked in the bathroom.

Noah stood on a stool at the sink, his dark hair matted in record-setting bedhead, his orange pullover clashing with his red track pants. His eyes were closed, nose scrunched and his head tilted back while he bellowed the song off-key with all his little might.

Dam—darn kid was adorable.

"C'mon, Pavarotti." She ruffled his hair. "You'll miss second breakfast at Mrs. Tanner's." He stopped mid-word. One eye scrunched open. "Is it pancake day?"

"I don't know, sweetie, but if you don't hurry and it is pancake day, you'll miss it."

It was amazing how one shoulder shrug could make him look so grown up and so small all at the same time. And he usually loved pancake day.

So long as he didn't start throwing fits over staying with Mrs. Tanner, Nat could survive his not loving pancake day. Mrs. Tanner was a godsend. She'd watched Noah since the floodwaters receded. After Mom died, she'd been the normalcy he had desperately needed.

"Mrs. Tanner says growing dinosaurs need fruit and protein," Noah said. "Did you know she can make bread from flour, Mom? When I grow up, she's going to teach me how."

So Mrs. Tanner made Natalie feel inadequate when it came to mealtime. But she got Noah two square meals a day, so that counted for something. "Great. Finish brushing. Time to go."

Noah went back to his singing.

Nat shook her head. She had the janitorial committee meeting this morning at the Rose and Dove. Plus, it had been raining since she got home from Suckers—the Queen General proving a point about being displeased with Natalie, no doubt—and unlike last week's weather, this time the rain had brought temperatures that had dropped near freezing.

That poor sunflower field wouldn't survive—the plants should be sprouting soon—and she had no idea what she'd suggest to Bonnie and Earl as a backup plan.

Or how she'd go about making that suggestion. "C'mon, Noah. The roads aren't pretty today."

"You should get them a dress, Mom. That would help."

Leave it to a four-year-old to put life in perspective. She pivoted so he wouldn't see her laugh. "One minute, Noah." God, she loved that kid.

She went downstairs and finished the dishes, mopped up her mess, and grabbed her leather parka and Noah's blue ski jacket. He finally moseyed down too. She hustled his arms into his sleeves and herded him out the door.

He came to a complete stop. "Mama—snow!"

She clamped down on her first reaction—to tell him to keep moving, they'd be late, he'd miss breakfast—and took a moment to stop and stare in wonder herself.

Snow.

In freaking April.

The sunflower field was doomed.

Last year's brown grass stood above the meager accumulation. What was there would melt before noon. But they probably wouldn't see the white stuff again until December or January, and by then, they'd be gone from Bliss.

Possibly in an apartment. Without a yard.

How could a little boy make snow angels or build snow forts or snowmen in an apartment complex parking lot?

Natalie's heart clenched. "C'mon, kiddo. Careful." She nudged him. He dragged his feet down the stairs, then turned toward her car, longingly brushing his hands over the snow-dusted evergreen bushes beneath the windows.

Natalie let him get four steps in front of her. She hesitated, remembering his terrified screams in the fountain, but then he paused.

Looked over his shoulder with a guarded hope.

She grinned at him, then leaned over, balancing on her heeled boots, scraped together a handful of snow, and lobbed it at him.

"Hey!" His shriek melted into a giggle. He dropped to his knees and raked at the ground until he had a half-formed snowball that he threw to get back at her.

She dodged it easily, but when she bent to scoop another pitiful snowball, Noah launched himself at her and dumped a puny handful into her hair. She snatched him in a hug, knocked herself off-balance, and they both fell laughing to the ground.

She checked her skirt to make sure her panties weren't showing, but she didn't care that her knee-high suede boots would probably never recover, or that she'd just ripped a hole in her tights.

These moments were rare and precious and they'd be gone too fast. "I'm gonna get you, Mommy!"

"Not if I get you first!"

Noah's breath hung in puffs like little clouds of happiness. His cheeks were rosy and his giggles and shrieks echoed through the neighborhood. Natalie struggled to keep up with him. She eventually settled for laughing on the ground while he dumped snow in her hair. "I got you, Mommy! I got you!"

She snagged him and pulled him down. Wet coldness seeped through her skirt, but she had a warm little boy squirming and giggling in her lap. "Now I got you," she said. She'd just found his perfect tickle spot when a shiver went down her neck and shoulders.

CJ stood ten feet away on the sidewalk, dressed in jogging shorts, a long-sleeve T-shirt and a ball cap. And just like the other day, he wore an inscrutable expression. Lips flat, eyes clear but scrunched, the same rosiness in his cheeks that Noah was sporting.

Judging her for being an immature, irresponsible mother, undoubtedly. After what she'd done last night at Suckers, this couldn't be a friendly visit. She had some crow to eat.

He blinked, and suddenly he was the quirky-smiled, goofball bartender who might've been the kind of guy she'd like to get to know better, had they both been someone else.

Her breath caught.

"Missing something?" he asked.

What an ego. And she had a problem if she thought that was endearing. "No." "So this isn't yours?"

"Hey!" Natalie slid Noah aside and sprang to her feet as quickly as her modesty would allow.

CJ had her wallet.

"Somebody turned it in after you left."

She took it and unzipped it enough to peer inside but not cause any other embarrassing scenes.

Yep, definitely her wallet. "I don't understand how this happened."

He stared at her like the how should've been obvious. She hadn't dropped it. She'd paid, then she'd handed it over to—

Lindsey. She'd handed it to Lindsey. Lindsey had taken all the purses and coats in her side of the booth.

This wasn't an accident. This was all Lindsey. Sneaky little bi—brat.

"Thank you," Natalie said. She needed to add I'm sorry. He'd been nothing but decent to her entire family since he'd come back, and she needed to let go of what had happened between them.

CJ wasn't the type of guy to intentionally kiss the wrong woman. And Derek hadn't been the type of guy who was cut out to be an Aisle husband.

Natalie's problems had never been CJ's fault. Lindsey was right about something else too.

Natalie needed to convince CJ to play in the Golden Husband Games. To make a point to the QG. Have some kind of psychological victory.

More, though—it was what Mom would've wanted.

"Hey, I remember you." Noah stepped out from behind her, one hand tucked around her knee. "You saved Cindy."

Natalie put a protective hand to Noah's shoulder, which earned her another inscrutable look from CJ. He squatted down to Noah's level. "And how's Cindy doing?"

"She's fair," Noah said, as if he were forty instead of four. "She's sad that we couldn't save her dress, but Mommy's going to make her a new one."

"Better give her a few extra hugs until then," CJ said. Natalie's heart might've gone a little soft at the edges.

Noah pointed to CJ's head. "Is that a Cubs hat? I only like to be friends with Cubs fans, but the Cubs are blue, and your hat is gray. Why's it pointing backward?"

"Noah—" Natalie started, but CJ twitched another eye at her.

He pulled his hat off and handed it to Noah. "You like the Cubs, little dude?"

Noah inspected it, wrinkling his forehead and squinting at the letters. "Yeah, but I wish they won more. They like to fall apart after the all-star game. If they were my team, I'd rename them the Dinosaurs and give them all dresses if they played good."

CJ smiled easily. "You like dinosaurs?" "And dresses. And the Cubs."

"You like planes?"

Noah gave a body-moving shoulder shrug. "They're okay." "Not every boy likes planes," Natalie said.

CJ ignored her and touched his hat. "Well, this is an Air Force hat. They fly planes and have a football team."

"A dinosaur team?"

"Sorry, little dude. They're the Falcons."

Noah's whole face scrunched up. "What's a falcon?" "It's a big bird."

Noah rolled his eyes as only a four-year-old could. "Dinosaurs can eat birds."

CJ chuckled. He brushed a few errant snowflakes out of Noah's hair, then abruptly stood. "Good kid." His gaze focused somewhere beyond her, and there was an unfamiliar note in his voice that almost made him sound simply human, rather than Celebrity Poster Boy for Knot Fest.

The idea of considering CJ normal among mere mortals caused a pinging sensation beneath her rib cage, and the pinging made her stop for an extra breath, which gave him time to look back at her.

Into her.

"You're lucky to have him." The raw sincerity in his words impacted her chest stronger than the pinging and deeper than her core.

She squeezed Noah's shoulder, as much to ground herself as to acknowledge CJ's sentiment. "I am."

He held her gaze a moment longer, then turned away with a ruffle to Noah's hair. "Have fun in the snow, little dude."

"Here's your hat." Noah held it out to him.

CJ grinned a grin that had probably given his mother a thousand heart attacks. "You keep it, so your dinosaurs have something to practice stomping."

"Cool!" point.

Natalie nudged him.

"I mean, thank you," Noah said. He shot a sly glance up at her. "And cool."

Natalie took a long, slow, deep breath, and willed her pulse to slow. Noah might've had a It wouldn't change anything, but he still had a point.

Chapter 9

CJ had promised Bob and Fiona he'd stop by today to investigate a noise in Fiona's car. Instead of driving to Willow Glen, though, he was crouched in the breeze on top of the wedding cake monument.

Felt nice to release some pent-up energy, but working out the physics of racing from the ground to the top tier with nothing more than rope and the columns between the layers hadn't worn him out. Muscles, maybe. Brain, no.

He couldn't shake Noah out of his head. Kid had his mother's eyes, but without the wariness and weariness. Noah offered the nonjudgmental, no-history, innocent kind of acceptance that made CJ ache for what he'd lost and for what he'd never have.

A family. Kids. Friends.

Huck and Jeremy and the regulars at Suckers were great, and much as CJ complained about Basil, hanging with his brother again was nice, but none of them got it. Neither would Noah, which didn't explain why the kid made him want a friend.

Climbing up here, breaking the rules, taking in the view, it was all supposed to clear CJ's head. Remind him he was here temporarily, just a stop on his grand tour of life. Instead, he was leaning against a mutant statue of a bride on top of a concrete wedding cake, his thoughts ricocheting from one unfortunate memory to another, with the occasional thought of a dark-haired pain in the ass.

He dropped his head back against the bride's dress and stared at the perfectly manicured courthouse lawn way down at the opposite end of The Aisle. At the white gazebo peeking through the bare trees to the left of the classic Federal-style building.

Seemed a hundred lifetimes ago that he'd stood there and said his vows. Reality was, it was only Serena's lifetime ago.

She'd died for her country, and what had he done since? Basil liked to rib him about needing to grow up, but aside from the lessons he'd learned traveling the world, CJ had grown up, once upon a time. He'd put himself through college and then he'd had a steady accounting job in a small government contract firm near Scott Air Force Base in southern Illinois.

Then Serena had come to town, an Air Force lieutenant on official military business. They met over dinner with a mutual friend.

CJ's world had stopped the minute she walked in the door. She'd had dark crescent eyes over round, dimpled cheeks, and the bounce in her step only added to the self-confident way she carried herself. She'd given him a disarming smile and offered to arm-wrestle him for his menu. He'd let her win. She'd called him on it. But one touch of her soft skin, and he was a goner. He'd asked her out before their drinks arrived.

She'd said yes.

They had gone into St. Louis for a Cubs-Cardinals game after work the next night. Night after, he took her up in the Arch, then accepted her invitation to join her in her hotel room. He proposed over stale biscuits and chewy bacon in the hotel lobby the next morning. After her meetings were over, she called her boss to get leave approved. He told his boss he needed the rest of the week off to get married, and they drove up to Bliss that night.

Let's start our adventure with a bang, she'd said.

Knot Fest had been the best days of his life. He'd thought it would only get better. But two months later, he was unemployed, living hundreds of miles from his family at

Gellings Air Force Base in southwest Georgia, and being invited to work at the base thrift shop and join the Officers' Wives Club for their monthly bunco-babes-gone-wild get-togethers.

Not his thing.

Any of it.

At first, when Serena was home, when it was just the two of them making dinner or playing board games or going out to the movies, life was good. The rest of the time he was either holed up in a silent house or handing out résumés to companies that all suggested he come back for temp work during tax season.

He started looking for jobs Serena could do when her commitment from her ROTC scholarship was up. Jobs in Chicago, so she could be near her hometown and he could be close enough to his own. Where he could find a job without employers asking when his wife would get orders to move somewhere else.

She suggested he enjoy being a man of leisure. That her next assignment would be longer, and he'd have a better shot at getting work then.

In another year or two.

They started fighting. Over her hours at work. How many video games he played while dishes sat dirty in the sink. The honeymoon she wanted to take when he couldn't see where they'd find the money to afford it. Her refusal to understand why their smartest financial decision was for her to get out of the service.

Because Serena didn't want to get out. She lived and breathed being an officer in the Air Force. She didn't have a job with a paycheck, she had a mission. And she was good at it.

He thought she could serve her country some other way. Some way where his life, his training, his career didn't have to suffer.

She disagreed.

Then he'd gotten the phone call.

His old company had a job opening in their Atlanta office.

CJ had suggested he and Serena try long-distance for a while. It was just a few hours up the road, and they could still see each other on the weekends. He'd have meaningful work, she'd keep her job—for now. Even with him renting a little place in Atlanta, they could afford to put money in his retirement account again and save enough for that honeymoon she wanted.

She said if they were going to be physically separated, she was going to war. They fought. More.

Eight months into their marriage, he took the job in Atlanta, and she shipped out for a voluntary deployment.

Three months after that, the military gave her full honors at her funeral.

CJ had given the flag to her parents, sold or gave away most everything they'd owned, stored a few essentials—like his old car—quit his job, and took off to get a grip on his life. He told his family he was going to do something he and Serena had talked about doing after her deployment. Lounge on a beach in Hawaii, or walk along the Great Wall, or parasail off the coast of France.

The Air Force sent him a big check, Serena's life insurance money, and selfish grieving bastard that he'd been, he did all three.

Those three months he'd been in Atlanta, he'd realized something. He'd screwed up.

He missed her. Work didn't make him laugh. Work didn't challenge him. Work didn't make him special.

He'd been an idiot to not appreciate what he'd had, and before he could tell her, she was gone.

So he got gone too.

Cori—short for Coriander, which he didn't tell people lest she share his real name—joined him for a camelback adventure across the Moroccan Desert about a year later. She'd been sent to talk him into coming home, dangling word that Bob and Fiona's house had flooded in storms that had submerged half of northern Illinois.

She'd shown him pictures on the Internet, including one of the wedding cake monument floating in water. He'd nearly been sick. Too many memories still.

Instead of going home, he'd sent Serena's parents her life insurance money to help with their cleanup. He still had most of it, partly because growing up with twelve siblings had taught him a thing or two about being frugal, more because it was blood money to him. He stayed in Marrakech, working at a club until he scraped up enough cash to move on to a new part of the world.

It was how he'd lived since. Without steady income, without a steady home, without any of the things he'd demanded Serena let him have. His grief had faded, but he'd still gone down a path of testing his own mortality. Seen how close he could get to what Serena must've felt in her final minutes. If he could feel her there again. Tell her he was sorry. Ask her to forgive him.

Didn't work.

Gave his family a few heart attacks though. He learned to hold back what he told them when he e-mailed or called for his monthly check-ins, shared less with Bob and Fiona in their e-mail exchanges—he was, after all, the only thing they had left of their daughter now—and no one bugged him about coming home and getting a real job.

Until now.

Because every day in Bliss was one more day to face his mistakes in his own marriage.

Something about being close to home made this feel more permanent than it should've. He still had rocks to climb and reefs to dive.

Voices below distracted him. He tensed, not eager to talk his way out of trouble if he'd been spotted by the wrong person, but when he listened closer, he decided he was safe.

Relatively speaking.

"No, really, I'll do it," Kimmie said to someone. "One of the port-a-potty guys got married last year. We did his cake. He'll give me a good deal."

"Honey," an overly patronizing male voice replied, "that's not necessary."

CJ peeked over the edge of the cake. Kimmie was trailing a sedately dressed middle-aged couple who looked as if they sampled wedding cakes every weekend.

"You keep giving Nat all the dirty jobs. That's not nice."

"Kimmie, this is the janitorial committee. Everything we do is dirty." "Not everything."

The woman put a hand to Kimmie's shoulder. "Hon, we don't like it any more than you," she said. She leaned closer to Kimmie. Whatever she said next was too soft to carry up to CJ. He caught references to your mother and off the committee and ordered us to. He strained to hear more.

Better than wallowing in self-pity.

Kimmie put a hand to her forehead. "My mother's not always right, you know."

"Damn shame it's come to this," the guy said. "Committee's gonna need more people like her in the next few years. If she weren't divorced…"

Wasn't the first time CJ had heard that sentiment. He'd picked up plenty of Knot Fest trivia at Suckers. The one thing the off-Aisle couples talked about most was how much respect they had for the woman whose favorite pastime was hating CJ.

She was making Gabby's wedding dress.

She'd helped the local trophy shop secure the order for the Golden Husband Games awards when they'd heard rumors the contract would go to a competitor in Willow Glen. Paid for them out of her own pocket, too, he'd heard.

She'd finalized a design for a Golden Husband Games commemorative T-shirt with the local screen printers since the husbands hadn't started their own designs yet.

She'd secured advertising in the program from half the small, non-Aisle shops in Bliss, and they were all honored to be included. So were the companies who had offered her gift certificates and other door prizes for the Games spectators.

She was living and breathing something she believed in, and everyone but Marilyn Elias loved her for it.

Marilyn Elias, the legendary Knot Fest chairperson who didn't tolerate anyone or anything smudging Bliss's Most Married-est Town on Earth status.

If Natalie were still married, she'd be ruling this place. Kimmie and the couple parted and went their separate ways.

A door slammed somewhere below him. Natalie herself marched out of the Rose and Dove Country Club, head down, absorbed with something on her phone. CJ's pulse rolled up to Class II rapids rates.

Smart man would've stayed put. Smart man would've kept his distance.

CJ, obviously, wasn't a smart man. Because his stiff muscles were moving, he was hooking up his gear, and then he was enjoying the feel of the cool air swirling around him while he rappelled down.

He hit the ground at the edge of the splash pad before he knew why he'd moved, or what he hoped to gain. Natalie was almost to the side cake on the walk that wrapped through the little park area. "Hey," he said.

Her short, sleek hair fanned up when she whipped her head toward him. Surprise, maybe a little irritation, maybe some regret, and finally blankness settled on her features. "Good morning. Again." She scooted a little farther along her path, sweeping her gaze about the cake as if she were checking for the nearest escape route.

But then she paused and looked at him again.

This time, there was determination in those dark eyes of hers.

CJ's ropes came down off the cake with a flick of his wrist. "I'm sorry for my role in your divorce," he said before she could steal the moment with whatever she was about to say. "I didn't know my mistake cost you so much."

Taking a woman by surprise was one of CJ's greatest joys in life. Usually resulted in blessed silence. Then there was the pride in getting the better of them for once. But Natalie's parted lips, wide eyes, and utter stillness felt less like a victory and more like a failure.

As if he'd said the wrong thing yet again.

She sucked in a big breath. Lot more than just air moved between them, as if his apology had created some kind of connection that shifted the atomic structure of his world.

Bliss was going to his head.

"Derek would've left me anyway." She spoke quietly, but he was so fixated on her pink lips that the words were imprinted on his brain. "I was an Aisle princess, he was the son of a janitor, and we got married for the wrong reasons. I made him compete in the Husband Games to show him the kind of life I wanted, but I didn't give any thought to who he was or what he wanted. I deserved to be left."

Underestimating this woman would be dangerous. "I'm still sorry, for what it's worth," he said.

"No, I'm sorry." She blew out a breath that sent her bangs scattering. "You made an easy scapegoat, but my problems aren't your fault. I'd be horrified if Noah behaved the way I have. You can't grow up in Bliss and not know how important it is to get marriage right the first time. I knew better." Her humorless laugh gave him chills. "You honestly did me a favor. He's never met Noah. Signed away all legal rights and ran. That's what I married. And now I'm living the consequences. That kiss"—she waved her hand, as if she could wave away the memory—"It wasn't the problem with my marriage. It wasn't your fault Derek left. It was mine. All mine."

CJ wasn't the same kind of asshole as her ex-husband, but he hadn't been a great husband either. He'd never know if he would've made it right with Serena, or if they would've ended up just like Natalie and her ex.

"We all make mistakes," he said. He waited for his brain to telegraph a shut the hell up now message, but it didn't come. Maybe because of everyone in Bliss, Natalie would get it. "Not so sure if I wouldn't have been in your shoes a while later myself."

Her eyes narrowed, and he realized he'd done it again. Rookie mistake. Don't let them see your weakness.

Even if they might get it.

CJ stumbled a half-step back and almost tripped over his ropes, his face gathering an unusual heat.

Natalie shook her head. "I'm the last person in the world to judge anyone else's marriage, but this town believes in what it thinks yours was. More than that, Bliss thinks you're its hero."

"I'm not a hero. She was."

"And you're all the world has left of her."

"Piss poor thing for her to leave behind," he muttered. "Should've been me." "Me too," she said.

He snapped his focus back to her.

She shrugged. "Mom should've had another twenty or thirty years. She should've been here to run the Golden Husband Games. If it'd been me instead of Mom, my son could still have playdates without anyone worrying about what the Queen General might think.

He could have good role models. The possibility of a future here. But it wasn't me. It was my mom. It was her time."

It was her time. That phrase should've been banished from the language. He hated it more than he'd hated anything in his life. "Heard that a time or two. You buy into that bullshit?"

"I don't like it, but I can't change it. Can you?"

He wished he could. God, he wished he could. "I drove her to volunteer for the deployment. She'd still be here if it weren't for me. We barely knew each other."

She cocked her head. "You were happy here in Bliss. You had something."

Yeah, they did. But he'd ignored what they had and concentrated on what else he wanted. "Wasn't enough."

"Not for me to judge," she repeated. No condemnation, no pity. Refreshing change, especially from her.

"But she's gone, and you're not," Natalie continued. "If I could play in the Golden Husband Games to give Noah a shot at being accepted for who he is instead of for who I'm not, I'd do it in a heartbeat. I can't. You can, though. Play. Remember the good times. Win. Use the publicity and the prizes to make a difference in someone's life. Be what they thought you were. Give someone hope that they can do it too. Your wife was a military hero. Whatever your issues, I'm sure she'd appreciate that."

She made it sound reasonable and logical. She made it sound right. "Then what?" He had no home, no long-term goals, no dreams. Just a cobbled-together future of chasing adventures around the globe, never again getting close enough to anyone to hurt them, one of thirteen kids, admired son and son-in-law. But completely, intentionally alone.

And she was watching him as though she knew it. Pity crept into her eyes, but it was worse than the you-poor-widower pity.

It was the you-poor-you pity.

She slowly licked her lips, never breaking eye contact. "Then you find your new happy." His happy? He didn't have a fucking clue how to find his happy. "Where do you start?" Her pulse fluttered in the soft hollow of her neck. "I don't know."

Another door slammed. They both jumped. "CJ? Is that you?"

Natalie blinked. She looked toward Vi's voice, then nodded stiffly to CJ. "Think about playing. You could do some real good." She turned, but looked back at him one last time. "I really am sorry," she said softly. "I won't mention the kiss again."

With that, she casually walked away, leaving him dangling and cursing Vi for interrupting.

Or maybe praising the Lord for her coming in and saving him from himself. Because he wanted to ask which kiss she wouldn't mention again.

"Come on up here," Vi called. "I have some flowers for the rectory."

He wouldn't find his happy in country club flowers, but he wouldn't find it in the woman who'd just retreated either.

He glanced back at her.

She might not be popular, and she might seem like she was hiding, but CJ suspected she could hold her own.

Lot better than he could, anyway.

* * *

Natalie fumbled into her car and started the engine. She couldn't breathe.

No, she could breathe. Easier, actually, for having apologized. But her chest was tight and her skin was tingly and her throat was dry.

She checked traffic—light for Monday lunchtime—and pulled out of the parking lot toward Bliss Bridal. She hadn't had all these symptoms together since Derek had asked her out.

Except Derek never would've apologized for something that hadn't been his fault. How many men would?

Apparently one. One who understood mistakes. Of everything she'd thought of CJ, she'd never expected him to be a kindred spirit.

Not that it mattered.

Because CJ may or may not play in the Golden Husband Games, but he'd leave Bliss when his commitments here were over. A guy like him wouldn't be satisfied with climbing a wedding cake statue every once in a while. He needed to be out in the world.

Not tied down.

Free.

She'd leave too, much as she wanted to stay. But she still had responsibilities. The best responsibility. She couldn't be a world adventurer. She got to live the adventure of motherhood.

And why would a guy like CJ want to raise another man's son with a woman who—up till now—had kept blaming him for something that wasn't his fault?

She arrived at Bliss Bridal and hustled into the store. Back near the dressing rooms, Amanda gave her a something's up look, then nodded toward the office.

A woman's voice wafted out. Natalie's mammaries shrank, partly instinctive fear, partly pure frustration that the woman wouldn't leave her alone.

Sorry, Amanda mouthed, along with something else Natalie didn't catch. But she recognized the male voice that answered the Queen General.

Dad was back.

"Are the dressing rooms clean?" Natalie asked Amanda. They'd been a mess yesterday. "Spotless. We have three new appointments tomorrow, and I already have the girls set up to prep for them."

"Good work."

Natalie smoothed her hair back and shoved CJ completely out of her mind. Then she stepped toward the office. Just beyond the register counter, though, she stopped cold.

"I gave you your six months," Marilyn was saying. "It's obvious Natalie can't do the job. You know I'll compensate you fairly for the space, and you can avoid the hassle of finding a broker and everything else you'll have to do."

Natalie's heart ripped in two. A violet haze blurred her vision. Dad was selling Mom's shop to Marilyn?

"No," Amanda whispered. She had moved beside the register, and she was staring in horror toward the office.

Nat couldn't breathe.

"I appreciate your patience," Dad said. "Selling the shop—it's—it's not—" He cleared his throat, and when he spoke next, his words came out less broken. Still sad, but less broken. "I'd like to see if I can find a buyer interested in keeping it as a boutique. Let another family have the legacy."

"Karen understood things would change. She'd want this to be easy on you."

"Maybe. But she wouldn't want you to be making things so difficult for Natalie either." Natalie's lungs moved, and she sucked in a surprised breath.

"Natalie made her choices," Marilyn said. "The Aisle is no place for a divorced woman with a young child. You don't have to drag this out and make it any more difficult than it needs to be."

"Actually, I do. And while you might be right about this not being where Natalie belongs, I've still lost interest in selling it to you."

Relief and fear mixed to leave a sour taste in Natalie's mouth.

He wouldn't do it. He wouldn't sell to Marilyn. But was he strong enough? How long could he resist? When Marilyn wanted something, nothing stopped her. Natalie was pretty sure her heart had quit pumping blood and was now pumping tears.

Dad couldn't sell Mom's shop to the Queen General. He couldn't.

"Arthur—" Marilyn started.

"I'm hiring a broker and seeking alternate offers," Dad said. "That's final."

The chair squeaked. Natalie jumped. She turned back to the register, fiddled with the mouse on the computer. Through one of the mirrors up front, she watched Dad and Marilyn's reflections in the doorway behind her. Marilyn was sporting her General side, with I-will-not-be-disobeyed stamped into her features. Dad caught Natalie's eye in the mirror.

Despite the pressure in her chest and eyes, she offered him a small smile. He'd stood up for her. He was fighting Marilyn. For Natalie.

He didn't smile back.

He didn't frown, but he didn't smile either. Since the health department incident, he'd simply been sad.

She had to quit letting him down.

A phone dinged. Marilyn dipped a hand into her apron and pulled her phone out. She glanced down, the diamonds in her ears sparkling in the boutique light, and the semblance of a smile crossed her lips. "Well," she said. "At least someone has come to his better senses. CJ Blue has agreed to play in the Golden Husband Games."

You're welcome. Natalie wanted to say it, but she just couldn't push the words out.

The Queen General lifted her head and gave Dad a regal nod that had entirely too much determination in it. "We'll speak again soon," she said, and then she saw herself out the back door.

Dad took two steps out onto the shop floor. Natalie turned to face him. "You were going to sell to her?" Every word put another shred in the tatters of her heart.

"She made me a good offer a while ago. Wanted to expand the bakery." His lips were still turned down, disappointment in Natalie still lingering in his eyes. He began to turn away, then stopped. "You won't ever get where you want to be if you don't fight for it, Natalie. She's one woman. Stop letting her push you around."

"I'm doing the best I can here." But it still wasn't enough.

"If you would stand up to her the right way once in a while, maybe—" he turned, head down. "Never mind. Doesn't matter. I'll get Noah tonight. Need some quality time with my little buddy."

She wanted to demand what maybe was.

But she didn't have the right. She'd given that up somewhere along the way.

Dad trudged out the back door too. Amanda was still lingering near the cash register. "He's selling?" she said. "It's true?"

"I'll have him put in a good word for you to whoever the new owners are." Nat's voice was wooden and pained in her own ears. "You've done a great job for my family. We'll always be grateful."

Amanda shot a look at the three bridal consultants on the floor—one working furiously on the computer, another searching through the rack of new winter dresses, the third poking through the display of tiaras and veils.

"Them too," Natalie said quickly. "It'll all work out. Just have a little faith in me." She had her work cut out for her. Because she still needed to find her faith in herself.

Chapter 10

A week later, Natalie got a phone call that should've been to her mother.

The Bliss-approved thing to do would be to call Bonnie and Earl Phillips and offer her assistance today. But the Phillipses would not only decline her offer, they would also report her presence to the Queen General, because there was no question where Natalie was going.

She had to see her mother's sunflowers before the rest of Bliss knew what they were.

She told Dad she had to get to the shop early, asked him to drop off Noah—who had slept with CJ's hat on last night, as he had every night the last week—and then drove across town, past the high school and Suckers and the civic center and beyond, to a patch of earth that sat a little ways past the boundaries of Bliss.

Where the first thing she saw was Duke and Elsie Sparks' Lexus SUV. A tingly, something's not right shiver went up her spine.

She made a mental deposit in Noah's college fund and drove past the farm. She passed a line of trees—a windbreak for the field—and whipped her car behind it.

These were Mom's sunflowers, dammit. The farmer had specifically taken the time to tell Nat that they'd survived the recent weather. She had every right to be here to see them.

She parked the car in the dirt and snuck through the spring growth of weeds beneath the trees. Probably should've worn pants instead of a skirt, but she hadn't planned on climbing around in the wilderness. Damn—dang weeds were taller than the sunflower sprouts she spied from the edge of the tree line, where she was hiding behind one of the thicker trunks to peer across the field.

Seven acres was what Mom's contract with the farmer had called for. Nat could barely breathe for the beauty of it. The individual plants were straggly green sprouts spaced in regular rows, but they made a green gauze over the ground that stretched on and on toward a farmhouse across the field.

She inched closer. She wanted to see their individual little leaf buds. To touch their green softness. She couldn't not experience Mom's sunflower sprouts. This would be the most epic Husband Games opening event in the history of the Husband Games.

The edge of the woods opened up to a small grassy strip. Natalie squatted low, close to the ground, and crept out from beneath the shelter of the trees. "You beautiful little sunflowers, you," she murmured.

"Tell me again how the maze will be cut," Duke's voice boomed out. Immediately to her left.

Oh, shit!

Natalie jerked back into the woods. She tripped over a weed and went down.

"Did you see that?" came Elsie's pinched voice. The woman could've been a girls' boarding school principal.

Natalie scrambled deeper into the woods on her hands and knees. Branches and sharp early weeds dug into her skin.

"Deer?" a semi-familiar deep voice said. The farmer. Closer.

Shit.

Natalie scurried to her feet, dodging trees, ignoring the wincing pain in her palms and knees and shins.

"It was a person," Elsie said.

Natalie broke into a high-speed run. Dashed through the wet undergrowth, tripped and went down once more, but she kept running, all the way back to her car.

She dove inside and peeled out onto the two-lane highway. Her chest was heaving, lungs burning, heart hammering.

Elsie and Duke would report her to the QG. The QG would cut her off the committee. Tell Dad she'd committed another egregious error.

No one was supposed to know about the sunflower field. Marilyn knew Natalie knew about the field, but Marilyn didn't know Natalie would come out here. And it didn't matter how the Sparks knew—if they saw Natalie, they'd tell Marilyn.

Shit.

Nat hung the first left she came to. There was a dull itch in her shins. A soft burn irritated her scraped palms. Her skirt and blouse were a mess, and a layer of dirt squished between her shoe and the gas pedal.

She couldn't go home for fresh clothes or Dad would know she'd been up to something, and she doubted he'd approve.

But she'd needed to see Mom's sunflower field.

A quarter mile down the road, her hands and legs began burning. A quarter mile after that, the burn had spread up her arms and down to her feet. Burning and itching and aching.

She rubbed at one hand, but it burned worse.

She circled back into Bliss, eyes stinging. Her skin felt like it had been pricked by a thousand flaming needles. Scratching made it hot and uncomfortable. She passed the civic center, but her vision blurred too badly to see it clearly.

She needed to pull over. Get help.

But what would she do? Call 911 and say the Queen General had somehow found out Nat was visiting the sunflower field and given her fast-acting poison ivy?

There was an unfamiliar car in the parking lot behind Suckers. It looked like the kind of beat-up old car Jeremy would drive.

Maybe he was prepping for the lunch shift. He could help her.

She didn't hesitate, just whipped her car behind the building. She tumbled out and banged on the door. "Jeremy?" She banged again, then stomped her feet, hoping the sensation would distract her from the flaming itch spreading over all her skin. "Jeremy, it's Natalie Castellano. I need help."

The door flung open, but it wasn't Jeremy standing there.

"Hell and damnation." There went a nickel and a dime into Noah's college fund, which she'd be raiding to pay for cortisone cream at the gas station across the way. She turned away, raking her nails over her hands and rubbing her knees together.

The gas station was only half a mile away. She could make it.

CJ latched onto her arm and let out a low whistle. "Where have you been playing this morning?"

Let go. She needed to say it. Not because she was afraid the QG would hear she'd seen CJ again, but because Natalie didn't trust herself with him.

But, dammit, her skin hurt. Raw welts were rising on her hands, worse on her knees and shins, and his grip on her upper arm was confusing her.

Because she didn't want to break the physical connection. Her breath came in heavy pants.

"You been rolling in poison ivy or itchweed?" He tugged her arm. "C'mon. Let's get you hosed down."

Hosed down?

He was grinning, a wicked, I'm-going-to-enjoy-this kind of grin. Distinctly lacking in that grin? Animosity.

For the first time since she'd seen him face-to-face, he seemed genuinely pleased to see her.

Probably because she was a mess. Still, this was a bad, bad idea.

"You gonna stand out here all day and wait for someone to see you, or you gonna get in here and quit itching?" he said.

She was going to go. Go to the gas station.

Except her wobbly legs ignored her better judgment and followed him into the Suckers kitchen.

He gestured to an industrial-sized stainless-steel sink with a large sprayer hose hanging on a hook on the ceiling. "C'mon over. This ever happen before?"

She followed him, her movements jerky and itchy and painful, equally suspicious and hopeful that he knew what he was talking about. "Broken out in hives while driving my car?" Her jaw clenched. She hurt so bad. "Yeah. Happens every day."

"You ever think of starting your day with a smile? Might help that grumpy-head thing you've got going on."

Her chest inflated, and she opened her mouth to give him a piece of her mind—her hands and legs were on fire—but he grinned down at her with the orneriest, most self-assured, heart-stopping smile, and her tongue was suddenly as capable of forming sentences as Cindy the Stegosaurus was.

He held her gaze. His smile slipped—his lips still tilted up, but the spark of mischief in his eyes faded, replaced with a curious intensity that magnified with every thump of her heart. She squirmed.

He blinked, and easygoing CJ came back. One hand on the sprayer, the other gestured at her. "Take 'em off."

"Mm-buh?" she said, with as much class and dignity as it was possible to put into gibberish. Which wasn't any at all, but she'd made a life of living with her own delusions.

"Strip. Best way to get it all off." His voice wobbled, as if perhaps he wasn't as comfortable as he wanted her to think he was.

"Hell, no." But he was right. She was starting to itch in places he couldn't see. Places she wanted him to—no. No.

Places she didn't want him to see.

Obviously her brain was breaking out in hives too. She pointed to the door. "Leave."

His eyes took on a stubbornness that reminded her of the man who had driven her father home two weeks ago. "You make a mess in here, I have to clean it up. We're doing this my way."

She squirmed. The itch burned higher and higher on her legs, rushing to meet another sensation traveling down her legs that she should've been worried about.

Nothing good could come of her attraction to him.

She forbade herself to scratch anything and glared at him. "I'll go do it myself in the bathroom."

His nostrils flared. "For God's sake, Natalie, I have eleven sisters. You don't have anything I haven't seen before. You want to feel better or not?"

Oh, yes. She wanted to feel better. She wanted to feel much better.

His eyes darkened. His gaze darted to her lips, then back to her eyes, and something else inside her lit on fire.

Something primitive and womanly and needy.

Something that made her see something primitive and manly and needy burning in his eyes.

As if he could feel it too. As if he liked it too.

She was imagining things. She hadn't given this man a single reason to like her. More, him liking her could cause them both more problems than he could understand or anticipate.

But she wasn't imagining things.

He was looking at her as though he wanted to kiss the argument right out of her.

He broke eye contact to yank on the sprayer hose. He pointed it into the sink, flipped it on full stream, then snatched her hand and pulled her arm into the sink.

Warm water pummeled her skin, washing away the sting.

Half her body sagged in relief. "Oooh, that's good," she breathed. It did nothing for the other sensations prickling to life deep inside her, but her arm—oh, God, her hand and arm were better. She thrust her other arm at him. "Do this one too."

He shifted behind her and guided her left hand into the water. "You should get some itch cream." His voice was rough silk in her ears, his body rigid behind her, and if her legs didn't hurt so badly, she would've gotten a few bad ideas about his proximity.

Who was she kidding? She was having plenty of bad ideas.

She should start charging herself for impure thoughts about CJ too. Double. At this rate, Noah could go to an Ivy League school on the IOUs in his college fund.

CJ pressed the hose into her hand. "Keep spraying." He stepped away, then came back with a box of baking soda. He touched her shoulder. "Stop scratching."

She hadn't realized she was rubbing her legs against each other. "Shoes off," he said. "And ditch the skirt. It's making it worse."

He was evil. He'd given her a taste of relief, and now he knew she couldn't walk away. He didn't look nearly as certain that he could handle this as he had at first.

Not as wicked either.

But he was right. Whatever she'd gotten into, it was all over her skirt. In her sweater too.

She gulped.

Then gulped again.

Then surrendered the hose so she could strip. Nearly naked.

In front of CJ.

"I need to text Lindsey." If she kept up a stream of conversation, she could pretend she wasn't unzipping her skirt or worrying about what underwear she'd put on this morning or if he'd notice her mostly faded stretch marks. "She'll bring me clean clothes."

CJ's full concentration seemed to be on mixing baking soda and water in a bowl. "Nicer than my sisters would be," he said.

"Doubt it," Natalie muttered. Because now that she thought about it, she wasn't so sure Lindsey would be helpful if she knew Nat was stripping to her Skivvies in front of CJ. She'd gone all lawyerly and danced around Natalie's questions as to how CJ ended up with her wallet. Which wasn't like Lindsey at all. She didn't play matchmaker. Nor did she usually cause hell just for the fun of it, especially when she knew how important the Golden Husband Games were to Natalie.

Natalie's skirt hit the floor. She made quick work of yanking off her sweater. One minute CJ was staring at the baking soda mixture, the next he was scooping Natalie up and depositing her at the edge of the sink. He thrust the water at her, and she got the impression he hadn't taken a single glance at her body.

It was almost disappointing. "Keep spraying," he said.

With her legs bent in the sink, she turned the sprayer on them. And once again, moaned in relief.

CJ's shoulders bunched. He was staring at the baking soda again. "My sister Pepper snuck out to a farm party one night in high school. Wore sandals. She got itchweed so bad, she couldn't stand socks or pants for a week."

Nat's hands stung again, so she alternated the spray between her arms and legs. CJ's green polo was getting damp from the mist off the sprayer.

"A week?" Natalie said. "I can't wear clothes for a week?"

Damn the man and his adorable upturned lips. "Week or two, I'd say."

A week or two? "Oh, hell, no," she started, but then she noticed the vibration in his shoulders.

He was playing with her. "You—"

He expertly flicked the sprayer out of her hands before she could turn it on him. "Hold still." He picked up the bowl and brought it close, eyes trained on hers. "This'll help."

Before she could ask what would help, he slopped the wet mixture in both hands, and then, with slow, sure strokes, he rubbed it down her arms and over her hands. Her breath caught.

"My sister, Margie, could tell you the science behind this, but she's as stuffy as Basil. I'd rather go to confession than listen to the two of them have a conversation. Makes your ears bleed."

He didn't flinch over the word confession, but she didn't believe he'd slipped it in there completely innocently.

But with his hands rubbing her half-naked body down with gritty white goop, it was overlookable. Her skin pebbled into goose bumps, both from his touch and from the cool air around her. The man had talented hands. Competent, confident, warm.

She'd need to go to confession with all the ideas his touch inspired. "You like your family?" she asked. She needed something safe. Something normal.

If he noticed her teeth chattering, he didn't comment. Simply piled more mix in his hands and went back to rubbing her down. "Most of 'em. Most days."

"How do you keep them all straight?" Her head had swum at the conversations whipping around her when she'd fixed Saffron's veil. She couldn't imagine keeping all eleven of them straight.

"You don't," CJ said.

Natalie laughed. He grinned at her, then moved to rub the goo on her legs. She shivered again. "Can you name them all?"

His hands stroked up and down her calves. "Nah, we just use numbers."

This time her laugh caught in her throat, because his fingers were massaging the goop into her skin with tiny circles. The pressure had her on the cusp between needing to squeeze her thighs together to relieve the tension building there, and wanting to shove him away for tickling her.

She closed her eyes and decided there was nothing wrong with enjoying a cheap thrill. She was still a woman, this wouldn't go anywhere, and it would probably be another five or ten years before another man touched her. "What number are you?"

"Numbers don't matter when you're the best."

She missed the cue to laugh again. His hands stilled, and she blinked her eyes open. He wasn't smiling.

He wasn't frowning either.

He was simply standing there, watching her watch him, his hands resting on her knees. Her pulse danced in her veins and her heart knocked in her chest. She made a quick swipe of her lips with her tongue, and his breathing went ragged.

Maybe he was enjoying rubbing her legs as much as she was enjoying having them rubbed.

Or maybe she was delusional. Delusional was probably the best scenario. Because she already thought about him too much, and nothing good could come of his thinking about her too.

And she couldn't fathom why he'd want to.

"How long does this stuff need to stay on?" Her voice wobbled, thick and low.

CJ took his time looking down to her legs. Under his gaze, the skin on her chest prickled, then the skin on her belly, around her belly button, beneath her panties.

He took one hand off her knee, grabbed the sprayer. "Feeling better?" he asked, and she was both relieved and terrified to note the husky tones in his voice.

She nodded.

"You'll want some itch cream for a few days." He took her hand, held it over the sink, and rinsed her arm, but this time, he wasn't watching her arm.

He was watching her.

Her face, her eyes. Her lips.

This was crazy. He didn't like her. She didn't like—no, that wasn't true. She did like him.

She liked him too much. So she needed him to not like her.

He switched arms, carefully rinsing off more of the hardened white goo. "You're very pretty when you laugh," he said.

"I wasn't laughing." "You should be."

He cradled her arm as if it were more delicate than a newborn, his touch as gentle as she would be with Noah. She had to swallow again, but nothing could cut the way her mouth had gone dry. She should've been cold. Instead, the kiss of the cool air against her wet skin made her feel more alive, more aware. "There's nothing funny right now," she whispered.

"Oh, it's funny. Pretty sure I just heard God laughing."

She needed to tell him to stop. Finish rinsing herself. Call Lindsey. Get to work.

Instead, her wet fingers drifted up to touch his cheek. "Thank you." She swallowed against the huskiness in her own voice. "For your help. Here."

He angled closer to her, his eyes never leaving hers. "Everyone needs help sometimes." "I don't think I deserve it."

He answered her whisper by twisting his wet fingers in her hair, his body becoming a solid shield between her and life's complications. "When's the last time anybody helped you with anything?"

"I help me."

But she wasn't built for it. She wasn't tough and driven like Lindsey, she wasn't the natural nurturer Mom had been. Deep down, she was still a spoiled princess who couldn't cope with the difficulties of living in the land of wedding dresses and cake monuments and

"Canon in D" without her prince charming. She did the best she could, but never felt that her best touched adequate.

And she suspected CJ saw every last one of her insecurities. It shouldn't have mattered, but she didn't want him to think she was weak. Didn't want him to see the rest of her faults.

Didn't want to confuse the fairy tale with reality.

But she couldn't move away when his lips lowered to hers. Because he was good with his lips. His hands. His tongue. And probably several other body parts she shouldn't think about.

So she gave up thinking, just for a little bit, and let herself kiss him back. Just for a little bit.

But kissing him without touching him was impossible, so she rested her hands on his chest, felt it rise and fall with the steady drum of his heart beneath the solid wall of muscle, and restarted the clock on just for a little bit. Because this was much better.

Better still was when he wrapped her closer, kissed her harder, nudged open that long-neglected part of her that still craved a man's touch. His touch was a uniquely thrilling combination, luxurious as silk and rough as starched lace. It left her aching for more, and she let instinct take over, squashing that part of her whispering a reminder that Noah's mom and the covert planner of the Golden Husband Games should not be kissing this man.

Or sneaking her hands to the hot skin beneath his shirt, or letting him dip his just-this-side-of-chilly wet fingers beneath her panties.

"I don't know why I want you so bad," he said. "Shut up and don't stop."

He took orders damn well. Before long, he'd hefted her out of the sink and up against the nearest wall, kissing her desperately, both of them fumbling with his clothes. Then he said it. "Protection?"

Gasped it, really, with the same needy desperation she felt all the way to her bones, but the word brought her back to reality.

She froze, pulled her arm back to hold her bra up. "You don't—?"

He winced, slowly backed away, letting her slide to the floor while he scrubbed a hand over his face. "I don't."

She was breathless, heart pounding. She was also suddenly painfully aware of how little clothing she had on and how big and open the kitchen was. "So, ah, I'm just gonna go wait. For Lindsey. In the bathroom."

At least, she hoped that's what she said. She couldn't hear herself speak over the Shit!

Dammit! What the hell was I thinking? chorus in her brain. She needed a second job to support her cussing habit. He stared at his feet. "Sure."

She hadn't been prepared for that to hurt. But the bigger surprise was that she wanted to launch herself at him and ask him to kiss her—just kiss her—a little bit more.

Make her feel special for a few more minutes. Make her feel wanted.

Make her feel like a woman again. Not a mom, not a daughter, not a surrogate shop owner. Just a woman.

She blinked against the sting in her eyes. She couldn't afford to feel like a woman. That never ended well for her, and she didn't have room for one more regret.

"Thanks again," she choked out. She snagged her purse and fled the kitchen for the bathroom, back to her regularly scheduled, CJ-free life.

Because that was reality, and reality was the only thing she could count on.

* * *

Women were trouble. It was a truth CJ had been born into, but knowing the truth didn't make living with it any easier.

"You got a bone up your butt, boy?" Huck said. He'd arrived to play cook today fifteen minutes after Natalie left with Lindsey's assistant, and he'd spent the last thirty minutes being more annoying than half of CJ's sisters put together.

Or perhaps CJ was simply in a foul mood. "Nope." "You break those bottles, you're buying 'em."

CJ took more care with the next beers he pulled out of the back cooler to stock the front, but he didn't reply.

"Two solutions to your problem," Huck called. "Forget her or do her." Forget her.

CJ needed to forget her.

"I vote you do her," Huck said. "Preferably tonight. Got some money on you." CJ spun on him. "She's got a kid, Huck."

"So?"

So was right. Two consenting adults could keep a kid out of it.

But CJ couldn't. Whether because Noah made a convenient excuse or because CJ liked the kid, he couldn't say.

He did know, though, that everything that affected Natalie affected Noah. Her job, her friends, her reputation. It all filtered to Noah one way or another.

"I'm leaving after Knot Fest," CJ said. And he was seventy percent sure it wasn't just his ego thinking that his leaving would affect Natalie.

"Long time away," Huck said. "Tell you what. You decide you like it here, I'll take that trip for you. Wouldn't mind getting away from the exes a while. Don't get married again. Ain't no such thing as being done with 'em when they still got their hands in your cookie jar after the divorce."

"Appreciate the offer. Don't need the advice though."

"Don't ever let anybody say I ain't a giver. Hell, boy. Ain't gonna hurt a thing for you to try her out. You know women. She'll decide you ain't all that in the end anyway."

"Watch your mouth," CJ growled. Growled.

For Natalie.

Shit.

Huck's laughter took on a gleeful edge. "Don't forget. I got tonight."

CJ went back to stocking for the lunch crowd. "Too bad you booked me for a double shift."

Huck let out a string of foulness that would've been worth a few dollars in Natalie's cussing jar. And when CJ realized he was thinking about Natalie's cussing jar—another tidbit about her he'd picked up from his customers in the last week or so—he added a few quarters' worth himself.

Knowing he was facing a revolving door of single women auditioning for the role of his Golden Husband Games partner tonight didn't help. He didn't mind the tips, but he wasn't in the mood for women.

Not when his curiosity about the wrong one had him tied up in knots that this festival couldn't fix.

Chapter 11

Saturday was busy, thank God, but with Noah underfoot, still wearing CJ's Air Force Falcons hat, the day felt like a bustle with two popped buttons. At least Natalie had recovered from her itchweed, if not from whatever insanity had prompted her to make out with CJ again.

Insanity. Right. Recovered. Right.

She'd seen him a few times this week. Once out jogging, which had set her not-anywhere-near-dormant-anymore parts all atingle. Once stepping into the tea shop across the street with his brother. And once at the Rose and Dove, where the QG had hosted a welcome reception for him in one of the private rooms that doubled as wedding chapels. Natalie had been leaving the country club after another janitorial committee meeting, and she'd glanced into the room just in time to catch the QG singing Kimmie's praises to him.

Also just in time to watch him notice her walking by.

Three days later, she could still feel the intensity of his gaze.

Not that she should've spent any time thinking about it. The panicked Husband Games e-mails and calls had tripled this week. She was working on Gabby's dress late into the night after dealing with shop issues and Knot Fest issues, and today, Dad was nowhere to be found.

Maybe he was having another secret meeting with the QG. Natalie had seen him with Marilyn a couple more times this week, and there had been something off about the way they had their heads tucked together.

Not comforting.

The QG was probably practicing mind control tricks to convince Dad to sell her the boutique. He'd interviewed some brokers this week, but until Mom's shop was sold—Natalie's heart withered some more—the QG still had a shot.

But since today's schedule was full, the parking lot was finally open, and nothing had gone obviously wrong, Natalie told herself Dad was above mind-control tricks. That he was probably keeping the QG out of Natalie's hair so Nat could do her job.

And her other, secret, self-appointed Husband Games job.

And keep her mind off CJ. Mostly.

Sort of.

Who was she kidding? Every time the doorbell chimed, she looked up to see if he'd stopped in. Not that he had any reason to. But she looked anyway.

As she had all week long.

Noah trailed Natalie everywhere. When they both started getting cranky with each other, she realized they'd missed lunchtime. She stopped in the middle of the floor and turned around so fast he ran into her hip. "Hey. You want ice cream for lunch?"

Noah pumped a fist in the air. "Yeah!"

"Me, too." She flagged Amanda, mouthed lunch, and went to the office for her purse. When they pushed out the back door two minutes later, Noah shrieked with glee.

"Grandpa! Guess what! Mommy's taking me to the Milked Duck for ice cream cones! You want to come?"

Natalie blinked. Dad was leaning against the side of the building between Bliss Bridal and Heaven's Bakery. He straightened quickly, eyes wide, face flushed.

The QG stood beside him in the alley.

"Hey, little buddy." Dad knelt down to Noah's level. "You being a big helper today?" "Yeah. Amanda sat on my crayon, and then this girl called another girl a quarter word, and then I let her play with my dinosaur so she would feel better, and we're having ice cream for lunch."

"Sounds like a good lunch," Dad said.

Natalie paused. Dad had never been the nutrition expert in the family—none of them were—but normally he would've commented on ice cream for lunch.

Something was off. Abnormally so.

"Crazy busy in there today," Natalie said. "We should get going." Marilyn made a commanding noise.

Dad's ears went red. He whispered something to Noah, then grunted and creaked while he pushed himself back to standing. Only when he again stood several inches above her did he look her in the eye. "Natalie, there's something I need to tell you."

Natalie's pulse skittered.

He'd succumbed. The Queen General had done her best, and Dad hadn't been strong enough. He was right. Natalie should've stood up to her too. Natalie should've fought back differently—the right way, whatever the hell that was—so that Dad never would've been in this position.

The QG had brainwashed Dad, and now she was about to destroy the shop that three generations of her mother's family had built.

Natalie's stomach clenched.

She didn't want him to sell the shop. She wasn't ready. She had to stall him. "Yes?" Natalie said.

"I'm entering the Golden Husband Games." "Please don't—what?"

He hadn't sold the shop to Marilyn. She still had time. Later, she'd think about why she was letting herself get delusional about her future. But now—she shook her head. "You want to play?" She looked between him and Marilyn. "That's what you two were out here talking about?"

He nodded once.

"But you'll need a stand-in wife," Natalie said. Someone to take Mom's place. No.

They were not having this conversation. They couldn't be. He couldn't replace Mom.

Dad and Marilyn shared a look. "We've been talking about possibilities," Dad said. Natalie couldn't catch her breath.

He could never replace Mom.

He couldn't. And yet there he was, plotting with Marilyn Elias—Marilyn Elias, the woman who'd declared outright that she'd go to whatever lengths necessary to get her claws into Bliss Bridal's business space—about how best to do it.

Natalie latched on to Noah's shoulder, squeezing too hard to cover the shake in her bones. "Great. We have to go."

"Natalie—"

"It's seriously busy in there. I have to get back ten minutes ago."

"You want to come, Grandpa?" Noah said.

Dad looked like he'd rather swallow a bolt of starched muslin. "I can't today, sport. Maybe tomorrow, okay?"

"Ice cream today and tomorrow? Awesome!" Awesome. Right.

Nope. Not even close.

* * *

Natalie's Saturday night plans hadn't included finding Noah a last-minute sitter so she could have an impromptu girls' night at Suckers, but today called for it. Gabby's dress and all the Knot Fest stuff and this week's payroll at the boutique could wait.

She wanted a drink.

After Dad's bombshell—and her subsequent realization that his #1 Grandpa mug and the Keurig had disappeared, which meant he was running his tryouts for Mom's stand-in out at his cabin—Natalie not only wanted a drink, but she was just masochistic enough to want to see CJ. Possibly it was more rebellion against the Queen General, but more likely, she was too weak to resist the ideas that her accidental visit to Suckers on Monday had prompted.

And tonight, watching him behind the bar, she wanted more of what she'd sampled in the Suckers kitchen. She was either incredibly stupid or incredibly lonely.

Possibly both.

CJ tossed bottles and glasses, filling orders with Jeremy and Huck for the waitresses handling the normal Saturday night out-of-town-wedding crowd. But unlike Jeremy and Huck, CJ was also flirting with six women vying for the opportunity to be his partner in the Games, and then flirting with Lindsey and Kimmie and Natalie with an easy grace. He looked like he owned the whole damn bar.

He owned the atmosphere, that much was certain. She couldn't take her eyes off him.

Especially when his back was turned.

His jeans hugged the curve of his ass, and she couldn't help a sigh of admiration. His was the nicest butt in Bliss. She remembered—vividly—that it felt even better than it looked.

She gulped her whiskey sour. The bar was hot tonight.

CJ circled back to check on them. "You ladies doing okay?"

"Define okay." Natalie's whiskey seemed to be talking. Because the whiskey was the only thing that could've put that husky, suggestive tone in her voice.

Yep, that was all the whiskey.

He propped his elbows on the bar, which put his face level with hers, and fixed his undivided attention on her.

There went her lady bits fanning themselves. With a few added whimpers.

They remembered what his hands and body and lips felt like too.

"Content." His voice was low and raw, his gaze penetrating and unwavering. "Happy. Completely, one hundred percent satisfied."

Her mouth went dry while the rest of her went up in needy flames that made her want to scratch the all-but-gone rash he'd tended so well on Monday. "Nope," Natalie squeaked. "Not okay then."

His eyes crinkled in the corners. Her feet flexed, ready to push her up over the bar so she could taste the smile on his lips. But even with the whiskey for courage, she couldn't overcome the weight of her responsibilities or her habit of keeping to Bliss's shadows. His gaze swept downward to her peach printed v-neck.

Lindsey—Nat's designated driver tonight—cleared her throat. "How about some refills?" CJ's gaze went back up to Natalie's face, lingering on her lips. "Sure. How about you?" Natalie blinked. "Me?"

"You want another?"

"Oh, yes. Please." Another kiss. Another taste. Another chance to feel hard male muscle and hot male skin. Preferably with all requisite precautions in place, and preferably with a satisfying conclusion.

Her libido was so totally out of hibernation she was surprised people weren't staring at the hungry growls coming from her long-neglected body.

His eyes went a darker shade of green. "Coming right up."

She wanted something else up. Her cheeks flared, and she felt a pull low in her belly—the kind she hadn't experienced since—well, since they'd made out here on Monday.

CJ straightened with a cocky grin. "Anything else? Kimmie—food or anything?" Kimmie shook her head.

He moved away.

Two sets of inquisitive stares, one on either side of Natalie, demanded she say something.

She squirmed on the barstool, tugged at her too-tight skirt, then lifted her eyebrows at her companions in turn as if she weren't the horny elephant in the room. "What? I haven't gotten drunk since I got pregnant."

Or laid.

Obviously.

"My mom is going to blow a bread basket when she hears about this," Kimmie said. Lindsey waved a hand. "What she doesn't know won't kill her."

"There's nothing to know." But even Natalie's whiskey couldn't convince her that was the truth.

"You have your eyes checked lately?"

"I don't think she was looking with her eyes," Kimmie said. "Of course, my vagina would know if a guy were watching me like that." Several nearby men stared at them.

"Can we leave our vaginas out of this?" Natalie whispered. The whole bar didn't need to know the status of hers.

Kimmie eyed CJ. "I can, but I don't know if he can. Yours, that is. Although, obviously, you'd have to be a willing participant, which didn't look like a problem, but—sorry. I know. Shut up."

"No, no, I'm enjoying this," Lindsey said.

Kimmie rolled her lower lip into her mouth, eyeing Natalie and Lindsey as though she couldn't decide whose side to take. "I had a dream last night I had a pet alligator that burped bubbles. I thought about trying to make a cake out of it, for kid birthday parties or something. Except when the bubbles popped, these rabid elves with flaming lightsabers came out and set up battlegrounds in my bathroom, and then these Swiss buttercream monsters came out of the tub. It was kinda weird."

The guy next to Kimmie flipped out his wallet, dropped two bills on the bar, and left his beer half-finished.

CJ came back and slid fresh drinks to Natalie and Lindsey. He glanced at the empty barstool next to Kimmie.

"My fault," she sighed. "I said vagina. Sorry."

CJ gave her a brotherly kind of smile that made Natalie like him a little bit more. "His problem, not yours," he said. "Unless you asked him if he had a vagina. Then you might've been out of line."

Kimmie looked temporarily horrified until Lindsey laughed.

"You're joking," Kimmie said. "Right. That's almost as funny as my mom and their—oomph!"

Lindsey straightened like she hadn't just reached around Natalie to poke Kimmie in the ribs. "So." Lindsey waved at CJ's cheering section across the bar. "You want to know who your best bets are over there?"

Before Nat could turn a glare on her sister, CJ shook his head. "Pass. Thanks." Lindsey gave Natalie an obnoxious You're welcome smile.

"You should use her," Kimmie said. "Not use her use her, but use her skills. She's super good at matchmaking."

"Preventing unwanted relationships," Lindsey corrected. At the R-word, CJ took a not-so-subtle step back.

Natalie's mood did too. If they acted on this—whatever it was—it would be temporary. An itch-scratching. Nothing more. What he needed was one of those women in his cheering section.

Not the divorced woman on The Aisle.

Her stomach folded over itself and cramped like someone had tied it in a bow. She should've stayed home and worked.

CJ cleared the money and the glass from the place next to Kimmie, already beating a quick retreat. "Let us know if you want something," he called over his shoulder.

Natalie slouched over the bar. "How do you do it?" she said to Lindsey. "Do what?"

"Date."

She meant to add casually. Something about Lindsey's three-dates-or-three-weeks rule.

Instead, the single word hung between them. "He's interested, Nat," Lindsey finally said.

"Remember that whole vagina thing?" Kimmie added. "But he needs a temporary wife, and I—I can't be it."

"Yeah, my mom would twist your pastry bags so hard, you'd shoot buttercream out the wrong end."

"Screw her. If you're leaving Bliss, go out in style." Lindsey's smile turned sly. "By doing something bigger than just calling the health department." "Hush. How did you—never mind."

Kimmie clapped her hands over her ears. "I didn't hear that."

"Mom wanted her last Games to be epic," Lindsey murmured. "Guarantee you no one would forget."

God.

There was no way in hell Natalie could be CJ's partner.

But she still wanted to date him. She wanted to date him and have sex with him and laugh with him. And the Queen General wasn't her biggest obstacle.

"But I don't date well," Nat whispered.

Lindsey's lips quivered, and Natalie caught her telltale eye crinkle.

"Don't laugh," Natalie said. "The only reason I had prom and homecoming dates in high school was because their parents made them take me."

"Please. Even if that was true, it was high school. No one dates well in high school."

"Or after, for some of us." Kimmie still had her hands over her ears, but she leaned closer. "Derek was the first guy to ask me out after I graduated college. Two years. No guys asked me out for two years after I came home. The single sons on the The Aisle? They'd all duck and cover when they saw me coming. Max, Luke, all of them. Jake Sydney convinced me he was dating his cousin when I asked him to the Husband Games reception once. None of them want me to get my claws in them."

"Natalie—"

"I made Derek marry me, because I was afraid no one else would." Lindsey didn't say anything.

Neither did Kimmie.

Probably because it was the truth. "How do you do it? How do you get a guy to just go on a couple of dates with you? How do you get what you want and then just move on?"

Lindsey's eyes pinched. Briefly, but long enough for Nat to notice. Lindsey had never talked about settling down. About having a wedding. About raising babies. Even before she picked her law specialty, she'd never had the princess dreams.

But Nat had wondered a time or two if her sister's love life was truly that simple. "Lindsey, I didn't mean—"

"There's a difference between enjoying a man's company because you can and taking a chance with the right guy because you should. I don't have a right guy. You? You might. But you won't know if you don't jump."

Natalie looked closer at her big sister. "How do you know you don't have a right guy?" "I just know."

Not the If-I-haven't-found-him-yet, he-doesn't-exist excuse Natalie expected. Because for someone who claimed to be good at spotting bad matches, Lindsey was damn good at spotting the perfect temporary hookup.

She'd also never said she didn't want a husband and a family of her own.

A déjà vu kind of shiver prickled Natalie's skin. "Oh," she whispered. "Who was he?" A rare show of color impeded Lindsey's normally placid complexion. "Who?"

"Don't lawyer me. You were in l-o-v-e once, weren't you? What happened?" Nat sucked in an excited breath. "Or who is he? Is he married? Is he a client? Ohmigod, Lindsey. Did he die?"

Lindsey's eye roll was so big, it nearly smacked Natalie off her stool.

"I believe we were talking about you," Lindsey said. The guy on her other side bumped her, and Lindsey hunched her shoulders in.

Sympathy and gratitude that Lindsey was here, braving the crowd on a busy night, overwhelmed Natalie's urge to keep prying. "Playing that card?" Nat murmured.

"Yep." "Spoilsport."

A burst of laughter at the top of the bar drew their attention. A few of the guys from the Bliss Bachelors baseball team were gathered around, listening to CJ and howling.

It was wrong that she'd spent so many years blaming someone so fun and full of life for the worst part of hers.

So wrong that he'd had to suffer all he had as well.

Lindsey squeezed her hand. "Your life's changing, Nat. Take a chance. Worst case, you've lost a few nights. Best case, you end up with something special for both you and Noah." She jerked her chin toward CJ. "Won't know if you don't try."

"What's with you? This isn't your normal kind of anti-pep talk."

"The guy has eleven sisters, he's living with a priest, spending half his week doing odd jobs for his deceased wife's parents, and he apologized to you for the kiss that wasn't his fault. If he's psycho, he's hiding it deep. So I formally have no objections. Further, I'd like to see you happy. Because you deserve it."

Did she? Could she? Natalie didn't know. "That's quite possibly the nicest thing anyone has said to me all day."

"It's true." Lindsey nudged her. "Mom would tell you to go for it." Natalie blinked at the hot tingle behind her eyeballs.

"Not till after Knot Fest though, okay?" Kimmie said. "I'm not kidding. My mom will toast your coconuts worse than she did Bonnie and Earl's."

Natalie swung all the way around, her blood suddenly zumba-ing through her veins. "She what?"

"Did I say toast? I meant flambéed. Mom turned the Games over to Duke and Elsie. You—you hadn't heard?"

Natalie shook her head. It explained why Duke and Elsie had been at the sunflower field.

And it was probably good news for the Games.

Very good news.

But it still should've been Natalie's job.

"And Bonnie and Earl are putting their shop up for sale," Kimmie said. "Apparently none of their kids want it, and after the shame of, well, you know, they're retiring."

Being kicked off the Knot Fest committee could do that to a couple.

Kimmie leaned closer. "Rumor is, they're not handling being empty nesters well. They've been secretly having marital counseling over in Willow Glen. And since you had everything with the Games under control…They kinda checked out a while ago, you know?"

Natalie had noticed. Hearing it was because of marital issues—that put a new light on things. Her sympathy for Bonnie and Earl went up a few thousand points.

But it still didn't change all that Natalie had done and would never get credit for. "Just the rumor I heard," Kimmie added. "They didn't tell mom the part about you." "Nat?" Lindsey said. "You okay?"

CJ had moved down the bar to his fan club again. To real women who had real chances of being a good partner to him in the Games. Mom's Games. That Duke and Elsie Sparks would get all the credit for. That Dad would be playing in with a woman who wasn't Mom.

That second whiskey sour was a bad, bad idea. "I'm tired," Natalie said. "Have you guys watched Outlander yet? I have it on

DVR. We could swing through Wok'n'Roll and get some sweet 'n sour chicken."

Lindsey looked across the bar at CJ, then back at Natalie. "We're already out. Let's stay and enjoy. I'm officially designating this an Aisle-free, Husband Games-free, man-free zone. If you're still tired in ten minutes, I'll take you home. Promise."

"Man-free?" Natalie smelled a trap.

Lindsey waved a hand at the three men crowding her on her other side. "We'll just pretend they're all eunuchs. Or have Kimmie yell vagina a couple more times."

"Jesus." The guy closest to Lindsey pushed his drink back, set a few dollars on the bar, and went the way of Kimmie's former barstool neighbor. The guy who was now closest to her shot her a scowl and scooted over one more, so now there were two seats between them.

"See?" Lindsey's shoulders relaxed, and the pinched look in her eyes faded.

Natalie laughed. "Man-free. Got it." She could ogle CJ all she wanted. Which was still a very, very bad idea. She pointed to the clock. "Ten minutes."

"You haven't had dinner yet, have you?"

"Nine minutes, and you're beginning to annoy me." Lindsey grinned. "Oh, honey, I'm just getting started."

She lifted a finger at CJ, and he crossed back to them. "Yes, ma'am?"

"We'd like some cheese fries," Lindsey said. "Bonus points if you can get some bacon on them."

"You got it." He signaled the kitchen.

The kitchen where he'd nearly made Natalie explode. Her thighs squeezed. "He can't do that in seven minutes," she said.

"Eight and a half. And it'll take the same amount of time to get to Wok'n'Roll and wait on an order there."

"Plus, this way you don't have to worry about fortune cookies." Kimmie dropped her voice and glanced around. "I probably shouldn't be here tonight. I got one the other day that said I should avoid public places until I'd made peace with my past."

Natalie smiled again. "What could you possibly have in your past to make peace with?" "You'd be surprised. Oh! Fries! Yum." fast.

CJ slid a plate of cheese fries, complete with bacon crumbles, onto the bar. "Enjoy, ladies." Gap-jawed, Natalie checked the clock over the mirror. "No way." That was entirely too

Impossibly fast.

"He's really good," Kimmie said.

"He is," Lindsey agreed. "Wouldn't you say, Nat?"

Her lady bits sighed in agreement. "How'd you do that?" "Fate. We were supposed to have cheese fries tonight."

Natalie pointed to the empty seat on Lindsey's other side. "He ordered some before you chased him away, didn't he?"

Lindsey grinned. "Eat up. You'll feel better once you get some food on top of your whiskey."

It was a decent enough theory to test, and the fries smelled pretty dang good, so Natalie dug in. And it turned out, cheese fries were way better than Chinese tonight.

So was hanging out at Suckers with Lindsey and Kimmie again. Between the food and the whiskey and the scenery, Natalie hardly noticed the next hour slipping by.

But then Kimmie sat straight and went pale. "Oh, pumplegunker." She dove under the bar.

Natalie craned to see what Kimmie had noticed, above or below the bar, but she couldn't pick out anything—or anyone—in particular. It was just the normal, non-Aisle crowd mixing with out-of-town wedding guests of the male variety, with CJ's fan club thrown in for good measure.

"Kimmie?" Natalie said. "Everything okay?" Lindsey added.

"Dropped something," Kimmie murmured from her hiding place. "Oh, no. Here it is." She glanced up, but didn't straighten or retrieve anything. "Um, guys? I think I left my shower on. I should—you know—go check on that. Don't want my house to burn down."

"Because you left your shower on?" Natalie wasn't that inebriated. She hadn't even finished her second drink.

"Oven! I meant my oven." Kimmie cast a desperate look across the room, still hunched over. "Stupid fortune cookie."

Natalie shared a look with Lindsey, then caught CJ's attention.

"Back door?" she asked him.

He didn't quirk a single eyelash at Kimmie. He did, however, scan the building before giving a subtle nod toward the back. "C'mon, Kimmie. I'll get you out through the kitchen."

"Thanks," she squeaked.

CJ strolled to the kitchen, upright like nothing was wrong. Kimmie attracted only a mild bit of attention by walking like a duck with back problems on her way out.

But it was Kimmie.

So the sight was only mildly unusual.

"His sisters trained him well." Lindsey scanned the crowd too, frowning, but her gaze didn't pause on any suspects.

CJ casually sauntered back past them. "Any idea if somebody needs his ass kicked?" he asked.

"Nope," Lindsey said. "She say anything?"

"Her toaster's been malfunctioning and she's afraid she left it out for the cats to turn on." "She'll tell us when she's ready," Natalie said.

CJ nodded. "Smart thinking there." He tapped the bar twice. "You ladies holler if you need anyone's ass kicked."

"Aren't you sweet," Lindsey said. "But we're perfectly capable of kicking ass on our own."

"I know. I want to watch."

There went Natalie's lady bits again.

Suckers was crowded enough that other customers quickly claimed the empty seats on either side of Natalie and Lindsey, but since one of them was Gabby, they didn't mind. She'd had her first fitting this week, and she was even happier with her dress than Natalie was. Gabby had final projects to tackle for her last semester of school, though, so she didn't stay long.

Shortly after she left, Lindsey got a phone call. She glanced at the display, and a frown the size of the wedding cake statue darkened her expression. "Right back," she said to Natalie, then slid off her stool and toward the bathroom.

A minute later, she was back, but obviously not to stay. She snagged her purse and coat. "Client emergency," she said tersely. "I've gotta run. You okay here?"

Natalie had only a vague idea what kinds of emergencies Lindsey dealt with, but she knew it wasn't good and the police would probably be involved. "Don't worry about me. You go." "Rain check on finishing," Lindsey called over her shoulder. She already had her phone back to her ear.

"Don't make threats you can't follow through on," Natalie called back.

But when the door shut behind Lindsey, Natalie realized that inebriation wasn't the only thing keeping her from getting home tonight. "Shit."

"That one of your quarter words?" CJ asked on his way past with a plate of onion rings. "How do you know about my quarter words?"

"People talk. Heard your dollar words are really bad." "Yep. I save 'em for Knot Fest meetings."

He flashed a smile at her—for her—but moved down the bar to deliver the onion rings to the CJ fan club.

Natalie needed to call a cab. Put an end to a night of fun, leave CJ to his real choices for a stand-in bride.

He was watching her watch him in the mirror behind the bar.

She blew out a slow breath. She shouldn't do this. The Queen General would torch her tiara. Or kick her off the Knot Fest committee. Or—or keep her from taking what could be the best risk of her life.

"Well, now, what's a pretty girl like you doing all alone in a place like this?"

Startled, Natalie tore her gaze from CJ. The guy sliding into the seat to her right was neatly groomed from his sandy blond hair and designer beard to his custom-fit blazer over a plaid button-down shirt and distressed jeans. There was something both approachable and off-limits about him. His cheesy grin said he knew exactly how bad the line was, and Natalie couldn't help smiling back.

"This seat taken?" he said.

CJ had turned back to his fan club. "Finders, keepers," Natalie said to the guy.

His smile shifted to half-friendly, half-flirty. It should've done something for her but didn't. She half-wished it would've. If she was thinking about dating, or scratching itches, better to do it with a guy the QG didn't care about.

He stuck his hand out. "Josh."

She shook it and glanced at CJ again.

He was talking to one of the waitresses now. "Natalie," she said to Josh. "You from around here?"

"All my life. You?"

"In from Chicago checking on some business."

CJ turned, and Josh made an I-need-a-drink gesture at him. CJ's eyes narrowed. Natalie's pulse leapt.

"You work on the weddings, or you from the other side of the tracks here?" Josh said. "The Aisle."

Josh laughed. "So you're one of The Aisle people too."

She had CJ's full attention now. And he wasn't smiling at all. Her pulse jumped higher.

"Only kind of," she said to Josh. "I'm the resident divorced single mother in the Most Married-est Town on Earth, living the dream in the wedding biz because of who my parents are."

Oh, God.

She just said that.

So she still wasn't datable, but now it was because she wasn't fit to be out in public. Maybe she should yell "Vagina!" too.

Josh's grin turned genuine. "Excellent," he said with a head bob. Natalie couldn't help it. She laughed.

CJ, though, glowered.

He was jealous.

Her heart was going at a full-on gallop now. If he wanted her, truth was, he'd have to put up with a lot of her shit. Might as well see what the man was made of.

She kept her smile and aimed it at Josh. "So what kind of business are you in, Josh?" Jewelry, she'd bet. Maybe music.

"Dessert."

His flirting was doing absolutely nothing for her. Nothing except for making sure CJ had eyes only for her.

How could she not smile about that? "On The Aisle?" "Unfortunately."

Her mind slowly caught up to the conversation. Dessert. Unfortunately. On The Aisle.

Natalie's whiskey sour rolled over the cheese fries in her belly. "Cake?" she sputtered. It could've been chocolates. Or the sweets shop. Even the tea house.

But she doubted it.

A rude cough from the other side of the bar interrupted them. "Soda?" CJ asked Josh. "Tea?"

"Dirty martini." Josh slid Natalie another grin. "I've earned it today."

He probably had. And Natalie might've understood Kimmie's bolting now.

The thought trickled in right behind her complete certainty that this guy had no interest in the well-being of Bliss. He had playboy written all over him, and that absolutely didn't fit with Bliss's Most Married-est image.

She felt an actual, honest-to-God pang of sympathy for Marilyn Elias.

"One dirty martini, coming up," CJ said. He turned an inscrutable emerald stare on Natalie, and her stomach flipped inside out. "Why'd you run off Lindsey?" he said.

"Work emergency." "That normal?"

"Happens occasionally. It's never good." She forced a smile. "Missing her help?"

His full-on, just-for-her grin made her girly bits sigh. "She's already given me everything I need." He winked at Natalie, then went back to work.

Josh eyed her, then CJ. "Your boyfriend?"

"No." Not yet. And probably not for long. But she definitely wanted to see what else his hands and mouth and body could do to her.

Josh twisted on his stool so he was facing her, so-let's-have-fun lingering in his grin. "Want to make him jealous anyway?"

She shouldn't have laughed. Josh—oh, boy. Josh. Danger zone. "Heaven's Bakery?" she said softly.

"Hey, now, no call for profanity." His easy grin went just brittle enough to confirm Natalie's suspicion. He was the Queen General's secret silent partner.

He propped his elbow on the bar, but the gesture wasn't as casual as she would've expected a minute ago. "No more work talk. What's a girl like you do for fun around here?"

She blinked. Then she opened her mouth, but realized she didn't have an answer. His playboy grin came back full force. "Gotta work on that."

It wasn't funny, but she laughed again anyway.

Chapter 12

"You got an itch, boy?"

Huck's question made CJ's shoulders bunch. Yeah, he had an itch. It got worse every time Natalie laughed at the tool sitting next to her.

Every time her lips so much as hinted at another smile for the idiot, he wanted to take some of the pressure off by flirting with one of the women crowding the bar tonight. And not because any of them had caught his attention.

Maybe the guy with Natalie wasn't the only idiot in the room.

CJ grabbed the soda gun. "Heard that microbrewery out on the edge of town takes special orders and makes batches for peoples' weddings."

Huck gave him the suspicious old man eye. "You been cheating on my alcohol?" "Been thinking you should have 'em brew up a Suckers' Punch."

"Look at you, getting all fancy with the ideas. Next thing you're gonna tell me you're good with numbers and can fix my books so I don't have to pay the exes so much in alimony."

Basil would've called Huck's request a sign from God. Something about growing up.

Something else about distracting him from his infatuation with the wrong woman.

But CJ hadn't had all those sisters to not see a setup coming. "Somebody told you I used to have a real job, eh?"

"I read that write-up on you on that Knot Fest blog they got." Huck's nose twitched like it did every time he said "Knot Fest." "Didn't mention where you're working now though, did it?"

This town was certifiable. In a lovable kind of way. "Don't think you're hurting for customers, Huck."

“Look at this place. Practically empty.”

It was almost midnight, and the crowd was thinning. They’d still done a hell of a lot more business tonight than the last two Saturdays. “You could add a karaoke machine,” CJ said. “Give Melodies some competition.”

Huck’s nose twitched so hard, his upper lip got in on the action too. CJ smiled.

“Not funny.” Huck surveyed the bar again. “Get out of here. Me and Jeremy got this covered, and you been itching to get at something else the last hour anyway.”

“Don’t know what you’re talking about. Love my job.” “Go on. Get.”

A man had only so much argument in him, so CJ nodded. “Will do. See you tomorrow night.” CJ did love his job. Loved it more when his tip jar overflowed like tonight. Had him well on his way for getting out of Bliss after Bob was back on his feet.

Across the bar, Natalie laughed at her companion. She looked over at CJ, and her cheeks went a delicate pink beneath her darkening eyes. She lifted her glass—mostly melted ice—and tipped it back for the last few drops, then turned back to the jackass beside her.

CJ closed out at the register, then ducked into the office for his jacket. Natalie was still chatting with the pretty boy, and CJ didn’t have an ounce of guilt over interrupting.

He tapped her on the shoulder. “I’m off. You want a ride?”

When she looked back at him, he was surprised no one else jumped from the electric shock of the sparks that passed between them.

She licked her lips. “Yeah.” She gave her companion a smile that CJ wished had been aimed at him instead. “Nice to meet you, Josh. Enjoy your time in Bliss.”

The guy couldn’t have been a total tool, because he cracked a grin at that.

CJ put his hand at the small of her back and led her to the door, ignoring a few curious stares.

She ignored them too, he noticed. Big change from the girl who tried to kick him out of her house with the rationale that she'd ruin his reputation.

The cool, dark air outside did nothing to diminish the charge between them. CJ steered Nat around the corner toward his car, anticipation drumming through his veins as if he were loading up in a Cessna 208, chute packed, ready to jump.

They reached his old car. He let his nose dip into her hair while he opened the passenger door for her.

She stopped short. Gave him one of those female looks. The is this really your car? kind of looks.

How far they'd come from the days when she would've just said it. "You walk a lot, don't you?" she said.

That was his girl. He stole another breath of her shampoo. "Get in the car, Natalie." She licked her lips. His heart kicked into hell, yeah rhythm.

"Or what?" she said.

"Or you're walking home alone. That really what you want?"

She held his gaze for that infinite moment of time that existed between pulling the rip cord and the chute snapping open. Voices spilled out into the darkness. Her head shifted toward the rowdy patrons—just barely, but enough—then her shoulders went back, and her half-smile answered his challenge.

"If you're sure it'll start," she said, her voice like warm silk.
"Oh, it'll start."

Her head tilted, her dark eyes fathomless in the night.

For one heartbeat, he thought she'd walk away. Chicken out. Leave him hanging.

Instead, she trailed her fingers down the front of his shirt, sparking sensations that made him shiver in anticipation. "Guess we'll have to see."

And while CJ stood there enjoying the feel of all his blood heading south, she tucked herself into the car.

* * *

Natalie directed CJ to a small wooded cliff overlooking the north side of Harmony Lake.

She shouldn't have—he needed a partner for the Games, not a quick hookup with his worst choice. But tonight, she wanted to be wanted. And when he turned the car off and focused on her with the same intense interest he'd worn when he'd kissed her in the Suckers kitchen Monday, she felt wanted like she'd never been wanted in her life.

He made her feel broken and whole and vulnerable and strong all at the same time.

Being wanted by this man, feeling worthy of being wanted, scared her more than anything else she'd faced the last five years.

Because he wasn't permanent. He wasn't hers. He never would be. He leaned toward her.

She lunged for the door and tumbled out into the night.

Across the lake, St. Valentine's was dark, save for the spotlight on the spire. The illuminated wedding cake monument glowed in the night. The Rose and Dove was bright and teaming with people. Hints of laughter and the "Chicken Dance" wafted across the lake.

That was her life. Other people's weddings. Other people's dresses. Maybe she'd have another shot at her own happily ever after, but it wouldn't be today, and it wouldn't be with CJ.

No matter how decent of a guy he was. So she had a choice. Go home, or let herself have one night.

His car door squeaked, then shut softly. His shoes crunched over the dried leaves and gravel.

She rubbed her hands over her arms, but not because it was cold out. Not when the cold came from doubts deep inside her.

"Nice night." His voice rumbled low and deep. His hands settled on her shoulders, thumbs along her shoulder blades, easing the tension she'd held so long, she couldn't remember when it began.

"I didn't thank you," she said. "For helping me. Monday. With the itching." "You started to."

The suggestion and amusement in his voice prompted a painful smile. She could've fallen for a guy like this. She probably already had.

His thumbs moved in soft circles beside her spine. She leaned back into his hands. "I didn't thank you either," he said.

Thank her? "For what?" "For being a pain in the ass."

She twisted to face him, expecting to find him sporting some cockiness or swagger or plain amusement at her expense.

Instead, his sincerity held a reflection of her own grief over everything she'd lost in the last five years. Her naïveté. Her marriage. Her mother.

Was his wife all he'd lost?

"You drive me crazy," he said. "Makes me feel like I'm at home."

A warmth she hadn't felt in months—maybe years—crept into her soul. "You really know how to flatter a girl."

He pulled her around to face him, toes to toes, her chest to his sternum, his hands gripping her hips, his fingers latching into her ass. "I can't stop thinking about your mouth."

Yes.

Heat pooled low in her belly. "This is crazy," she whispered.

"Inevitable," he murmured back.

She pushed up on her tiptoes, closer. "Why do you do this to me?" "Could ask you the same thing."

His fingers thrust up in her hair. His lips joined hers. She melted into her fantasy world, letting him be her strong, gallant prince setting fire to her hopeful princess heart.

She pushed his jacket out of the way and pulled his shirt out of his jeans, then slid her hands up his hot, silky skin and over the ridges of his muscles. "Tell me you have protection."

"Whole damn box."

She laughed into his kiss, but the urgent pull of his lips and the instant response of her body to his exploring fingers turned her laughter into needy gasps. He wasn't just touching her body.

He was touching something in her soul, lifting her burdens, making her feel feminine and competent and whole.

Desirable. Worthy.

CJ cupped her rear end and nestled her hips against his. "You feel so good." He licked his way down her neck to the sensitive spot over her shoulder.

"Don't stop." He was satisfying emotional cravings she didn't know she had.

His body was satisfying some gratuitous lusting she'd been aware of for a while now.

She grabbed his hair, held his mouth against her collarbone while her other hand gripped his rock-hard ass and her pelvis pushed against his erection. "More."

"Mmm." He boosted her up. She wrapped her legs around him, then he twisted and pushed her back against the car, kissing and stroking and holding her.

This wouldn't happen again, so she intended to enjoy the hell out of it. From the smell of his jacket to the texture of his skin to the sound of his voice to the slide of his tongue, she imprinted every last detail in her brain to savor over and over and over, after they went back to being two people who were totally wrong for each other despite all the ways they felt so right.

She wanted to go slow, but she couldn't calm her frantic tug at the button on his Levi's. His hands fumbled under her shirt, thumbs finding her nipples beneath her bra while he cupped her breasts. He rained kisses on her neck, behind her ears, over her jaw, working his way to her mouth, pulling involuntary moans from deep in her throat, staying there, kissing her, holding her, touching her, until he owned her.

No blindfolds. No tricks. No hiding.

This time, he knew exactly who she was. This time, she knew who he was too. "More," she whimpered.

"God, Natalie." He was hoarse, muscles vibrating against her, hands desperate as they pushed her skirt up to her hips to grind his pelvis against hers.

There was still too much material between them. "Please," she gasped. She yanked at his belt loops, but her legs were clamped around him, her hips thrusting against him, and she couldn't find his skin.

"Wait."

She froze. Her eyes popped full open, then she snapped them shut and dropped her head back. Wait? Was he kidding? "No." She hadn't been here in so long. Too long. And now, he was taking it all away.

And chuckling about it while he pulled back.

"Natalie." He traced a finger up the lace edge of her panties, then pressed his lips back to the hollow in her neck, sparking her nerve endings and nearly making her come right there. "Logistics, honey."

He shifted and pulled one arm away, then shifted again, then did a little shimmy, and suddenly the denim was gone from his hips and her legs were wrapped around hot, slick skin, the head of his penis rubbing her lace panties.

"Oh, God, yes," she moaned.

He chuckled again, but it ended in a strangled noise when she thrust against him. "Wait," he said.

"You are such a tease."

A wrapper crinkled. She dropped one arm from around his neck and reached for the condom.

"Hold me." He hissed out a breath, but he anchored her tight against the car, staring into her eyes, unblinking, unflinching, while she used shaky fingers to roll the condom down his hot, hard length.

"Now, please," she said.

His fingers dipped into the side of her panties, and she gasped out his name. He pushed the lace out of the way, and then he was in her, filling her, spurring her body to feelings and emotions she'd missed for so long, she almost couldn't remember what they were supposed to feel like.

Everything about making love to CJ felt more. Rougher. Stronger. Better.

"Nat," he gasped. Her whole body clenched around him, spasming too soon, too fast, too intense.

Too right.

He followed her over the edge, breathing hard but holding her steady against the side of his car, in the middle of the night, while party noises and soft lake sounds drifted over from the real world.

Natalie's legs had all the consistency of chiffon. She struggled to catch her breath, and she could feel CJ's heart pounding against her rib cage along with the rapid rise and fall of his chest. "Oh my God," she said.

"Yeah."

He was still inside her, but real life was slithering back. He wasn't hers. He couldn't be hers.

That grief made it more difficult to breathe than the physical exertion had. She shifted, lowered one hesitant leg to the ground.

He pulled back and looked at her. Even in the darkness, she could see the affection, the hope shimmering in his unguarded expression.

She should've stayed home tonight.

She needed to ask him to take her home. Right now.

Instead, she closed her eyes and leaned into him, pretending—just for a few more minutes—that he could be hers.

* * *

When CJ had woken up this morning, he hadn't expected to end the day perched up on the hood of his car under the moonlight overlooking Harmony Lake, telling old family stories to a firecracker of a woman who was a hell of a lot more everything than he would've given her credit for in a confessional a couple of weeks ago. He wasn't entirely sure what to make of her.

But he didn't need to know.

All that mattered was that tonight felt right.

She was laughing again, wrapped in his coat, her shapely legs curled up against him while she leaned into his shoulder. Those eyes of hers turned up to him in the moonlight, and he was hit with an unexpected happy peace.

"Nuh-uh. You honestly expect me to believe you've milked goats?" she said. "What, you haven't?"

Her laugh got him every time. Throaty, but with a ring to it. Sent his blood pulsing south.

Again.

"Seriously," she said.

"Sure. We all milked the goats. Except Margie. Scared her when she was little, and she never got over it."

Natalie's fingers tiptoed up his thigh. "How's she fit with the others? Rosemary and Pepper and Ginger and Basil…?"

"Short for Marjoram."

Then she got The Look. The one he would've recognized half a mile away in a blinding snowstorm in the dead of midnight in northern Alaska.

She wanted to play the name game.

He sighed and shook his head, but with her so relaxed and free and fun beside him, instead of uptight and guarded, he couldn't stop his smile. "Don't do it."

She squinted hard, then tipped her head back in another laugh. "I am the worst cook. I can't come up with a single guess."

"That makes you about my favorite person on the planet." "Is it that bad?"

"Worse." He tugged her fingers to his lips and brushed a kiss over her chilled knuckles. He should take her home.

But he wasn't ready to let go. Not tonight. Maybe not tomorrow either.

"You want to be my stand-in wife?" CJ said.

Her eyes went wide, and every bit of her stiffened. "You—who—what?" Horrified disbelief wasn't the answer he was hoping for.

"Will you be my partner in the Golden Husband Games?" he repeated.

It was too dark to catch the nuances of her expression, but he heard the brain grinding.

Smelled the what's-his-angle questions.

Felt the yes he knew she wanted to say.

But there was a dam going up. Frost tickling the edges of the warm atmosphere between them.

He wasn't wrong. She wanted to say yes. But she was shaking her head no.

"You have so many better options than me."

Maybe. Maybe not. What did he really know about Natalie? Not much.

Not enough.

"I don't have a lot of experience being a good husband, and you irritate the shit out of me half the time, but you and I, we have something I can't fake with anyone else." Nat rubbed the heels of her palms into her eyes. "CJ—"

"I'm not asking for a commitment," he said. "I just need a partner. And the thing is, you—you're the only one who gets it."

She did. She understood marital failure. She understood not fitting into her own life. But she wasn't saying anything.

"Hey, we've already got that blindfolded kissing thing down," he said.

He expected an eye roll. An irritated huff. Maybe a good shove in the ribs.

Instead, he got a shaky breath, a swipe of her eyes, and the feeling that she was sliding further away.

Smooth, jackass. "Sorry, bad joke."

She shook her head. "It was a very good joke."

She was stroking his ego. Bad sign. "Got lots more where that came from. Think about it.

A whole month and a half of this guy right here for your personal entertainment."

He didn't like begging. Wasn't his thing. And she was right. He had several options.

Her lips slanted up, just a hint at the corners, and in that moment, he would've done anything to see her full-on smile.

She was a different person when she smiled. Friendly. Approachable. Damn near perfect. Because even smiling, she kept her stubbornness. She'd push him when he needed pushing. She didn't think he was any more special than the rest of the world, and she treated him that way.

Everything he needed from the woman who would stand in Serena's place. "Plus you'll get to boss me around." No way she could resist that.

Her smile crept higher. But when she tilted her head up at him, her eyes were still bleak. "These are my mom's last Games."

There was something significant in her statement, something he was apparently supposed to understand. "Then you should be up there too."

Her lips parted. He waited for the yes. It was just a breath away. "Natalie?"

"You need a real partner for the Games." "What's real?"

"Someone your family and your in-laws won't be ashamed of."

He tensed. He wanted to shake her. "The only person ashamed of you," he growled, "is you."

"You don't know a thing about me," she growled right back.

"I know you're hurting more people than just yourself by letting some Queen General dictate who you should and shouldn't associate with. What kind of example are you setting for your son?"

Some of her spark flared back to life. "Line. Crossed."

"Truth. Hurts." And the truth was, he wasn't making his case to her. He was pissing her off.

In his admittedly limited experience, a pissed-off Natalie wasn't a cooperative Natalie. It was a sexy, desirable Natalie, but for once, he wanted the cooperative part back.

Abruptly, she drew back. "You don't understand." "Explain it to me."

She pressed her palm to her forehead above her eye. "I will not create another scandal in my mother's Games. Especially not the Golden Husband Games. Bliss needs this, and they need it right. They need you to be right. With someone who can shine for Bliss. And that's not me."

She was the most irritating female he'd ever met, and that was saying something. "You could shine."

She shook her head.

As if she didn't want to shine. As if she liked being the black sheep in Bliss.

Far cry from the girl who had wanted to be the Queen General. From the girl who called this place home.

"You could," he said, stronger. "You could shine. Might find out you still belong. You made your choices. Got a pretty great kid out of it. But you keep letting a moment in time, a signature on a couple pieces of paper, and a bully's opinion of you define who you are and what you can do. So maybe you're right. Maybe you can't shine. Until you're willing to fight for yourself, no one else will either."

She didn't look at him, but instead slid the rest of the way off the hood. Her shoulders sagged like she was trying to hold up the damn wedding cake monument all by herself. "I need to go home."

He didn't want to take her home. He wanted to pull her back up onto the hood of the car and talk some sense into her. Failing that, he'd take kissing some sense into her. Nuts as she made him, mad as she made him, he wanted to take care of her.

To prove to her that she wasn't alone.

He might've been hiding from himself all over the world, but he'd always known his family was waiting for him. She had her sister and her dad, one little boy who counted on her to be his everything, and a whole damn town of people who were afraid to stick up for her because of one bully of a woman. "Nat—"

"I understand if you'd rather I walk."

He slid off the hood and caught her at the waist. She pulled back, her wariness chilling the night and chasing away her soft scent. "I'm tired, CJ."

He was too. But he couldn't let her go. Not yet. Not like this.

He needed to kiss her. Softly, with no demands, no expectations, no delusions, letting his lips warm hers one last time. Hold her tight and solid, so she could lean on him.

And for a brief moment, she let him. One last time, she let him kiss her, let him caress her, let him try to be enough to take care of all of her.

Too soon, she pulled back. Dashed her hand over her cheeks, then wordlessly climbed into his car.

He didn't want to, but he drove her back to her dark house. Back to the real world. They were silent most of the way. Before he let her go, he gripped her hand. "Let me help you."

"CJ—"

"Promise if there's anything I can do, you'll let me do it."

Her sigh sounded less like surrender and more like an indulgence in humoring him. "There won't be, but thank you." She turned her dark eyes on him for the first time since they'd left the lake, and she squeezed his fingers. "Thank you for tonight. It—it meant the world to me." She brushed a quick kiss against his jaw. "Good luck finding a partner."

Then she was gone, dashing out into the night and up the stairs to her real world. Leaving CJ to ponder his own world.

Chapter 13

CJ would never go so far as to say he was smart about women, but after growing up with eleven sisters, he liked to think he was no dummy.

He was about to prove otherwise.

Even knowing he was about to prove otherwise wasn't enough to stop him.

He gave himself every opportunity to chicken out. He walked instead of driving. He passed a few donut shops he could've stopped in. He passed half a dozen churches he should've stopped in. If ever there was a time for divine intervention, it was now. But his feet carried him through the streets as Bliss slowly came to life, churches opening for Sunday services, robe-clad residents yawning over steaming mugs of coffee and plucking their papers off their porches, dogs and cats and birds doing their business, until he stopped in front of a neat two-story apartment building in a functional part of Bliss just south of downtown.

A smart man would've kept walking. A not-dumb man would've at least spent five or ten more minutes debating with himself.

But CJ walked right up the sidewalk, said a good morning to the elderly gentleman who held the door for him, and then made his way to apartment 2A where he knocked with all the ignorant confidence of the idiot that he was.

The door swung open—of course it did, because he wouldn't have planned his own self-destruction at a time when fate could've intervened—and Kimmie's already round blue eyes went rounder.

"Oh! Oh, no. Did I forget to pay last night? Ohmigod, I'm so sorry. I'm always doing that. Hold on. I'll get money."

"Kimmie. Wait. I'm not here about the bar."

She paused, her body halting awkwardly with one arm mid-air and her hips off-center.

Bafflement clouded her eyes, and her wavy hair seemed to stand at an extra level of confusion. She twisted back toward him, lowered her arm, and swung around, expertly avoiding the pile of cat toys on the floor. "You're not?"

The way she wrinkled her nose reminded him of Cinna trying to puzzle out some of the more mature—or rather, immature—jokes he and Cori and Pepper used to make before she was old enough to get them. "Nope. Wanted to ask you something."

She kept gaping at him.

He could appreciate that. He'd felt the same a few hours ago. Except when Natalie threw his world off its rotational axis, there'd been some hurt thrown in with the disbelief.

He should've been grateful she shut him out, because holding her, touching her, knowing her—it might've inspired ideas. Sneaky little ideas about family and forgiveness and acceptance. With some love and laughter and light thrown in.

Screw that. He had some rocks in Utah to climb. Marriage and family—it wasn't his thing.

Especially not with someone who didn't know any more about it than he did. "Can I come in?" he said to Kimmie.

"Oh!" She pulled the door wider and kicked a pile of clothes out of the way. "Yeah. Um, don't mind the mess. Darn cats, right?" She gave an awkward half-laugh, half-snort.

He could've done worse. If his biggest objection was who her mother was, then he didn't have any real objections. She wasn't always predictable, but her heart was in the right place.

That counted for more than what anyone else wanted him to do.

She led him past an efficiency kitchen and into a living room strewn with clothes, books, and cake magazines. "Your cats left the toaster alone?" CJ asked.

She flushed. "Yeah, they were good."

One of the felines in question, a gray tabby, darted from beneath the sunshine orange couch to lick her paw in the window. Kimmie shoved a pile of kitchen towels off the matching recliner and gestured for him to sit. "You want some breakfast? I have these toaster pastry thingies in the freezer. Or cupcakes, but they're not exactly decorated for company."

He wasn't sure what constituted decorated for company, but now he wished he'd looked closer at her kitchen.

Wasn't why he was here though. He settled into the chair and tried to decide what to do with his hands.

Didn't fit right on his knees. Or hanging between his knees. He thrust one through his hair. "I'm good. Thanks."

She flitted about the room like a hummingbird. "Coffee? V8, maybe? Everybody needs their vegetables."

"No, thank you." He pointed toward the couch. "You mind sitting?"

"Oh! Right. Sorry." She plopped down, tucked her hands in her lap, then smoothed them down her lime green pants, then folded them again.

Maybe this wasn't such a good idea.

"I haven't had any more dreams about you." A half-frown dimmed her vibrating energy. "At least, I don't think the vampire cow was you. Pretty sure that was somebody else."

"You having trouble with somebody?" That, CJ could solve. "Oh, no," she said quickly.

Too quickly.

With too much emphasis on wagging her head back and forth. "You sure?"

"No, no, no trouble at all," she insisted. "I just—yeah. No trouble. Everything's fine." She stood, shot a nervous glance at him, and sat again. "So. You're a morning person?"

"Sometimes." He gave her an easy smile, but he couldn't tell if the flush on her neck meant it was working or not. "How about you?"

"Depends on the dreams."

He opened his mouth. Then closed it again.

"It's okay," she said. "You don't have to pretend I'm normal." "Normal's overrated."

"Can you tell my mom that?" "Ah—"

"Never mind. She wouldn't listen anyway. Unless you're like the second coming of Prince Leopold."

"Prince…?"

"Leopold. Father of the modern wedding cake. Kind of. When he got married—sorry. You're not here for a cake history lesson, are you?"

No, but it was infinitely easier than talking about why he was here. "Always happy to learn something new."

"If you stay too long, my mom will start to get ideas." She lowered her voice. "And believe me, she hears everything."

CJ swallowed a smile. "I've noticed."

"So?" Kimmie said. "What can I do for you?"

CJ sat straighter, linked his fingers while his hands dangled between his knees. Now or never.

He hadn't had the biggest balls in his marriage, but he'd never been a chicken. Wasn't about to start now.

"I need a partner for the Golden Husband Games."

Kimmie flashed him a duh look. "And you're getting short on time. I was pretty young at the Silver Husband Games, and nobody's saying yet which games are on the schedule, but everyone knows it was the how-well-do-you-know-your-wife quiz that totally turned the tide twenty-five years ago. And if it's not that, it'll be something else. You need to quit stringing all those women along and make a decision, or there's no chance you'll win. Plus you'll be late with getting the team designs to the T-shirt shop, and my mom will julienne your carrots if you don't do a few interviews." She clamped a hand over her mouth. "Sorry," she said, muffled. "No right to nag you."

"No, you're right. I need to decide." Pick a partner or bail on the games.

Over the last few hours he'd given plenty of thought to bailing. But he always circled back to not being a coward.

And to remembering that he'd promised Serena that they would spend their fifth anniversary here. That he'd play in the Husband Games again for her. Natalie was right. He had a chance to honor his wife and help Bliss at the same time. Serena would've appreciated that.

Kimmie swayed on the couch. "Still, your fake wife's the one who should nag you. Practice, right?"

He lifted his eyebrows at her.

"Ohmigod," she said. "Nuh-uh." She jumped up and launched into her hummingbird impersonation again.

This was the tough part, and not just because she was moving so quickly about the room that CJ couldn't entirely concentrate on what he had to say. "All I'm looking for is a friend," he said. "I know I'm asking a lot, but—"

"What about Natalie?" Wasn't that the question?

He could've done the dumb guy thing. What about her? Could've simply pretended she didn't exist.

But he owed Kimmie the truth. "She said no."

Swift injury flitted across Kimmie's features, then an almost cheerful resignation set in. "Figure it's best if I'm honest with you," he said. It'd worked for his parents for years.

Couple of his sisters too.

"She really said no?" Kimmie said. CJ nodded.

"I guess that makes sense. My mom would pretty much cream everyone's butter if Nat played, and Natalie's working so hard to make sure the Games are everything her mom wanted them to be, and after the way the last Games she played in went—erm, I mean—"

"All good, Kimmie."

She was right. Natalie was scared. And maybe CJ was being an ass, asking Kimmie to be his partner this soon after Nat said no, but being an ass was what he did.

Especially when it came to holy matrimony.

Kimmie's gaze darted over him, then to the rest of the room, then back to him. "Then if you're sure—"

"I'm sure."

"Wow. Thanks. It's not like I'll ever play in the Husband Games for real, you know?" She gave another one of her little half-laughs. "My mom's gonna pass raspberry ganache when she hears this."

He'd considered not asking Kimmie for exactly that reason. He was absurdly grateful he wouldn't have Marilyn Elias as his mother-in-law the rest of his life. On a temporary basis, though, he was eighty percent sure he could handle it. "This won't cause problems for you, will it?"

She waved his question away. "Are you kidding? After this, I could knock over a cake in the middle of a reception and she'd still weep tears of joy." She froze. "So are we, like, exclusive? Because I've never non-dated a temporary fake husband before. This isn't the kind of thing they teach in Bliss's public education system. You'd think they would though, wouldn't you?"

Crazy-ass town was growing on him, because he could see her point. "I won't be dating anyone else. But if you meet someone and want out, I'll understand."

"That would be weird, even for Bliss."

"Kimmie, I've been around the world, so you can take this to the bank," CJ said. "There's nothing too weird for Bliss."

* * *

Natalie had every intention of proceeding with her life on Sunday as though everything were normal. And she did pretty well, too—she sold a few dresses and got next week's schedule done, she kept Noah happy by letting him play dinosaurs in the shop basement, and she only caught herself looking out the window in hopes of glimpsing CJ every other minute.

But facts were facts.

They'd had mind-blowing, life-altering sex, and then she'd let him go. And he'd let her.

Obviously, they had no future. Only memories.

She made it through the Knot Fest meeting without drawing any attention to herself.

Kimmie was conspicuously absent, and Marilyn had been positively giddy. Which was frankly terrifying.

For many reasons.

But Natalie didn't have the strength to deal with Marilyn drama today. Or any more drama.

She'd given herself enough in her personal life.

Or so she thought, until Duke and Elsie made their report. The Golden Husband Games were back on track.

Without Natalie. Because of all that she'd done, and she was still fielding calls and e-mails from people who didn't yet trust Duke and Elsie or hadn't yet heard the news. But to the rest of the world, the Games were on track without Natalie.

By the time she stumbled back home after the meeting Sunday night and paid Noah's second sitter of the weekend, she wanted to curl up and cry.

But life had one more kick for her, in the form of a phone call near midnight.

Mrs. Tanner, Noah's day care lady, was in the hospital for emergency bypass surgery following a heart attack.

Facing the mortality of the woman who cared for Noah forty hours a week made Natalie feel as if she were living through Mom's final moments all over again. The shock. The fear. The denial.

Nat didn't sleep the rest of the night, and she felt only marginally better when she got word early Monday morning that surgery had gone fine and Mrs. Tanner was expected to make a full recovery.

It was the news she never got when Mom collapsed on the shop floor. That night, when she'd gone to pick Noah up from day care, Mrs. Tanner had held them both while Nat told him Grandma wasn't coming home.

Thank God she didn't have to tell him he'd lost someone else.

No time to dwell on it though—which was probably a blessing—because Nat had a shop to run and short-term day care to find.

And when she failed at the latter, she didn't have much hope that the former would be easy. Especially when Noah started wailing as soon as they pulled onto The Aisle.

"I forgot Baby Dinosaur," he cried. "We have to go back for Baby Dinosaur!" "Baby Dinosaur? Noah, you don't have a baby dinosaur."

He broke down in blubbers she couldn't understand, so she turned the car around and headed for home to figure out what he was talking about. She couldn't not. Because Mrs. Tanner would be okay, but odds were good Natalie and Noah would be gone from Bliss by the time she recovered, and they had to make this new arrangement work until then.

Fifteen minutes later, they left home again, this time with Baby Dinosaur strapped into a booster seat beside Noah. Cindy the Stegosaurus had apparently undergone a name and personality change. Noah happily chatted with the stuffed orange dinosaur, shrieking and giggling and squirming with all the pent-up energy of a four-year-old boy.

Keeping him at the shop the next few weeks wasn't a good idea. He needed a safe place to run and play and yell and be a kid.

She needed to figure out a solution. She needed to call Dad.

Ask him for help.

But she kept letting him down. Kept letting him fight her battles. It was no one's fault Mrs. Tanner had had a heart attack—not even the QG could be that cruel, even if she could cause another person's health problems. Natalie still needed to handle her issues herself.

To be a grown-up, and to do the grown-up thing.

When she walked into Bliss Bridal, though, one more bombshell dropped.

Amanda was waiting with news.

She made eye contact with Natalie's hairline when she asked if they could talk a minute. Back in the office, she stared at Nat's left cheek. "I've been grateful for the opportunity to work for your family so long," she started, and Natalie knew.

Her manager, the longest-running employee at Bliss Bridal, was leaving. "Will they take good care of you?" Nat interrupted.

Amanda flushed, but she nodded. "It's a good package." Finally, she looked Natalie in the eye. "I don't want to leave you hanging, but with everything so uncertain here… I can't turn it down. It's in Chicago, and if I'm ever going to see life outside of Bliss, I need to go now."

"Sure," Natalie said, though she was having a mild panic attack. And by mild, she meant epic. "If I didn't have family responsibilities here, I'd look at moving to Chicago too." She choked on her own words though.

Because she didn't want to move to Chicago. She didn't even want to move to Willow Glen.

She wanted to stay here. In Bliss. Running her mother's shop. Being a respected, valued member of the Knot Fest committee and Bridal Retailers Association. Making Dad proud.

Fulfilling her dream.

"I'll do what I can to help find my replacement," Amanda said.

But they both knew it was futile. Word had leaked that Dad was selling the shop. Between the boutique's uncertain future and Marilyn Elias's interference, there wouldn't be another manager until the shop had new owners.

Happily married, well-adjusted owners. "Thank you," Natalie said anyway.

Because one day soon, she could be asking Amanda for a job. The front doorbell dinged.

"Nat, I really do hope everything works out for you." But there wasn't much optimism in her words. "Thanks. Let's get to work."

Helping brides plan the day of their dreams was hard today, but Natalie put on a bright smile anyway. Because she had to.

Until a somewhat familiar woman stepped inside the shop an hour later.

The brunette swept an assessing gaze about the room. Her light green eyes met Natalie's, and Natalie's heart twisted into knots.

Smiling, she approached Natalie with a painfully familiar confident ease. "Hi." She stuck her hand out. "I'm Pepper Blue. You fixed my sister's veil a few weeks ago."

She didn't add, And you boinked my brother Saturday night, but she might as well have. For all of Pepper's wide smile, Natalie couldn't have smiled back if she wanted to. She wanted to plead cramps and run and hide in the back office for the rest of the day.

Or maybe the rest of her life.

"Natalie Castellano." Natalie shook Pepper's hand. "Welcome to Bliss Bridal."

"No, Baby Dinosaur!" Noah suddenly shrieked from beneath a rack of dresses. "It's not polite to look up girls' skirts!"

"Sorry," Natalie said. "Day care issues."

Pepper grinned. "No problem. You've met my family. Trust me, I grew up with worse." Natalie tried to smile back. She did. But smiling didn't usually sting her eyes.

Or her heart. "How can I help you?"

Pepper leaned across the counter and lowered her voice. "I heard a rumor the owner's selling."

Natalie opened her mouth, but no sound came out.

Probably good, because if it had, it would've sounded like a wounded animal, and Bliss Bridal was struggling enough without Nat going protective cavewoman.

"I'm in management at Bridal Universe," Pepper said.

Natalie's veins iced over. "No." No question, no doubt, no hesitation. No way in hell—and forget the damn nickel—would she let Dad sell Bliss Bridal to an impersonal bridal retail chain. Hell no. Fuck no.

The brides in the room stared at her. So did the consultants. Pepper drew back a step.

Natalie's head was shaking. So were her hands. She couldn't stop either, and she didn't want to. "I'll see this place burned to the ground before I let my mother's shop become a franchise for Bridal Universe."

Pepper's cute little nose wrinkled, her perfectly groomed brows furrowed.

And then she laughed. "Oh, no." She reached out and put a smooth, cool hand over Natalie's. "Honey, I'm not interested in fattening their corporate wallets with a place like this. I'm asking for me. I want to buy the shop."

Fragments of CJ's stories from Saturday night floated into the forefront of Natalie's mind.

Penny stocks. Pepper. Brilliant. Fortune.

Pepper slid a card across the counter. Natalie couldn't move. Mom's shop had an interested buyer.

A viable, smart, interested buyer.

A buyer who would satisfy Dad's terms of keeping the shop as a bridal boutique, and probably inspire Marilyn to up her game to get the space too.

Natalie was going to throw up.

"Excuse me," she heard herself say, "I have cramps."

* * *

Bliss didn't have many opportunities for CJ to scratch his risk-taking itch, but asking Kimmie to be his partner in the Games had proven to be the next best thing to climbing the wedding cake.

Pretty sad when a clandestine meeting to exchange "life history binders" in an alley behind a bakery on a Monday morning was his new version of adventure.

"Sorry for making you meet me out here." Kimmie gestured at the sweet-smelling Dumpster with her pink binder. "Mom's still on her equivalent of a sugar high over the news. You'd think I told her I was pregnant with the next generation of Keebler elves. Not sure she's grasped the whole it's-only-for-the-Games thing yet. Although she was hoping for someone more financially—I mean, she's delusionally happy for us. It's kinda scary, actually, and I'm used to her."

She leaned in and lowered her voice. "Plus I dreamed Lindsey put a hit out on me to make you a 'single man' again."

"Are your dreams often psychic?" Wouldn't surprise him. The hit or the psychic dreams. "Not like fortune cookies."

Before he could decide if he wanted to go down that path, the door one shop down banged open. Natalie shot out into the alley. She stopped short and doubled over, heaving like she'd run a marathon.

"Holy cupcakes, Nat." Kimmie shoved her binder at CJ and half-trotted to her friend. "You okay?"

Natalie looked up sharply. Her normally smooth hair was rumpled, her creamy shirt wrinkled, her face was so pale it wasn't far from blue. "I'm good." There was a punctuated crack in her voice. After one quick glance at CJ, she focused on Kimmie and Kimmie only.

Felt like a sucker punch.

He sauntered after Kimmie, binders tucked under his elbow. "Mondays," Natalie said. "You know."

"Yeah, my Tuesdays are usually like that. Sometimes my Sundays, depending on the week." Kimmie put a palm to Natalie's forehead. "You're clammy. And you look like fried marzipan. Are you sick?"

Natalie swiped at her nose with the back of her hand. "Stressed." Her gaze drifted toward CJ, but snapped back to Kimmie before it got there. She took a deep breath, as though she were putting her world back in focus.

Lining up which problem she wanted to share with them.

She blinked twice, and her voice was almost steady when she spoke. "Noah's sitter had a heart attack last night."

"Oh, no," Kimmie whispered. "Oh, Nat."

"She's going to be okay." Natalie shivered, her gaze somewhere not in the alley. "I just—I'm worried about Noah."

CJ didn't know a lot about parenthood, but he knew something about grief.

A few months after Serena died, he'd been in the Swiss Alps. Checked his e-mail right before heading out for skydiving and found a message from Margie that one of their high school friends had almost died in a car accident.

Couldn't remember the guy's name now, but he remembered being so shaken up, he cancelled the dive. Sitting in his hostel, wishing he could sleep, thinking about going out and getting drunk, unable to quit trembling.

Because he kept remembering the moment he'd gotten the news about Serena. He hadn't wanted to remember.

He'd been useless for about a day—felt longer, but it had only been a day. And the sad truth was, he hadn't been useless to anybody but himself. The moment that realization had hit him, he booked transportation to France and went skiing.

Ordered himself to get over it. Told himself afterward that it worked, but the truth was, it had taken a while.

Nat looked as if she could use some skiing. Maybe a day at the beach. A massage.

He was decent with his hands. And he wouldn't have minded having his hands on her skin again.

All of her skin. Maybe get his mouth on her skin again too. "Does Noah know what happened?" Kimmie asked.

CJ gave himself a mental head slap. Not the time.

"No." Natalie's color was coming back. "I need to find temporary care for him. He's never gone anywhere else. I don't know how he'll handle it."

"Children are adaptable," an unfortunate voice said behind CJ. "Kimberly had dozens of sitters growing up. Your son will be fine."

Natalie squared her shoulders and stared back at Marilyn with a mixture of animosity and respect sparking across her face. "Yes, he will."

"In the meantime, Kimberly and CJ can help you with your little problem."

An awkward silence settled in the alley. Natalie glanced between Kimmie and CJ, then looked closer.

CJ felt his cheeks turning the same shade as his hair.

"Are you—" Nat stopped herself. Set her dark eyes like black onyx. Her nostrils flared.

Just a little. He had to watch her close to notice.

But he couldn't take his eyes off her.

"The official announcement was in the Bliss Times this morning," Marilyn said. Natalie's shoulders squared tighter, her color came all the way back, and she faced the Queen General straight on. "That's kind of you to offer, but we wouldn't want Bliss's most celebrated couple to be linked to that divorced woman on The Aisle, now would we?"

Marilyn made a noise that would've been a pfft coming from any other woman. "Bliss's most celebrated couple will be lauded for their charity work."

"Charity," Natalie echoed.

The frozen steel in her voice gave CJ the chills. Made him a little hot under the collar too.

This could get interesting. Dangerous, even. CJ suspected Natalie had just stomped the shit out of that line she'd mentioned the other night, and she was about to start flinging flaming justice out of her fingertips.

Natalie's eyes subtly shifted toward CJ, commanding his full attention. He gulped.

He'd wanted adventure in Bliss. He was about to get it.

"Mr. Exalted Widower," she said in another of those female tones, this one loaded with the power and danger of the mother of all nuclear weapons, "are you sure you're up to the task of taking on my son as a charity project?"

Something's burning was the right and wrong answer. He was physically incapable of putting Natalie and char—chari—He couldn't do it. Charity deserved its own sentence. Far, far away from any thought of what Natalie needed.

On the one hand, he couldn't tell her no. Couldn't refuse a challenge. That would make him seem like a chicken.

But when staring at Mama Bear Natalie, who was wearing a touch of Pissed Off Lover Natalie beneath the Mama Bear thing, being a chicken might've been CJ's wisest option.

Of course, if he refused the Queen General's suggestion, he'd be screwed in an entirely different way.

Kimmie took one of those about-to-launch-into-a-story breaths. The back door of Bliss Bridal opened, and Noah stuck his head out.

His head that was still sporting CJ's Falcons hat. "Mommy?"

Natalie beckoned him with one hand, still glaring at CJ. She slipped an arm around Noah's shoulder. The little boy curled into her.

Despite this being a highly inappropriate time to remember how she'd felt with her legs wrapped around him against his car Saturday night, he had plenty of brain cells—among other body parts—dedicated solely to the task of wondering what it would take to get them there again.

The combination of royally pissed and motherly was hot. He clearly needed to talk to a professional about this. "Well?" Natalie said to CJ.

"Of course they'll do it." Marilyn dusted her hands. "Problem solved." "You don't get to solve my problems," Natalie said.

"Miss Castellano, I already have." Marilyn consulted her elegant wristwatch, then pinned CJ and Kimmie collectively with an I-will-be-obeyed look. "It would behoove the two of you to experience parenthood. For the sake of your relationship. You have my blessing to babysit."

She turned on her heel and strode to her car, apparently oblivious to the animal she'd just unleashed in Natalie.

"Excuse me," Natalie said to Kimmie. "I have work to do."

The QG's engine purred to life. Kimmie stepped forward before Natalie could disappear back into the shop. "Nat, I know you don't like it since my mom suggested it, but I—erm, we would love to help you with Noah. CJ mostly works nights, and we could use the practice pretending to be parents if we're going to pull this thing off at the Husband Games, so…win-win, right?" She glanced back at her mother's retreating car, then gave CJ a questioning glance. "I don't think Mom will interfere more. And Noah's not short enough to be an elf. Technically. So we can do this, right?"

Natalie leveled a flat stare at CJ that a lifetime of living with too many women had fully prepared him to interpret. She wanted him to say no.

But despite the danger rolling off Natalie in heavy waves, he still had full possession of his balls, and truth was, her kid was adorable.

CJ squatted down to Noah's level and tipped the hat back so he could see the boy's face. "You wanna see the Bachelors practice, little dude?"

"Can Baby Dinosaur come?"

"You bet. You, me, and Baby Dinosaur will do all kinds of man things." "Awesome!" He yanked on Natalie's hand and jumped. "Mom, isn't that awesome?" "Sweetie, I know you don't understand," Nat said, "but this is complicated—"

"The hell it is," CJ said softly.

Natalie's glare went so icy he wished he had a jacket.

But more, he wished he had the right to kiss the ice out of her. To melt her frozen heart. To heat her from the inside out until she couldn't find her frost.

He wanted another night. A week. A month.

Her hostility wavered. She stepped back, her pulse fluttering in her throat. As if she'd read his thoughts.

"And you know I love Noah," Kimmie said. "Terms of payment?" she said crisply.

"Oh, no," Kimmie said. "We couldn't take your money. You're doing us a favor."

A ghost of a smile teased Natalie's lips. The haunted kind of ghost, not the friendly kind, but seeing the corners of her mouth lift gave CJ an unexpected sense of relief that her muscles were still capable of bending that way.

The boutique door opened again, and one of the shop girls stuck her head out. "Natalie? You've got a phone call."

Natalie looked at Kimmie. "If you're sure you have time—" "Completely sure," CJ said.

Kimmie nodded. "It'll be fun. Nat, he's such a good kid, and you deserve some peace of mind on something. This is what friends are for, right?"

"Go ahead, Noah," Natalie said on a shuddery sigh. "Go play. Be good. I'll call and check on you, okay? And I'll find you a real babysitter so we can get back to normal soon. I promise."

Back to normal. CJ got the message. Loud and clear. He wasn't their normal. He was temporary. Because that was his life. His choice.

Shouldn't have pissed him off, but it did.

"Love you, Mom!" Noah darted away from her to launch himself at CJ. "We're gonna be men today, huh?"

Probably not.

But they would at least try.

Chapter 14

Charity.

Marilyn Elias thought Natalie was a charity case. Fuck that.

As soon as Noah danced out the back door—danced—to go have a man day with CJ, Natalie gave her heart a whipstitch patch-job, then pillaged the locked bottom desk drawer.

There wasn't enough petty cash to cover the purchase Nat was about to make, so she grabbed her personal credit card too. She stalked out to the floor where Pepper was still waiting, none the wiser that her brother had just danced off with the best thing in Natalie's life.

"You have experience with brides?" Natalie asked without preamble.

An achingly familiar spark lit Pepper's green eyes, exactly as Nat had hoped and feared. Pepper liked a challenge as much as her brother.

"Eight years," Pepper said.

"We're short-staffed. You're hired." Natalie signaled Amanda. "Back in five." She marched out the front door, turned left, and stormed the bakery.

One of the bakery girls looked up from the pristine white desk where she was assisting a customer. Her eyes flared wide. Natalie stalked past, straight to the checkout counter. "Kimmie?" she called.

The half-door to the kitchen swung open. Kimmie darted out, a smear of purple frosting on her nose. "Did they forget something?"

Natalie slapped the cash and her credit card on the counter. "I want all your cupcakes." Kimmie gawked at her.

"All of them," Natalie said.

"Um, Nat, that's like, three hundred cupcakes."

In all of the last five years, Natalie had never felt herself smile so ugly. "Perfect."

Kimmie visibly swallowed. "Are you going to cupcake my mom's house?" she whispered. "She only went for a short Knot Fest meeting. She'll be back in half an hour."

"Worse." Natalie's smile grew until the very act of smiling almost made her feel happy.

"Much, much worse."

Kimmie eyed her with a healthy mixture of fear and respect. She slowly reached across the counter to take the cash and the credit card. "Mom's gonna bake our Alaska," she breathed.

"Let her try."

Let her bring all she had. Because Natalie was done.

Done being that divorced woman. Done being the pimple on the face of The Aisle. Done being a second-class citizen.

She'd planned most of the Golden Husband Games. She'd done every task asked of her for the janitorial committee. She'd kept Bliss Bridal in the black. Barely, but still in the black.

She was better than Marilyn Elias could ever be, and she was done taking that woman's shit.

"So I'm ringing these up in your dad's name," Kimmie said. "Use mine."

Kimmie winced. "Nat—" "Use. Mine."

This time, Kimmie didn't argue.

Fifteen minutes later, the kitchenette and the office at Bliss Bridal overflowed with Heaven's Bakery cupcakes. Strawberry shortcake cupcakes, Key lime pie cupcakes, lemon blueberry cupcakes, blackberry fudge cupcakes and piña colada cupcakes covered every surface. Kimmie and two of the shop assistants at Heaven's Bakery had boxed and delivered Natalie's purchase. As soon as they scrambled out the back door, Nat locked it and jammed a chair under the door knob.

She knew better than to underestimate the QG's powers against a door lock.

Downstairs in storage, she located the easel her mom had kept on hand to advertise summer specials and trunk shows, which Natalie had been unsuccessful in booking since her mom died.

But Nat didn't need anything more than chalk and her own determination to accomplish this mission. The bridal consultants and Amanda and Pepper had all looked curiously at her when she dragged it up, but after seeing what she'd written on it, every last one of them—even Pepper—stared at her as though she'd stabbed the wrong pincushion.

Free Heaven's Bakery Cupcakes for All Bliss Bridal Customers and Parties Today! No Appointment Necessary!

"You know ninety percent of our brides are on diets, right?" Amanda said.

"And one hundred percent of them walking by today will think Heaven's Bakery endorses Bliss Bridal as the best place in town to get a gown." Natalie's heart thrummed like her sewing machine on a power surge. "So will all the other shop owners on The Aisle."

A chorus of gasps trickled through the group. "She'll kill you," Amanda said.

Or up her game to outbid Pepper for the shop, but if Dad could fight Marilyn there, Natalie would too. "Let her try."

Natalie put the easel outside, then posted notices on Twitter and Facebook to the same effect. The first hour was slow. Two brides stopped in, each with only their mothers. Lunchtime came and passed, and four bridal parties came in to check things out.

But then—then Natalie got a text from Luke Hart down at the chocolate shop.

LMAO. Sending some people your way.

Natalie wouldn't have minded laughing her ass off right along with Luke, but she hadn't had enough takers on the cupcakes yet to work up even a smile.

Claudia Sweeney walked past, saw the sign, and did a double take just outside the front window. She looked back toward Heaven's Bakery, then grinned big and gave Nat a thumbs-up before scurrying down the street.

Twenty minutes later, Bliss Bridal was more packed than the foyer of St. Valentine's had been when CJ's sister got married.

Brides logged in on their phones and tablets, right there in the store, and followed Bliss Bridal's Pinterest boards and liked its Facebook page. They browsed the gowns, both for themselves and for their bridesmaids. They took impromptu tours of the alterations room upstairs and splurged on tiaras and clutch purses.

And they booked appointments.

They booked appointments until Bliss Bridal's calendar was full for the next three weeks, with other brides fighting over their places on the waiting list.

And when the inevitable finally happened—when Marilyn Elias herself marched through the door a while later, horrified disbelief marring her normally unflappable demeanor— Natalie smiled even bigger. "Ladies," she called over the din, "meet Mrs. Elias, proprietor of Heaven's Bakery. Aren't these cupcakes wonderful?"

God bless them, every last member of every single bridal party stopped to clap.

The General portion of Marilyn's personality roared to life. Her eyebrows slammed together, her lips thinned, and Natalie could see the I will end you threat coming.

Right there.

In the midst of all the applause.

The QG was going to totally lose her shit in front of dozens of women.

Nat snagged a cupcake and raised it in a mock toast. "My dad says thanks for your generosity," she said over the applause.

Marilyn's eyes flared. She blinked around at the brides complimenting her, and her queenly side came back in full force. The regal smile, the hand flutter over her chest, the head tilt to make her diamond earrings sparkle, all the while moving back to the door. She made her gracious excuses about getting back to the bakery, and wished all the brides a wonderful day in Bliss.

And then, with one last This is not the end glare at Natalie, she disappeared out the door. "That woman is scary as hell," Pepper whispered. “She looks like she wanted to kill you.” “Or something worse, no doubt.” Natalie surveyed the room again, took in all the happy, glowing women chatting and shopping and enjoying themselves. It was a sight that would’ve made her mother proud. “But I would do it again in a heartbeat.”

* * *

Turned out four-year-old boys and women had something in common. They both had the same air intake valves that kept their mouths running while their ears were shut off. Difference was, the four-year-old just wanted to talk. No subtext, no secret agendas, no land mines.

And he was the funniest character CJ had ever met.

CJ had taken the assignment to prove he wasn’t a chicken—and also because Natalie needed the help—but Noah didn’t understand any of that.

He simply understood that the guy who saved Cindy the Baby Dinosaur Stegosaurus wanted to hang with him for a few days.

The whole ride to Willow Glen, Noah jabbered away from his booster seat in the back of Kimmie’s Outback, which she’d insisted CJ borrow for the day after she saw his old car. So he didn’t break down with a four-year-old in tow, Kimmie said.

Noah told CJ all about the Cubs, his dinosaur, things his mom said, what Mrs. Tanner could bake, places his grandpa had taken him, anything and everything that crossed his mind. When CJ pulled up in front of Bob and Fiona’s house, Noah gave CJ an earful about his grandma’s flower beds. On the way up the walk, he explained the difference between lace and tulle. But when Fiona opened the door, he went so still and quiet, a part of CJ’s world seemed to disappear.

“And who is this?” Fiona asked.

CJ opened his mouth, but Noah sprang back to life and stuck his hand out. “I’m Noah. How are you today?”

CJ understood Fiona’s rapid blinking and softening expression all too well. He’d felt the same near-grief over the grandkids she’d never have more than once over the years. But as he expected, she steeled herself and squatted down to Noah's level. "I'm very well, thank you. And you?"

"Yeah, it's been a kind of a day," Noah said with an overly adult nod. "His mom's having some day care issues," CJ said.

"What's your mommy do, Noah?" Fiona asked.

"She sells pretty dresses and keeps all those crazy couples in line at Knot Fest meetings, and when I grow up I'm going to wear a pretty dress and kiss a girl and get married and we're going to play in the Husband Games like CJ."

"And your daddy?" she said.

"I don't have one of those." Noah nodded gravely, as if confirming Fiona's worst fears. "It's hard enough to manage one parent."

How could anyone resist this kid?

Fiona melted into a puddle of grandmotherly adoration at his feet. "Has anyone ever told you you're adorable?"

"Oh, yeah. My grandma used to all the time. She's in heaven now, you know. Is your grandma in heaven?"

"She is," Fiona said.

"Do you think they're having a tea party together?" "I certainly hope so."

The scent of nostalgia and heartache made breathing difficult. "Bob tape the Cubs game yesterday?" CJ asked. "Noah here's a big fan."

"So's Baby Dinosaur," Noah said. "And CJ's taking us to see the Bachelors practice tomorrow."

Fiona straightened. "He usually does. Come on in."

Noah and Bob hit it off instantly. Bob seemed to be having a good day. Fiona made them mid-morning popcorn, and they sat in the living room like long-lost buddies, discussing how far into the season the Cubs would make it before they choked. CJ left them to their baseball and headed to the garage to tackle the door opener that had fried itself out.

"So you're dating his mother?" Fiona said from the doorway into the house. She huddled in it as though she were cold, though he suspected the pleasant spring temperature was the last thing on her mind.

"Not dating anyone right now," CJ said. He moved to the fuse box and looked for the right switch. "Just helping out. Noah's a good kid."

"And his mom is your partner in the Games?"

He'd called yesterday to tell them he'd picked a partner. "Ah, no. Kimmie's another friend. Not his mom."

A crease almost as deep as her frown appeared on the bridge of Fiona's nose. "It's complicated," CJ said. Lamely.

He rummaged through Bob's toolbox, not sure what he was looking for, but unable to stand there and face Fiona for fear she'd judge him for being the type of guy who'd ask one girl out to make another girl jealous.

It wasn't like that.

It was way more complicated than that. Obviously. Because women were involved.

Women always overcomplicated things.

"It's okay if you move on, you know," Fiona said.

He stopped his hunt. "Been moving the last four years, Fi."

She stayed in the threshold and leaned her head against the doorframe. Bringing Noah had changed their dynamic.

Shouldn't have. CJ wasn't auditioning for the role of Noah's next father. Even if he wanted to, he couldn't.

The kid—and his mother—needed more stability than CJ had to offer.

More dependability in the husband and father department too. Not something he could share with his mother-in-law.

Because that would involve telling his mother-in-law that he'd made her daughter miserable.

"She was a stubborn girl." Fiona's wisp of a sad smile left no doubt who she was talking about. "Beautiful, perfect and stubborn. But you two would've worked everything out."

CJ dropped the tape measure he hadn't realized he'd picked up. She knew?

"Oh, come now," Fiona said. "Of all people, you should know girls talk to their mothers." She had him there.

"The year Bob and I got married, we fought every night over how he washed the silverware. My mother told me I should've appreciated having a man willing to wash the silverware back then, but we still fought about it. And you know what?"

CJ swallowed before he found his voice. "What?"

"She was right. I should've kept my mouth shut. Because he hasn't washed so much as a damn fork for the last thirty years. But he's kept the lawn mowed and the plumbing in good order and paid the mortgage, and I wouldn't have wanted to share this life with anyone else. I wish you and Serena had had each other long enough to find your compromises. Because she was a wonderful woman, and you're a good man, and she missed you. And I don't believe you'd be here now if you hadn't missed her. You would've worked everything out, and I know you would've been happy forever."

She blinked quickly, then stood and tucked her hands in her pockets. "But reality is reality. I wouldn't stick my nose in your business if you looked happy, but you, my dear, have the look of a puppy who just watched the mailman skip your house. And whatever—or whoever—you need to put the joy back in your life, Bob and I support you." She glanced back into the house, where Noah's little voice still drifted out. "Some things mean more than the world. They don't come easy, and you'll still hurt sometimes, but the effort of making it work is worth it. I believe in you, honey. It's time you believe in yourself too."

She cleared her throat. "Well. I'm going to go see if the boys need anything. Don't need to be out here distracting you all day."

"Fi."

"Hm?"

"Thanks." It was inadequate, but it was all he could manage for the moment. He hadn't realized he'd wanted her forgiveness until she gave it, and he still wasn't sure about her permission, but the relief at not having to pretend to have been Serena's superman anymore was overwhelming.

"I'm only sorry I didn't tell you sooner," she said.

She disappeared into the house, and with her departure went a chunk of his guilt.

It wasn't everything, but it was more than he'd found on his own the last four years.

* * *

CJ and Noah left Bob and Fiona's place late afternoon. Fiona had magically unearthed a pile of toys and games, and Noah had played his little heart out.

Fi would've made a terrific grandmother.

The thought sat heavy in CJ's gut all the way back to Bliss.

Bob was doing well with his treatments. Their house was getting back in shape. After the flood renovations, the big projects like the garage door were few and far between. Mostly CJ had done their spring maintenance and helped Fiona with errands. They wouldn't need him much longer. He was pricing tickets to Utah and keeping an eye on airfare to Australia.

He'd gotten his scuba certification with the Great Barrier Reef in mind. Be a shame to waste that now.

Noah yawned in the backseat. "Are we going home?"

"Not yet, little dude." According to the schedule Natalie had texted CJ this morning, she wasn't off work for another hour. He had to be at Suckers not long after that. Kimmie had initially offered to take Noah late afternoon, but then she'd sent him a message about a cupcake emergency and that her mother was scrambling somebody's eggs. No way was he wading into that.

So they went to the rectory so CJ could get ready for work and Noah could have some downtime.

Kid was tired.

But Noah wasn't the only one who needed downtime at the rectory, apparently. When they walked in, Pepper was there, sprawled across the couch. She lifted one eyelid with what looked like a great deal of effort when CJ and Noah walked in.

"Is this supposed to be a good surprise?" CJ said. "That's the last time I offer to buy a bridal boutique."

An involuntary shiver rattled CJ's spine. "You came here to buy Bliss Bridal?"

"Mm-hmm. Great little shop. Crazy-ass owner." One eye lazily slid to Noah. "So that's where you went, little dude."

And there went his sisters, leaving him speechless again. No wonder Natalie had been so strung out.

She was losing every last one of her dreams.

Not his problem, he reminded himself. This part of his life was temporary. "You're still standing," Pepper said. "Should've traded jobs with you today."

CJ sucked in a breath. Time to be the brother she expected. "Big crowd at the bar. I've gotta go help. You got Noah for a while?"

Pepper whimpered.

CJ kept his game face. She could open her other eye and focus enough to call his bluff any minute. "And Natalie called," he lied. "She has to work until nine tonight. Something about a computer glitch."

Pepper's whimper went deeper, but then she came up like she'd been shot off the couch with a slingshot, tossing a couch cushion at him. "You are so full of shi—" She shot a glance at where Noah rested his head against CJ's leg. "Doody. You're full of doody."

"What? You don't believe me?" Damn. He was still rusty with the family pranks.

The grin spreading over Pepper's cheeks reminded CJ of the time they'd hidden one of each of Saffron's special socks so she didn't have a single matched set. "Nope. But after today, it wouldn't surprise me if she was working late. That woman—the Queen General? She's scary. But Natalie showed her who's boss today, and packed Bliss Bridal in the process. It was epic. I'm surprised the fire department didn't come in and chase everyone out for building capacity code violations."

CJ felt a grin coming on despite his own wobbly standing with Natalie. "So she had a good day?"

"Oh, yeah. She sent everybody home and said she was closing up half an hour ago."

Pepper hooked a thumb toward the kitchen. "By the way, cupcakes are in the kitchen if you want some."

It would take more than cupcakes to distract CJ from the rest of the story. "You really want to buy the shop?"

Her animated smile morphed into a line. "Yeah. Drama aside, it's a great shop in a great location with a great history. I would love to buy it. But they're not selling."

"They're not?" The news made him happier than it should've. Nat's future was none of his business.

"Depends on who you believe," Pepper said. "She gave me her dad's contact information and the name of his broker. But she doesn't want to sell. You can tell. Honestly, watching her work—I don't get why anyone would object to her. She's good."

Yeah, she was. At a lot of things. "So you're giving up?"

"Oh, I didn't say that. She's not the only one who was born to sell dresses, and an opportunity like this doesn't come around every day. If she's dum—er, if she wants out, I'll happily step in."

CJ opened his mouth to tell Pepper to back off, but when he realized the words would have been more of a growl, he turned the lecture on himself.

Who was he to get upset with Natalie's choices? He tapped Noah's shoulder. "You want a cupcake, little dude?"

"Did Kimmie make them?"

"Kimmie," Pepper said. "We should talk some more about her." Pepper's evil side was as big as Basil's, but twice as happy.

"Mommy never says quarter words about Kimmie," Noah said. "I like her cupcakes better."

"Kimmie made 'em," CJ assured Noah.

"Interesting choice for a stand-in wife, Princess," Pepper said. "Back off."

"Her, sure. You, never." Her gaze drifted down to Noah again. "We all like you close to home. Far be it from me to stop reminding you how much you like it too."

CJ nudged Noah toward the kitchen. "Might want to change your tactic." "You know what's interesting?" Pepper said.

"Anything but this conversation?"

"How much you and Natalie have in common."

She had more of a point than he'd ever admit. To her, anyway.

Skipping Utah and heading straight to Australia was beginning to sound like a very, very good plan. The sooner, the better.

* * *

Despite all the good coming out of Bliss Bridal today, when Natalie got home, a weary sadness settled into her bones. The Queen General hadn't counter-attacked, which meant something big, bad, and most likely horrifying would be coming soon. Nat was half-afraid to close her eyes tonight.

But she had a more immediate problem first. Noah was due home any minute.

Her heart shuddered. The cupcakes had been a decent distraction from thinking how Noah was getting to know CJ. About trusting CJ with the single most important person in her life.

About how CJ was giving the Queen General exactly what she wanted in his choice of Golden Husband Games partner.

Nat didn't want to hate Kimmie. But CJ had replaced Natalie.

Already.

No amount of logic could convince Nat that it was right. That Kimmie deserved her moment in the limelight. That everything was better this way.

Because Natalie liked CJ.

She didn't want to. Not for CJ's sake, but for her own sake. He was off-limits. He'd picked Kimmie. He was leaving.

Her phone buzzed, announcing a text from CJ that they'd arrived. She squared her attitude and went to meet them in front.

Noah tumbled out of Kimmie's car and streaked across the yard to launch himself at Natalie, stories tumbling out at a hundred thousand miles an hour.

The basics came down to I love CJ, Mom. I can't wait to do this again tomorrow.

Natalie hugged him tight, ignoring the shadow she felt approaching. "Were you a good boy?" she asked in the midst of one of his infrequent pauses for breath.

"He was great," CJ said.

"I was, Mom. And I got a cupcake. Can we have cupcakes for dinner? Pepper said Baby Dinosaur wouldn't fit in her dress if we gave her any cupcakes, but you can just let the seams out, right, Mom?"

Pepper. Pepper, who would take over her mother's boutique one day. One day soon. At least one good thing would come of getting out of Bliss.

Natalie would have the energy to enjoy Noah's enthusiasm for every bit of life.

He had a frosting ring halfway around his upper lip, subtle smudges beneath his eyes that spoke of a hard day of playing without a nap, and he was still vibrating with excitement. He'd mentioned CJ's in-laws—Natalie knew enough CJ Blue trivia to recognize the names—along with Pepper and Father Basil, and he looked about to launch into My Day, Part Two: A Narrative. Natalie tapped his lips. "Save some for dinner conversation, okay, kiddo?"

"But, Mom, CJ used to be married, and his wife died in a war. Did you know that?"

CJ's sudden stillness balanced Natalie's suddenly painfully pounding heart. "I did." She patted his back. "Go on in and get washed up for dinner."

"Can we have cupcakes?" he asked again.

Three hundred cupcakes delivered to Bliss Bridal this morning, and there had been fifteen left at the end of the day. Total success in Nat's book. She had sent most of them home with the rest of the girls, but she had two inside for Noah and herself. "If you eat your SpaghettiOs."

"Cool!"

He scampered inside, singing. "Oooh, girl," he crooned. "I'm having cupcakes! With my dinner! Washing my hands! With Baby Dinosaur!"

Natalie suppressed a smile, then rose to snap on her grateful mother face.

CJ hadn't moved. One of his eyebrows crinkled, and he was watching her like he would a crazy person.

"Thank you for your assistance today," she said, more stiffly than she intended, yet still more friendly than she wanted.

His face relaxed, and his shoulders subtly did too. "Heard you had your hands full." She almost smiled. She wanted to smile.

Getting the best of the QG—even though she'd surely pay for it later—had made her feel invincible. But CJ was still the man who'd slept with her and then asked the QG's daughter to be his partner in the Golden Husband Games.

"Handling crises is in my job description," Nat said.

One corner of his mouth hitched up. The warmth in his eyes made her want to hide. She didn't, of course. But she wanted to.

He watched her a beat longer, and the other corner of his mouth joined the first. He nodded. "Looks good on you."

"Wh-what?"

"Your confidence. It fits you. You should wear it more often."

The compliment slipped through a crack in the iron case protecting her heart. Warmth spread from her breast to her fingers and up into her cheeks. "I do what I have to do."

"You're doing it right." He shoved his hands in his pockets, still watching her, making the warmth spread higher and hotter in her face. "Kimmie's got the morning shift with Noah tomorrow. She'll swing by and get him around eight, unless you need her earlier. I'll take him at lunch."

"I don't need charity."

Damn man smiled bigger. But it wasn't the bigger that bothered her so much as the softer.

Affection from CJ was dangerous.

Addictive.

"Only a fool would make that mistake, Nat. Your day care lady back to work tomorrow?"

She shook her head. Mrs. Tanner would be out for several weeks, and he knew it. Which meant the right thing to do was to call Dad.

But she'd solve this herself. She would.

"I have a few calls out," she said. "This is a temporary solution." And she'd pay them the same that she paid Mrs. Tanner.

"You like being difficult, don't you?"

"You like sleeping around, don't you?" she fired back.

Then instantly wished she could take it back. Not because CJ minded. He laughed. He actually laughed, as if she'd told a funny joke. But Natalie felt like a petty little bitch, and she didn't want to be a petty little bitch.

She wanted to be worthy of a guy who put his own plans on hold to take care of his in-laws and a babysitter-less kid.

She wanted a different kind of life.

"Who would you have picked for me?" he asked.

No one. She would've picked no one. But that wasn't an option, which meant she'd pick— Kimmie.

Dammit, she would've picked Kimmie. "Quarter word?" CJ said.

"Don't you have to be at work?" She squeezed her eyes shut and blew out a slow breath before opening them again. He'd asked her first. She'd said no. Aside from a brief flirtation where they both knew the score, he hadn't given her any impression that he was playing in the Games for any reason other than to honor his dead wife. He deserved the opportunity without judgment from her. "I hope Kimmie is everything you need from a partner."

"She wasn't my first choice," he said.

Her heart grew baby wings and beat against that iron casing. "I also hope you don't have to endure too many family dinners with her mother present."

His grin was significantly less amused this time. "Me too." He checked his watch. "Noah had a lot of questions about Serena today. You might get a few more."

"He likes you." "He's a good kid."

They stared at each other another moment. "I need to go—"

"Gotta get to—"

Natalie smiled, and CJ smiled back at her. "Thank you," Natalie said.

His hand rose, as if he wanted to reach for her, but then he dropped it and stepped back. "See you tomorrow."

When he turned back to Kimmie's car, Natalie gave herself a moment to ogle his ass, then took one last clear breath and headed inside to have dinner with the little boy who was her world.

She'd earned it.

Chapter 15

After a couple weeks of playing part-time parent, CJ had a new respect for anyone who'd ever raised a kid. Working the late shift at Suckers every night this weekend had wiped him out, but Monday morning, when Noah barreled at him full-steam, still wearing CJ's Falcons hat, CJ wouldn't have traded it for anything.

He squatted, and Noah tackled him with a hug. "Hey, big dude!" CJ squeezed him back. "Hey, little dude."

Natalie was on the phone at the register, rubbing her temples as if she were warding off a headache, but her smile for him made him both lighthearted and light-headed. And maybe a tad frustrated.

He wanted to do more than make her smile. Preferably with both of them naked again.

Not exactly appropriate given that he was holding her son in a bear hug—he'd missed his favorite buddy this weekend—but it was the truth. "Ready to go?" he asked Noah.

"Yeah! Can we have cupcakes for second breakfast?"

Cupcakes. With CJ's temporary stand-in wife, who felt like his twelfth sister. His life was currently on the messed up side. "You bet, kiddo."

They waved at Nat. She smiled again, and CJ decided getting out of here for cupcakes was a very good plan.

Otherwise he might start getting ideas about sticking around after the Golden Husband Games for a single mother he had no business getting ideas about.

Next door, Kimmie greeted them with a wide, open, sisterly smile. "Second breakfast?" she asked Noah.

"Yeah!"

"Broccoli cupcakes or eggplant cupcakes?"

Horror and disbelief flashed across Noah's features beneath the Falcons cap. CJ was stuck between gagging and laughing. He swung the boy up. "She's teasing, kiddo. How about a s'more cupcake?"

"With extra marshmallows?" Noah said.

"I'll see what I can do." Kimmie let just enough disapproval color her words to remind CJ who her mother was.

She disappeared into the kitchen. CJ put Noah down, and the two of them discussed which of the display wedding cakes looked most delicious until Kimmie returned with a box big enough for two cupcakes. CJ nudged Noah.

"Thanks, Kimmie," the little boy said.

She handed over her car keys, then gave Noah a hug. "Be good today, okay?" "Yep. We're gonna do man things."

Kid was freaking adorable.

Kimmie cast a quick glance back at the kitchen, then squinted up at CJ. "Hey, listen," she said softly, "it's not too late if you want to switch partners."

Her words were like ice and inspiration at the same time. He shot a look at the kitchen too. "You meet somebody?"

"No, no, nothing like that. You just—you two—you three—" She shook her head. "You'll do best if you're with somebody you like. You know, like that. And you do."

Noah was watching them as if he understood every implication of what Kimmie wasn't saying, in addition to what she was.

CJ's hammering heart swelled up to nearly choke him. "It's okay if you don't want to play."

"I do. I'm in. I just thought—never mind. I read it wrong."

No, she read it right. He was getting too close. Getting those ideas. "We're good." CJ tried for a reassuring grin. "Besides, team T-shirts are already ordered. Can't waste a good design."

"That's the stupidest reason ever," she whispered. Her unique jagged flush crept up her cheeks. "I just wanted to make sure."

CJ could appreciate that. He wasn't so sure of a lot of things lately. "You're a good friend, Kimmie."

"Can we eat cupcakes yet?" Noah whispered. Kimmie smiled down at the boy.

CJ rubbed his hat. "Soon as we decide what we're doing today."

"I want to go see Grandpa."

Kimmie's gaze darted back to the kitchen, and her cheeks took on a darker hue. "You boys have fun." She took two backward steps, then dashed back to work. "Where's your grandpa at?" CJ asked Noah.

"His cabin. We fish like men when we're out there. Do you think he's ever coming back?" "Sure he is. Let's see if I can get an address, and we'll track him down, okay?"

"Yeah!"

The only thing Nat ever said about her dad and his absence was that he deserved to enjoy retirement. But her tone always said something more. Something that implied she and her dad were having some issues. Life with CJ's sisters had taught him to avoid emotional land mines, so he texted Lindsey for the address instead of asking Natalie.

They exited the bakery's front door, then circled around to Kimmie's car at the back of the Heaven's Bakery parking lot. Noah somehow managed to both walk and dance the whole way, singing an impromptu "We're Going to See Grandpa" song.

Kid was hysterical and adorable. Might've had a pretty firm grip on that little organ in CJ's chest too.

He got Noah strapped in, and was just about to open his own door when a woman exited the back of the bakery, heels clicking and thunderclouds brewing around her.

"CJ," the Queen General said. "Lovely to see you this morning."

There was a set to her jaw that said it wasn't so lovely at all. She continued her approach.

Inside the car, Noah's song went silent.

The trouble coming smelled so bad, it should've set off emergency sirens. But CJ's sisters had also inspired him to master the art of acting dumb and happy. "Marilyn. Lovely to see you too. You wouldn't happen to have an address for Arthur's cabin, would you?"

She stumbled to a stop, and a delicate pink stain with jagged edges crept up her cheeks. "Why would I be in possession of that knowledge?"

She was definitely in possession of that knowledge. What he couldn't immediately grasp was why a woman like Marilyn Elias would have any reason to pretend she wasn't. "Because you've been shop neighbors for thirty years," CJ said.

"Oh. Of course." The pink got pinker. As if she were embarrassed for being embarrassed. As if she were caught.

Holy shit.

Maybe she was caught.

Holy double shit. Time to go dig a bomb shelter.

Because if Natalie caught wind of what CJ suspected, there wouldn't be a safe corner to be found in Bliss. Possibly in the whole state of Illinois, and some of Indiana and Michigan too.

Marilyn's blush receded so quickly it might not have been there. "I assume you're going to let the boy visit his grandfather and for no other purpose?" Marilyn said.

CJ squinted at her.

She gave him the laser death stare back.

Not too different from the way she'd smiled at him over dinner at her house last week, but enough to put a chill in the air and make CJ's nerves stand on end. "What other purpose would I have?"

"You seem to have become quite attached to your ward's family." His ward? This lady was nuts. "That a problem?"

The General part of Marilyn's personality bloomed, which he wouldn't have been able to recognize before last week when Natalie had demonstrated the difference. Damn funny impersonation she'd done. He'd laughed his ass off.

"It certainly might be," Marilyn said. She spread her legs, tucked her arms behind her back as though commanding her troops. "By the power vested in me as a community leader in Bliss, it is my duty to remind you that there are certain expectations of the honored participants in the Golden Husband Games."

"You wanna spell out exactly what those expectations are?"

Marilyn spared a glance toward Noah. CJ wished he could reach into the car and give the kid a hug, but he stood his ground with the QG.

"To be precise," Marilyn said, "despite my daughter's misguided and ill-advised intentions, there will be no divorced women participating in the Golden Husband Games."

"Does Arthur know you talk about his daughter like that?"

Her lips tightened, and a hint of color touched her cheeks again. "My personal and professional obligations unfortunately do not always perfectly align."

"How do you sleep at night?"

"Tread carefully, Mr. Blue. Your time in Bliss is limited, is it not?"

Yeah, he got it. She was the Bliss Queen, and even if he was the Exalted Widower, she'd still keep him as much in his place as she could while he was here. But aside from personally,

Nat wouldn't be a problem for the Queen General much longer.

However, Natalie had something in Bliss that Marilyn didn't.

She had friends. Quiet friends, but friends nonetheless. If enough of them stood up to Marilyn—

Holy shit again.

That was the issue.

The whole issue.

"You don't care that she's divorced," CJ said. "You do this because you're afraid of her." "Don't be absurd."

But it wasn't absurd.

It wasn't absurd in the slightest. "If you're not, you should be. She's strong enough to shake up everything in Bliss. Has the friends to pull it off too." Friends like Kimmie, born and bred and indoctrinated in Bliss, yet willing to defy her mother for a smart, strong, compassionate woman who had once made a mistake.

Friends like CJ, who had found a place here and had friends in his own right.

Marilyn's laser death glare should've inspired terror, but if Natalie could stand up to this woman, hell if CJ would back down.

“Don’t underestimate me, Mr. Blue.”

“I have eleven sisters, Mrs. Elias. I never underestimate a woman. Any woman.” He gave her a mock imitation of her own regal nod. “Enjoy your day. Noah and I are gonna go catch some fish.”

He pulled out of the parking lot with Marilyn scowling in his rearview mirror, but a grin on his own face.

Score one for Team Natalie. Damn if that didn’t make him happier than he’d been in a long, long time.

* * *

Natalie’s good mood had been growing by the day, but today, she was giddy. Giddy.

She was still stressed—Pepper would probably buy Mom’s store and Nat still had Golden Husband Games and janitorial committee issues, but Noah was happy. Gabby’s dress was nearly done. The QG had apparently launched an unspoken truce since the cupcake incident, which probably either meant she knew something Natalie didn’t about the future of Bliss Bridal, or she’d changed her mind about wanting it for herself. And Natalie had safely ensconced herself in a farce of epic proportions about her relationship with CJ.

Someone knocked at the door, and her heart smiled. The boys were home.

Her boys.

She was delusional, but she couldn’t stop thinking of them both as hers.

CJ hadn’t touched her since that night at Suckers, and he never stayed long when he dropped Noah off, but he was melding into her life as if he’d been there all along. As if he’d found where he belonged. Listening to him and Noah talk about their day was so natural, she felt more home than she’d been since before Mom died.

And he was here. Again. Now.

She pranced on light feet to fling the door open, but her smile died a quick death.

“Miss Castellano,” the Queen General said in all her queenly, General glory. “A word, if you please.”

Natalie didn't please, but Marilyn sailed through the door anyway. Nat wrapped her arms over her chest to ward off the chill slinking into her bones. "Mrs. Elias. How may I be of assistance?"

"I'm concerned about the Golden Husband Games."

Natalie's pulse missed a stitch. "It's my understanding that Duke and Elsie are working hard to catch up."

"I'm not discussing the planning of the Games, though we could have another interesting conversation on that topic, now couldn't we?"

So much for that truce. "I did what my mother would've wanted me to do, and I'd do it all again."

"Your loyalty is charming, but the Games were never about your mother." Marilyn eyeballed Natalie's parents' wedding picture on the entryway table. Something flickered in her eyes. "The Games are about bringing Bliss back to its full and complete place in the wedding industry, and this, Miss Castellano, is where you've failed."

"I've failed?"

"You've grown rather fond of disregarding my instructions to you. Going behind the Golden Husband Games committee's backs to complicate the planning of them."

"The Games would've flopped without me, and you know it."

"Continuing to associate with CJ after your ill-advised visit with him in a confessional." "You told Kimmie and CJ to watch Noah."

"Interfering with Kimberly's attempts to capture his attention." Marilyn shuddered. "Next you'll be encouraging him to associate with your sister as well."

"My sister is a good person working for a good cause," Natalie said. "Your sister is a disgrace to Bliss, as are you."

"And you're a nasty old woman on a power trip."

Marilyn didn't flinch, but her lips flattened. "Since you're so determined to ignore me, let the record show that I've requested you to discontinue your attempts to secure CJ's affections by sharing top secret Golden Husband Games event information with him."

Natalie sucked in a lungful of air that didn't deliver any oxygen to her body. Her marrow crystallized with ice. "You wouldn't dare—"

"Bliss has certain standards, Miss Castellano, and you do not meet them. And then you proceed to meddle and interfere with our Games and try to be better than every other hardworking family on The Aisle? Were your mother here, she'd echo my sentiments."

"My mother would tell you to go to hell. Who plans the Games means nothing. That they're done, that they're done right, that they're a tribute to what Bliss stands for is what's important."

"Done right and done by the right people are one and the same. You, Miss Castellano, are not the right people. And your mother knew it. That is why you were denied her position on the committee. She didn't want you to have it."

Natalie hardly recognized her own deadly quiet voice. "You're lying."

"Come now, Miss Castellano. Despite your own delusions, you must've known she was looking for a Husband Games apprentice. The single sons on The Aisle are simply taking too long to find wives, or she would've had her replacement trained years ago."

"That's ridiculous." But possibly true. Mom had mentioned concerns over the future of The Aisle a time or two. In conjunction with Knot Fest activities? Natalie couldn't remember. It was all too hazy.

Too long ago.

God, she wished Mom were here now.

"But the more immediate point," Marilyn said, "is that your mother would be horrified to learn you've been encouraging an honored guest in Bliss to cheat. I daresay she'd kick you out of her house for disgracing her and the town she loved so much. She's rather lucky she's already in her final resting place, isn't she?"

"Get out," Natalie breathed.

Marilyn didn't budge. "All the work you think you're doing? If word gets out what you've done, it will be for nothing. Your mother understood the unique value of Bliss's celebrations of wedlock better than anyone. She understood the value of Bliss's status as the Most Married-est Town on Earth. It's why she ran the Husband Games for so many years. You, Miss Castellano, are not your mother."

No, she wasn't. She never would be. She'd always known that.

What she'd never fully comprehended, though, was how much better Bliss could've been if her mother had run it instead of Marilyn.

"Now, let's start again," Marilyn said. "And let's see if perhaps this time you learn your place."

Natalie snapped.

It wasn't a physical snap. Didn't come with a loud clang, or even a subtle pop. One minute she was standing there, shocked motionless, and the next, Marilyn said learn your place, and poof! Natalie's life shifted into complete focus.

First she swallowed the lump that had been forming in her throat. Then she cleared her eye of any threat of weak emotion. Next, she pulled herself taller than she'd been before Marilyn knocked on her door.

Natalie turned on her heel. She marched into her sewing room and pulled a file from the desk, then marched back to stare down the Queen General.

"My notes," she said. "On everything." She shoved them into the QG's chest, gratified when the older woman's eyes went uncharacteristically wide. Better was watching her take a step back.

Natalie followed.

"You win," she said into the rapidly narrowing space between them as she advanced on Marilyn and Marilyn backpedaled for what had to be the first time in her life.

"No more divorced woman marring the sanctity of your precious committee," Natalie said. "I quit. I quit the janitorial committee. I quit the Golden Husband Games committee. I quit the Knot Fest committee."

Marilyn tripped another step back.

"Now," Natalie snarled, "get the hell out of my house. We're done here."

Whether Marilyn had gotten what she'd ultimately come for, or whether she'd recognized Natalie as a threat to her physical well-being, the QG listened.

The neighbors probably wouldn't have noticed, but as Natalie stood tall, proud of finally fully standing up to Marilyn, watching her retreat and knowing the work Marilyn had just given herself, Nat saw less regality and more evil old witch in the QG's stride.

Because no doubt, the QG was an evil witch. She'd just ensured that it wasn't enough for Natalie to quit the Knot Fest committee. To leave her mother's final Husband Games. To step back into the shadows of Bliss, where Marilyn wrongly thought Natalie belonged.

No, Natalie couldn't stop there.

And that knowledge was what ultimately broke her.

She slammed the front door. Took four steps into the house, and crumpled into herself.

She'd just let her mother down. But she couldn't let herself mourn her failings just yet. She had a few more disappointments to hand out first.

* * *

CJ smothered a laugh on his way up Natalie's front steps. Noah was rocking his completely inaccurate rendition of the new Billy Brenton tune they'd just heard on the radio. Legs kicking haphazardly, head back, arm bent like he had an invisible microphone, the kid crooned with all the might in his little heart. CJ needed to remember his camera so he could tape stuff like this and send it to Saffron. She'd left Billy's band when she got married, and video footage of Noah mimicking the country rock star would have her rolling.

Hanging out with this kid took him soaring into a completely different stratosphere. Better, CJ had a pizza in one hand, a pack of juice boxes in the other, a pretty lady waiting inside, and nowhere to be until tomorrow morning.

The past few weeks, he'd come to think of Natalie as a friend. When she let her guard down, she was funny. Nice. Frustrating in that wonderful way women could be when a guy wanted to touch them but couldn't.

Tonight, he could stick around. Have dinner with his friend and her son.

Accidentally cop a feel, maybe. If his hand happened to brush Nat's ass when he reached around her for a slice of pizza, he'd apologize. Pretend he hadn't enjoyed it. Try to do it again.

Give some thought to that idea Kimmie had sparked. Give some more thought to the kind of unique comfort he'd be able to offer Nat when Arthur finally told her what he'd confessed to CJ today.

Maybe not help her make sense of it, but there would definitely be more feel-copping in the course of his comforting.

The door opened, and his plans stepped in a pile of goat shit.

"Mom, look! Me and CJ went fishing with Grandpa, and we brought pizza for dinner. And I'm gonna do the dishes and wash my face and be a big boy and everything."

Natalie's cheek twitched—effort of holding something in, if he knew anything about upset women—then she squeezed Noah's shoulder. "You want to wear your dinosaur cape to dinner? It's on your bed."

Her voice was froggy, but Noah didn't notice. He jumped and pumped a fist in the air. "Yeah!"

Natalie looked past CJ, swept a gaze up and down the street, then stepped out onto the porch. She gestured limply toward the pizza. "How much do I owe you?"

His heart turned into a glacier. "Nothing."

She scrubbed her hands over her cheeks. Her eyes wrinkled up, but she blew out a slow breath and blinked twice before looking up at him with bloodshot eyes. "Don't be ridiculous. I'm not a charity case."

"Nat?" Something was wrong. And acknowledging that there was something wrong with his friendship with her made him acknowledge that this was more than friendship.

Her humorless laugh sent an icicle through his heart. "I'll write you a check for the babysitting."

"Are you—" He swallowed, because this conversation had I'm breaking up with you written all over it.

They weren't actually dating, and she was breaking up with him. "What the hell, Natalie?" She met his gaze evenly. "What the hell is my life. And I need you to stay out of it." "Why?"

"Marilyn threatened to ruin me." "Tell her to piss off."

"She threatened to start a rumor that I helped you cheat in the Games." Her dinner splatted onto the porch about like his world just had.

Fucking Games.

It was always the fucking Games.

CJ shook his head. "Enough. I'm done." He reached for his phone. Natalie stopped him with a soft hand on his arm.

Soft.

Not a feeling he normally associated with her, but there it was. Softness. In her touch, in her face, in her voice. "You have to play." Her voice wobbled. She took a hiccupy breath, but she held herself together. "I quit the committee. I gave her all my notes. I'm done. But I wanted—I can't—they're my mom's last event."

She was the least helpless woman he'd ever met. A titanium brick wall reinforced with lead couldn't stop her if she decided to go through it. But tonight, she looked broken.

"Your mom's gone," he said.

Stress accentuated the tight lines in the corners of her mouth. "Yes. She is. But as long as I'm not, I'll honor her memory by doing the right thing."

"You're not doing this for her," he growled. "You're doing it for yourself."

He'd anticipated the flare of irritation in her dark eyes, but when she followed it by schooling her expression in blankness, his gut twisted.

"And what are you doing for yourself?" she said.

Some menacing calm in her voice would've been nice. Instead, it was just as flat and empty as the fight in her eyes.

"You're leaving," she said. "You have eleven sisters and a brother who adore you, but you won't trust any of them enough to let them in. You're so fixated on being wrong once, you can't conceive of taking a chance on something that might be right. So who's wrong, CJ?" Her voice cracked. "Me, for wanting to honor my mother and not make my father endure any more embarrassment on my behalf, or you, hiding from your life because you're not man enough to take another chance?"

He wasn't hiding from anything. He was standing here, wanting to eat a pizza with the woman she was ten minutes ago. At least, he should've been. Red haze crept into his vision. A roiling sensation in his gut had him clamping down on the trembles starting in his core.

She hadn't just hit a nerve. She'd hit his worst nerve. "You need to leave," she said.

Little footsteps echoed inside the house, and grief flooded his veins. The door flung open. "Mom! Mom! Look, I'm super-dino-man!" CJ stepped back.

He didn't belong here.

He never had. He'd just been pretending for a while. A different kind of adventure, that's all it was. He thrust his hands through his hair, then squatted when Noah barreled at him. "I've gotta go, little dude. You take care, okay?"

Noah flexed his puny little bicep. "I'm the man of the house. I can take care of everything."

Life sucked eggs sometimes. "Counting on you, sport." "See you tomorrow, CJ!"

No, he wouldn't. But that was a problem Natalie would have to deal with. It was time for CJ to move on.

* * *

Dad got home around nine. Calling him hadn't been easy, but it was the only option Natalie had left. Mrs. Tanner was still recovering and wouldn't reopen her day care until after Knot Fest, if she reopened at all. Natalie didn't want to waste time and effort and emotions finding Noah another sitter. She wanted him with family.

Family was all she had left to count on. "You look tired," Dad said.

Not tired. Stretched so far she'd snapped.

They were in the living room on opposite ends of the molded leather couch. When she called, Dad hadn't asked much, and Natalie hadn't offered much. Just that she needed help. Now, he was eyeing her as if he was sizing up her mental state, but she didn't have the energy for anything beyond the basics. She held up her hands in surrender. "I've made a mess of everything."

He shook his head. "I was wrong, Nat. You can handle anything life throws at you, and Noah's a lucky little guy to have you. You've done real good here."

Her eyes stung. She didn't know if she'd fooled him or if he was saying it to make them both feel better, but the conviction behind his words wrapped around her like a warm, safe blanket on a cold night. "I've had help." She still did. She was still living in Dad's house, working at Dad's shop, now calling Dad to watch Noah.

"Nobody can do it all by themselves. But what you have done is amazing. Your mother would be so proud of you. So proud."

She swallowed a sob. She wasn't amazing. She was a fake. A big, posing phony who still had to call good ol' Dad to fix her problems. "It's not enough." She curled her legs beneath her and pressed her palms into her eyes. "God, I'm tired." Tired of work. Tired of the festival. Tired of her life.

She wanted to disappear for a couple weeks at a spa. She'd even raid Noah's college fund and take herself skydiving if a certain someone she'd just kicked out of her house would go with her.

Just so she could pretend for another couple of days. "I'm so tired of being a grown-up." "Got a real good offer on the shop from someone who wants to keep it as a boutique," Dad said. "Suppose you probably heard about that though."

Natalie was going numb. Numb was good. She was tired of feeling. "You should take it." "Don't have to decide today. Got a week or so."

She took a deep breath. "Waiting won't change who I am or who I've been. Pepper's a great choice for a new owner. She's smart, she knows the wedding business, and if anyone has the personality and background necessary to work on The Aisle without a husband, it's her. Not me." Besides, with all the single sons on The Aisle, Pepper wouldn't be lacking in the husband department for long.

Dad didn't say anything.

Natalie huddled closer into herself. "And the truth is, I'd rather be Noah's mom than have a million boutiques. I can't ever repay you for all the help you and Mom have given Noah and me, but I can make sure I'm there for him the way you've been there for me."

"Been thinking a lot lately about how your mom and I had each other. How much of a difference that made for you girls."

Natalie nodded. Her parents had worked hard—the shop wouldn't be what it was today if they hadn't—but Dad had always gotten Natalie and Lindsey to dance lessons and softball practices while Mom ran the shop and did other Aisle business. By herself, Natalie couldn't do the same for Noah.

"If you had the right partner, you could do it too," Dad said. Nope. Not all the way numb yet. Because that one hurt.

She blinked her stinging eyes back into submission. "I'm not getting remarried, Dad." "Mistakes are only mistakes if you don't learn from them."

"It's not a mistake to not marry a guy who doesn't love you." That, she'd learned. Much as the thought threatened to turn her stomach inside out, CJ didn't love her. She didn't know if she loved him. He made her laugh, he frustrated her, and he twisted her heart so hard it had wrinkles, but that couldn't be love.

As if it mattered. Because if it was love, she'd killed it efficiently tonight.

CJ was right. Mom was gone. And Natalie had kicked him out so she didn't put a stain on her mother's memory.

But who else would care if Marilyn Elias spread those rumors? Who besides Natalie and Lindsey and Dad? They all knew better.

Natalie wished Marilyn an eternity in boxed-cake-mix and divorce-support-group hell.

Dad heaved a Dad-sigh. "You take another look when Knot Fest is over. This isn't the time to make big decisions. I'll tell Pepper we're not ready."

"We're ready." She couldn't feel her heart anymore. Thank God.

"Honey—"

Nat held up a hand. "Dad, I can't do this another year. Pepper can turn Bliss Bridal back into what it's supposed to be. Everything it's supposed to be, eventually with the husband and all. I can't. Even without Knot Fest and all the other stuff, I can't. You should sell it to her. Mom"—Natalie's voice cracked, and she dug deep to embrace the numbness again—"Mom would like her. You can't take the chance that the next person who makes an offer won't have the experience or the personality to make it work. I'd rather Pepper have it now, before I break it."

Or before Marilyn broke Dad, and convinced him to let her expand the bakery in the boutique's space.

"Natalie—"

"We've always known, Dad. We've always known I couldn't do it forever. Let me out with dignity. Please." She wouldn't cry. If she cried, if she bent the smallest amount, he'd know she didn't want to sell any more than he did, but the timing didn't change the facts.

Natalie didn't belong on the The Aisle.

She belonged in a dress shop. Her own dress shop, where she could dabble with modifying and designing gowns again, where she could hire the best bridal consultants and managers, where she could sign exclusive contracts with highly sought designers and popular wedding planners. But that dress shop couldn't be in Bliss. Not as long as Marilyn Elias ruled here. Nat had successfully stood up to the wicked old bat a time or two. But what kind of life would she give Noah if she had to fight Marilyn every day?

Dad was studying her again. "If you're sure you want out."

"I'm sure."

He shifted deeper into the couch, then fiddled with the remote. "While we're talking about difficult topics, I have something else I need to tell you."

The numbness in her chest plummeted to her stomach.

He was dying. He'd been hiding because he'd been diagnosed with cancer or heart disease or tuberculosis, and he didn't know how to tell her.

Her throat wouldn't work. Neither would her tongue. Or her lungs.

But she ordered her body to snap out of it, and she kept her eyes clear and steady when she looked at him. "Whatever it is, we'll deal with it."

He opened his mouth.

Natalie braced herself. She'd get through this. She had to, for Noah's sake. For Dad's sake.

For Mom's sake. She owed it to all of them to be strong and hold it together.

He sucked in a breath. "I've asked Marilyn to be my partner in the Golden Husband Games."

Natalie's spine went so rigid it cracked. No.

No.

Dad's gaze was steady, his hand half out to her, as if it were a peace offering. An apology and a plea all in one.

Her relief that he wasn't dying was swallowed whole by her horror, and she didn't care. She'd earned the right to be horrified.

At least if he'd been sick, it wouldn't have been his fault. "No," she said. "Natalie—"

She ignored the warning note in his voice and sprang to her feet. This wasn't happening.

He hadn't just said that.

"Replacing Mom is bad enough. But with her? How could you? How could you?" "She's not the devil, Natalie."

"That woman marched in here tonight and threatened to publicly accuse me of fixing the Golden Husband Games."

Dad's eyes flared open, then snapped narrow along with his flattening lips. He didn't believe her.

This wasn't happening.

Natalie had to leave. To run. Take Noah and get as far the hell from this demented town as she could. She turned to the door.

"She's not already buried in the backyard, is she?" Dad deadpanned. Natalie stopped.

"Sit," he said.

She shook her head. She pinched her lips tight to keep from howling.

"Nat, hon, that's what happens to a person when she thinks she's doing it all by herself for too many years."

"You're excusing her. You don't know—you don't know how awful she's been. The things she's done. And Noah—Noah's terrified of her."

Natalie didn't have to turn around to see him rubbing his temples. She could hear it in his sigh. "People aren't perfect. Even Queen Generals. I knew she wasn't happy when I told her about Pepper's offer, but I didn't think she'd take it out on you. I'll talk to her."

"Talk?" Natalie was screeching. She knew she was screeching, and she couldn't stop herself. She spun back to face him, barely aware of the ground beneath her feet. All she knew was her own pulsing core of horrified disbelief. "Talk?"

"Lot more effective than revenge." His lips twitched in a half-grin. "But, that cupcake stunt you pulled—that was a good one."

"I quit the committee because of her. I kicked CJ out of my life—out of Noah's life—because of her. Mom's Games could be ruined because of her. And you know—you have to know the only reason she's being nice to you is because she thought she could convince you to give her the shop. She's brainwashing you. Don't you care?"

"Natalie…" The warning was back. The tension was back. She'd called him home. She'd asked for his help. And now she was attacking him.

Justifiably, but if he was far enough off his rocker to ask that woman to stand in Mom's place, he was obviously far enough off his rocker to not realize that this time, he was the one who was wrong.

"Sit," he said.

She sat.

Not happily, but she sat.

She'd lost enough already. She didn't want to lose Dad too. "Do you love her?" Natalie said.

Dad barked out a surprised laugh, but there was no flushing, no hiding, no fidgeting. "No." His simple answer was mildly soothing. Like putting a Band-Aid on a twisted, mangled, compound double fracture.

"I love your mother," he said. "No one will ever be to me what your mother is to me. But I miss having someone to talk to. Marilyn's been missing having someone to talk to for so long, she doesn't know she's missing it. Ah—" He held up a hand at Natalie's snort. "Think about how hard you've been working. About all the difficulties of being a single mother. Not having time to date or have friends or a social life. Then imagine living like that for over twenty-five years."

She was too irritated to consider the point. "You think your companionship will cure Marilyn of her—" Natalie waved her own hand and let Dad fill in whatever insult he felt appropriate.

"I think some of the best battles are fought when the enemy doesn't know you've snuck behind their lines."

Natalie couldn't say much to that.

Because she didn't know who Dad considered to be the enemy—her, or Marilyn. She did know, though, that he was her dad. She'd just have to trust him.

Chapter 16

Having eloped during Knot Fest, CJ wasn't prepared for how seriously Bliss took their festival. He should've picked up on the clues. Like the obvious one when Natalie kicked him out of her life almost two weeks ago so there would be no hints of anyone marring the sanctity of her precious Games.

He hadn't been this upset by a woman since Serena shipped out. Damn good sign of something he didn't want to think about.

So was the fact that he'd started his own cussing jar. Pissed him off that he owed it more change now. But at least Marilyn had gotten too busy to bother him. No more invitations for dinner or hospitality receptions. Not that he minded. Last time he'd braved the Fortress, as he liked to think of Marilyn's house at the top of Natalie's subdivision, she'd come right out and asked him what he was worth financially. Kimmie was nearly as bad in her own way. Since Natalie had handed over all the work she'd been doing on the Golden Husband Games, Marilyn was working triple-time to help Duke and Elsie Sparks keep up, which meant Kimmie was working triple-time covering for her mother at the bakery. Kimmie could barely utter a sentence without a mention of a dream or a fortune cookie lately.

But he'd escaped all of them today and taken an extra day shift at Suckers. Bob's last treatment was today—great way to spend the Friday before Knot Fest week—and Fiona had forbidden CJ from stopping by.

There was a possibility CJ had been a bear lately.

While he banged around the bar getting set up for what could possibly be the last normal day he'd ever have in Bliss, he told himself the comforting lie that Fiona didn't want anything to distract Bob from getting his rest before Knot Fest.

Because they were coming to watch him make an ass of himself at the Games next weekend.

The back door banged open, and something that sounded like Huck singing drifted from the kitchen to the bar.

And was that—yep, CJ knew the song. "If You Want To Be Happy." He'd sung it to every one of his sisters at some point in their lives. He'd always meant it as a compliment, obviously. A wish for them for long-term marital success. Getting to call them ugly in the song was simply a bonus.

Huck skipped out of the kitchen and shimmied his saggy sixty-five-year-old hips all the way to the front door, which he unlocked with a flourish. Braid swinging, an uncharacteristically happy smile splitting his cheeks, he danced back through the tables.

"Get an ugly one for wife number four, Huck?" CJ said. "Careful. She might stick." The old guy let out a gleeful laugh. "Hell, no, boy. I'm getting my freedom."

A quieter presence behind CJ made him look back.

"Who in the hell is that?" Jeremy said with a nod at Huck. "An anti-zombie in Huck's body?"

"She's getting maaaarrrrried," Huck sang in a tune CJ didn't recognize. "She's getting hitched. She's alllllll hiiiiiisssss!"

"Dude's lost his last marble." Jeremy moved to the nearest table and started pulling chairs down for the lunch crowd. CJ hadn't expected Jeremy here until later, but today apparently wasn't normal.

"Get a bottle of champagne," Huck said to CJ. "Gonna have us a celebration." The front door opened. CJ's pathetic little heart sputtered.

First time Lindsey had walked through that door in weeks. And it took everything he had not to strain to see if her sister was behind her. Dressed up like she was—in a power suit that could've done battle with some of Marilyn Elias's getups, and with her hair back in a tight bun—Lindsey obviously wouldn't have Nat, or Noah, with her, but CJ looked.

He couldn't help himself.

The disappointment that she was alone twisted the log of a splinter that had taken up residence in his chest about two weeks ago.

"I take it he's not talking about you getting married," CJ said.

Lindsey snorted delicately. "Not a snowball's chance in hell."

Huck hooted. "Sing it with me." He puffed his lungs up, but Lindsey leveled a look on him that must've been inspired by the power suit.

"I don't sing," she said.

"Sad truth, that," Jeremy said.

Lindsey ignored him and claimed the table he'd just cleared of chairs. She pulled a file out of her messenger bag. "What's the emergency, Huck?"

Huck pointed to the file. "You boys see that? That right there's my freedom. Number two's getting hitched to some old geezer with a Swiss bank account and a faulty pacemaker."

Much more glee, and the guy would need his own pacemaker. His gray braid frizzed with all the excitement.

"So now she has to support you?" CJ said.

"Hell, no. Means I don't gotta pay her alimony no more." He poked Lindsey. "Right? That's what my prenup said, right? Tell me I'm a free man. Go on. Tell me." Lindsey's lips quirked up. "This is not an emergency."

"Best case you've had in months, though, ain't it?" Huck poked her again. "Lot better'n that custody problem you had last month. Go on. You tell me I'm free, I'll pay you overtime." He snapped his fingers. "Where's that champagne?" He scampered back behind the bar.

Jeremy shrugged at CJ and went back to work clearing the rest of the tables. "You want something to drink?" CJ said to Lindsey.

She lifted a water bottle from her bag and waved it at him without looking up. Like it was his fault Natalie kicked him out of her house.

Except it was.

He'd been too mad to realize it that night, but the next day, when Kimmie had stopped by the rectory to drop off cupcakes, everything had clicked.

He'd pushed Marilyn's buttons. He'd told her she should be afraid of Natalie, and she'd made Natalie pay for it. Made Kimmie pay for it too.

A prince among men, that was CJ. Always punishing the women in his life. He propped his hands on the bar. "Haven't seen you around much lately." Lindsey didn't look up. "Been busy."

"How's Noah?"

He knew better than to show weakness to any woman. But he wanted to know. Losing Noah was as bad as losing Natalie. Worse, in some ways.

Because Noah was so easy to love.

Lindsey dropped her pen. "Are you leaving after Knot Fest?" Simple question. Loaded, but simple.

He looked down at the row of vodka bottles beneath the bar.

"I saw you last Knot Fest," Lindsey said. "When you kissed her."

Everything inside him went still. Utterly, completely motionless. From his pulse to his nerves to his ego, everything—everything—stopped.

And waited.

"You were a married guy kissing my married sister. That doesn't bother me. It's the Games. It happens. But you and Nat—you weren't a bad match. That bothered me. It bothered me for a long, long time."

His body slowly moved back into motion. He lifted his head, inhaled fresh bar air, and studied her. He didn't believe all this voodoo anti-matching crap.

But he still had to ask. "And me and my wife?"

"Is there any good that can come out of either answer I give you?" No.

He didn't have to think about it. Because there wasn't. He'd either been a good match or a bad match for Serena, and he couldn't change it now. They'd made their choices. She'd died for it, he lived with it every day.

He shook his head. "You think something good could come of telling me that me and Nat aren't one of your bad matches."

"Something very good," Lindsey said softly. Almost wistfully. CJ's breath came out long and slow.

Something very good. Like a home. A family. A best friend and lover. Weekend T-ball games. Playing dinosaurs. Reading Dr. Seuss.

Giving up his freedom, he reminded himself. Never making it to the Great Barrier Reef.

Seeing his family every holiday.

Seeing his family every holiday. Belonging somewhere again. Laughing.

Dammit, who turned off the AC?

"But if you're going to use that plane ticket," Lindsey said, "none of it matters, does it?"

He was sweating. A cold, steamy, life-changing sweat. He hadn't mentioned to anyone that he'd bought his ticket to Utah last week. "How do you know about that?"

She smiled. Dammit again. She'd gotten him with one of Sage's favorite tricks. Pretend you already know, and they'll admit it.

"I hear all kinds of things," Lindsey said.

The kitchen door hinges squeaked. "Saddle up, boys! The champagne wagon just pulled into the station. Yeeee-haaawww!" Huck plopped a bottle down beside CJ. "You figure out the rest of it yet?" he said to Lindsey.

"I need half an hour."

"Quit bugging the lady so she can work," Huck said to CJ. "Ain't paying you to stand around with your thumb up your butt, am I?"

"Have been the last couple of months, haven't you?" Jeremy said. He'd worked his way close to the door, and now he frowned at one of the small side windows. "We open early today?"

"If they're paying," Huck said. The door swung open again. "Aw, hell," CJ muttered.

"Good to see you too, Princess," Pepper said. But she wasn't alone.

She'd brought more of them.

He pinched his eyes shut. If he didn't look, if he didn't see them, they weren't here. But if they were here, on a Friday, then they'd be here tomorrow on Saturday for the parade, and then again on Sunday.

"Is this place sanitary?" Margie wanted to know.

Eleven sisters, and he knew each of them by their voice alone. It was a curse. "Some days," Basil said with an audible sniff.

CJ surrendered and opened his eyes again. The whole Blue contingency from the northern part of Illinois was trooping into Suckers.

Cori paused to run her fingers over the purple rope lights circling the door. "Pimpin'." She stumbled forward, propelled, apparently, by an overeager Cinna.

An overeager Cinna who, last CJ checked, had been living with Rosemary in St. Louis while temping as a receptionist and taking night classes in… something. "Totally pimpin'," his baby sister agreed. She crossed her arms and surveyed the room. "Who's in charge here? They still hiring?"

Holy hell. He was too old to work with his baby sister in a bar. But the thought wasn't as unappealing as it should've been.

Actually, it wasn't unappealing at all. He had a fun family. Having family to make him smile and laugh now—that was priceless.

"What brings you all here?" he said.

Cori, who wore her personality like Cinna but her hair like Pepper, grinned the famous Blue grin at him. "We're here to cheer you on."

"Is that our code word for heckling?" Margie—a redhead who could've been Basil's twin except for the eleven years between them—didn't twitch a single eyebrow. Cori and Margie bookended him in birth order, and he was all but certain they'd been the two who had ultimately driven Basil to seminary.

"Heckling, support, it's all the same," Pepper said.

She'd given notice at her job and was staying at the rectory while she looked for a house and filled in at Bliss Bridal until the purchase paperwork went through.

She was also being stubbornly tight-lipped about it.

Because she didn't want to bore him with the details or remind him of what he didn't have the marbles to fight for, she said.

"You all know the Games are next weekend, right?" CJ said.

"We've taken time off our respective lives to spend some quality time in preparation for the heckling," Margie said.

"Your skin's gotten a little thin," Cori added. Margie nodded. "Think of us as your coaches."

Huck grunted. "You gonna stand there gossiping, or you all gonna order something to drink?"

"Think we're out of Kool-Aid," CJ said to the group, "but I might be able to dig up some milk and cookies."

"We're all legal to drink, you dingbat," Cinna said.

Margie lifted an insufferable eyebrow. "I believe he was attempting to incite hilarity with an implied question of our maturity."

"Didn't work," Cinna said. "What else you got?" "A headache," he offered.

Basil blew out a Holy Constipated Breath. "Our female siblings are correct. If two minutes with them gives you a headache, you're in need of training." He looked down at the four girls and shuddered, then took a seat at the bar. "Double shot of vodka, please."

Pepper introduced the rest of the family to Lindsey, who politely but firmly informed them that she was working. And then let her shoulders relax when they backed up to take seats at the bar instead.

He set his siblings up with a round of drinks, half-listening to their idle chatter while he and Jeremy finished prepping the bar to open for the real lunch crowd. Sage was looking at buying her first house. Rosemary's oldest hit a home run in her softball game last weekend. Ginger's husband finally got snipped.

All the good stuff.

"All signs would indicate whoever picked May second should receive the pool," Margie said.

CJ nearly dropped a tray of glasses.

Pepper visibly choked. Lindsey looked up from her books, first to CJ, then to his sisters. He was going to kill Cinna and Margie.

"Did they—" Lindsey shook her head. "Never mind. Don't want to know." She motioned to Huck.

"I'm free?" he said.

She nodded. "As the day you were born."

"So I can sell this heap of sticks and retire to Tahiti and she don't get any of it?" "As soon as she's married."

"Hot damn!" He poured himself another glass of champagne and slammed it like it was tequila. "Hear that, boys? I'm putting this place up on the auction block soon as that ol' hag has a new ring on her gnarled fingers."

Jeremy frowned.

"Thought she would've been a looker, Huck," CJ said. "I heard what you were singing about marrying ugly girls if you want to be happy. And we all know you weren't happy."

"Oh, she's a looker," Lindsey said. "This one won the first Miss Junior Bridesmaid pageant. Huck, unfortunately, sees her through alimony goggles."

"See her for what she is," Huck said. "And I ain't telling her new husband anything about it."

Jeremy's frown was growing more menacing by the second. "How's that all work out? You're getting to sell because of her getting married?" Huck pointed to Lindsey. "Tell him. Go on."

Lindsey slid the files away. "Long story short," she said, "with his second wife remarrying, his various prenups and divorce settlements have now played out in a fashion that entitles him to sell the bar and keep all the profits to himself."

Those weren't just thunderclouds forming on Jeremy's face. It was a hurricane. "Who you think you're gonna sell to?" he said.

"Hell if I know," Huck said. "But I got a feeling one or two of them minor league guys will snatch this place up quick."

"Unless one or two of your current employees made you an offer first?" Lindsey said. She was still shuffling papers, still calm and cool and indifferent as one would expect of a divorce lawyer, but CJ knew better.

She was nudging fate.

His sisters had stopped their yammering, and each of them wore her own particular brand of thoughtfulness. Margie's matched Basil's constipated look, Cori did a head-tilt, Pepper went quiet but alert, and Cinna chuckled with unrestrained glee. "You still got that big retirement fund you were working on, old man?" she asked CJ.

"Shut it, Cinna," he growled.

Not one of his finer comebacks. But his head was spinning too fast over the idea of settling—of owning a bar, of owning Suckers—for him to effectively deflect his sisters' attention.

What scared him the most was how much settling in Bliss didn't scare him.

Should've terrified him down to his toenails. Wasn't anything exciting in Bliss. A golf course, a couple minor league teams, a bus to Chicago. No scuba. No BASE jumping. No skiing.

"Don't have much capital," Jeremy said, "but I got the heart, man. Don't want to work for a bunch of jocks."

CJ's chest prickled. His foot bounced. He'd seen Huck's books. The guy wasn't talking about running away to Tahiti because Suckers wasn't profitable. He was taking off for Tahiti because he was old and tired of working and wanted someone else to wait on him.

Once in a lifetime business opportunity here.

If Huck were selling because Suckers wasn't profitable, this would be an easy decision. CJ still had plenty of old accountant left in him.

He also had the part that broke out in hives at the thought of dipping into retirement funds to buy a bar.

"You should do it," Cinna said. "I'll be your manager. Fun job, right?"

"We could do cross-promotions with the boutique," Pepper said. "Buy a dress from me, get a free round for the bachelor party from you."

"Mathematically speaking, that gives CJ no benefit," Margie said.

"And he needs some financial benefit," Cori agreed. "Unless you offer a free round for the bachelorette party instead. Then he's getting some benefits, if you know what I mean."

"I believe it was previously decided that he received his benefits on May second," Margie drawled.

Basil waved his shot glass at CJ.

"Tarra totally won the pool," Cinna said. "But we don't have to tell her. She always wins. CJ, you think you could try to get laid again?"

"First thing we could do is ban them," Jeremy said, hooking a thumb toward CJ's sisters.

Lindsey slung her bag over her shoulder. "You all have a pleasant afternoon. I have marriages to correct." She glanced at Huck. "Next time you make me clear my schedule for an emergency, make sure it's an emergency."

"Next time, I'm flying you to Tahiti," Huck said. He saluted her with his champagne flute, then danced back to the kitchen, singing his freedom songs.

Jeremy leaned a hip into the bar and stared at CJ. "Think it over. We make a good team." Yeah, they did.

But he'd made a good team with other people in other places. Places without ridiculous rules about who could cavort with whom, without antiquated royalty structures based around marital status. Places without complications, places that didn't require leaps of faith or facing his demons or underestimating Queen Generals.

Places that weren't as colorful.

Places that didn't have sharp-tongued women with wounded eyes and little boys who believed in the power of stuffed dinosaurs.

The door shut behind Lindsey.

Bliss had grown on him. Owning Suckers? Not a bad proposition.

Except when the Games were over next week, the real draw in Bliss wouldn't be around much longer.

She'd be moving on. Starting over. Having a new life adventure.

And the fact that he was thinking about Natalie in conjunction with his future meant he'd been here too long. He'd gotten too comfortable.

He'd gotten delusional.

He wasn't what she needed. She'd made that abundantly clear. Because even if it had been his fault Marilyn made her choose, she hadn't chosen him.

And that still hurt.

He could hear his sisters holding their breaths.

Hurt to shake his head. He did like this place. But—"Can't, dude. Not sticking around in Bliss."

He recognized the disappointment and sadness in his siblings' faces, because he felt it too.

He'd miss them. All of them. Even Basil.

"But I'll be back for the holidays," he said.

For the first time in four years, he couldn't imagine being anywhere else.

* * *

After a crazy, did-I-remember-to-put-my-pants-on kind of Friday, Saturday morning was remarkably slow. Every wedding venue was booked, the hotels and bed and breakfasts overflowed with wedding parties and guests, reservations for a round of golf at the Rose and Dove were going for twice their normal rate, the paddleboats had been released on Harmony Lake, and the scent of love was in the air. The Aisle itself was packed, but not the stores on it, because everyone was gathered outside to watch the Bridal March, the parade that launched Knot Fest week. More people came in asking to use the bathroom than to browse the dresses, though there would be a massive influx once the parade was over.

Lindsey had used vacation time to help watch Noah so Dad could help Natalie man the store the last two weeks. They'd been booked since the cupcake incident, and Natalie had even been able to hire more help.

Dad had ducked out an hour or so ago to join Marilyn before the parade. Natalie still wasn't happy about it, but every time she expressed the slightest bit of displeasure, Dad had insisted that friendship and forgiveness were the two strongest weapons a man had in his arsenal.

Natalie didn't entirely agree, but since he'd been back, he'd seen Marilyn a handful of times—she was too busy with Knot Fest to see him much more—and every time he saw her, he came back happy. He didn't get misty-eyed and sad talking about the future or the past or the shop. He was excited about something other than spending time with Noah or at his cabin. She'd heard him whistling while making coffee this morning.

Didn't mean Natalie was ready to see him with Marilyn firsthand though. The prospect that Dad would get hurt—by the Queen General, no less—had put more cramps in Natalie's gut. The sale of the shop wasn't final yet, and Natalie didn't trust that Marilyn wouldn't pull something still. Lindsey might've been able to overlook all the injustices the QG had piled on her since she'd come home a divorce lawyer, but Natalie was still learning how to be that big of a person.

She wasn't sure she had it in her.

So she'd asked Gabby if she wanted to march in the parade, and when Gabby said no, Natalie had scheduled her final dress fitting for this morning. Their wedding was still two weeks away, but Natalie wanted all her projects cleared up long before the Games were over so she could mourn her past and look to her future without distraction.

"I'll pay you back for this one day," Gabby said while they settled into one of the fitting rooms.

Natalie closed and locked the door. "No need. It was an honor to make it. Just promise to never have reason to burn it, okay?"

She had enjoyed making the dress. If she hadn't gotten divorced—no. No, she was done with if she hadn't. She had, and now she had the chance to start a new future.

Gabby stripped down to her underwear, then answered Natalie's questions about their small ceremony and reception and honeymoon while she changed into the right undergarments and, finally, the dress.

"Can I ask you something?" Gabby said while Natalie fussed with the row of pearl buttons up the back.

"Sure."

"What happened between you and CJ? He's been moping around Suckers like a lost puppy dog."

Natalie's fingers stilled. They weren't entirely alone in the shop. Someone could overhear.

"Who said anything happened between us?" She'd read every blog on the Knot Fest Web site, followed every article in the Bliss Times about CJ—along with the few interviews he'd given to the Chicago papers—and nowhere had she picked up hints that he was anything less than perfectly devoted to Serena's memory while being Kimmie's pretend husband, or that he'd been caught sneaking around with Bliss's most notorious divorcée.

Gabby shot a look toward the open air over the door, then back at Natalie. "I know he took you home from Suckers that night," she whispered. "Jeremy said you both looked really happy. And then all that time he spent with your son. Then—nothing. Except for sad CJ. He's a great guy."

He was more than a great guy. And he would never be Natalie's, because she'd screwed it Pushed too hard for something that wouldn't make her happy for the rest of her life. Picked the wrong battle.

She shouldn't have asked him to stay in the Games after Marilyn's threats.

Nat did Gabby's last button, then reached for the veil. "Quit squirming. Almost done." "Was it something he did?"

"It's complicated. We just—I don't do well in relationships." She set the veil on Gabby's head and pinned it in place. "There. Here, turn around, then we'll take you out in front of the big mirrors.

Gabby peeked in the small full-length mirror behind her and gasped.

Her skin was pale against the eggshell color of the vintage-cut gown and fabric flower crown of her veil, and her eyes stood out big and bright. Her arms glowed beneath the flowery lace. But Gabby's chin trembled, her forehead creased, and her eyes went red and leaky.

Natalie's heart flopped. She'd ruined the dress. She'd ruined Gabby's wedding.

"Here." She flung the door open. "It'll look better out in this light."

Gabby didn't move. She stared at her reflection, eyes crinkling harder and lips pouting wider and wobblier. Voices carried into the dressing room, but Natalie couldn't understand them over the roar of panic in her ears.

Gabby turned abruptly and tackled Natalie with a hug that smelled like satin and itched like lace.

"Thank you," Gabby sobbed. "It's perfect."

Air rushed back into Natalie's lungs.

"Sorry," Gabby sniffled. "It's just so—I—It's like Nana's here again." "You—you like it?"

Gabby choked on another sob. "I love it." She pulled back, forehead still creased, dress in danger of the same. "Sorry. I know. I'm an ugly crier."

Natalie blinked, still catching that relieved breath.

She caught sight of three women outside the dressing room. Pepper, and two others who were obviously her sisters. All three staring at Gabby with jealousy-colored wonder. The hallmarks of a crowd admiring a bride and her perfect dress.

"I owe you so much more than I can ever repay." Gabby's words were wet and cracked and sincere. "Thank you. Thank you so much."

Natalie felt a little choked too, but she couldn't tell if it was happiness that Gabby loved the dress, or her own simple jealousy over Gabby's happiness. "My pleasure."

“Can I just look at it for a while longer?” “Absolutely. Here. Come see in the big mirrors.”

Natalie led her to the large, wide panel of mirrors in the corner and let Gabby get a good look from all angles.

Pepper stepped up beside Natalie. “Beautiful,” she said. “That’s the one you’ve been making?”

“Finishing,” Natalie said. “For her grandmother.”

Pepper’s sisters were wandering around the shop. They waved off the two bridal consultants on hand to prep for the post-parade crowd.

“Bliss doesn’t have any original designers, does it?” Pepper said.

A tingle tickled Natalie’s neck. “We have contracts for exclusives with a few designers, and so do Mrs. and La Belle Bridal.”

“But not originals,” Pepper pressed. “Not originals.”

“Girl, we’re gonna put you to work.”

How she wished. Someday. But not in Bliss. “That dress was half-designed already. I just had to finish it.”

Pepper stared her down. “I heard about your design degree. And I’ve seen Noah’s dinosaurs’ dresses.”

“You don’t own this place yet,” Natalie said. “And even when you do, you won’t be bossing me around.”

One of her sisters—the redhead—snickered. “I was under the impression you’d made Pepper’s acquaintance before,” she said, sounding strangely like CJ’s impersonation of his oldest brother.

“Margie?” Natalie said without thinking.

Pepper’s grin spread slowly. “Impressive.” She jerked her head toward their other sister. “Which one’s that?”

Cori. Short for Coriander, though Natalie wasn’t supposed to know that part. Brown hair, looked a lot like Pepper. They both favored their dad, CJ had said.

And they both hated being teased with one particular wrong spice name. "Nutmeg?" Pepper and Margie both laughed. Cori didn't. "I'm gonna kill him."

But the shop girls were watching them, and so was Gabby now, and Natalie didn't want any more attention about how well she knew CJ. "Pepper told me to say that."

Pepper gave her a look that suggested Natalie was in for it. "Yep," she said. "All me." As if it mattered. Natalie would never see CJ again. He was done with her. "Gabby, whenever you're ready, we'll get your dress hung back up. I'll make sure it's pressed before your wedding."

And she went back to the business of running her mother's shop for a few more days. She'd get over CJ.

Eventually.

In the meantime, she had a new life to create.

Chapter 17

CJ wasn't ready when Arthur picked him up Friday afternoon to check in for the Games.

Physically, yes.

Emotionally, he was as big a mess as his sisters during their high school years. He'd signed up to honor Serena. Fulfill a promise. Forgive himself.

Funny thing was, since Fi had given him permission to move on, he felt like he'd already done all three.

"All this buildup, and it'll be over by ten o'clock tomorrow night," Arthur mused. He navigated the Jeep through the back roads, avoiding Harmony Lake and The Aisle and the crowds that had taken over Bliss this week.

"You nervous?" CJ asked. His knee was bouncing as hard as his heart, and he couldn't help feeling that his life was tilted on the wrong axis.

"I'm playing to honor and remember my wife," Arthur said. "After thirty-four years of being a good husband, this is nothing to be nervous about."

And there was the big difference between them.

They arrived ten minutes early at the back door of Heaven's Bakery to pick up the Queen General and her daughter. CJ and Arthur both climbed out of the Jeep, and Arthur glanced toward Bliss Bridal.

Soon enough it would be Pepper's. That was wrong.

Everything was wrong. Even the scent of cake was wrong. Cold sweat simmered beneath CJ's skin. This wasn't how he wanted to play these Games.

Arthur knocked on the bakery door. It flung open, and wrong was suddenly too weak of a word.

The kitchen was in pandemonium. Two of the bakers' assistants were crying, a third appeared to be hyperventilating. Pink frosting splattered the walls, smoke drifted up from the industrial-sized mixer in the corner, and in the middle of the chaos, Marilyn and another girl leaned over Kimmie on the floor.

CJ's lungs froze.

He'd killed another one.

"It was the fortune cookie," Kimmie said.

His breath wheezed out. He steadied himself against the door frame. Kimmie was okay. She was okay.

"It said a lack of prioritization would land me on my rump," she said. "I should've listened."

"Hold still," the QG commanded. Kimmie complied with a whimper.

"Marilyn?" Arthur said. "What happened?"

"A series of unfortunate incidents," she said. Dryly. As if she had a sense of humor. "Kimberly requires medical attention."

"It's just a little flesh wound," Kimmie said.

"She hasn't slept in three days," the older lady who'd opened the door whispered to CJ. "Somebody forgot to put the shield up on the mixer, and poor Kimmie slipped on the frosting and bonked herself in the head with her icing spatula. Some of it got in the electrical outlet and shorted everything."

Marilyn stood and issued orders to her staff, things about contingency plans and Cake Readiness Condition Four. She clapped her hands, and the motion in the room went from disorganized panic to smoothly coordinated purpose, despite the two girls still crying.

"Holy shit," CJ muttered.

Arthur gaped at the scene, some fear leaking into the admiration in his eyes.

One of the younger girls helped Kimmie up. She clutched a bloody rag to her ear. CJ jumped forward, but Marilyn held up a hand.

"Gentlemen, by the power vested in me by me, it is my extreme displeasure to announce to you that Kimberly will be unable to compete in the Games."

Something akin to relief prickled CJ's skin.

If Kimmie couldn't play, neither could he. A guy couldn't play in the Games without a wife, stand-in or real.

"I'm so sorry," Kimmie said. She winced and readjusted the rag. "I'm not a klutz. I'm not."

"She is not." Marilyn's eye twitched. "Usually."

"It's okay." CJ took another step into the kitchen. Marilyn stopped him with the death eye.

He held a hand out to Kimmie. "C'mon. I'll get you to the ER."

"One of the girls will deliver her to the hospital," Marilyn said. "We practice drills for this kind of thing. Now, we need to find you a stand-in for your stand-in wife."

Was she out of her ever-loving mind?

Kimmie was bleeding from a head wound, but keeping CJ in the Games was more important?

"What's wrong with you?" CJ said.

Arthur cleared his throat, but the QG donned the full force of both the queenly and the General parts of her personality and glared at CJ—God, he missed Natalie—with all the power that came with her title. "Kimberly has a simple laceration requiring stitches, which the emergency room is fully equipped to handle. The Games must go on."

"You okay, Kimmie?" Arthur said.

She nodded. "Yeah. Ellie will take me to the hospital." She gave CJ a sorry look. "You should go. See if you can get a new wife."

"Kimmie—"

"Stitches are a hazard of the job. Well, that and frosting in unfortunate places." She and her companion stepped toward the back door. "You're not playing for me, CJ."

Even Marilyn didn't correct that.

"Go on," Kimmie said. "Go find a wife."

The girl helping her nodded. "Kimmie's in good hands."

"They're all well-trained," Marilyn said. "Kimberly, call us from the hospital."

When Arthur stepped aside so Kimmie and Ellie could pass, CJ did too. Arthur was a smart man. If he trusted Kimmie's judgment, CJ would do the same.

Wasn't sure what it all meant about the Games for him.

But his heart had an idea. And his world was shifting back toward the right axis.

Marilyn dusted her hands of imaginary flour. Despite the carnage throughout her bakery kitchen, she was still spotless. "Now then. Let's find you a wife." She peered around the room, at all of her assistants mixing and frosting and washing and doing God only knew what. Marilyn's frown grew almost as dark as Jeremy's had been at Suckers every day this week. "Unfortunately," she said, "I am unable to spare any more of my assistants."

He didn't want one of her assistants. He wanted— "Natalie's available," Arthur said.

Natalie.

He wanted Natalie.

He cut a glance at the QG. She looked at Arthur. Cleared her throat. Lifted her chin. Arthur tilted a brow at her.

"If that is his wish," Marilyn said.

Huh. CJ would've thought she'd morph into a human praying mantis and eat Arthur whole for that suggestion.

Arthur gave Marilyn an approving nod. And CJ realized he was a moron.

He didn't need some Queen General's stamp of approval on his choice of stand-in brides.

He could've taken Basil out there with him if he damn well wanted to.

But CJ wanted Natalie.

He walked out of Heaven's Bakery. Turned left. Strolled one shop down. Banged on the door.

When it didn't open fast enough, he let himself in. Natalie was talking to someone—he could hear her.

And he could smell her, that lingering bit of oranges and baby shampoo hanging in the air, as if she'd just walked out of the kitchenette and back to the office.

He followed the music of her voice. She sat ramrod straight on her metal folding chair, phone to her ear, frown on her lips, but—unlike the last time he'd seen her—eyes clear, bright, and well-rested.

His heart stirred again.

She was beautiful. Strong, determined, and unstoppable. Just how he liked 'em.

She stopped mid-sentence, leaving something about a shipment of dresses dangling in the air, and stared at him as though he were a mirage.

"Kimmie's on the DL," he said.

She blinked, her brows furrowing briefly before she cleared her face of all emotion. "I'll call you back," she said into the phone. She disconnected, then gave him a once-over. "DL?"

"Disabled List. She's on her way to the hospital for stitches. You're up. Say no, and I'll hog-tie you, toss you in your father's car, and drag you to the Games anyway. So, are you going to be my partner the nice way, or are you going to be a pain in the ass about it?"

"That's a dime," she said. "Nickel."

"Quarter, if you keep arguing."

Damn, he'd missed her. "Easy way or hard way, Nat. I'll give you to the count of three to decide."

"Fine way to start a fake marriage." Her pulse fluttered in her neck as fast as his blood flew through his veins.

"One..."

She leaned back in the chair and gave him a do it look. "Two..."

Her head shifted. Left. Then right. Just enough to broadcast that she didn't believe him. "Three."

He stepped forward.

"Are you still playing for Serena?" she said.

He was playing for himself. For Serena's memory, for his freedom, for his future. "That depends," he said. "Are you?"

He didn't give her a chance to respond. Instead, he scooped her up, tossed her over his shoulder, called toward the shop floor that Natalie was leaving for the day, then carried her out the door.

He couldn't think of a better way to start his last few days in Bliss.

* * *

The sunflowers were perfect.

Natalie couldn't say whether anything else was perfect about today, but the sunflowers were. And here, in the middle of the sunflower maze, with nothing but the blue sky and pretty yellow flowers standing tall around her while she waited for CJ to find her and take her back to the stadium for the opening ceremonies of the Golden Husband Games, she had her first chance to breathe since he'd banged on the back door of Bliss Bridal.

First he'd tossed her in the back of Dad's Jeep, then climbed in beside her. Then he and Dad had talked baseball and other random baloney the whole drive.

At the stadium, CJ had explained to Duke and Elsie why Natalie was subbing for Kimmie. He'd gotten them checked in, then handed Natalie her team T-shirt. The men were whisked away to their bus while the women were shown to theirs. Keys and phones were surrendered—though Natalie held onto hers until Lindsey texted back that she'd keep Noah tonight.

Nat had gotten a couple of weird looks on the bus, but more, she'd gotten smiles.

Encouragement.

Welcome.

After that, she'd made a point to talk to everyone. Everyone.

Including Marilyn.

What more could the Queen General do to her? Dad was closing on the sale of the shop next week, and he insisted that Marilyn had agreed to not interfere. Pepper had offered to let Natalie stay on, which Nat appreciated, but once Knot Fest was over, she had an interview in Willow Glen.

And a few patches to put on the iron case around her heart.

Because CJ's little Neanderthal act, his staking a claim and dragging her out here, had blown a few bits in the protective covering she'd been welding around her poor little organ.

Someday she'd take the time to process it all.

But not today. Because today, she had to put on a show for the Games.

She blinked up at the blue sky again, and she could almost feel her mother's smile.

Warmth spread in her heart.

Mom would've been glad Natalie was here. For Nat's sake.

And, Natalie was surprised to realize, she was okay with that. CJ had been right. She had made the Games about herself. About doing in private what she'd failed to do in public. But now she had her chance to say good-bye.

And hopefully not make a fool of herself this time around.

She'd miss this when she was gone. Knot Fest, the Games, The Aisle. When she left Bliss, she'd leave a part of herself behind.

Gilbert lumbered around the corner to Natalie's left. He was alone, which meant he was still looking for Vi.

He squinted at Nat in surprise, which she barely noticed for trying not to gawk at his violet T-shirt emblazoned with I'm the Dove in huge green letters.

She'd seen Vi in the complementary shirt—I'm the Rose—and she still couldn't help staring. Nor did she have the right to stare, given the shirt she'd been ordered to change into. Damn Neanderthal.

"What's your clue?" Gilbert said.

Natalie shook herself. "If you've found her, go on, if you're still looking, go back," she recited for the fifteenth time. All twenty-eight of the wives were positioned inside the maze with clues to help the husbands get through, and hers had to be useless since she was supposed to say it regardless of which direction the men came from. So far they'd all come from Gilbert's direction, though, so maybe there was logic to it.

The only people who knew for sure were the farmer who'd cut the maze and the dozen cameramen situated on platforms around the field, live-streaming the event to the stadium for a crowd waiting to cheer them on.

Gilbert grunted. He moseyed back the way he'd come, and Natalie went back to pretending she didn't know her every move was being videotaped.

"Natalie?" an achingly familiar voice said softly from beyond a row of sunflowers. She stiffened, but she didn't reply.

It was against the rules to say anything other than her clue until her "husband" found her. "Hope you're staying out of the itchweed this time," he said.

Half of her wanted to deck him. Mr. Hotshot Know-It-All.

But the other half wanted to laugh. She could hear the teasing grin in his voice, and she knew all the way through her soul that he wasn't trying to hurt her.

But she would still hurt. Tonight, she got to pretend she was his. Tomorrow he'd be Kimmie's, and Tuesday—

Tuesday, he had a flight out of Bliss.

Pepper hadn't denied it when someone mentioned it at the boutique the other day. So it had to be true. His sister would've known otherwise, and his sister had looked so exasperated with him, he had to be leaving.

CJ didn't say anything else, and Natalie went back to alternating between watching a few fluffy clouds drift by and admiring the sunflowers. She fingered a leaf on the nearest plant. Her pink nails caught her eye.

When Lindsey and Noah had dropped by the boutique with lunch this afternoon, Lindsey had bullied Nat into taking an hour off to get a manicure and pedicure. To give her an extra boost before the big days, Lindsey had said.

Natalie had assumed she meant the last big days at Bliss Bridal. But could she have known—Nat shook her head. She was getting crazy thoughts, and they didn't matter. Kimmie would be back tomorrow, and life would go on as it was supposed to.

Still, Nat might take a few hours to look at the video footage of today.

See if the maze was cut to look like the wedding cake Mom had envisioned. Lindsey had an ex-boyfriend at one of the news stations. He'd get them a copy.

CJ stepped into view around the corner to her right. His eyes met hers, the green a perfect match for the sunflower leaves, and an honest, happy smile lit his face. "Hey, temporary wife. Missed you."

He walked down the path, his jeans rustling, his arms loose. He wore an American flag–inspired T-shirt with Team CJ and Kimmie—Dream It, Do It emblazoned across the front. The red and blue striped cotton fabric stretched from one of his shoulders to the other, with a lot of solid chest underneath.

And he had a singular concentration on her, as if he meant what he'd said. He'd missed her.

She tried to swallow, but her tongue had gone sandy and rusty at the same time.

His smile took on a knowing bent, still hypnotic as ever. He stopped just within arm's reach. "Miss me too?"

God, yes. She swallowed hard. She had to keep it together. "My clue is that you're supposed to keep going once you've found me."

His eyes narrowed. Thoughtfully, as though he were looking for the words she wanted to say instead.

"Keep going in the maze?" he said slowly. "Or keep going somewhere else?"

The man had an evil streak. "The maze," she said firmly. Helpfully. Like a dutiful daughter of Bliss.

"Because there are a few places I'd like to go with you." Her stomach tightened. So did a few areas farther south.

She pointed left. "So we should probably go that way." He crossed his arms. Lifted a brow.

There she went, being bossy again. "Unless you'd prefer to lead. I can let you lead." "Good," he said. "Because first, we're going to do this."

He stepped forward. "I—" she croaked, but his hands settled on her waist, and she instinctively copied his movements to hook her fingers through his belt loops, and suddenly he was brushing a soft kiss against the corner of her lips.

She recoiled.

Not because she didn't want to kiss him.

But because she hadn't earned this. Being here today. At Mom's last Husband Games.

Kissing a guy she couldn't keep.

It wasn't right.

"Smile, beautiful," he murmured. "Cameras are watching."

It took a minute for the message to break through the haze of feelings coloring her world.

But when it did, it killed every happy thought she'd had about him in the last hour.

"You ass—jerk." She shoved him away, and considered adding a kick to the shin for good measure.

He laughed.

Laughed.

Her temper spiked, but he slipped an arm around her and pressed a friendly kiss to her hair. "That's the Natalie I was looking for. I missed you. What say we get out of this maze? Heard a rumor we might have a few minutes alone on the ride back to the stadium. We could make out."

There went her mouth doing the not-working-right thing again. All because his mouth went and did the saying-all-the-right-things thing again.

"So, temporary wife, which way's out?"

She looked at him, then in front of her, then behind, her fury and confusion and doubts colliding. "I don't know."

He flashed her another classic CJ grin. "Then let's go figure it out." He twisted back to face the path, linked his fingers through hers, and pulled her along.

And she went, because he was holding her hand, and he was treating her to those wonderful, terrible smiles he used so well, and even if he was pushing her buttons, he was here.

He dragged her along, cracking jokes and teasing her. Five turns later, they stumbled across Marilyn.

She was squatting, pushing frantically at the straw and dirt. Natalie and CJ stopped.

Marilyn looked up, then stood. Bits of straw stuck in her hair and to her black pants, dirt was streaked across her white Going for Gold T-shirt, and instead of showing off her queenly or General sides, she wore a human expression with something akin to grief dragging at her eyes. "Head north, and you'll soon be back south," she said.

She touched her ear, then did a weak impersonation of her normal nod of dismissal. Her diamond earring was missing.

CJ was squinting at her. He started to turn around—of course he knew which direction north was—but Natalie stopped him. "Did you lose it here?" she asked Marilyn.

Marilyn didn't speak. But she gave a single nod. Her eyes shone. She blinked twice, and they went back to normal. She dropped back to the ground, searching in the straw.

Natalie looked up at CJ. She could hardly believe what she was about to do, but maybe Dad was right. And she knew her mother would approve.

The earrings were obviously special.

Natalie stepped closer to Marilyn. She squatted a few feet away. "Have you looked here yet?"

The shine came back in Marilyn's eye. She shook her head.

CJ joined them, and all three of them combed the ground, looking for the earring.

There were three more events tomorrow. Natalie's gut tightened. He was on his own for the last two. If he had any chance of winning, he needed to do well in the sunflower field. She needed to not slow him down.

But maybe—just maybe—life was about more than the Games. For all of them.

* * *

CJ had been right the first time he asked Natalie to be his partner. Would've preferred it hadn't taken Kimmie needing stitches, but Natalie was with him now.

They'd finished the sunflower maze and they were sitting onstage in front of a packed stadium, listening to the roar of a crowd the likes of which he hadn't heard since the last time the Cubs made the play-offs. Highlights of the maze race flashed on a giant screen behind them. Sunset was coming on, and in the soft light, with Kimmie's T-shirt hanging too wide on her shoulders, Natalie glowed.

He'd been surprised when she stopped to help Marilyn. She was one hell of a woman, not only stopping to help her biggest enemy, but then doing the impossible in finding the diamond amidst all that straw. But after she'd pulled that earring out of the ground, she'd looked at him, told him to haul ass, and then she'd sassed him the rest of the way through the maze and all the way back to the stadium. He'd been certain she was enjoying herself. But now, she was near mute.

He got it. Being semi-alone in a freaking amazing sunflower maze was worlds away from sitting on a stage before over five thousand people, playing husband to a woman who drove him crazy—good crazy and bad crazy—while he was supposed to be here honoring Serena.

He squeezed Nat's hand. She jumped.

"Thanks," he said. "Couldn't do this without you."

"You're you. You could've done this with or without anyone. But thank you for asking me. Again."

"Ladies and gentlemen," an irritating female voice boomed throughout the stadium. The sound was so loud, CJ's teeth rattled. "Welcome to the Golden Husband Games."

The crowd roared. Natalie half-smiled at CJ, then turned her attention to the woman who had taken her mother's place.

The crowd's cheers grew. So did Natalie's half-smile. Thinking about what her mother would've thought about the crowd, he'd bet. She looked around the stadium, at all the people, at the couples around them, then back at CJ. "Kimmie will enjoy this tomorrow," she said.

He didn't bother correcting her misconception. She'd fight him about it, and this was a talk best had in private.

Fine with him.

He didn't want her soft and easy. He had just a few more days with her, and he wanted her for her. Getting an excuse to visit her tonight—all the better.

CJ smiled, and Natalie turned back to watch Elsie introduce the couples. The Games had just begun.

* * *

Natalie's feet ached, her head pounded, and when she caught herself about to snarl at Dad over a SpaghettiOs splatter on the counter she'd just wiped down, she grabbed the bottle of red wine Pepper had slipped her while she was trying to escape the post-opening-events festivities, and she took herself out onto the swing on the back porch.

She hadn't bothered with a cup, and she didn't know enough about red wine to know if she were guzzling a ten-dollar or a fifty-dollar bottle. She did, however, appreciate the warm glow the first two gulps had given her belly.

If only the glow would spread faster. "Nat?"

"Yeah?"

"I'm going to bed." Dad's loafers shuffled behind her. He touched her shoulder. "Real proud of you, hon."

The warmth in her belly spread to her lungs. "You too, old man," she said. "Fourth place is nothing to sneeze at." Despite stopping to search for the earring, CJ had taken second tonight.

"I meant for all your hard work." Dad ruffled her hair, then kissed it. "Marilyn's earrings?" he added. "They were the last present her husband gave her before he died. Meant a lot to her." He stepped back. "Don't stay up late. Long day tomorrow."

No kidding. She'd called Kimmie, who insisted she was fine. So Natalie would be glued to the public access channel tomorrow, watching CJ and Kimmie and Dad and Marilyn play Mom's last Games.

She wasn't strong enough to watch in person. "Night, Dad."

He shuffled back to the door. Natalie dropped her head back and closed her eyes. He was right. She needed to get to bed too.

Her swing shifted beneath her as if a boulder had suddenly sat down on the opposite end.

She snapped upright and gaped like an idiot at her Highland warrior Neanderthal.

"Your dad said you were out here," CJ said before she could speak. He stretched out, his arm draping across the back of the swing, his fingers brushing the skin above her tank top. He nodded at the bottle. "Any chance you're sharing that?"

She wordlessly handed it over.

He put the bottle to his lips—the same lips that had kissed her no fewer than three times at various points this evening—tipped it back, and took a long swallow.

Then he pulled back and gave a loud shudder. "That's disgusting."

She felt the pull in her cheeks, a helpless desire to smile growing despite the uneven fluttering of her pulse.

"Jeez, who'd you piss off?" He held the bottle for inspection in the low light. "Somebody calls this wine?"

Now her diaphragm was getting into it, pushing her to give in. To laugh. "It's from your sister."

"Eleven of 'em, and not a one has a bit of taste. You saw Ginger's husband tonight, right? The guy leaves the toilet seat up. Can you imagine?"

She'd seen his whole family tonight. All of them, every one of his sisters, his three brothers-in-law, his seven nieces, his grandma, Father Basil again, his parents. His in-laws.

"And that's why I need the alcohol," she said, more to herself than to him.

He laughed, and she gave in and smiled back. Before CJ, she hadn't ever been funny. It was surprisingly enjoyable.

"So, tomorrow," CJ said. "I'll pick you up at eight."

She eyed the bottle. One gulp couldn't affect a person that fast. "Pick me up? Don't you have to be at the reception at seven?"

He pushed the swing into motion. “In the morning.” She choked on the question, For what?

Because for what was suddenly obvious. She shook her head. She shook her head, and she couldn’t stop. “Kimmie’s fine. She’s back. You don’t need me anymore.” But she was also giving herself a mental beating.

Because she wanted him to want her just as badly as she wanted to not want him when she couldn’t have him. Distance was her best ally.

And he kept stripping her of it.

“I miss being your friend,” he said.

There was a loneliness in his voice, a whisper of a reminder that they could’ve been friends. Real friends. Real lovers. Real—no. No, they never could’ve been more. “Were we friends?”

“We were something.” His thumb brushed her neck. Need pulled her nerves tight, low in her belly. His voice turned husky. “Something good.”

“You’re leaving.” Not something she wanted to think about tonight, but it was her reality.

His thumb drifted higher, his fingers joining in the party at her hairline, and for one beautiful moment, she thought he might correct her.

Tell her he’d stay. Tell her she was worthy of him. Tell her he’d missed Noah too. That he wanted to try.

He tilted her chin up, stared down at her as if he’d heard her thoughts, but needed to see her to know he’d heard right. As if he needed to hear her ask him to stay.

But she couldn’t do it.

If CJ wanted to stay, if he wanted to take a chance with her and Noah, he would say so. And if he didn’t, he wasn’t the man she needed him to be.

Heartbreaking as it was, her reality was that simple.

He touched her cheek. “Get some rest,” he said. “Long day tomorrow. See you at eight.” He pressed a hard kiss to her temple, and then he was gone.

Leaving her alone. As she was apparently supposed to be.

Chapter 18

Nat's stomach was putting a different kind of knot in Knot Fest. As promised, CJ had arrived at 8:00 a.m. to pick her up. He must've sweet-talked someone at the T-shirt shop, because he'd brought new team shirts. Today's were a flattering periwinkle printed with a new logo: The Second Chance Misfits.

If she hadn't been in danger of falling for him before, the shirts would've done her in.

They'd certainly made up for his leaving last night. And for not kissing her.

Every time she thought of kissing him, she thought of this afternoon's Games, and her stomach knotted harder.

This morning's event was about skill and strength. Then came the events about love.

That knowledge may have kept Natalie up half the night.

She and CJ were at the edge of the end zone. The field wasn't large enough to accommodate all twenty-eight couples at once, so the couples were going in three groups. They were in the first.

The high school marching band finished "Chapel of Love," and the last of the couples took their place at the starting line.

It was go time.

Three couples down, Dad was smiling. Nat had heard both him and Marilyn laugh once or twice in the hospitality tent before the festivities officially kicked off this morning.

It was strange to see Marilyn acting human. Even after yesterday, Nat couldn't shake her suspicions and distrust.

Old habits died hard.

Beside her, CJ bounced on his toes. "Ready?" Natalie swallowed and nodded.

On the side of the field at the fifty-yard line, Elsie stepped onto the platform with today's judges—a local news anchor, a Methodist minister from Willow Glen and a nationally syndicated radio talk show host who had recently moved to Bliss.

"Gentlemen," Elsie said into her mic, her voice booming through the stadium, "welcome to the Hubstacle Course."

The packed stands erupted in cheers and hollers. Midway up to the right, a portion of the crowd wearing periwinkle T-shirts waved white foam fingers and signs for the Second Chance Misfits.

"Before you is a series of challenges to test your skill as husbands," Elsie said. "Judging will be not only on your time, but also on your style, and you'll have the opportunity to earn extra points at the stations along the way, as detailed by the instruction sheets you'll find there."

Nat's heart gave a sentimental pang. Mom should've been here.

She'd dreamed up the Hubstacle Course two years ago. One morning, she'd charged into the kitchen wearing a green striped bath towel, her short blonde-gray hair dripping onto her shoulders, and declared, I've got it! The pinnacle strength challenge will be a Hubstacle Course. Points for time and style! Then she'd scurried out of the room with a "Be right back, have to write down a few things" tossed back over her shoulder.

And now the Hubstacle Course was here. In two hours, it would be over. All of Mom's ideas and dreams and hard work, all here, now, without her.

Natalie caught Dad's eye. He smiled, gave a rueful shake of his head, and she knew he was remembering too.

CJ squeezed her hand. "Okay, Nat?"

She nodded. "Thank you," she said softly. She was still afraid she'd do something to embarrass Dad or Mom's memory or CJ, but more, she was so, so grateful to be included today.

CJ swept a gaze around the stadium. "You people are nuts." His lips tipped up, his fingers fidgeted, and determination settled into his features.

He wanted to win.

Natalie smiled. Whom he wanted to win for didn't matter. That he was here, fully committed, excited, was wonderful.

It reminded her of the CJ who had come to Bliss five years ago. The thought that he'd made some peace with his past the last couple of months made her happy for him.

"We'll see you at the other end zone, gentlemen," Elsie said. "On your marks!"

CJ grinned at Natalie. He waved up at his family, eliciting a call of "Go, Princess!" "Which one was that?" Natalie asked.

"Rika."

"Is that a spice?"

"Short for Paprika. Poppy's twin." "Get set!" Elsie said.

More "Yeah, Princess!" cries erupted. "Go!"

CJ grabbed Natalie's hand and dragged her to the ten-yard line. He skidded to a stop at their designated table, grabbed the index card with this station's instructions, then eyeballed their equipment. Coffeemaker, pitcher of water, and canister of Folgers.

"Black?" CJ said to Nat.

He knew how she took her coffee? "Usually. How—"

His grin cut her off. "Ninety-eight percent success rate with knowing what will make a woman happy. Remember?"

He made laughing so easy. "Such an ego." "You like it."

She did.

He slid open the basket on the coffeemaker. No filter.

Looked like one or two of the other tables were missing filters as well. CJ plowed ahead.

He grabbed the Folgers, measured out two scoops, closed the basket, and then added the water to the machine and started it.

"I sincerely hope I don't have to drink that," Natalie said.

"I kinda hope you do." He slid her a grin, and she laughed again.

"We should make out while it brews." He settled his hands at her waist. His eyes gleamed with mischief, but there was a hint of uncertainty in them. As if it mattered to him whether or not she wanted to kiss him.

She rested her hands on his chest. "For the judges?" "Sure. For them too."

His shirt was warm, his muscles tight beneath his shirt. She could've kissed him. She could've kissed him so easily. "You want to gross out your sisters?" Nat said.

"You're a pain in the ass."

"That's a dime. And your coffee's not brewing."

"Hell." He released her and bent under the table, then popped back up. "Unplugged. All fixed."

Cameramen wandered around the tables. Duke followed, giving the audience a blow-by-blow of each husband's difficulties.

And the crowd loved it.

By the time CJ's coffee was ready, most of the other couples were already at the next obstacle at the twenty-yard line. CJ poured the coffee cup three-quarters full, then, still holding both the mug and the coffeepot, jerked his head down the field. "Let's see some hustle."

Nat pointed at the coffeepot. "You can't—"

"Sure I can." He grinned. "Rules said carry a full cup to the end. Didn't say I can't take refills."

That was exactly the sort of thinking that had won him the Husband Games five years ago. "Go, Nat."

Together, they raced to their pile of two-by-fours at the twenty-yard line, then backtracked like the other couples, searching for the screws in the grass so CJ could build a free-standing doorframe. The cameras circled. Duke entertained the crowd with his running commentary, and Natalie wished the Hubstacle Course could last forever.

CJ started on the frame when he had enough screws. Natalie kept searching. When she had eight, she darted to deliver them. His drill wrenched out a sickening squeal that ended in an abrupt sputter. He pulled the trigger, but nothing happened. "Huh."

He dropped the battery out, glanced at it, shoved it back in, and pulled the trigger again. Nothing.

"Oh, no," Nat whispered.

"Ye of little faith." He reached into his back pocket and whipped out a multitool, then flipped it open to the screwdriver. "Need six more, Nat. Get back to work."

"Fine way to talk to your wife."

"If you were my wife, I would've slapped your ass too."

She stared at him a beat too long. She did love the feel of his hands on her ass.

"Go get the screws, Natalie." But there was a heat in his eyes that hadn't been there a minute before, and she felt an answering pull low in her belly.

"You dirty talker, you," she murmured.

He clamped a board in place between his thighs and lined up the edge with the last piece of the square frame. "You haven't seen dirty yet."

Nat scampered back to scour the grass for more screws. There wouldn't be dirty talk—not after what was coming next—but she was here to support him, so she'd find the screws.

By the time CJ finished his door frame, most every other couple—including Vi and Gilbert—were at the next obstacle. CJ handed Natalie the coffee mug and pot, and then—

"Ohmigod," Nat squealed.

He hefted her up in his arms, sloshing coffee over both of them. "Style points, right?" He marched her through the doorway, all the way from the twenty-yard line to the thirty-, where he deposited her gently at the edge of the next obstacle.

A temporary floor was laid out, and secondhand couches and recliners and lamps were scattered haphazardly on top of it. CJ plucked the instructions off a torchiere floor lamp. "Put it all in its place," he read. He grinned at Natalie. "'Bout time I get to use these muscles for something."

He hefted her into a chair, and then he went to work.

Three floors down, Dad was heaving against a purple floral recliner while Marilyn pointed to a mark on their portion of the floor. The couple closest to Nat and CJ, a younger couple that had won sometime since the flood, were pushing a pockmarked leather sofa to a strip of yellow tape that roughly matched the couch's length.

CJ heaved and shoved at the furniture on their floor. Natalie couldn't deny her primal satisfaction at watching him go caveman on the furniture.

He did have nice muscles.

And all too soon, they'd done their job. He had moved up to fourth place, behind Dad and Marilyn.

CJ carried the mug and the coffeepot while they raced to their next station at the forty-yard line. When they arrived, Natalie's heart cramped.

Mom was up there in heaven laughing right now. She should've been here though. On the field. Watching. Celebrating.

This obstacle was the reason she'd created the Hubstacle Course.

Another folding table held three glass mason jars full of a brown substance. CJ set down the coffee. "Open these?" he said. "That's it?"

"That's it," Natalie said. He twisted the first lid.

And grunted when it didn't budge.

No doubt, Mom was watching from her cloud in heaven, cackling gleefully at finally disposing of the stash in the attic.

CJ tried the lid again.

And again.

"Natalie," he said between grunts, "where the hell did these things come from?" He twisted and twisted, but nothing gave.

"Grandma Stella," Nat whispered.

CJ stopped. Looked at her. Wiped his forehead. "How"

He shook his head, then whacked the jar on the edge of the table. This time when he twisted, the band came off.

"I think you have to pop the seal too," Natalie said.

He flipped open his multitool and pried the lid off. "Holy mother," he gasped. "What is that?"

Natalie's laughter came from deep, deep inside her.

Around them, other couples were groaning and moaning and shrieking.

But Natalie couldn't stop laughing. Mom would've loved this. "Beets," she gasped. Hands on hips, CJ turned to face her. "How long's Grandma Stella been dead?"

"S-seven y-years." "Jesus."

He grabbed a second jar, whacked it against the table, then twisted. When the lid didn't budge, he yanked his shirt off.

The crowd whooped.

So did a few of Natalie's not-anywhere-near-dormant-anymore bits, despite her uncontrollable laughter.

CJ covered the lid with his shirt and twisted again, and this time, the lid came loose. He held the jar as far away as possible and popped the lid with his pocket knife. "Good God."

"Get it off! Get it off!" Claudia Sweeney shrieked four tables down.

"Gilbert, go get that damn drill," Vi shouted. "We're getting done with this once and for all."

There was laughter, there was chanting, there were cameramen gagging and backing awa from the tables.

This. This was what Mom had envisioned. A new challenge, nothing anyone had seen before, with reactions to rival the best reality television anywhere. They'd go viral on YouTube, get mentioned on Good Morning America, and Bliss's place in history would be re-secured.

She'd done it. Mom had done it.

Natalie's hands shook. Her laughter faded, a thicker, heavier emotion took its place. Her throat clogged and her eyes stung.

Mom had done it. She should've been here to see this. To dance and laugh with Dad. To celebrate her victory. To rule her final Games.

CJ grabbed his last jar. "Where's the hazmat unit?" She didn't answer.

She couldn't. "Nat?" CJ said.

She waved her hands at the jars. "Keep going," she said, but she had to push the words out. "You're crying."

He sounded completely dumbfounded at the thought of a woman crying. He had all those sisters. She couldn't comprehend how he couldn't comprehend a woman crying.

"You're crying," he repeated.

"Oh, my God, what is that?" the young wife at the next table shrieked. Her husband gagged and spilled the congealed, God-only-knew-how-old beets all over the grass.

The crowd went wild. This was Mom's heaven.

She'd done it. And she wasn't here to see it.

"Hell, Nat." CJ pulled her into a hug against his warm, solid body. "They're just beets." "Quit." She shoved his chest, then swiped her eyes. "Win. I—I'm good."

He muttered something that sounded suspiciously like damn women, but he let her go and grabbed his last jar again. "So your cooking skills are inherited?"

It was impossible to pretend to be insulted, and the laughter felt good. "Nobody had the heart to tell her the beets were terrible." "Nobody?"

"She gave them to half our neighbors, and they gave them back to us." Natalie's laughter was born from her soul this time. "Mom couldn't bring herself to throw them away, so she stored them in the attic. Every year, she made Dad buy new jars and wash them so they looked like the jars we'd eaten and saved for her. We lost so much sentimental stuff in the flood, but the damn beets survived."

He grunted into the jar lid, then banged it on the table again. "You people make my family look normal."

A cheer broke through the crowd. A loud, rambunctious, female-voiced chant. "Princess! Princess! Princess!"

"What's that about normal?" Natalie said.

She was being obnoxious and she knew it. But he treated her to one of his charming smiles, and she giggled. Soon, they were both laughing.

The last lid gave way. He popped the seal, deposited the open jar on the table, shrugged his shirt back on—damn it—then grabbed the coffee. "Let's get the hell out of here."

Two couples were ahead of them, three keeping pace, and Dad and Marilyn were right on their heels. The last visible obstacle was at the fifty-yard line. Finish line tape stretched across the end zone, but first, they had to tackle a Christmas tree.

CJ groaned at the pile of Christmas lights on the ground beside the fake tree. Natalie huffed out a laugh. "Memories?"

"Nightmares." He handed over the coffee, then grabbed the tangled string of lights. "Didn't get what you wanted for Christmas?"

"After Basil left for college, I was the designated light stringer. If we had one tree, we had five. Every year."

"So this'll be no problem."

He gave her the dubious eye, but he was already untangling the chaotic mess. He was a natural competitor. But more, he was fun to watch. Engaging.

Hypnotizing.

"You're doing really well," she said.

He ducked his head, but she caught the glimmer of light in his smile. "I'm having fun."

"I'm glad." Glad that the shadows in his eyes were gone, glad that he was able to enjoy himself, glad that she was here with him.

And so very, very sad that this was almost over. The next two events were all on him. He wouldn't need her anymore.

Too soon, they'd untangled the lights. CJ instructed Natalie to stretch the strand out in a straight line on the ground. He picked up the tree, turned it sideways, wrapped the end around the top of the tree, and gave her a completely unfiltered CJ grin at the chant of "Princess! Princess! Princess!" erupting again. Behind him, sprinklers sputtered and erupted past the fifty-yard line.

General cheering overtook the chant. The cameramen covering the tree-lighting from behind darted for cover. Nat's stomach pitched.

The last obstacle.

Her time with CJ was almost over.

"Hope you brought your rain jackets, gentlemen," Duke said over the speakers. "Keeping your wife dry is part of the next challenge."

Dad's tree flickered on, the colored lights tiny pinpricks beneath the bright sky. Another tree lit down the line. Then another on their other side. Three couples, heading into the water.

CJ glanced behind him, then back at Natalie. His next word was drowned by the crowd, but his feelings about the final obstacle were obvious.

Despite knowing she'd end this event soaking wet, despite knowing it was nearly time to let go, Natalie grinned. "That's a dollar."

He shrugged, then rolled the tree down the line of lights Natalie had stretched out.

When he reached her, he straightened, took the plug end from her, and jerked his head back toward the electrical cord. "Haul ass, woman."

She did. Claudia and Wade were in the sprinklers. So were Dad and Marilyn, and the sound of Marilyn shrieking—shrieking—under the spray was music.

She didn't have superhuman water-repelling superpowers. Who knew?

By the time Natalie caught up to CJ, he'd plugged in the tree. The white lights glowed, the crowd hollered, and now they were facing half a football field of water.

CJ cracked his knuckles. "Wife dry, coffee cup full." He handed Natalie the coffee mug and pot.

A fifth couple waded into the sprinklers.

"Strategy," CJ said.

Claudia took a spray across her front and shrieked. The sixth couple moved into the water.

CJ's eyes shifted farther down the field. A brief frown furrowed his forehead, then he held his arm out in gallant fashion. "Natalie, may I have this dance?"

"You're going to love watching me get soaked, aren't you?"

"Oh, yeah." He grinned, guiding her closer to the water. The spray on their right was coming back toward them, the spray on their left headed away.

CJ shifted so he was on her right. "Keep walking straight. Go as fast as you can without spilling."

Another shriek echoed on the field. The crowd roared.

Natalie stepped forward, one eye on the coffee, one eye on the approaching stream of water.

"Keep going, Nat." CJ positioned himself between the water and Natalie. When it hit, he sucked in a sharp breath, but he didn't squeal.

Mist dusted Natalie's bare arms. "Quicker," CJ said. "Keep going straight."

He pivoted behind her and came up on her left. "Little faster, Nat." He gripped her elbow and nudged her to speed up.

To get closer and closer to the finish line. To end her time with him.

The coffee cup was less than half-full, and the pot had enough for maybe only three-quarters of a cup. The more they had at the end, the better, because he wouldn't win the Hubstacle Course based on their time alone. They needed the style and bonus points. "Don't be so bossy. You'll make me spill."

"You've got this. Trust me. Faster." She stepped quicker. Not for herself. For him.

"It's coming back on your right, Nat. Gotta move. Now." She scuttled faster.

"Now this way," he directed.

They zigzagged up the field, Natalie's feet responding to CJ's orders to move faster, turn this way, stop here, go there. Five yards from the end zone, he lifted her over a sprinkler head, and the crowd went nuts. Dad and Marilyn—both soaked—were already across the finish line. So were the younger couple. Vi and Gilbert were halfway back, hollering at each other. Claudia and Wade were right on CJ and Natalie's heels.

But other than the coffee spills, Natalie was barely damp, whereas the other women—Marilyn especially—were looking pretty drippy.

Just before they crossed the line, CJ took the coffeepot and refilled the mug, then he hefted Natalie up in his arms to cross into the end zone. He set her down, a giant grin on his face, everything about him completely sopping wet.

"Way to go, wife," he said.

He handed the coffee mug and pot to Duke for measuring, and right there in the end zone, three feet from her father and Marilyn Elias, CJ kissed Natalie.

Full on the mouth. His fingers tangled in her hair, his body pressed against hers, their breathing in sync.

Perfectly.

As though everything about this moment was meant to be.

CJ pulled back from the kiss, but he took Natalie's hand, twined his fingers through hers, and squeezed.

Vi and Gilbert, the last couple, stumbled into the end zone. Natalie's lungs compressed.

Moment over.

It was time for her real life to begin.

"Gentlemen," Elsie said, her voice booming over the speakers, "your wives will now be taken for fresh clothing. But you will be moving on to begin your next challenge. Duke, lead the men away."

"See you soon," CJ said, that happy, confident, easy smile still lighting the stadium. Nat gripped his hand, pulled him down once more, and pressed a hard kiss to his lips.

"Thank you," she said one last time.

Because he wasn't hers any more.

* * *

A love letter.

As soon as the men had arrived at the husbands-only hospitality tent behind the stands, still soaked, they had been instructed to sit down and write their wives a love letter.

Which they would read. Out loud. In front of thousands of people. And which the Husband Games organizers would then post on the Internet so the whole world could vote on the best love letter.

CJ's clothes had dried in the two hours since he'd finished the Hubstacle Course, but he was sweating like he hadn't sweated since he came to Bliss. He was about to take the stage to read his letter. In front of his in-laws. His family. Natalie and her family. God knew how many strangers.

And he didn't know if he'd written the right letter.

Too late now. Elsie Sparks was announcing the husbands' arrival up on the stage in the end zone. The Hubstacle Course had been cleared, and rows of chairs now lined the football field, adding another few thousand people to the spectators. The wives were already there, seated and waiting. Like the Hubstacle Course, the couples were going in three groups.

CJ followed the line of husbands—followed Arthur—to his spot behind Natalie.

She had a small pack of tissues in hand, and she twisted in her chair to look at him with upturned lips. But there was more wariness, more questions, more insecurity than anything else in the tilt of her chin and the crease between her eyes.

She'd known this was coming. She'd known all of this was coming. And she'd agreed to play with him anyway.

He smiled back with no more confidence than she seemed to have. This wasn't anywhere near as fun as dancing in the sprinklers.

Elsie announced the challenge and explained to the crowd that they'd get to vote online for the winner after the last letter was read, then reached into her magic bag of names to pick the first husband.

CJ held his breath. He wanted to read his letter. He wanted to be done.

He was scared how the crowd would take it. How his in-laws would take it. How Natalie would take it.

These were the Husband Games. And not just any Husband Games.

The Golden Anniversary Husband Games. The Games that Natalie had dedicated her life to since her mom died. Her mom's last Games.

He didn't want to be the person who put a stain on her mom's last Games. Elsie leaned into the microphone and read a name.

Not CJ.

In her chair in front of him, Natalie was breathing almost as fast as he was. He wondered if her heart was pounding as hard too. She'd been a champ the last twenty-four hours. A pain in the ass at times, but he liked that about her. She didn't take any of his shit, but she wasn't stingy with her appreciation either. Her smiles. Her casual touches.

Her own unique brand of sunshine.

The first husband—the youngest guy—led his wife to the microphone so he could look at her while he read his letter. CJ's stomach rolled like it had tumbled out of a life raft.

Would Nat go up there with him? Should she?

He barely heard the first guy's letter. He saw the wife smile, heard her laugh, watched her wipe a couple of tears. Then the crowd cheered, and Elsie dipped back into her magic bag of names.

CJ's gut tightened.

He could be up.

"Arthur Castellano," Elsie announced.

Nat went rigid as a mountain, white-knuckling the life out of her tissue pack.

CJ cupped her neck, ran his thumb along her hairline. And when she relaxed back into his hand, he felt the same thrill as if he'd just hit the summit of Mount Everest.

Arthur said something to Marilyn, then approached center stage alone.

At the microphone, he cleared his throat. The sound bounced around the nearly silent stadium. "Dear Karen," he began.

Natalie's breathing audibly hitched.

Arthur straightened his paper. The microphone picked up the crinkling. "I wasn't supposed to be here today," he read. "Thirty-four years ago, you made me two promises. First, if I won you the Husband Games, you'd never ask me to play again. And second, that you'd let me go first."

Nat trembled. CJ dropped to his knee and put an arm around her shoulder. A little voice in his head whispered something about happiness.

"But here I am," Arthur said, "playing in the Husband Games for you. And here I am, carrying on after you went first. I've spent a lot of time wishing I had one more hour, one more minute. What we'd say. What we'd do. But mostly, what I'd ask."

A single tear rolled off Nat's cheek and landed on her hand. CJ opened her pack of tissues and gave her one.

"Thank you," she whispered.

Arthur's voice echoed in the speakers. "If I had another hour with you, I would ask for directions. You always knew where to turn for help, how to steer the girls, when to pack a flashlight and when to stay home and wait for the storms to pass. When I lost you, I lost my guide. I'm having to be my own guide now. I'm stumbling, but you left me two amazing young women who are so much more than the world gives them credit for."

CJ squeezed Nat's hand. She squeezed back. Warmth spread through his chest.

"If I had another hour with you," Arthur continued, "I'd share you with them. When we got married, I wanted to go first so I wouldn't have to suffer through the pain of losing you. After Lindsey was born, I wanted to go first so she wouldn't have to live without her mother. When Natalie joined us, I knew I could never do what you do. I want you back for one more hour for our girls and our grandson. Because some days—no, most days, I'm not strong enough for them. Not by myself. I never was."

Natalie shook her head, leaned into CJ.

"If I had another hour of your time, I'd ask for your secret," Arthur said. "How you could pack so much strength, so much spirit, into one beautiful human body. I'm in pretty decent shape for an old guy, but next to you, I'm weak as a baby. I sometimes wonder if I'd been stronger, stronger in body, in mind, in soul, if I could've willed you to stay longer in this world with us."

Arthur had lived. He'd lived a full life, with the woman he loved. He hadn't hidden. He'd lived.

And look what he had to show for it. A beautiful family. A belief in the future. A life. A right to stand in front of a stadium full of people and read a love letter to the woman who'd been his everything.

"I would still trade places with you if I could," Arthur said. "But until I find the magic formula, I'll be here, with our family, missing you and loving you. Forever."

He stepped back. He handed his letter to Duke, then retreated to his spot behind Marilyn.

Marilyn…who was dabbing her eyes with a pristine handkerchief. She stood and hugged Arthur, then kissed him on the cheek.

"She's been good for him," Natalie said. Confusion and resignation and a bit of bewilderment creased her brow.

A slow rumble had begun in the crowd, and now half of them were on their feet. Yelling and cheering and wiping their own eyes.

Because as far as husbands went, Arthur Castellano was a hero.

"You gonna be okay?" CJ said to Natalie.

She visibly swallowed, wiped her nose, and then steel shone through her eyes. She nodded.

Definitively.

CJ grinned. She smiled back at him, and he went lightheaded. "That's my girl."

Those pink lips of hers slanted farther upward, this time with a pretty pink blush adding to the mix.

She was beautiful.

Elsie pulled the next name out of her hat. Gilbert and Vi were up.

Then one of the younger couples from out of town. Three or four husbands down the line, CJ's subconscious started connecting some themes, solidifying what he'd noticed in Arthur's letter.

The good times. The bad times. The inside jokes. Their children. Their lives.

Every one of these men—some not much older than CJ—had full, rounded, sometimes overwhelming, perfectly imperfect lives.

And they were embracing every moment. CJ's letter didn't belong here.

Elsie pulled a name from her magic bag and stepped up to the microphone. "CJ Blue." Natalie cast a questioning glance at him, her chest rising and falling rapidly.

He swallowed hard, then pressed a kiss to her hair. "Back in a minute."

He approached the microphone alone with eight thousand pairs of eyes staring at him. Ten cameras were lined up in front of the stage, several more situated around the stands to capture the crowd's reactions.

And every last person in the place had gone more silent than ghost whispers. Wasn't even a bird or a bug chirping.

He twisted the microphone stand, pulled it tall so he didn't have to stoop. Looked out at the crowd, found his family several rows back in the chairs on the field, all of them in their Second Chance Misfits T-shirts. They waved their foam fingers at him.

"I had a letter written," he said into the microphone, "but my family's goat ate it."

Basil cringed the Holy Wince of Embarrassment. Rosemary and Ginger wore matching horrified expressions. Margie groaned. But the rest of his family—sisters, brothers-in-law, nieces, his grandma—laughed. Bob and Fiona smiled. Confused, worried smiles, but they smiled.

Some of the crowd laughed too.

CJ smiled into the mic. "My sisters will tell you, the one thing a man does best is to mess things up. That's pretty much where I'm most competitive as a husband. I screwed up a lot. There's a lot I'd do better if I could."

That much was true. And that much was in the letter in his back pocket.

But now, the letter wasn't what he needed to say. "I'm not here to win," he said. "I'm here to remember the good times Serena and I had. I'm here to fulfill one last promise I made to her. It's an honor to compete in the Golden Husband Games. But these gentlemen behind me, these are the men who are what husbands are made of. I barely had a year at it, but I thank you all for letting me play in the Games anyway."

He glanced back, at his fellow competitors, at Duke and Elsie, at Natalie.

Her head was tilted, eyes narrowed thoughtfully, as though he were a puzzle rather than the man who was sitting out an event in her mother's last Games. Her hair brushed her shoulder. CJ wanted to kiss her there. Among other places.

God bless Kimmie for finding her klutzy side and giving him a few more days with Natalie.

He turned back to the mic. "Let's hear it for the husbands."

The crowd cheered for the men who had earned the honor, and CJ retreated to his spot. "Just when I think I have you figured out," Natalie said. The affection in her voice and the warmth in her smile made CJ feel as if he'd won something much bigger than a silly crown.

She rose and squeezed him in a hug. She still smelled like oranges, but not like Serena's oranges.

Like her own, unique, special oranges.

He closed his eyes and hugged her tighter.

Wherever he went, whatever he did, he would remember her for the rest of his life.

Chapter 19

CJ and Natalie could've stayed in the hospitality tent and had lunch with the rest of the couples, but he wanted a minute alone with Natalie.

He had too few minutes left, and he wanted to pretend to fit in here just a little while longer. And there was a part of him that wanted to show her his letter. His real letter.

Because she would get it.

But as soon as they hit the parking lot, a cacophony of squawking burst out so loud, it actually made the sunlight flicker.

"CJ! Wait up!" one of the twelve most irritating voices in the world called. "Hell," he muttered.

"You're up to about seven-fifty." Nat flashed him a cheeky grin and bumped her hip against him. "Might want to quit while you're ahead."

The horde overtook them, and in the face of all his family, Natalie shrank back. Natalie hiding—from his family, no less—was wrong.

"Great letter, Princess!"

"Did you have to take your shirt off to get that jar open? Eew."

"Natalie, we could've told you he'd make you cry. He's male. He can't help it." "My favorite part was watching you get wet. Who knew you had a chivalrous side?"

"Mommy!" Noah darted through the mass of CJ's family and launched himself at Natalie. He was perfect, in a T-shirt that matched theirs, CJ's Falcons cap still on his head, still holding a piece of CJ's heart, even if he didn't know it.

Natalie snagged him in midair and lifted him for hugs and kisses. They whispered to each other, private things CJ couldn't hear over his sisters' yapping, and CJ had an ugly moment of being jealous of a four-year-old.

"You know what the marching band between acts made me think of? That time we had to hide Sage's violin bow."

"You mean times?"

"Shut up! I wasn't that bad."

"Saffron! Dylan! You guys should talk to the person in charge of entertainment here. You could get Billy to perform next year."

"Yeah, and he could do commercials for Pepper's boutique." CJ spun on them.

"You guys," Pepper hissed. "Hush."

Hush was right. That was still Natalie's boutique they were talking about.

One by one, between CJ's glare and Pepper's admonishment, they went silent save for one tiny voice.

"So CJ's like my dad today, huh?"

And that's when CJ noticed Fiona and Bob nestled between Basil and Lindsey at the edge of the group.

"No, honey," Natalie said softly. "CJ will always be your special friend, but Mommy's just helping him out right now."

Special friend. That felt wrong too. "Since his real wife died?" Noah said. Natalie nodded.

"So he's gonna leave us again like last time?"

CJ's heart took a running leap without a parachute. He jerked his head at Pepper. "Lunchtime," she announced. She grabbed Poppy's shoulder with one hand and Tarra's with the other and steered them both away from CJ's car. Ginger and Cinna and Gran were next. "And I have to get back to the shop," Pepper continued. "Natalie, don't let him give you any shi—crap." Rika and Sage and Saffron retreated by themselves. So did Rosemary and Margie, who herded CJ's nieces. His three brothers-in-law gave him sympathetic man-grimaces. Cori shot a glance at Lindsey and the parental units, who hadn't moved, but Pepper grabbed her by the arm and hauled her away too, sweeping their parents along with them toward the back of the parking lot.

"They're fun," Noah said. "They say dime words."

Natalie gave Lindsey a sisterly look CJ recognized all too well. There was an invisible ass-chewing going on, something that may have involved exposing Noah to CJ's family. Or possibly to the Games at all. "You and Noah have lunch plans?"

Noah wriggled in her arms. "We're going to tea with Mrs. Fi and Mr. Bob."

"If that's okay with you," Fi said quickly.

"Of course." Natalie's voice hitched, and unguarded vulnerability flashed through her face. "Noah talks about you a lot. We'd love to see you again after—after we're settled after Knot Fest."

Something tingled in CJ's chest. Felt suspiciously like his heart had found that parachute.

Natalie had just offered Fiona a grandkid. A kid who didn't have another grandma. And she knew it.

Fiona blinked as rapidly as she nodded. "We would like that. We would like that very much."

"Come with us, Mom," Noah said. "Mrs. Fi is gonna order me a dinosaur sandwich at tea! Isn't that awesome?" "It is."

"You can come too, CJ," Noah said. "There's enough dinosaur sandwiches to go around."

CJ's heart swelled into his throat. He'd obviously been forgiven for abandoning his favorite little buddy. Leaving this kid again would break his heart.

Natalie was giving him the wary eye again. "You up for it?"

So long as he didn't think about that plane ticket he had for Tuesday. Because even though she was here with him, now, he still wasn't so sure she would've chosen him. He was cheating, using borrowed time to make a few more happy memories before he went back to his life of fun. "Sure."

Noah pumped a fist in the air, then wriggled out of Natalie's grasp. "Oh, yeah!" he crooned. "Going for dinosaur sandwiches with my big dudes!"

"Cupcakes for breakfast again?" Natalie said. Lindsey grinned.

"C'mon, Mom." Noah grabbed her hand. "Let's go eat some dinosaurs!"

CJ trailed along behind them. If he couldn't be alone with Natalie, he had the next best thing.

* * *

After lunch, Natalie and CJ were almost late getting back to the Games. She had barely had time to brush up her makeup before it was time to go out on the stage with the rest of the wives. And now that she was there, memories and fears were once again threatening to destroy all that had been wonderful about today.

For this last event, all twenty-eight women were lined up.

The sun beat down on Natalie's hair and shoulders. Her belly churned much like it had the last time she'd been in this position.

But last time, she'd been wondering how much longer her marriage would last, instead of knowing exactly when this charade would end. She'd thought for sure the love letter challenge would've ended things. That CJ would write a love letter to Serena, and that Natalie wouldn't have been able to handle it.

That instead they'd had lunch together with Noah and Serena's parents after CJ declined the challenge—no. No, Natalie couldn't afford that kind of hope.

Nineteen blindfolded husbands had already crossed the stage. Thirteen had kissed the wrong women, and Natalie herself had had the distinct privilege of being groped by Wade Sweeney and kissed by one of the out-of-towners.

Neither of which she'd enjoyed, but both of which she'd handled with significantly more grace than she had five years ago.

She'd also had the distinct privilege of watching her father kiss Marilyn Elias. On the lips.

Without kissing any other women first.

She hoped Lindsey had shielded Noah's eyes. Or, better yet, taken him home for a nap instead.

Natalie shifted on her stiff legs. Nine husbands to go. CJ would be one of them.

Elsie announced Gilbert, and Duke led him up onto the stage. Natalie held her breath until they passed her by.

She'd been doing a lot of holding her breath since CJ hadn't read a letter. Because she was starting to hope he might stay.

She wasn't a fool. She came with the kind of baggage a charismatic bachelor didn't need.

She was mouthy and stubborn and a poor compromiser.

Most important, she didn't know if he cared for her the way she cared for him. Why would he? She'd banged into his life with an announcement that she hated him for ruining her marriage. She'd worn her Bliss's Biggest Loser badge with frigid pride every time she'd seen him. He'd taken special care of Noah, and she'd kicked him out of her life because of fear of Marilyn Elias.

CJ was special, and he deserved better.

But he made her feel special. As though she deserved happiness too.

A rowdy cheer went up from the Blue brigade. Elsie announced CJ, and his family cheered even louder. Despite their teasing, they obviously adored him.

As they should've.

He arrived onstage with assistance from Duke. Even blindfolded, he appeared comfortable with his surroundings, his cocky half-smile teasing his lips and every available female in the stadium, his stride slow but steady, his limbs loose.

And he was here to kiss her.

The bottom dropped out of her stomach. She hoped he kissed her.

Only her.

And that when he kissed her, he was thinking about her.

Only her.

If he kissed her, she would kiss him back. She would kiss him back with everything she had. Every last person in the stadium would watch her kiss him, and every last one of them would know she wouldn't have minded kissing him forever.

She hoped he didn't kiss her.

Because if he kissed her, he'd also have to stop kissing her, and then the Golden Husband Games would be over, and then she would have to move on.

Ironic how this event in these Games on this stage seemed to always break her life.

He passed the first four wives with barely a waver in his step, Duke at his side counting the women off. On the fifth—Marilyn Elias—CJ paused.

Natalie's heart stopped.

CJ's lips twitched up in a move Natalie recognized as his gotcha! smirk.

She pressed a hand to her chest, felt her heart kick into gear again. She was going to kill him.

Several thousand people roared with appreciation.

He passed two more wives. In five, he'd be in front of Natalie. No pausing. Two.

Her lungs quit working. Her heart jumped around her chest like Noah in a bouncy house.

He wasn't going to stop.

He was going to walk right past her.

Make a statement about his wife not being here. He'd walk past every one of them. Give Serena one final bow. She was why he was here.

One more step, and he'd be past Natalie. His legs kept moving—

Then stopped.

He turned his face toward her, the confident smirk fading away, mild curiosity taking its place.

His nostrils wavered.

As if he could smell her adrenaline pushing her pulse past healthy limits. "This one," he said to Duke.

Natalie's breath caught audibly.

The crowd was screaming. The sun too bright. Her knees as solid as wet lace. CJ stepped toward her. His hand found her cheek. Natalie's eyes drifted shut. He was going to kiss her.

"Good thing we practiced five years ago," he whispered.

Natalie whimpered out a pathetic laugh, but then his lips were on hers, his hand tangled in her hair, his other hand holding her against him.

And he kissed her. Soft, gentle kisses at first, just his lips brushing against hers. Enough to satisfy the judges. He could've stopped.

He probably should've stopped.

But his lips lingered on hers, then his mouth opened, and he suckled at her bottom lip.

She wrapped her arms around his neck, and she kissed him back. She kissed him for bringing her father home. She kissed him for rescuing Noah's dinosaur. She kissed him for every drink he'd poured her at Suckers, for returning her wallet after Lindsey stole it, for talking to her in public even though she told him not to. She kissed him for understanding grief, she kissed him for kissing her itchweed boo-boos, she kissed him for making love to her in the moonlight. She kissed him for hiding in the confessional.

She kissed him for changing her life.

If she never experienced love again, she wanted to put it all into this one, perfect last kiss.

And it was perfect. Hot and long and unrestrained, full of promise and excitement and desire. The kind of kiss that could change a girl's world.

The kind of kiss that could make him stay. With her.

She shuddered.

She couldn't. She couldn't manipulate him. If he were staying, if he wanted her, he had to want her on his own. For all of who she was. Not because of a kiss.

Not because she made him.

The crowd was too loud, the sun too hot. CJ let her go, but he pressed his forehead to hers. "Jesus, Nat."

"You may remove your blindfold and stand behind your… person," Duke said over the crowd.

Natalie flinched.

The statement wasn't meant to get to her, but it was all getting to her. Dad and Marilyn.

The Games. The crowd. The welcome she'd received from the other husbands and wives.

How CJ kissed her like he never wanted to stop.

He lifted his head and blew out a shaky breath, then pulled his blindfold off. She wanted to flinch again under the weight of his stare, the questions and promises and hope lingering between them.

She refused to blink. If there was any chance he wanted to explore this attraction between them, she wouldn't let fear stop her.

Not with CJ.

Duke cleared his throat. The as—jerk.

CJ slid him a look, then slipped behind Natalie, one hand at her waist, the other on her shoulder. "That's a dollar twenty-five," he murmured in her ear.

She looked back at him while they waited for the next husband. "My language is improving, thank you very much."

There went his all-CJ grin, lighting up the stage. "Mine's not."

She laughed, right there onstage at the Golden Husband Games. And with a roaring crowd all around them, CJ kissed her again.

Vultures. Squawking vultures.

* * *

The Games were over, and instead of hiding in the nearest corner making out with Natalie—which was CJ's only priority for the next twenty-four hours—he was stuck in the hospitality tent between his family and her family, with Marilyn Elias thrown in for good measure.

"We're having dinner at the bistro in an hour," Arthur was saying to Natalie and Lindsey. "You girls want to join us?"

"Can't," Lindsey said, all breezy and natural. "I have to take Nat shopping for a dress for tonight."

"But—" Nat started.

"And we have exactly ten minutes before her emergency pedicure," Lindsey said. "We're late."

Devil woman. Natalie was CJ's today. Based on the grip she had on his hand, he didn't care if she went tonight in a paper sack and ragged nails. She wanted him too. "I'm gonna help," Noah said.

Arthur looked between his daughters as though he couldn't decide whether they'd conspired against him to stay away from Marilyn, or if they were telling the truth, but in the end he shrugged. "We'll see you at the reception then."

"Can I go?" Noah tugged on Nat's hand. "I wanna go to the reception. And see all the pretty dresses."

Lindsey tugged on Natalie's other hand, toward the door. "What? Then who's gonna watch Shrek and eat s'mores with me?"

"Good lord," Natalie murmured. "More sugar?"

"Take it out on my kids some day," Lindsey said with a smirk.

For the first time since they'd been swarmed, Nat looked up at CJ. But her exasperation was comforting. At least he wasn't alone.

"I need to go," she said to him. "I'm apparently busy right now."

"Yeah." He got it. She was a girl. Had to do girly things. Then make sure Noah was taken care of. CJ was temporary. They were her real life. "Anything I can do to help?"

"You can go get ready to treat her like a princess," Lindsey said. "After nails and shopping, she has to get dressed and do her makeup. And Noah and I have an appointment with a pizza parlor right after, so we need to go. Now."

They were busy. He'd seen his sisters prep for prom and weddings. He got it. But— Lindsey winked at him. He glanced down at Nat's fingers.

He'd seen enough manicures in his life to recognize a fresh manicure when he saw one, which was a skill he hadn't fully appreciated until this moment. He was willing to bet her toes looked the same.

And since when would Natalie not have a reception dress? This had setup written all over it.

Huh. He was starting to understand why Huck and Jeremy gave Lindsey free drinks.

CJ touched Nat's shoulder. When she blinked up at him, he leaned down and pressed a kiss to her cheek. "I'll pick you up in a bit."

"Don't be late."

His groin tightened at the hints and promises coloring her words. "I won't be."

"Hot damn, getting warm in here," Saffron said behind them. "Get a room, you two." Marilyn cleared her throat.

CJ resisted giving her the finger.

Natalie laughed a beautiful, rich laugh that put a little more brightness into CJ's world. He let his sisters swallow him into their group while Nat and Lindsey and Noah walked away. For the first time in four years, he kept up with all the teasing and the jabs and inside jokes flowing around him.

His family annoyed him and irritated him and pushed him. And he loved it.

* * *

Natalie shared a cone with Lindsey and Noah at the Milked Duck Ice Cream Shoppe around the corner from Bliss Bridal while they waited for a text from the neighbors that Dad and Marilyn had left for dinner. Noah's sugar crash tonight would be epic, but Lindsey would deal with it.

Lindsey dealt with a lot of things. Including making sure that Natalie's nails were done yesterday.

"Was this planned?" Natalie asked Lindsey while Noah finished off the last of the cone. "An excuse to get you out of dinner with Dad and Marilyn? Was there any doubt?" "Me being CJ's partner. You and Kimmie rigged it, didn't you?"

"Nat. Seriously?" Natalie stared at her. Lindsey stared back.

"God help Kimmie if Marilyn finds out," Natalie murmured. And God bless Kimmie for stepping aside. The last day—she would remember this until the day she died.

Lindsey's phone buzzed. "They're gone. House is yours." They climbed in to Lindsey's car. When they reached Dad's house, Lindsey shoved three condoms in Nat's hand before pushing her out of the car. "Enjoy," Lindsey called. She and Noah waved, and then they drove off, leaving Natalie to prepare for the rest of her night.

When she went inside, she left the front door unlocked.

But she'd barely hit the stairs when she heard the knock. With light feet, she dashed back and flung it open.

CJ stood there, devastatingly handsome in a tux, his hair styled as though his sisters had gotten hold of him.

"You alone?" he asked.

She nodded. He stepped inside, shut the door, and then his arms were around her, lifting her against the wall, his lips devouring her. He kissed her mouth, her jaw, her neck.

Natalie wrapped her legs around his hips. "I want you," she gasped. "I'm all yours, Nat. All yours."

He kissed her again and carried her to the bedroom, and just for a little bit, she let herself believe in her own happily ever after.

Chapter 20

After their own intimate pre-party, Natalie and CJ were fashionably late to the reception. It was in the exhibition hall of the Bliss Civic Center, and the room was packed. Tickets were sold out for the first time in ten years.

Mom would've been overjoyed. Of everything Natalie was grateful for today, that Mom's final event had been such a spectacular success was near the top of her list.

All the newly wedded Knot Fest couples were being introduced on the stage where the Golden Husband Games winner would be crowned next. Linen-draped tables with elaborate floral centerpieces were scattered about the room. Waiters and waitresses circled with hors d'oeuvres. Cameras flashed, voices mingled over the string quartet playing at the opposite end of the hall. Two local news stations had crews on scene, and both had interviewed CJ already. Now, they were in the center of a group that included not only his family, but also several regular patrons from Suckers and a handful of couples from the Knot Fest committee.

"Your mom would be so proud of you," Claudia Sweeney had whispered. She'd given Natalie's hand a squeeze, and then let go so Vi could move in. "You did this, young lady, and don't think we aren't grateful."

Elsie Sparks had stopped for an air kiss. "Thank you," she'd said, and then moved on. CJ had produced a tissue, proving once again how much he knew about women.

Natalie didn't want tonight to end.

Even so, when she spotted Kimmie at one of the wedding cake tables around the ice sculpture, she squeezed CJ's hand and excused herself.

Kimmie was in her bakery best—a floral sundress, orange sneakers, hairnet, and a white Heaven's Bakery apron. Natalie gestured to the bandage across Kimmie's temple. "Does it hurt?"

"Oh, no." Kimmie's self-deprecating snort rose above the din of the couples around them. "Not really."

Natalie leaned closer. "Next time you want to play matchmaker, try not to cut yourself, okay?"

"I wasn't supposed to," she whispered. "I was just supposed to pretend to twist my ankle. Mom knows I'm bad at being a klutz, but she thought I could—" Natalie grabbed Kimmie's arm. "What? Your mom?"

Kimmie went pale. Her chin pulled in, and she took a step back. "I didn't say that. Did I say that?"

Natalie followed, whispering fast. "I thought you and Lindsey set this up."

"Me and—Lindsey! Yes. Me and Lindsey." Kimmie nodded furiously. "It was me and Lindsey. Don't tell my mom, okay? She'd fry my bacon. All that trouble with the hospital and Cake Readiness Condition Four… that puts her in a mood, you know? Did I tell you I had a dream—"

"Why?" Natalie said. "Why would she do that? Did Dad make her?" A commotion at the edge of her vision caught her attention. Josh was here. Marilyn's secret silent partner. And he had supermodel look-alikes on each arm. "Was it him?" she whispered to Kimmie. "Did he have something to do with it? Ohmigod, she's going to stop Dad from selling Bliss Bridal so she can buy it outright, and then move and get rid of him, isn't she?"

"You know about him too?" Kimmie had gone past pale to ghost. "She's gonna light my candles for this."

"I'm not going to tell." Natalie pointed to Kimmie's bandage again. "After all you've done for me?"

"Since my candles are already lit, listen. Mom's given up on buying Bliss Bridal. Crazy as it sounds, she values her friendship with your dad too much to keep causing problems."

"Seriously?"

"Yeah. He's been really good for her."

Natalie gestured to Kimmie's bandage again. "Did he know you were going to do that?" "No, Mom's too embarrassed to admit she played matchmaker after all the trouble she caused you. She won't say that, of course, but I can tell. Nat, she knows you make CJ happy. And he makes you happy. And you being happy makes Arthur happy. Your dad says my mom's been so invested in the economics of love that she's forgotten the mechanics of it, and I think that made her stop and think. Don't hold your breath for an apology or anything, but she's trying."

The commotion following Josh was getting closer. Kimmie's complexion had recovered and was now in competition with the roses scattered over the cake table. "I need to go check on the stove. I think I left the water running," she said. "Enjoy CJ, Nat. See you later."

She scurried away.

Natalie gathered a few plates of cake, then headed back to join CJ and his family and their friends.

Their friends.

That had a nice ring. But he was leaving. And she'd have to live with that.

She was halfway to the group when another commotion near the stage caught her attention. Two ovens were being rolled out.

The pit of her stomach met the floor. Ovens.

She knew exactly what ovens meant.

"Nat?" CJ stepped up next to her. "Everything okay?" "Ohmigod," she whispered.

Elsie Sparks took the stage and approached the microphone. "Ladies and gentlemen," Elsie said, "Golden Husband Coronation will begin in fifteen minutes."

That was their cue. Their cue to line up for the crowning of the Husband of the Half Century.

But this wasn't coronation. Coronation would come.

First, there would be one last Game. Because ovens meant only one thing. A first-place tiebreaker.

* * *

Bliss loved to draw out the drama, and they did it with flair.

The screen behind the stage flashed a slideshow from the Games. The crowd was whispering and murmuring and pointing to the ovens. CJ knew Natalie knew what they were for, but she wasn't saying.

And now CJ was parading onto stage with Natalie and their fellow Husband Games competitors while the string quartet in back played the wedding march. They were in alphabetical order, which put Arthur and Marilyn beside Natalie and CJ. The music faded out, and the flash of the screen behind them dimmed, then stopped.

"Ladies and gentlemen," Elsie said into the microphone at center stage, "it is my distinct pleasure to present to you your award winners."

Natalie had a death grip on CJ's hand. She looked half-scared, half-excited.

All this would be over too soon. He'd miss her. He'd miss her more than he wanted to admit.

Elsie started the awards with a few goofy prizes presented first to the guys who hadn't done so well. Most creative path through the sunflower maze. Longest letter. Most wives kissed before finding his own. Fewest screws used in the doorframe. Best gag reflex over the beets.

Soon, only half the couples were left.

"And now, ladies and gentlemen," Elsie said, "what you've all been waiting for. The announcement of our Golden Husband."

The audience clapped. A few people whistled. CJ's family took up the Princess! chant again.

They were lucky he loved them.

Elsie opened the envelope. CJ's pulse kicked up like he'd been out jogging.

He'd done well in most of the events. Duke and Elsie had transcribed his non-letter and posted it on the Web site for voting, but even then, CJ didn't expect he'd win anything.

And he was okay with that. He meant what he'd said in place of his letter. All these men were better representatives of husbands than he was.

"Second runner-up," Elsie said, "is Mr. Wade Sweeney."

The video screen behind them flashed. CJ glanced back, saw pictures of the Sweeneys' wedding and their families, along with a few pictures taken the last two days during the competition. Once the crowd's applause died down, Elsie read a bit about Wade and his family. Wade accepted his trophy, kissed his wife, and exited the stage.

Nat squeezed CJ's hand harder.

He took a glance up and down the row of remaining husbands. Arthur.

Arthur would win. He deserved to win. He was everything a Golden Husband should've been.

And one of the younger guys—the one whose wife was expecting. They'd performed great. They'd take first runner-up.

"First runner-up," Elsie said, "is Mr. Joe Jeurgens."

Just as CJ hoped. A relieved breath slipped from his lips. Natalie's hand trembled.

A little tremble, but a tremble all the same. Arthur eyed CJ.

And while the Jeurgenses' life played out to a Kenny Chesney song, CJ got a funny feeling in the pit of his stomach.

The Jeurgenses exited the stage. A hush fell over the hall.

"Ladies and gentlemen," Elsie said, "for the first time in Husband Games history, we have a first-place tie."

The crowd gasped, then went wild.

Bliss knew how to throw a set of Games. Holy hell. CJ's lungs suddenly shrank to the size of a button. Holy hell.

No. Just—no.

Natalie looked at her dad.

Arthur looked back. His eyes went misty over a sad smile, an expression CJ couldn't read or understand, and Natalie reached out with her free hand to grip her dad's.

"We will have one final event for the tiebreaker." Elsie gestured to the ovens in front of the stage. "For our final, tiebreaking challenge, each of our husbands will be required to make dinner for his partner. Final judging will be based on the partner's reaction to the meal, and also by a taste-test done by an impartial panel of judges picked from the audience."

Partner.

She'd said partner.

"Your final competitors, ladies and gentlemen," Elsie said, "Are Mr. Arthur Castellano, and Mr. CJ Blue."

CJ's family—his whole family—stood near the stage, jumping and yelling and celebrating. Fiona was crying.

Bob was too.

But Natalie—Natalie was shaking her head.

She met CJ's eyes. Mouthed, I'm sorry, then pulled her hand away. She'd already dropped her father's hand.

Before CJ could begin to understand what she was sorry for, she marched away. Right to Elsie Sparks.

CJ started after her, but Arthur stopped him.

Elsie turned, probably expecting CJ and Arthur. In her moment of surprise, Natalie stepped forward, and Elsie stepped back.

CJ moved again.

"Mrs. Sparks," Natalie said into the microphone, "on behalf of CJ and myself, we respectfully withdraw from the Golden Husband Games."

Her voice, clear and confident, echoed throughout the hall.

She'd captured control of not just the microphone, but the attention of every last person there.

"My father has dedicated the last thirty-five years of his life to Bliss and everything it stands for. He was a wonderful husband to my mother, and I would give anything if she could be here to see this today. I would say there's no one in Bliss who deserves this award more, but it's not entirely true."

A few surprised gasps went up from the guests. Arthur inhaled sharply. His eyes went shinier, and his chin wobbled.

"There's one person on this stage who's given more. A person who's been both mother and father, both husband and wife. She's been married to Bliss for longer than I've been alive, and God knows I've spent a lot of time hating her. But she's been a friend to my father when he desperately needed one, and so she's been a friend to my family."

This wasn't like the cupcake incident. Sincerity shone in every syllable Natalie spoke. CJ's chest swelled. With pride. With respect.

With love.

He loved her. How could he not? She was magnificent.

She turned, looked back at her father and Marilyn, her eyes clear, her shoulders straight, her voice strong. "Marilyn, thank you for all that you've done for Bliss, and for all that you've done for my father."

She wasn't just magnificent.

She was ten times the woman Marilyn Elias was. And if the crowd couldn't see that, they were blind.

CJ didn't care what title the Knot Fest and Husband Games committees wanted to bestow on any of them. He hadn't played for a title.

He'd played to win her. Even before he'd known it, he'd been playing to win her. To give her this moment.

Natalie turned back to the crowd. "Please join me in congratulating the Golden Husband, my father, Arthur Castellano, and his partner, Marilyn Elias."

She stepped back from the microphone so she was facing them. She met CJ's eyes, only the barest hint of a question in them.

He grinned.

She smiled back, and his heart soared.

Arthur turned to CJ. "Go on," CJ said. "She's right. You deserve this."

"Her mother would be very proud of her." Arthur blinked against his ever-dampening eyes. "I am too."

While he and Marilyn approached the microphone, CJ ducked behind the row of husbands and wives still onstage. Natalie mirrored his movements in front of the other couples, and neither of them stopped until they hit the stairs.

He loved her. She was his, and he loved her. "Natalie," a commanding voice boomed around them.

They linked hands and turned as one. Marilyn stood at the microphone, her shoulders draped with a royal red robe. Arthur was beside her, trophy in hand and a red velvet crown balanced on his graying hair.

"By the power vested in me by the Knot Festival committee, I declare your mother's spot on the committee to be yours for as long as you'll have it," Marilyn said. "Thank you for your own sacrifices and commitment. You will always be a welcome member of The Aisle."

Natalie inhaled sharply, put her hand to her throat.

Marilyn's head dipped in a single regal nod. She turned back and waved at the crowd. A crowd that was now whooping and hollering louder than before while the spotlight rested on the true star of tonight.

And there in the spotlight, with her entire hometown cheering her on, Natalie smiled. She smiled so hard, so big, so thorough, that the force of her smile made CJ step back.

It was a smile of absolute wonder and happiness. The smile of a woman who had finally found how she fit into her own skin, where she fit into the world, and in a single instant, it transformed her from his Natalie to Bliss's Natalie.

To the Natalie she'd always been inside, but never allowed to be outside. It was beautiful.

It was beautiful, and it was terrifying, and it was wrong.

CJ's gut quaked. Deep, deep down, under his lungs, behind his stomach. It didn't start as a small tremor. It hit hard and fast. A shiver crashed over his chest. His shoulders bunched.

The spotlight shifted off Natalie. Arthur's voice overtook the noise in the hall. Natalie turned her blindingly happy smile on CJ.

The quaking slid down his thighs.

She couldn't want to stay. To give more of herself to the Knot Fest committee. To sacrifice her free time. Her self-worth. Her family.

Could she?

No. No, this was wrong.

Natalie skipped down the steps, dragging him along. They hit the ground behind a floral arrangement the size of Mount Kilimanjaro, and her verbal floodgates opened. "I'm sorry, I should've asked you first, but Dad can't even boil water, none of us can, and it felt so right, and you—you know you're golden too. Right?"

He needed to answer.

Just nod.

Breathe.

But he'd done it again.

Again.

He'd fallen in love with a woman who had a higher purpose.

"Will you stay?" he choked out.

He had to know.

He had to know that she thought more of herself than that. That she knew she was better than the games that went on in Bliss. That three sentences from Marilyn Elias—three sentences that didn't include the words I'm sorry—weren't worth shit.

He loved her.

He adored her.

He wanted her to have the life she wanted to have.

But he couldn't stay here with her. Because if he told her he loved her, if he stayed, he'd make the same mistakes that had led Serena to leave him to go to war.

The tremors in his body reached his heart, and it doubled over on itself. "Will you stay?" he repeated.

Her smile dimmed.

He'd broken her smile.

This wasn't right. He didn't want to break her. He wanted to save her from here. Save her from herself.

"Pepper's offered me a place at the boutique," she said slowly. Hesitantly. As if she didn't know, which wasn't like his Natalie at all.

But she wasn't his Natalie. She never had been.

"It would be different, working for her," she said, "and I didn't expect this, but—but Bliss has always been home."

"You'd stay." CJ needed to shut up. He needed to shut up, and he needed to get out of her way.

But he couldn't. Because he'd seen what she'd sacrificed to make this happen. He knew what she'd sacrifice to do it again.

And again.

And again.

Until it killed her.

Just like Serena's sacrifices had killed her.

"CJ?" Her eyes were crinkling, uncertainty and hesitation dulling her glow. "What's going on?"

He had to go.

Now.

Because she had to stay. She was born to stay.

To lead the Knot Fest committee into the next generation.

She had a destiny. A destiny bigger than her, bigger than him, bigger than both of them together.

Well, CJ, I'm off to war. He loved her.

He loved her, but he couldn't have her. Because he wasn't a big enough man to live through being second in a woman's life again.

She put a hand to his arm. "CJ?" she said again. "What's wrong?"

"Thank you," he managed. It wasn't sufficient, but it was all he had. He brushed a kiss against her cheek. "Good luck."

It wasn't enough that he loved her. So he did what he did best. He left.

* * *

When CJ couldn't get his flight bumped up, he cleared out of the rectory and put himself up in a hotel room near O'Hare Airport instead.

He'd thought about bumming a room off Pepper, but she liked Natalie. So did Jeremy.

And Kimmie.

And Fiona and Bob and—and basically, everyone CJ liked in Bliss. Everyone who had liked him. Until now.

He hadn't been more than three feet outside the civic center before his phone exploded. Even over text messages, his sisters squawked. And if they hated him for leaving, the rest of Bliss would too.

He gave Cinna his car, told her to spread word that he needed a break, turned his phone off, and disappeared from the world. Not from himself, but from the world.

When Tuesday morning finally arrived, when it was finally time to board his shuttle to the airport, he packed his bags, took the elevator downstairs, stepped into the lobby—and came face-to-face with Basil.

"How the—"

"Don't underestimate a man of God," Basil said. Endearingly pompously, of course said.

CJ's ticket sat like a lead weight in his back pocket. "Got a plane to catch." "Taking the chicken way out, you mean."

As if CJ didn't know it. "Fuck off."

"You're a damn fool to not love her because you're scared." CJ didn't need Basil's lecture.

He'd been giving it to himself for the last two and a half days. "She doesn't need me," he said.

"God only knows why, but she wants you. You. Don't suppose it's easy to love a strong woman, but before you get on that plane today, you ask yourself if you're leaving because you think she's better off without you, or if you're leaving because you're too afraid to be the one man who can stand by a strong woman and help her be stronger."

Didn't have to ask. CJ knew. He was a worthless shithead.

Basil sighed the same heavy sigh CJ had heard Arthur make once or twice. "Don't stay away too long. The girls aren't the only ones who miss you when you're off trying to kill yourself. And they won't be the only ones who miss you if you finally succeed."

Basil turned, head down—all his holy pompousness, all his obnoxious righteousness, all his eldest sibling insufferableness gone. He wasn't Father Basil.

He was simply CJ's brother, and truth was, CJ would miss him.

He'd miss Basil. And he'd be jealous of Pepper being around Bliss, of them seeing Jeremy and Gabby, seeing Kimmie, and Arthur.

And Natalie. And Noah.

CJ squeezed his eyes shut. His chest was tight with grief and self-loathing and disappointment. And now Basil was walking away too. Leaving him alone.

Completely, utterly, miserably alone. He was a dumbass.

Basil was right. He had a choice. Face his fears, or isolate himself for the rest of his life. He could fail. Natalie could tell him to take a flying leap.

Or he could man up. Press past his fears. Be what she wanted. What she needed.

Have a place in her life. In Noah's life. In his own life.

"Dammit," he growled. He reached into his pocket, pulled out his phone. "When's Pepper closing on the shop?"

Basil's smirk wasn't as smirky as CJ would've expected. "Now."

"The hell she is." CJ punched her number on his phone.

He loved Natalie.

He loved her, and he trusted her, and he would win her. Even if it took the rest of his life.

* * *

After CJ had fled the reception and then refused Natalie's phone calls last Saturday night, she did what she'd gotten entirely too good at doing.

She picked up the pieces of her life. Or tried to, anyway.

She'd packed herself and Noah, and they'd headed north. Initially, she'd intended to go to Chicago for a few days, but they ended up in Wisconsin Dells instead.

Chicago was too close. Too close to home, too close to old memories, too close for breathing room.

She'd fallen in love with CJ, but he didn't love her back. And this week, he was flying out of Chicago. So they went to Wisconsin instead.

Being welcomed back into her hometown—it was surreal. Especially since, as of Tuesday, Bliss Bridal belonged to Pepper. Dad had given her one last chance to change her mind, but she couldn't run Bliss Bridal by herself. Nor did she want to.

Natalie tried to lose herself in the water parks with Noah. On the Duck tour. Reading that Mae Daniels book while Noah was sleeping.

It hadn't worked. And Noah—innocent, optimistic, perfect little Noah—had asked about CJ every couple of hours.

Watching the Husband Games had obviously been confusing for him. Natalie could relate.

But how could she explain to a four-year-old that she needed a man who not only loved and accepted both her and Noah, but could also understand that Bliss would always be a part of her?

Derek hadn't understood. Natalie hadn't either. Not fully. But she'd grown up in Bliss.

She'd adored dresses and weddings and being a member of the Most Married-est Town on Earth. She'd spent five years trying to flip that switch in her brain, to convince herself that the town was right to shun her, to accept that she needed to shun herself.

She'd been wrong.

So now, a week after CJ had walked out of her life, a week after she'd discovered what true heartbreak was, she was going back to Bliss. Back home. To make her own mark on her world.

Not because Marilyn had given her permission. Because she'd given herself permission.

Playing in the Games, then standing on the stage and giving up her own grievances against Marilyn—Dad had been right that she'd needed a friend, and he had too—Natalie's world had shifted into focus.

She'd accepted herself.

If she could accept herself, they damn well could too. And CJ could—

No. No, she couldn't go there. She had to stay strong. For Noah, if not for herself.

So Saturday, a week after the Golden Husband Games, while Dad was off somewhere enjoying retirement, Natalie dropped Noah at Lindsey's. They were all due at Jeremy and Gabby's wedding soon, but first, Natalie had a stop to make.

Bliss Bridal. Pepper's shop.

Just inside the familiar front door, the scent of wedding cake smacked her in the face. It was thicker in the shop than it had been on the street. One of the bridal consultants abandoned a bride to hug Natalie. Three others moved toward her, but Natalie held up a hand. "Where's Pepper?"

"The office."

No one stopped her—she'd have to talk to Pepper about propriety and ownership. Until the bridal consultants accepted that Natalie was no longer their boss, Pepper wouldn't have the authority she needed.

Not that Natalie intended to make a habit of interrupting operations on the floor. Today, though, they needed to talk.

But back in the office, Pepper wasn't alone. Dad was there too.

He jumped to his feet when she stopped in the doorway. "Hey, hon." His tight hug brought tears to her eyes. "Where's Noah? Miss that little guy."

"He's with Lindsey." Natalie blinked quickly. "I need to speak with Pepper a minute." Dad and Pepper shared a look, then he gestured her into his seat. "Of course."

He propped himself against the file cabinet. "Alone."

Dad and Pepper shared another strange look, but then Dad shrugged. With a loaded nod to Pepper, he left.

Nat and Pepper stared at each other for a minute, Natalie to gain courage, Pepper with a sort of fascinated curiosity. "You want to stay at Bliss Bridal?" Pepper prompted.

"I want you to sell my designs."

Before Pepper could speak, Natalie rushed on. "I don't have much in the way of a collection yet, but I will. For now, I'd be happy to work on custom alterations and bridal personalizations, and I'm willing to negotiate terms. But I know you recognize the value of an original line of designs from Bliss, so I'd strongly urge you to consider carefully before you make me an insulting offer."

She was being brassy and bold, but she knew what she was worth. She knew what the Bliss name was worth. And she wouldn't settle for anything less than what she deserved.

She knew she'd have to negotiate, and she expected Pepper to be tough. What she hadn't anticipated, however, was for Pepper to laugh.

Natalie's pulse boiled and her skin burned. She didn't have much money, but she wouldn't tolerate being laughed at.

Especially by CJ's sister.

Natalie turned. "Won't be so funny when La Belle and Mrs. launch a bidding war over me."

"Wait, sit, sit," Pepper said.

"Too late. You know what? I'm done with your whole family."

"He's an idiot."

Mollification seeped into Natalie's bones, despite her willful resistance to it.

"Honestly, I might be too," Pepper said.

This time, Natalie spared her a look. Pepper pointed to the chair again. "Have a seat. We need to talk."

Chapter 21

"Thought you were headed to Utah," Jeremy said.

"Had a wedding I didn't want to miss." CJ lounged in the doorway of the groom's quarters at St. Valentine's. His buddy was getting dressed in a tux courtesy of Bliss Bridal, Natalie's last thank you to Jeremy for stepping in as the boutique's sponsored bachelor in last year's bachelor auction.

"That the only thing you're here for?" Jeremy said.

Not even close. Although, fear of screwing that up had him nervous. Especially since he hadn't stopped Pepper in time.

Jeremy quirked a grin and went to work on his bow tie. "Crow don't taste all that bad, man."

"Yeah, about that…" CJ rubbed his neck. "I can help you work up a budget so you and Gabby can buy Suckers. If you're interested."

"You serious?"

"I'd buy into it with you, but my money's tied up." Tied up with his heart.

Or would be, as soon as he found Natalie. Because she had his heart, and she'd disappeared.

He could've called. Could've called Tuesday, Wednesday, Thursday, Friday. But every time he pulled up her number, he couldn't dial.

He couldn't grovel and beg over the phone. He couldn't use a phone call to prove to her that he had what it took to stand by her side and support her while she soared.

If he wanted to be Natalie's partner, he needed to be her equal. No way in hell she'd take the chicken way out behind a phone call if she were the one who needed to do the groveling and begging.

Jeremy jerked his head to a chair in the corner. "What kind of budget?"

"Don't need to interrupt your wedding day. Just wanted you to know I won't let Huck sell while you're gone, if you're still interested."

"All this is formality, man." Jeremy plucked at his bow tie. "Sit. Wedding don't start for another half hour. Tell me what we've gotta do."

CJ sat. Jeremy's best man arrived—he'd been sent to fetch the rings that had been forgotten at home—followed by Jeremy's family. Good folks, all of them.

Five minutes before the wedding, Basil poked his head in, the Holy Constipated Look of Exasperation making a lovably familiar appearance. "Both God and I would be extremely grateful," he said in his long-suffering, Holy Piousness way, "if you people would quit marring the sanctity of my confessional."

CJ's pulse skyrocketed. The quaking launched in his stomach. He bolted up, and barreled toward the door.

"Good luck today," he called to Jeremy.

"You're gonna need it more than me," Jeremy called back. That was the truth.

* * *

Natalie stood in the small, semi-dark room, sweet scents tickling her nose, and stared at the red vinyl chair.

She shouldn't be here, but she couldn't come to St. Valentine's without taking one last look.

Gabby and Jeremy's wedding would start soon. Lindsey and Noah were already seated.

But Nat was in the confessional, staring at her past.

CJ had sat there. Almost three months ago, he'd sat there, listening to her pour her heart out while she hid from Marilyn Elias.

She lowered herself into the seat, as much to see if she could feel him there as to give her wobbly legs a break. Today was overwhelming. A lot of her life lately was overwhelming.

She'd handle it, and she'd be a stronger person for it. But she didn't want to.

Not alone.

The door on the other side of the screen banged open, then slammed shut. "Natalie."

"Ohmigod."

"Not even close, Nat. Thought that'd be obvious by now." CJ.

Her heart tripped. She squeezed the armrests and shrank back into the chair.

He was gone. He'd flown to Utah. Except there he was, scooting around the screen, so tall and broad he barely fit.

Her chin wobbled. Her eyes stung.

"I lied." He dropped to his knees before her. "A goat didn't eat my letter. I didn't want to read it because it wasn't for them. It was for you."

She wanted to touch him. She wanted to touch his cheek, his lips, his hands. But if she touched him, she'd want more.

She already had so much.

Why did she keep wanting more? When would she stop always wanting more?

"I'm sorry, Natalie." His hand hovered over hers as if he was as afraid to touch her as she was to touch him. "I shouldn't have left. I panicked. You—you're one of the strongest, most amazing women I've ever known, and I didn't know—" He blew out a short breath. "Can I read it to you?"

She wanted to hug him and make that scared, broken sound in his voice and that uncertainty in the bend of his shoulders go away.

But she couldn't move. Because if she moved, if she touched him and he wasn't really there, if she misunderstood why he was here, she wouldn't recover.

He pulled a wrinkled paper from his back pocket. It was folded in fourths, the edges bent, the paper wrinkled. When he opened it, she saw smudged writing.

He looked at her.

She nodded.

He sucked in a big, audible breath. "Dear Serena," he began. Natalie squeaked an indignant sputter.

He glanced up at her, mild amusement lightening the shadows under his eyes. "It gets better." He lowered his head to the letter, but he put his hand over Natalie's, his solid, strong, very real hand, warming her skin and her heart. "I'm supposed to be writing you a love letter to read at the Husband Games. My sisters must've helped dream this one up, because this is probably the hardest thing I've done since that camel and I had a disagreement in Morocco a few years back."

A reluctant smile tugged Natalie's lips.

She missed him. She missed him so badly.

"I've spent the last four years wishing I could tell you I was sorry," he read. "But I've spent the last few months learning that I can't be sorry for the rest of my life. Instead, I need to try to do it better next time. Were our positions reversed, had I made the ultimate sacrifice while you stayed here, I would've wanted you to move on and be happy."

His eyes lifted once more, a question in them. Natalie nodded, and he went on. "God knows we had our problems, most of them my fault. You had a few faults too, though. All that hair in the shower drain, always using the last of my shaving cream without telling me, the way your boots stunk to high heaven… and you know what? If I'd died and you spent the rest of your life regretting that you never got Odor-Eaters to satisfy my olfactory sensibilities, I'd be pretty pissed at you."

He was cheating, using his unique charm against her.

He shifted on his knees, closer to her, head down over the letter. "I know not supporting you and your career—your calling—are orders of magnitude worse than not leaving enough room for my clothes in the closet. I still wish I could change things, but living in constant regret is an insult to you. In hiding from life instead of living it, I've put a shadow on your memory." His voice went husky. "And so one last time, I ask for your forgiveness, this time for moving on and finding happiness in the life that I've been gifted with."

"I've met someone." He wasn't reading anymore. He was looking straight at Natalie. "She's strong. Independent. Stubborn." He tucked her hair behind her ear. "She puts me in my place, even before she knows why I deserve it. She challenges me. She's been bearing her own grief, but instead of hiding from it, she's used it to make herself stronger."

Natalie's breath wobbled.

He set the letter aside. "A goat should've eaten the rest of it, because I really got it wrong after that."

"Don't tease me, CJ," Natalie whispered.

He gripped her chin, held her face while he gazed ferociously into her eyes. "I love you, Natalie. I've loved you since the first time I kissed you on purpose, but I was just too slow and scared to admit it. You've turned my world upside down, and I like it better this way. I love you, and I want to love you forever."

He wrapped his arms around her, all warmth and strength and comfort. "I'm gonna mess up, Nat. I'm gonna mess up a lot. But I'm here. I'm here for you, if you'll have me."

She didn't know what she'd done to deserve everything she'd ever wanted, but here he was.

The last piece to make her whole.

She buried her face in his neck, inhaled the scent of his skin, gripped him as tight as she could. "Are you sure?"

"I'm a little terrified. You're a hell of a woman to keep up with."

He'd meant to be funny. She could hear it in his voice. But based on what Pepper had told her this morning, he still didn't know everything he was signing up for.

Pepper and Dad had kept a huge secret. And he needed to know. She pulled back to look at him. "CJ—"

"I cleaned out my retirement accounts," he said. "I'll get you the boutique back. Whatever it takes. I'll buy Pepper a different dress shop, and I will get yours back for you. I'll watch Noah and all our other kids when you go to Knot Fest meetings, and I'll play in the damn Games every year if that's what you need me to do. I know it won't be easy, Nat, but you were born to shine. And I want to be the man who stands behind you and helps you shine as bright as you can."

Everything in her world stilled.

No more panic. No more stress. No more fears. She studied the earnest, honest openness in his eyes, the serious bent to his lips, the stubborn determination in the set of his strong jaw.

"I love you, Natalie. All of you. The strong parts and the stubborn parts and the soft parts. The parts that want to fit in and the parts I don't understand and the parts that drive me crazy. You are my everything. I will never be whole without you, but I don't deserve you if I ask you to sacrifice the parts of you that make you you. I know what Bliss means to you. I know what the boutique means to you. And I want you to have them both."

Tears rolled down her cheeks while irrepressible laughter bubbled from her core. "I do," she said. "I already do."

"You—?"

"Dad only sold half the shop to Pepper. He gave me a business partner." She understood the words she was saying, but the reality had barely sunk in. She'd earned her place on the Knot Fest committee, overseeing the Husband Games with a full committee to delegate to. She still had Mom's boutique.

And now CJ was offering his heart. He'd stayed. He'd stayed for her.

CJ visibly swallowed, and unless she was mistaken, he was thinking at least a quarter word. "So my first challenge is accepting that someone else got to be your hero."

"But you're my favorite hero." Her fingers were shaky when she stroked his cheek. "And since you don't have to buy me a dress shop, maybe you can think about buying you a bar."

His lips parted, and the hope springing to life in his eyes told her everything she needed to know.

He belonged at Suckers, and he knew it.

"You need to fit too," she said. "You can't just be the person who watches Noah while I work. You deserve your own happiness. And if that's what will make you happy, that's what we'll do. We'll make it work. For both of us."

He threaded his fingers through her hair, pulled her close, and he kissed her, right there in the confessional. She didn't know much about confessionals, but she knew this probably wasn't what it was designed for.

Still, she kissed him back with all her heart. "I love you, CJ," she said. "Chervil," he said. "My name is Chervil."

She blinked. Then blinked again. His name was—"Really?" she squeaked. "What, exactly, is—"

"It's French parsley, and I'd appreciate it if we stick with CJ," he said. "No wonder you don't mind the Princess thing."

A warning sparked in his expression, but he'd claimed he loved her. That he wanted to spend the rest of his life with her.

That he was up to the challenge.

Smiling had never felt so perfect. "What's the J stand for?"

He was already shaking his head. "Nuh-uh. For that one, you've gotta marry me."

Marry him. Love him. Make him happy. "Now how's a girl supposed to turn that down?" "She's not."

* * *

Natalie hadn't imagined when she woke up yesterday that today she'd have a new home, a new outlook, and a new future, but Sunday morning dawned clear and perfect, sunlight washing over the mattress on the floor of CJ's new master bedroom.

The house he'd rented was a cute little thing, a one-story ranch in a quiet older neighborhood between Suckers and The Aisle. The backyard was fenced, the front porch was big enough for a couple of rocking chairs, and miniature roses bloomed beneath the windows.

But the best part wasn't the house. The best part was the people inside it.

"Mom! Mom! Did you know the neighbors have a dog? Can we have a dog, Mom? Can we?"

She checked that the navy blue sheet was covering her naked bits and elbowed CJ behind her. "Are you dressed?" she whispered.

He grunted and wrapped his arm tighter around her waist.

Noah bounded onto the mattress, his knees inches from Natalie's nose. "Did you guys have a slumber party? Can I come to the next one? Can I have donuts for breakfast? Are we going to the park today? Do you think Grandpa's fishing? Is CJ still going to be my new dad? Can I have a goldfish? Can we go watch the Cubs play?"

"You bet, little dude," CJ said through a yawn.

Natalie tried to grab her shirt, but she couldn't reach far enough. "How about bacon and eggs?" she said.

Noah squinted at her. CJ choked on a laugh. "We ordering out?"

"It's bacon and eggs." She snuggled her rear end back into something extremely inappropriate for Noah to see. "I have every faith in your ability to figure it out."

"Can we have sprinkles on it?" Noah jumped back off the mattress, and Natalie got her first look at his epic bed head. She gingerly felt her own hair. Probably wouldn't be much better.

"You go run around the chairs in the living room fifty times, and I'll put frosting on it too," CJ said.

"Awesome, dude!"

"Ohmigod," Natalie said when Noah shot back out the door.

CJ nibbled on her shoulder. "It's okay. Lindsey offered to watch him this afternoon. She loves getting him when he's already sugared up."

"She does no—" She flopped onto her back and noticed the twinkle in his eyes. His special, just-for-her morning eyes. "You're going to keep me on my toes, aren't you?"

"Every last minute of our lives."

"You have to tell Noah that he can't have frosting and sprinkles on his eggs. You know that, right?"

"That's five times!" Noah yelled from the living room.

CJ's hand slid up to Natalie's bare breast. "Give me five minutes," he said, "and you're gonna be begging for frosting and sprinkles too."

"Eight times," Noah called.

"No cheating," CJ called back. But then he did something with his tongue and fingers, and Natalie forgot what he was talking about.

"Seventeen!" Noah hollered.

"Think Lindsey could take him early?" she said. "Already texted her. She's busy."

"Dammit."

"Better watch it. You're getting near ten bucks after all that dirty talk last night."

She shoved him playfully, but her whole body tingled in memory and anticipation. "Oh gods totally don't count when we're not in a church."

"Guys?" Noah panted into the doorway. "What comes after twenty?"

"Good lord." Natalie checked to make sure she was still covered while CJ choked on another laugh.

"Twenty-one," CJ said.

Noah frowned, then burst into giggles. "Oh, yeah." He scampered off. Natalie snuggled into CJ's chest. "He'll be back in about three seconds." "Probably—"

"What's after twenty-two?" Noah said from the doorway.

"Cheating, little dude. No way you're on twenty-two already. Go start over." Noah giggled again and disappeared.

"Are you sure Lindsey's busy this morning?" Natalie asked. "Mediation."

"On a Sunday? For what?"

"Setting ground rules for your dad's friendship with Marilyn."

Crap. Now Natalie's eye was twitching. But Marilyn truly was good for Dad, and apparently vice versa, and ground rules would help all of them.

"Guys, I'm at seven again," Noah yelled. "Is it time for donuts and bacon yet?" "Almost, keep going," CJ called back.

He shifted on the mattress and tipped Natalie's chin up. "Best morning I've had in years." She pulled him down for a kiss. "Best morning of my life." Today was the happiest, brightest, most perfect dawn she'd ever experienced.

No more shadows for Natalie. From now on, she would live in the light of her very own happily ever after.